THE 4TH DEMON

THE TRIAL OF THE 3RD DEMON

THE CHRONICLES OF JONATHAN STEEL
BOOK 9

BRUCE HENNIGAN

MY BOOKS

Hope Again: A Lifetime Plan for Conquering Depression (with Mark Sutton)
The Homecoming Tree
Our Darkness, His Light
Shadow Merchant (A Jack Merchant Medical Mystery)
Just a Bite of Something Sweet: At Christmas
Death by Darwin (Jonathan Steel Prequel)
The 13th Demon: Altar of the Spiral Eye
The 12th Demon: Mark of the Wolf Dragon
The 11th Demon: The Ark of Chaos
The 10th Demon: Children of the Bloodstone
The 9th Demon: Time of the Cross
The 8th Demon: A Wicked Numinosity
The 7th Demon: The Pandora Stone
The 5th Demon: Demoneyes
The 4th Demon: Trial of the 3rd Demon

For my readers. You have steadfastly believed in me and I hope I have created stories that intrigue, but mostly, inspire.

INTRODUCTION

This was supposed to be two books.

This book tells the story of the fourth and third demons and their stories are so intricately intertwined with Jonathan Steel's life I could not separate them without throwing major cliffhangers at my readers! It would also mean purchasing two books to complete the story and I do not want to take advantage of my readers.

For that reason, just be warned. This book is long. It is actually three parts. The first and last part focus on the demons. The second part is the totality of Jonathan Steel's backstory. I wrote that portion of this book way back in 2000 when I decided to extend Jonathan Steel's story from just one book, "The 13th Demon" into a series. I had to know then where we were headed as we approached the end of the Council of Darkness.

This book also references two other characters mentioned in my other books. Ruth Martinez is the main character of "Death by Darwin" and that book is a sort of prequel and introduces Jonathan Steel. Dr. Jack Merchant has his own series with the recently published "Shadow Merchant", a medical mystery.

This book can be enjoyed without referencing those works,

but the depth and richness of the characters can be enhanced once the reader knows their backstories.

Enjoy
Bruce Hennigan
November, 2022

PART 1 – THE SCALES OF ANUBIS

The Lord detests dishonest scales,
but accurate weights find favor with him.
When pride comes, then comes disgrace,
But with humility comes wisdom.
Proverbs 11:1-2 (NIV)

A person may think their own ways are right,
but the Lord weighs the heart.
Proverbs 21:2 (NIV)

PROLOGUE

Nigel Hampton paused before one of the five doorways at the base of the spiral staircase in the altar chamber. The Pandora stone pulsed in a small, wooden box. He withdrew the glowing stone from the box and calmed his racing heart. He was about to face a formidable foe and he hoped his plan would work.

Hampton placed the empty box aside and pressed the Pandora stone against the stone doorway. It grated as it slid aside. A mirrored surface wavered before him and he drew a deep breath as he stepped into the Void. His head swam as he passed through the inter-dimensional rift connecting one location on earth to another. For a second, he sensed the yawning, empty Void slide over him like some slimy wave of evil. It beckoned to him and threatened to pull him into its cold, clammy grasp. Voices of the dead and suffering assaulted him. Something touched his cheek and he glanced to the side. With his demonically powered eyes he saw ghostly figures swirling in an inky blackness. Their mouths opened in groans of misery. Empty eye sockets gazed hungrily in his direction. In the far distance he saw something long and mechanical. Some kind of ship? But it was unlike any ship he had ever seen on Earth, a ship that plied the stars. It disappeared through a flashing hole in the Void and Hampton took one more step and returned to the real world. The stone door grated closed behind him. He turned to study the wall where the door had been. A blank wall had replaced the doorway through the Void. He shivered and turned his back on the cold, beckoning emptiness of the Void sliding the Pandora stone in his pocket. He faced the woman at her desk.

"Jonathan Steel has been arrested for murder." Hampton said.

Dr. Sno sat behind a glass and chrome desk, her totally white eyes focused on the vista outside the windows of her office. From the office's high perch in the tallest building in the world, she looked out over a desert being transformed into a paradise. Hampton fought for patience. In time, he would take her place but for now, he would play the toady.

"At times, I regret giving up my normal vision. I wish I could see the world as I once did." Sno turned her white eyed gaze on Hampton. "However as much as I miss the mundane, I relish my enhanced view of reality." She frowned at him. "Is this why you chose to come to my office today? To tell me what I already know? Besides, you have a most unpleasant odor."

Hampton wore a wrinkled suit and a tieless shirt beneath. His white hair was a bit awry and he smoothed it down. The past few days had not treated him well. He had even lost his bowler hat.

"I have been hiding in the bloody altar chamber of the mansion in Austin, Dr. Sno. The police are keeping an eye on the mansion. Therefore, I have not had the opportunity for proper hygiene and sustenance."

"I assume these police are looking for you, correct?" Sno said with a sneer.

"Yes. I only barely managed to escape with the photo album when Steel defeated the unholy triad and I've been hiding in the altar chamber for days. Fortunately, the buggers haven't been able to open the library doors. I overheard the servants talking of Steel's arrest while making a food run to the kitchen. When I learned of this news, I came through your door to make sure you knew." He shivered at the memory of traveling through the Void and glanced over his shoulder at the empty wall. "I haven't been through that door before."

"You saw something in the Void?" Sno stood up and her blue embroidered saree was draped elegantly around her tall, lithe form. Her salt and pepper hair hung down around her shoulders.

Hampton tugged at his shirt neck and cleared his throat. "The bloody space is filled with ghosts of the past and specters of evil." He brushed his cheek with his hand. "One of them touched me." He shivered again.

"Our kind should not disturb you." Sno moved around her desk and walked to the wall behind Hampton. It was empty of decoration. When a Vitreomancer talisman, approved by Sno, was placed on the wall, it would open a passage through the Void to the chamber beneath the mansion.

Hampton tucked Pandora's stone into his pocket. He recalled the day he had first met Dr. Sno at a flea market in Canton, Texas. He had been searching for the Ark of the Demon Rose. Dr. Cephas Lawrence had been there that day and had been pointed in the proper direction by Dr. Sno. He still resented her for that! But she had given him the Pandora's Stone! His recent plan to control the mind of Joshua Knight with the stone and extract the Elixir of Life had been thwarted by Jonathan Steel. "That chamber always messes with my mind. So much blood spilled."

"Why are you so disturbed? You designed the mansion." Sno said.

"Yes, but *he* built it and added the chamber. I had no idea it existed until years later." Hampton said. And, one day, he would abandon that foul place and this office would be his!

"Pentagram altar and five doors leading to the locations of

each member of the Penticle." Sno said. She caressed the wall and sighed. "The chamber is a mystery to us all." She glanced at Hampton with white eyes. "Who is 'he'?"

"Oh, no." Hampton shook his head. "We do not speak of him. We do not speak his name. Ever!"

Sno tilted her head. "You're frightened."

"Very. You have no idea what this man is capable of." Hampton swallowed hard and tried to hide his growing uneasiness. He couldn't let Sno know of his secrets!

"He designed and built a five walled chamber with doors that open through the Void to the office of each member of the Penticle." Son said. "How did this man know of the Penticle? Is he a member of that group?" The Penticle, according to legend, was composed of five very powerful individuals who controlled all the world's power and commerce.

"No. Besides, you are a member of the Penticle." Hampton said. "You should know those answers." He avoided her relentless gaze.

Sno returned to her desk. "I am the only member of the Penticle with a relationship to a demon. While I do not know the identity of the other four members of the Penticle, I have it on reliable grounds the other four members are free of demonic influence." She paused and smiled. "Well, now there are only three with the unfortunate death of Dr. Faust."

"And they have no idea you are a Vitreomancer?" He touched the Pandora Stone in his pocket. "How would you know?"

Sno pursed her lips and sat back in her desk chair. "I have been in the physical presence of each member at our annual gathering. We are all swathed in secret cubicles, of course. I can sense if one of them is possessed. And if they knew I was in league with my demon I would already be dead."

Sno's white eyes shifted and she gazed at Hampton's pocket. "You like the stone, don't you? What is your ambition, Hampton? Do you plan on replacing me on the Penticle? Is that it?"

Hampton blanched. "Of course not! That's rubbish."

Sno snorted. "Your love for the stone is too great, Hampton. You have been blinded by its possible potential. When I gave you the stone, I hoped you would use it to locate other arcane stones for our purposes. But you chose to follow your own path with this silly Elixir of Life rubbish and in so doing, aligned yourself with the Unholy Triad of the seventh, sixth, and fifth demons of the Council of Darkness. I am very displeased with your actions. You deserve to rot in the altar chamber!"

Hampton swallowed hard and removed his hand from his pocket. He glared at the witch and vowed he would have his revenge. In time, he counseled himself. In time.

Sno glared at him with her white eyes. "No, the members of the Penticle have no idea I am the leader of the Vitreomancers. Now, why have you come here today to tell me news of which I have already been informed, Nigel? Why are you wasting my time?"

"I am here to talk about Steel. He will soon be in prison. He just eliminated three members of the Council of Darkness and I fear the Council will see to it that someone in prison will take him out of play. Wouldn't you agree he is still useful to us?"

Sno nodded. "Yes, I agree. We need him to continue to decimate our rivals. Perhaps we have someone who can make certain he doesn't suffer mortal harm?"

Hampton took his handkerchief from his coat pocket and dabbed at sweat on his brow. "I think I know someone who can be very subtle."

Sno raised an eyebrow. "I hope this person is more subtle than your last suggestion, Drake! The man killed someone in Louisiana. Not at all subtle. And then, he aligned himself with the Third demon!"

Hampton nodded and swallowed. If his plan worked, he would no longer have to cower to Dr. Sno. "The Crimson Snake was once in my employ. I think we can coerce her to use her 'influence' on someone in the prison to make sure Steel survives."

Sno frowned. "Snake? Better than Drake! See to it."

Hampton turned toward the office door. "Where are you going?" Sno barked.

Hampton froze and slowly turned to face her. "Anywhere but back to that chamber."

Sno stood up. "I have much to do and can't have you mucking about in the world. Soon, a replacement on the Penticle will be chosen. I must work towards the end of having one of our people replace Faust. That will keep me very busy for a while."

Hampton reddened. There was no way she would choose him! But, this was not over.

Sno frowned. "You have already pointed out the usefulness of your presence at the mansion. These servants will keep track of Steel's whereabouts. Such information is useful and you have already proven you have an ability to skulk about the mansion without detection. No, Nigel. You will go back to the chamber and remain at the mansion until I decide otherwise. That way, I can keep an eye on you." She glared at him with her unholy white eyes. "Or shall I revoke your association with the Vitreomancers? With one snap of my finger, I can remove the influence that gives your white eyes the ability to see. Do you want to be blind and helpless?"

Hampton sighed. It had been worth a try. He vowed once again to remove this pretentious fool from her position of power and assume her place. Patience, he cautioned himself.

"Very well." He said tightly and returned to the blank wall. He took the Pandora stone and placed it on the wall. A rectangular area rippled and formed a mirrored surface. Taking a deep breath, he stepped once more into the Void.

CHAPTER
ONE

THANKSGIVING DAY, the lake house

Jonathan Steel — Previously

When Steel opened his eyes, the first person he saw was the last person he expected. Inspector Goudreaux stood over him with hands on her hips and a huge smile on her face. She was a short, trim woman with coffee-colored complexion. Her hair was short and framed a plump face. Her dark brown eyes gleamed with malice. She wore a tight, dark blue business suit with smartly creased slacks and a white shirt buttoned to her neck beneath a matching blazer, just as he had remembered from their first encounter in Switzerland. Steel sat up from where he had fallen to the floor. Behind him, his friends and family still sat at the table.

"You can run, but you cannot hide, Jonathan Steel." She handed a folded piece of paper to another man standing beside her. He was a middle-aged man with a U. S. Marshal badge on his belt. He wore a cowboy hat and a khaki shirt and jeans.

"Jonathan Steel, you are under arrest for a murder in London,

England of Margaret McGuire and also for the deaths of over 200 passengers on flight 4551. Also, for aiding and abetting the escape of a known international criminal, Reginald Drake."

Goudreaux stepped closer and leered at Steel. "And an accessory to the murder of Dr. Faust."

Steel froze. "What? Faust is dead?"

"Murdered by your accomplice." Goudreaux grinned from ear to ear. "Not to mention associating with a known criminal mastermind known as the Geisha. You can't get out of this one, Steel, even with the help of Max. And we have an arrest warrant for her, too!"

Another man appeared behind her from the kitchen door. "Stop!"

Steel looked up into the eyes of Special Agent Franklin Ross. "This man is under arrest for federal crimes."

Goudreaux and the U. S. Marshal froze. Goudreaux shook her head. "Oh no, Ross. This is of no interest to you. I was here first."

Ross stepped between her and the U. S. Marshal. "This man," he pointed at the marshal, "Knows that any arrest made on U. S. soil for crimes committed here in the U. S. takes precedent over international crimes. Jonathan Steel belongs to me."

"On what charges?" Goudreaux growled.

"For one, assaulting a federal officer." Ross looked at Steel. "More than once. And aiding and abetting a known criminal, Theophilus Nosmo King. And there are many more." He held up an arrest warrant. "You can call my office to get a copy of this list." Ross helped Steel to his feet and turned him around. He whispered in Jonathan's ear.

"You owe me big time!" As he put cuffs on Steel, he recited Steel's rights to him. Ross turned Steel back to Goudreaux.

"Officer, I protest." Goudreaux said.

The U. S. Marshal handed the arrest warrant in his hands back to Goudreaux. "I'm afraid Special Agent Ross is correct. He has precedence. You can file a grievance with the American Embassy and seek extradition."

Goudreaux slapped the paper out of the man's hands. "I've already done that, or we wouldn't be here!"

"I'm afraid all of this is now null and void pending the FBI's case against Mr. Steel." He took of his hat and tilted it toward Goudreaux. "Good day, Ma'am."

Goudreaux screamed in frustration. "I am not a Ma'am!"

The Marshal let himself out and Ross pushed Steel toward the door. "You are in a heap of trouble, and you need the best lawyer money can buy, Steel. This arrest will only delay things a short while."

But the words were lost in the whirling and buzzing in Steel's mind as he reeled under the knowledge that his other self; his violent self; the man in his heart was correct. Who cared who was dead now? He had murdered his own mother!

I heard nothing as the officers hauled me from the lake house to the waiting van. It was all a blur of mixed-up images of Inspector Goudreaux's screaming and Special FBI Agent Franklin Ross screaming back at her. Josh had been held back by Jason Birdsong while Faye held her hands to her face to shut down the tears. They pushed me into the unmarked van and attached my handcuffs to a chain on the floor, then buckled me into the back seat with more chains.

The painful flashback changed everything. I couldn't get the image of my dead mother's face out of my mind. Had I killed my mother? I knew I wasn't guilty of killing some woman in London. But I wasn't sure about my mother.

"I'm saving your butt!" Ross said as he slid the door closed. He had arrested me for assaulting a federal agent to keep me from being extradited to Great Britain. The van lurched and bounced as it headed up the driveway.

The long drive gave me plenty of time to think. What would happen to Josh? He was still a minor. Would he go back into the foster program in Texas? I tried to put my head in my hands, but the chains kept me from doing so. I leaned back in the seat and my heart sank in despair. If I had truly killed my own mother, then Josh was in danger around me. How many times had my anger exploded after we first met? How many times had I only barely repressed the violent urges that overtook me? Yes, maybe Josh was better without me. The best thing for me was to confess my crime. Get it over with. The sooner the better and throw myself at the mercy of the court. Josh would be eighteen in a few short months and he had the trust fund left to him by Cephas Lawrence. I closed my weary eyes and fell into a restless slumber. Four hours later the officers pulled me from the van. We were parked in front of a low-lying beige building surrounded by fence topped by razor wire.

"Where are we?" I asked.

"Rockwell County Detention Center." The officer said. "The Rockwall County Detention Center is the only holding facility in the county and accepts prisoners from eight different law enforcement agencies. You'll be processed here and arraigned then transferred to Seagoville Federal Correction Institute. Pray you won't be here very long." The officer pushed me toward the doors leading into the prison.

"Where's Ross?" I asked.

"Doing paperwork to keep you from being extradited." The agent growled as he ushered me through the door into a crowded waiting room filled with noisy people. Half of them could have been the dregs of the earth, like me. The other half, officers. For a fleeting moment, I caught the eyes of an African American woman with bright yellow hair, Detective Citronella Jones. She did a double take when she saw me. The officer took me down a hallway into a small office. I barely heard what the officer said to the uniformed woman sitting behind a desk. They read me my rights. They swabbed my mouth for a DNA sample, fingerprinted me, photographed me, and took me from the small office to a locker room. The officer shoved me down onto a bench.

"Take your clothes off. You'll be strip searched and then given prison clothes."

I held up my hands. "How do I do that with handcuffs on?"

"Take off your bottom half first and then I'll take off your handcuffs. You're less likely to try and run out of here without your pants. Though many have tried." He smiled at me, and I shivered. I did as I was told. Some Thanksgiving!

CHAPTER
TWO

"HONEY CHILD, what have you done now?"

I looked up into the face of Homicide Detective Citronella Jones. The last time I had seen her was during the affair with the eleventh demon. She wore a red blouse under a dark blue blazer and matching blue slacks. We stood before the properties room desk. I had signed the log after handing over all my valuables and clothes. My orange jumpsuit was a size too big and my shoes had no laces.

"I killed someone." I said.

Citronella's eyes widened, and she glanced at the attendant behind the property room glass window and then at the guard standing next to her. "I got this, Lane." She took my arm and pulled me toward a bench against the wall. Lane, the prison guard, shrugged.

"Why don't you run get some coffee?" Citronella said. "I want black. Take your time."

Lane nodded. "Fine by me, Nella. Why are you interested in this perp?"

"I was here to pick up a suspect and take him downtown. That's all you need to know." She motioned toward the door. "Go now. Get!"

Lane motioned for the attendant behind the grill to open the door to the properties room. The door buzzed and Lane left.

Citronella turned to face me, her hands on her hips. "Have you lost your ever-loving mind?"

"No. Yes. Maybe." I said.

"Don't go telling nobody around her you killed someone. Everyone here is innocent, you hear? Whether they are or not! They put Lane and Marcus over there on the stand and you're dead meat." She pointed to the listless man sitting behind the bulletproof glass fronting the properties room.

I looked away. "But I'm not sure what I did. I remember holding my mother's head in my lap. She was dead."

Citronella ran a hand across her face. She sat beside me. "Your mother? Look, I know something about you. After we met, I looked into your history. It's a blank slate. No mention of a mother or father. No mention of anything."

"I have amnesia. But I remember my mother's dead eyes." I pushed back a swell of emotion.

Citronella sat back against the wall. "Honey child, when you showed up out of the blue just now, I asked the officer that brought you what was up. He told me you killed a woman in London. But you're being tried for assaulting an FBI agent."

"I didn't kill that woman in London. Ross arrested me to keep from being extradited." I said. "But I'm still a killer."

Citronella placed a hand on my arm. "This memory you had, you sure you killed someone? Maybe you just found her after she was already dead. You told me about your amnesia. Your memories are coming back and they can get all jumbled up."

I looked into her intense brown eyes. "I wished that were true. How many people have I killed in my lifetime? I have no idea."

"Don't go putting those turquoise peepers on me, honey child. You already got my sympathy. I don't think you are a killer. My instincts are good." She stood up. "Watch yourself in here. This detention center is supposed to be for holding prisoners only. But there are a few frequent flyers who end up staying longer and they are bad news. I gotta go take my suspect downtown, but I'll see what I can do to help you."

Lane returned with two cups of coffee. He handed one to Citronella. "I'm going to put him out in the yard."

She took the cup. "You just wait a few before you take him to the yard, Lane. Put him in his holding cell."

Lane shrugged. "I've been told to take him outside. You're not even on his case. He's being tried for assault, not murder." Lane grabbed my arm and jerked me to my feet. "Come on, man of steel. Time to face the villains."

Before Citronella could respond, Lane pushed me out the open door and down the hallway toward my fate. I deserved every minute of what was coming!

CHAPTER
THREE

IT WAS like the scene out of every prison movie ever made. Or at least, it must have been. I couldn't remember seeing any prison movies except for one that Josh asked me to watch, Shawshank Redemption. Lane ushered me down the hall and he pushed me through a door out into an open yard enclosed by fence topped with razor wire.

"After recess, I'll take you to your cell." Lane smiled and shut the door on the hallway. It was cool outside, and gray clouds obscured the sky. Most of the inmates had jackets on. My jumpsuit had short sleeves. I had no jacket. I wandered around the yard for a few minutes making sure I didn't make eye contact.

After a while, a short guy with a knit cap over his head rushed up to me. "Nylon's the name. Like the hose. I got whatever you need. You're the rookie, and before anybody gets to you, you'll want to be my friend."

He had close set dark eyes and a shadow of a beard with ears that belonged to a chimpanzee. Nylon's eye twitched.

"The average stay in this detention center is approximately 30 days. However, depending on their sentence, inmates can spend a longer period of time. With few exceptions, inmates would spend no more than one year at the Rockwall County Detention Center. That's a quote! I've been for three months. My fourth visit."

He glanced nervously over his shoulder. "Look, the Black and Blue Angels will be here in a minute. The BBA. They've been here nine months. The prisons are almost full around here. No defunding the police in Texas! They've been waiting for you. Don't know how they knew you were coming here." He giggled. "I'd tell you to run, but there ain't nowhere to run."

Four inmates sauntered up behind Nylon. The largest inmate easily weighed over three hundred pounds, none of which looked to be fat. His head was the size of a watermelon with small, pinpoint eyes swimming in fat. Long, stringy black hair surrounded the man's face. His skin was festooned with a dozen poorly drawn tattoos over his cheeks and jawline. His breath would stun a mastodon. He put a huge hand on Nylon's shoulder.

"Beat it, Nylon. This one belongs to us."

Nylon's eyes widened, and he grinned. "Yeah, sure, Muck." He winked at me and threw me a kiss and disappeared behind the massive wall of flesh before me.

"Let me guess, I'm fresh meat and you guys are hungry." I said.

"Something like that." Muck said. "I'm Muck. My brothers here run things around this place. Heard you slapped a feebie."

"I also killed someone." I said.

A tall, thin African American with a knit cap giggled. "They call me Hatrack. I thought everyone was innocent."

"Not me." I said. "Just leave me alone."

Muck pointed to the other two BBAs. A short fellow with more hair coming out of his jumpsuit than on his head glared at me through piggish eyes. "This here is Ball, as in wrecking ball." Ball pounded one fist into the other. Muck pointed to the other man about my height with blonde hair and dark eyes. "This is Boomboom. He likes bombs." Boomboom just shrugged.

"I don't care." I said, and turned to walk away.

"You ain't walking away from this one! It is customary to introduce yourself." Muck growled and his huge hand closed on my shoulder. Here we go!

CHAPTER
FOUR

AFTER LEAVING Steel at the mercy of the BBA, Lane nodded to Bellows behind the entry desk. "I'm taking a break." Bellows pushed the button to open the door, and Lane hurried out to the parking lot. Was she here yet? He ran to his pickup truck and, sure enough, an old yellow Volkswagen Beetle sat next to it. Steam puffed from the tailpipe and the driver's window lowered.

"Hey, sweetheart. How'd it go?"

Lane smiled at the red-haired woman seated in the driver's seat. "I did as you told me to. Now, how about we run down to the bar for a quick drink? There's a place not five minutes from here. All the guards go there."

The woman winked at him. "I don't think you have time. But, sugar, I got something inside that will warm you up. Hop in."

Lane climbed into the passenger side and had trouble squeezing his legs in. Sitting between the two seats was a paper sack. He had met the woman in a bar the night before and the memory of that encounter was still fresh on his mind. And body.

———

Lane nursed his third beer and leaned over the counter. Wendy, the barkeep, stopped before him. "What's eating you, Lane?"

"Oh, I got to work tomorrow. Thanksgiving day." He burped.

"Let me guess, you were going to spend the day with your loved ones hunkered over roast turkey and dressing and waiting for the kickoff." Wendy leaned on the bar. She had short, black hair and almond-shaped eyes.

Lane frowned. "You know I don't have anybody."

"You could come spend it with me." She stood up. "But I don't think my girlfriend would like that." Wendy tensed and looked over his shoulder. Lane turned on the bar seat.

The woman sauntered across the crowded room. Her hair was the color of fresh carrots. She wore a low-slung sweater with a turkey on the front. The turkey's eyes flashed with every step. The only disconcerting thing about her was she only had one arm. She kept her gaze frozen on him until she sat in the seat next to him.

"What will you have?" Wendy said tersely.

"Bug out, sweetheart. He's all mine." The woman said with a sultry voice. Wendy rolled her eyes.

"Gladly." Wendy put a hand on Lane's arm and he barely noticed. "Be careful, Lane." She walked away.

"I thought she'd never leave." The woman said. She took the beer mug from him with her one hand and guzzled it down. "Now, that's a good start. What's your name?"

Lane swallowed hard. Something about the woman's eyes enchanted him. And also scared him to death. "Lane."

"You're a guard at the prison, aren't you?" She plopped the mug down on the bar. "Hey, barkeep, how about another one for my boyfriend and bring me one also?"

"Correction Institute." Lane said lamely and then cleared his throat.

The woman put her hand on his and he shivered. It was as cold as ice. Wendy put two more mugs of beer before them and sloshed suds on Lane's hand. The woman cut a deadly look at

Wendy and the barkeep moved away from them. The woman's eyes cut back to Lane.

"Look, here's the deal. I'm cold. It's cold outside. I'm from out of town and I don't have any place to sleep tonight. I'll come stay with you if you're willing to do me one little favor." She sipped her beer and smiled at him.

"Whatever you want." He said.

————

He reached for the paper sack and took a quick sip of whiskey. She took the bottle from him and guzzled it. "You're still on duty. Now, did you do what I asked?"

"Yes. I made sure your friend met the Black and Blue Angels."

"Good. I just want him roughed up a bit but not dead. You do that for me and I'll stay over again tonight." She smiled at him.

A thought had wormed itself into his brain, his police brain, not his primitive brain. "We met last night, and Steel wasn't arrested until today. How did you know he would be here?"

"I had inside information, sweetie." The woman smiled. "Old Uncle Nigel knew the FBI would intervene and arrest Mr. Steel. When I found out, I wanted to make sure my, uh, uncle's friend was not in any mortal danger."

For a moment, alarm bells went off in Lane's head. Did this make any sense? Was she just using him? Did he care? He reached for the bottle again. She pulled it away with her only hand. "Not so fast. Just a taste is all you get. But there will be more. Now, go make sure Jonathan Steel doesn't get in too deep. I want him alive."

Lane reluctantly opened his door and slid out. He savored the taste of whiskey and recalled the taste of her lips. The fact she had only one arm had never crossed his mind.

————

Jonathan Steel

Pain lanced down my arm when Muck grabbed my shoulder. There are times when my memories return with such abrupt clarity it is disorienting. I heard my father's voice.

"Son, the bigger they are, the quicker they fall."

I ducked under Muck's hand and drove my fist up into his throat. I held back from crushing his larynx. Hatrack grabbed me by the nape of the neck. I spun, and taking his hand in mine, twisted his shoulder out of joint. The other two goons fell back as Muck fell on the ground, gasping for air. Hatrack screamed in pain.

The door behind me opened, and Lane appeared. He ignored Muck and Hatrack. "Steel, you've done enough damage. Let's go."

I glanced once at Muck. He sat up and caught his breath. "I'm going to kill you." He whispered.

Lance glanced at Boomboom. "Y'all get them to the infirmary. Now."

I followed Lance down the hallway, massaging my fist. He chuckled. "Thanks for that. It was nice to see someone take out Muck."

I glanced behind me at the doorway leading out to the yard. The BBA had been waiting for me. Someone had told them I was coming. I paused.

"Someone told you to put me out there. You set me up. I have a good idea who is pulling the strings. Wouldn't sit too well with your boss here at the center if I told all this to my lawyer."

Lane's eyes filled with a modicum of fear that quickly turned to an angry glare. "What do you want?"

"A yellow legal pad and a pen. Time for a hand-written confession."

Lane shrugged, and his expression went back to one of indifference. "Whatever. You're on."

CHAPTER
FIVE

My name is Jonathan Steel. At least, legally it is. I do not know what my real name could be except for a set of initials, JJ. I have come so far since I woke up on a beach totally naked, bruised from torture by my father, with no memory of my past life. I had no intention of falling in love with Dr. April Pierce. I should have known better. She died at the hands of a monster. Then I fell in love with Claire Knight. She died, and I adopted her son. He almost died. Everyone I love suffers.

I am a follower of Christ and I know this because I have one singular, powerful memory of my heart and mind changing for good when I invited his lordship into my life. That memory is buried in a sea of forgetfulness. But it is so powerful, it resonates throughout my entire life, amnesia or not. Since then, bits and pieces of my past have surfaced without warning and often without context.

I have taken on the mission of fighting evil. First, the 13th demon proved to be a creature soaked in the blood of centuries of human sacrifice. Next, the 12th demon who could not slake its thirst for human blood. Then, a fallen brother to other demons, the 11th demon spawned countless conspiracy theories. Following that, the 10th demon, an "extraterrestrial" Fallen had his eye on the untouched worlds beyond the Barrier. And then, the 9th demon, obsessed with changing the past and stopping the one Sacrifice that would save all who would come to Christ. Not long after that, the 8th demon, a being with a third eye, opened an alternate reality in which its evil spirit moves and captures the minds of all humanity. The most recent were the 7th, 6th, and 5th demons who tried their best to ensnare me in their foul plans, much to their destruction. And now, I am a prisoner of my past. I must answer for actions that led to the death of Margaret McGuire who was unwittingly serving a minion of the rival demonic force, the Vitreomancers. I do not know, but I am certain that my incarceration is the work of the next demon in the Council of Darkness. If so, I will defeat that demon as well.

But first, I must face the consequences of my past actions. A memory as powerful as that of my conversion has shown me the death of my mother, perhaps by my own hand. Could it be? Am I an assassin, a murderer, a creature of the dark powers as evil as any of the demons and their hosts I have defeated? It may be so.

———

WE SAT at a table in a meeting room in Rockwall Detention Center the Friday after Thanksgiving. I placed the papers on the table before me and looked at my attorney sitting across from me. Silence fell, interrupted by the clacking of my manacles on the metal table.

"You will not show that to the judge." Ruth Martinez said, pointing at the papers. Her short, dark hair framed her round face. Dark circles rimmed her eyes. Agreeing to represent me in a murder trial should never have been her fate. Lying to her and using her to help my adopted son, Josh, had sullied what little trust she had for me.

"I need to be truthful and honest." I said quietly. It was time to pay the piper.

"A little too late for honesty, isn't it?" She said.

"I'm sorry I lied to you."

"Jonathan, the evidence against you is very damning." Ruth

said as she tapped the papers before me. "Generating pity from the judge does not help."

"Ruth, I stood right behind you when you met Dr. Frank Miller. Did you think he was a murderer?" I had helped clear that man's name when I first met Ruth Martinez in what seemed like an eternity ago. She had since become a full partner in her law firm in Dallas.

Ruth tucked a strand behind her ear and averted her gaze. "I wasn't sure."

"Exactly. You were put in an impossible situation by your boss. Defend the un-defendable and you become a full partner. Fail and you might as well stay on as a law clerk."

Ruth raised an eyebrow and glared at me. "What is your point?"

"I helped you then. You listened to me, and you cleared Dr. Miller from murder. I am in an equally impossible situation. I know you're mad at me for what happened with Drake." I had released the serial killer Reginald Drake from his tracking anklet to gain information so I could save Olivia Monarch, and ultimately, my son, Joshua Knight. Ruth had given me the code to the anklet to find him, not let him go. I had betrayed her. I would do anything to save my son. Anything. But not murder! "But we need to focus on now. By the way, who called you to be my lawyer?"

"Dr. Liz Washington called Grace Pennington yesterday. I have my entire family at my house for Thanksgiving and I dropped it all to come help you." She ran a hand through her short hair. Even though she wore no makeup and her hair was roughly brushed, she was a sight for sore eyes.

"Thank you for coming. When I thought I would have a court appointed lawyer, I decided to play on the sympathy of the judge." I pointed to the papers before me. "I will need the sympathy of the court to get through this."

Ruth crossed her arms and leaned back in her chair. "Let's deal with the elephant in the room. Or, for more clarification, the serial killer." She sighed. "Yes, I am furious with you for what happened with Drake. You lied to me."

"I had good reason to."

"But appealing to the court with this narrative is a waste of time." She rubbed her eyes with both hands. "Look, bringing up your crusade against this Council of Darkness will fail. A jury will never believe that your adopted son was given a deadly virus on purpose for some kind of international evil conspiracy plot."

"But you have no problem believing it?" I said.

Ruth seemed to deflate. She glanced down at her hands. "Of course not. I know you. I know about the demons you've faced."

"Then you are a believer?"

"In both senses of the word. I believe in you, and I believe in Christ." She said. "But that means nothing in a court of law, Jonathan."

"Then you must believe the choice I had to make was to save Josh's life, no matter what the consequences. I must face those consequences now and I'm willing." I said. "All I can hope for is leniency. And that starts with me telling the truth, no matter how inconvenient or incomprehensible." I sat back, satisfied with my argument.

Ruth studied me and leaned forward on the table. She tapped the tabletop with the tip of her pen. I tried to relax some more but the manacles on my ankles and wrists were too tight. Lane did not like me.

"Did you kill that woman in London?" Her gaze met mine.

"No." I swallowed hard as another memory returned. "But I might have killed my mother."

Ruth closed her eyes and swore beneath her breath. She slammed the pen down on the table. "Stop saying that."

"I had a flashback, Ruth. I had that flashback yesterday, right before Inspector Goudreaux showed up to arrest me. In the flashback I was holding my mother's body."

"And, in line behind Goudreaux were London policemen

wanting to arrest you for the murder of Margaret McGuire, the receptionist at Hampton's Museum of the Weird in London." Ruth said. "Look, Special Agent Franklin Ross saved you when he intervened and arrested you for assaulting a federal officer, thus preventing your extradition. He helped you, Jonathan. I'm here to help you. We all want to help you."

I rattled my chains as I tried to stand up and then slumped back into the chair. "Surely there are records of my mother's murder. In my flashback, I was fifteen. A juvenile murdering his own mother would be all over the news. There would be records in the system. The guards let me talk to Jason last night. He's looking into the murder in London." Jason Birdsong was my investigating partner.

Ruth shook her head and stood up. "Jonathan, stop! Juvenile records are sealed. If you were exonerated, the trial would have been sealed so you wouldn't have to face the consequences of the publicity as an adult."

"And, if I was convicted?"

"You would still be in jail." She started pacing. "Can we focus on the present? Ross' charges will not hold you for long before Goudreaux bypasses the extradition ban. It won't take her but a few days and you'll be turned over to Interpol and then off to Europe, where I have no jurisdiction." She stopped pacing. "We must sort this out now. Forget your mother. Forget your flashback. The FBI will eventually drop the charges. Don't you understand? Ross was doing you a favor by pressing those charges. He was able to stall your extradition to buy you some time."

"But, I was on an airplane bound for Austin when McGuire was murdered." I said quietly. "How could I have killed her?"

Ruth hurried back to the table. "Yes, but we have no independent records of that. You flew on a private transport. We only have Jason Birdsong and Dr. Merchant's testimony and their testimony will be seen as tainted by your relationship with them."

"Dr. Merchant is an assistant medical examiner." I countered. "That counts for something."

"That doesn't matter. He's your friend. Both he and Jason would lie for you. We need more concrete evidence. Video footage of the murder. Witnesses in London who saw you board that airplane. The pilots, for goodness sake!"

I sighed. "Jason is already trying to track them down. But they worked for Hampton." Dr. Nigel Hampton had turned out to be an operative of the Vitreomancers and had orchestrated the infection of my son, Joshua Knight for his own purposes. He had disappeared along with my grandfather's evil photo album. Yes, I said evil. The thing exuded evil.

"Then who killed McGuire?" Ruth sat back down.

My face burned with rage. I clinched my fists. "Had to be Drake."

Ruth was silent. She closed her notebook. "Exactly. And you took his anklet off. At worst, you'll be an accessory to murder, Jonathan. They'll paint you as an accomplice."

I sat back in my chair as the far door opened. Jason Birdsong walked in. He was tall with long, black hair pulled back in a ponytail. He wore a leather jacket over a denim shirt. His jeans were tucked into hiking boots. "Sorry I'm late. Traffic was terrible." He just stood there looking at me with an expression of relief. "You okay?"

"So far. How's Josh?" I asked.

Birdsong hesitated as if he wanted to hug me. Technically we were "brothers" since his grandmother had declared it so. Instead, he sat in the chair next to Ruth. "He's fine. Dr. Washington has been busy. She's already reached out to Judge Bolton to let her keep watch over Josh instead of putting him back into the foster program." Birdsong glanced at Ruth. "Problem is, she has to go back to the university after the first of the year. She's on break right now for Thanksgiving and Christmas. Bolton probably won't let Josh go with her."

"I have to be free before then." I glanced at Ruth.

Ruth laughed. "I thought you were wallowing in guilt?"

"I don't want to stay in prison, Ruth. But I want to find out about my mother's murder. It's my past. It's the key to everything I forgot."

Ruth sat forward. "Then focus on Drake and the murder in London. I got you a preliminary hearing tomorrow before a judge and I'm moving for a trial without a jury. That would expedite matters and it is possible you could be free by Christmas. So, there won't be a jury to hear you read this letter. And believe me, it took a number of repaid favors to get a judge to see you on Thanksgiving weekend."

"He'll be free if we clear up the murder in London." Birdsong said. "Jonathan, I talked to Max. She has arranged for me to head to London to look into the matter."

"How is Max?" I said.

"Under house arrest." Birdsong said. "Goudreaux."

"She won't stay that way for long. She's more slippery than an eel. What about Vivian?" I asked.

Vivian Darbonne, without the apostrophe, had recently become a follower of Christ and had renounced her evil ways. Long in league with demonic forces, the FBI had turned Vivian over to Max in exchange for information on her exhaustive criminal connections.

Molly Alexandra Xavier, also known as Max, had the extraordinary ability to pull off almost any seemingly impossible task. She was the true love of my mentor, the late Dr. Cephas Lawrence, and she had taken on combating evil from her Cephas. Living in Switzerland, Max had made an enemy of Inspector Goudreaux and was currently under house arrest for her association with the known terrorist, Jonathan Steel. Yes, me. Max had pulled a few strings and had taken Vivian under her guardianship. Vivian was currently going through the dossier of victims of the assassin, Raven. Her job was to locate the survivors and offer them recompense from Raven's holdings.

"Vivian's working out of Max's chalet, from what Max said.

In secret, I would guess." Birdsong said. "What a mess, Jonathan."

"Yeah, what a mess."

Birdsong's phone warbled. He answered and hurried to the corner of the room, away from the prying eyes of the guard in the hallway behind me. I heard him whispering in conversation. He glanced over his shoulder and nodded.

Birdsong slid the phone into his pocket and sat at the table. "That was Jack. He wants to help." Dr. Jack Merchant was a radiologist associated with the medical examiner's office in Louisiana. He had been pulled into the dealings with the unholy triad of the seventh, sixth, and fifth demons.

I shook my head. "Absolutely not! I don't want him in any more danger."

"Too bad." Birdsong smiled. "He has credentials, you know. With the medical examiner's office. Says he can do some digging around in the archives in Austin to see if he can find out anything about," Birdsong hesitated. "Your mother's murder."

Ruth stood up. "No, Jason. He can't do that. All we need right now is more evidence that Jonathan is capable of murder."

"Too late. He's on his way to Austin."

My face grew warm, and I felt the old anger, the old fury burn in my chest. I slammed my hand flat against the table. Ruth and Birdsong both flinched. "I need to know if I killed my mother." I looked away and massaged my temples, which were difficult with the manacles. I heard a tapping on the door behind me. I glanced over my shoulder as Lane glared at me. I raised my hands and nodded.

"Got it! Sorry." I looked back at Ruth. "Look, Jack is an innocent doctor pulled into all of this. But he is a good man. I don't know. Maybe he could help." I had to admit I needed help from my friends. My friends? I had friends! I drew several deep breaths and felt the anger die down.

"Okay, maybe looking into the records will keep Jack away from this trial and what is going on in London." I looked at Birdsong. "Tell him to investigate away. I need to know. But only if he thinks he will be safe."

"What could possibly go wrong?" Birdsong said. "Whatever happened with your mother has nothing to do with the murder in London."

Ruth glared at me. "Let's hope not, since nobody is listening to me."

Birdsong tapped the table. "There is one other thing. Max wants Faye to come with me to Europe." Faye Morgan was a nurse practitioner who had watched over Josh while he was infected with the deadly virus. She had discovered Hampton and the unholy triad of demons were keeping Josh sick as leverage over me. To her credit, Faye had taken great risks to protect Josh from harm.

"Why?" I said.

"She wants Faye to help with Raven for some reason. Faye has agreed to go once I filled her in on what happened to Raven. Faye has an autistic sibling she worked with for years." Birdsong paused and swallowed. "I don't want anything to happen to Faye."

I nodded. I had seen them together. They had grown close. I glanced at Ruth and a familiar shiver ran down my spine. Even in her disheveled state, she was lovely. No! I couldn't go there. Not now!

"Max will protect her. As long as Raven is safe and hidden, Faye will be safe." Raven, the assassin, had once been a tool of my father, the Captain, and had performed many missions for that vile man. Dr. Monarch, a gifted neurosurgeon, had operated on me and on Raven implanting a device my father used to erase our memories. Recently, Dr. Monarch had taken Raven to her laboratory in London and had tried to neutralize the implant, only to erase Raven's mind. If Faye was accustomed to helping someone with mental difficulties, she might help with Raven's therapy.

"I don't know that much about Max, but she has bent over

backwards to help Jonathan." Ruth said to Birdsong. "There's not much you can do here to help me with Jonathan's case." She looked at me with a raised eyebrow. "Except a wild goose chase after an old murder."

I sighed. "Jason, go to London. See what you can find out about the murder I'm accused me of." I looked at Ruth. "Does that make you feel better?"

"Yes." Ruth nodded and then put a hand on Birdsong's hand. "And take care of Faye."

CHAPTER
SIX

I SAT in the silence of my cell. Dinner had been gratefully uneventful. The BBA were nowhere to be seen. I heard shuffling feet outside my cell and a shadow fell over me. I looked up into the eyes of Muck. His throat was surrounded by a cervical collar and his eyes were red.

"I'm not done with you, Steel." He croaked. "You can't hide in that cell forever."

"How's Hatrack?" I asked.

Something dark passed over Much's face. "He's in the infirmary. Surgery on Monday for a broken arm bone and dislocated shoulder. You did a number on him."

"He should have left me alone. Who put you up to this?" I said.

Muck leaned closer and his foul breath made me grimace. "Let's just say a NUMBER of people." He grinned at his own joke. Number? As in a numbered demon? Did Muck know that much about the Council of Darkness? Was he inhabited by a demon? I reached out with my spiritual "sensors" and felt nothing supernatural.

"Move along, Muck." I heard Lane's voice. Muck glanced over his shoulder down the walkway and moved on. Another guard out of sight opened Muck's door and locked the inmate in for the night. Lane appeared and glanced at his watch.

"You got a date?" I asked.

Lane glared at me. "I hope so. She was supposed to meet me outside on my break."

"Didn't show?" I asked.

Lane's eyes filled with fire. "Steel, all I have to do is disappear and Muck and his ilk will take you out."

Something about the way he said those words tickled the back of my brain. "Someone put Muck up to killing me. Are you saying someone has asked you to protect me?"

Lane stiffened. "I didn't say that."

I nodded. "I think you just did. Who asked you to help me?"

Lane glanced at his watch again. "I never said anything about helping anyone."

"She ditched you, Lane. You've done what she asked and now she's moved on. Who was it?"

Lane grimaced and looked away for a moment. "Red haired chick. One arm. But what she could do with one good arm!"

A cold shiver passed down my spine. "Snake?"

Lane looked at me. "Snake? What are you talking about?"

"The Crimson Snake." I sat back and my mouth felt like cotton. Why was Snake trying to help me? The last thing I knew, she had been working with my father. But Snake was fickle. She worked for the highest bidder. "Could it be the Captain? Why would he try to help me?"

"Who's the Captain?" Lane asked.

"My father."

"Why would it be so hard to think your father wanted to help you?"

I looked at Lane. "Daddy issues."

"Ah! I got those, too." He rubbed his chin. "So, you know this chick?"

"She tried to kill me. And she has considerably more finesse than Muck. Look her up. She's an international assassin on every wanted list from here to Moscow. You're lucky you're still alive. She doesn't like to leave witnesses." I said.

Lane sighed. "Just my dumb luck to fall for a one-armed assassin." He nodded. "Okay, Steel. Watch yourself. The deal is off. From now on, you're on your own and no one will be keeping an eye on you. I'm going to check the parking lot one more time." He walked away leaving me to my misery.

CHAPTER
SEVEN

THE COURTROOM WAS EMPTY. No audience. No jury. I sat at the defendant's table with Ruth and we waited. And waited.

"How long do we wait?" I said tersely as I shifted my manacled hands.

Ruth sat stiffly beside me. "As long as it takes. Judge Meridian is doing us a favor showing up on Saturday."

The door behind the judge's desk opened and a short, stocky bailiff with a comb over entered the courtroom. "All rise for the honorable Judge Matthew Meridian."

I stood, and my manacles rattled on the table. Lane was right outside the outer door and it had taken some pleading from Ruth to keep him out there and not be by my side. Ruth stood up quickly.

Judge Meridian emerged from his office and mounted the steps behind his desk. He was an imposing figure with stark white hair and black eyes set in a cadaverous face. His long, splayed fingers intertwined before him as he settled into his seat and his gaze turned to the papers before him. He looked up at us, and from behind black rimmed glasses with large lenses, the darkness in his eyes seemed to intensify.

"Ms. Martinez, I could complain about you pulling me into my courtroom on a holiday weekend. But the truth is my wife wanted me to go shopping with her. You saved me!" He crossed his arms. "You have made a most unusual request to fast track your client's trial to a judge only trial. May I ask why?" His voice was deep and resonant.

"As my brief states, Mr. Steel is also being wanted by authorities in Europe and I believe the evidence of this trial will exonerate him and prove he was here in the United States when the alleged murder occurred in London. The sooner we get on with the trial, the sooner we can get those charges dropped."

Meridian lifted an eyebrow. "The D. A.'s office hasn't yet assigned a prosecuting attorney, Ms. Martinez. I see no reason to expedite these processes."

"Your honor, I believe my old partner, Bryan Nicholas, has agreed to take on the case. Unfortunately, he is out of town for Thanksgiving But will be back on Monday." Ruth took a paper from her folder on the desk. "May I approach the bench?"

"Certainly."

Ruth walked quickly up to the desk and handed the paper to the bailiff. "Here is a letter from the D. A.'s office agreeing to allow Bryan to represent the prosecution."

Meridian glanced down at the paper and frowned. "I don't like surprises, Ms. Martinez. You should have told me of this before now."

"I just received this by email five minutes before walking into this courtroom, your honor."

"Five minutes is plenty of time to inform me of these developments." He placed the paper on his desktop. He looked over Ruth's shoulder at me. "There is something you are not telling me."

"Your honor, there is the matter of Mr. Steel's adopted son, Joshua Knight. Your associate, Judge Bolton, has approved a temporary custody arrangement under Dr. Elizabeth Washington, who is on leave for the holidays. But she must return to her teaching position by the second week of January. The sooner Mr. Steel's case is dismissed, the sooner he can have his son returned to his care."

Meridian sat back. "Bolton is far too lenient, if you ask me. How old is Joshua?"

"He will be 18 in August." I said.

Meridian looked over at me and his eyes filled with fire. "Mr. Steel, approach the bench, please."

I stood up and shuffled across the empty space. My manacles and chains rattled on the floor. Meridian waved his hand at the bailiff. "Bubba, remove Mr. Steel's manacles. I don't think he is a flight risk."

I looked at Ruth and she shrugged. "I don't understand." She whispered.

The bailiff unlocked my manacles and placed them on the table behind me. Meridian nodded to Bubba. "Now, take Ms. Martinez to my office and close the door, please."

Ruth stiffened and glanced at me. "But, your honor, I protest."

Meridian leaned forward. "Do you want me to consent to this trial or not? If so, go with Bubba. I wish to speak to Mr. Steel alone. Off the record."

Ruth looked at me, and I rubbed my wrists. I nodded. "Go ahead."

"This is most irregular, your honor. I will note it in my records."

Meridian sniffed. "Note away. Bubba, take her to my office."

"Don't say or do anything you will regret later." Ruth said and followed Bubba out of the courtroom.

Meridian drew a deep breath. For a second his chest inflated and his eyes almost rolled back in his head. He blinked, smiled, and sat back. "Well, well, well. Here we are, Mr. Steel."

An icy wave seemed to flow across his desk, stirring his papers. The wave washed over me, and my skin crawled. The hair stood up on the back of my neck. Nausea gripped me and I swallowed down bile. "You're one of them."

Meridian chuckled. "I, that is my mortal self, am one of many hosts, Mr. Steel. Many of us serve our master." He said, and his eyes opened wide. "Booo!"

I flinched. "Which one are you?"

"Well, you've only got four left, don't you?" Meridian stood up and made his way from behind his desk. He walked over to the prosecuting table and ran his long, spindly fingers over the fine-grained wood. "Imagine, Mr. Steel. A long sitting judge in my position has control over many of the most unsavory criminals in this city." He turned. "In fact, I am one of the most sought after judges for relocating highly profiled cases from their origin cities to my courtroom." He smiled and massaged his face with his long fingers. "To assure a fair trial, of course."

Meridian hitched himself up and sat on the edge of the table, his long legs dangling beneath his black robe. "In fact, there are many cases I adjudicate that never see the interior of a courtroom. Cases that never leave the sanctity of my chambers. Therefore, your attorney has sought to have your trial in my courtroom. I have unprecedented power, but I am only one person."

Meridian rubbed his hands together. "But there are a dozen or so men and women in powerful positions, just like me, who have sold their souls to a very powerful demon. You would know him as the fourth demon. And he does not inhabit just one individual. No, he moves among us from time to time."

"What is to keep me from sending you off to your eternal torment?" I said.

Meridian laughed and pointed at my hand. "Does it hurt?"

I glanced down at my left palm. A faint blue glow pulsed under the skin. "No." I had received some "shards" of a device known as the Grimvox from Vivian while in Numinocity. Those shards were part of a supernatural device that housed the history of the Council of Darkness. However, for me, it had become a conduit of divine power. But only when God saw fit for it to function that way.

"It should hurt, Mr. Steel. All knowledge comes with a price." He stood up and moved towards me. "For instance, I should not be able to touch you. If I did right now, I would be the one hurting."

He closed the distance between us, reached out with a bony finger and touched my cheek. I flinched. He smiled and raised his hand to my face. "See, nothing. No blisters. No pain for me. Now, if I had been burning from your supposed righteous anger, then you would have taught me a lesson. A painful lesson. Instead, I have taught you something. And while the pain is not physical, I guarantee it will be mental. Why was I able to touch you? Hmmm?"

Meridian tilted his head like a dog studying his potential prey. I raised my palm and studied the faint glow. Why hadn't he burst into blisters? Always when someone affiliated with a demon tried to touch me, they would suffer.

"I see you are somewhat stymied." Meridian retreated to the prosecutor's table and perched on its edge again. He massaged his lips with his long fingers. "You are now tainted, broken, fallen into sin. Working with the triad tarnished your soul, Mr. Steel. You conspired with demons! And you have recovered a memory, yes?"

My heart raced, and I tried to control the growing panic. Meridian hopped from the table and hurried over to me. He pushed his face into my line of sight. "It was your mother, wasn't it? Her eyes so full of life. At least you thought so. But she was dead, wasn't she?"

I closed my hand into a fist and fought the growing anger. I glared at Meridian. "How did you know?"

"I know the truth about you. I know who is responsible for the death of your mother."

I stumbled back away from this creature and slumped against the defendant's table. "So, it is true? I killed my mother?"

Meridian straightened and chuckled. "Now, that is the question, is it not? That is what trials are for. To determine the truth. And, Mr. Steel, I could tell you many tales from days past that would cast shadows on the truths you hold so dearly. Number Four has a long memory." He pulled a chair from behind the table. "Sit. Relax." He motioned to the chair.

My legs trembled with weakness and I slid off the table and into the chair. Meridian took the other chair and positioned it in front of me, then sat facing me. He reached out and grabbed my knees in a vise grip. I shuddered at his touch; cold, clammy, and filled with the sharp spikes of evil. Meridian laughed.

"You have no idea what a triumphant moment this is for me, Mr. Steel."

"What is the lie?" I mumbled.

Meridian paused and gave me that tilted look again. "What did you say?"

"What is the lie?" I said. "Satan is the father of lies. What do you know of truth? Actual truth?"

Meridian gave me a lopsided grin. He reached forward with one finger and paused before touching my palm. "Let me show you." He plunged his finger into my palm and the blue light exploded around me and I was somewhere else.

———

Micah gasped in delight at the sight of the Son of God. How glorious the bruises on his face. How wondrous the blood trickling from the corner of his mouth, the mouth that had spewed self-righteous bile at his colleagues. Where were his precious disciples now? Micah rubbed his hands in eager anticipation of the trial to come. A few mumbled words here and there to the members of the court had raised the level of anger and disgust. Now it all hinged on the high priest.

The court of the Sanhedrin had assembled. At first, Jesus of Nazareth appeared before Anna, Caiaphas' father-in-law, while the court was assembled. Once the court was complete he had come before

Caiaphus. Micah slipped through the crowd until he was within arm's reach of Caiaphus.

"Caiaphus, I have the scroll." He offered a rolled up document. "I have written down the charges for the record."

Caiaphus, dressed in his heavy dark robes, and his white and black striped headpiece, glared at Micah. His eyes were bright with eager anticipation. He stroked his beard. "I do not need your scribblings, Scribe. I know what needs to be said."

Micah bowed his head and backed away. Caiaphas paraded back and forth in front of Jesus. His face was twisted in anger with a touch of victory.

"Whoever is deserving of death shall be put to death on the testimony of two or three witnesses. He shall not be put to death on the testimony of one witness. Who will come forward to give testimony against this criminal?" Caiaphas said.

Silence gripped the crowded men. Slowly, tentatively, men asked questions, good questions of why this was occurring at night. Not everyone here was committed to seeing Jesus killed and this made Micah nervous. He had planned for this eventuality and slipped into the back of the room. Four men stood awkwardly in the shadows. Micah placed coins in the hands of each man and nodded.

"Now is the time for you to speak." He prodded them forward. The four men came forward. With strident and angry voices, they gave testimony of things that Jesus had said and did. Micah winced because their testimony never agreed. But he knew the leaders of this assembly were not interested in the truth. They only wanted the Son of God to cease to exist, to disappear, to die. He smiled and licked his lips.

Caiaphus raised his voice to silence the crowd. He paced back and forth before Jesus and his gaze met Micah's. Micah held up the scroll and nodded encouragement.

"Do you answer nothing?" Caiaphus asked Jesus of Nazareth. "What is it these men testify against you?" He paused. "Well, we will have the truth this night. Are you the Christ, the Son of the Blessed?"

The voices in the room fell silent, and a stillness gripped the air. Micah smiled. This was the moment. The question was like asking,

"Does your mother know you are stupid?" No matter what answer Jesus gave, he was condemned. He moved closer to see and hear.

Caiaphas looked around the room as if feeling a change in the air. He wiped his hand across his bearded face and once again paused, glaring at Jesus of Nazareth.

The voice that came then was the single most powerful thing Micah had ever heard. No, he didn't just hear it; he felt it! It was low and almost a whisper and yet it echoed and resonated around the chamber like a mighty wind assailing the ears and hearts of all who heard it. *"I am. And you will see the Son of Man sitting at the right hand of Power and coming with the clouds of heaven."*

Micah felt the power within him wither and pulse and then it was gone. He knew that the power known as Four would come and go. Four had other hosts in his legion of influence. And now, with the power gone and the words of the Son of God echoing in his ears, he felt his world was ending.

Four was nearby. But unlike the power he sensed in the past, Micah sensed fear. Four cowered in the shadows. Desperately, Micah wanted the power to return. But, that voice! It was the voice that spoke the universe into existence; the voice that quieted the storm that night on the beach; the voice that convicted every sinful heart of every sinful thought and deed. It was the voice of God!

"You have failed!" Four whispered in his ear and Micah was gutted, empty.

"This is not over. The law is everything!" Micah glanced at the scroll in his hands. He looked back at Caiaphus whose gaze was focused on Jesus of Nazareth.

Caiaphus' face flushed with red and immediately after, a new sound emerged. It was harsh and painful and selfish and evil all at once; a guttural, deep throated screeching that set the nerves on fire. The sound of rending cloth accompanied it, and Micah smiled as Caiaphas tore the cloth of his robe.

"What further need do we have of witnesses?" Caiaphus shouted. *"You have heard this blasphemy from his very mouth. What do you think? Does he not deserve death?"*

The surrounding men all joined in, calling for the death of Jesus. Their voices intertwined and reverberated with hate. As the emotion built, men rushed forward to Jesus. They spit on him and beat him with their bare hands. One man wrapped a cloth around Jesus' eyes and his raucous laughter followed with his harsh words. "Prophesy! Tell us who hit you." And then his fists smacked as they fell against the face of Jesus of Nazareth.

Micah released his held breath and retreated into the shadows. He searched for Four and for a fleeting moment, Four returned. He felt the power flood into him. Micah hurried into the alleyway behind Caiaphus' house.

"You are back! Never leave me! I can't live without you!" He whispered to the surrounding shadows.

"No, you can't live without me." Four said in the back of his mind. From the shadows before him, the figure materialized. It stood a foot taller than Micah, and its face and head hid in shadows. It wore a long purple robe and golden wristlets. As it stepped into the meager light, Micah gasped. Its face was that of a jackal with tall, pointed ears and a dog's snout. The eyes burned with red and it held up a golden set of scales. Two shallow dishes hung by chains from a golden bar.

"It is time for the weighing of your heart." The fourth demon said in a deep, raspy voice.

Micah grimaced and clutched the scroll to his chest. "What?"

"This ritual is mine to perform. You would ordinarily be asked if you had committed any wrongdoings or broken any laws. Since I have seen your mind, I am well aware of the many wrongdoings of your life. So we move to the next step. The weighing of the heart is the most critical part of the ceremony, since the results will dictate whether you will cross into everlasting paradise or into the underworld. In one pan will reside your heart. In the other a feather."

The fourth demon looked around the alleyway. Nearby, a white dove regarded him with a tilted head. Quick as a snake, his free hand snared the dove. One squeeze and the dove was a mass of dead flesh. One white feather floated in the air. The fourth demon dropped the dove and plucked the feather out of the air.

"Just so you will know I am giving you the benefit of the doubt, this feather will replace Maat's feather." He placed the white feather on one of the pans. The scales tilted slowly in the direction of the feather. "Now, if your heart is as light as this feather, you will cross over into paradise, a place of everlasting joy."

Micah shook his head in confusion. "But I'm not dead."

The fourth demon stepped closer and his pink tongue played across his teeth. "A mere inconvenience."

Micah grimaced from pain as his heart constricted. He fell back against the wall and clutched at his chest.

"No! What is happening?" He cried out.

"You have outlived your usefulness, and it is time for another host to take your place." Four said.

Micah screamed as the pain gripped him, and he fell into the shadows of the alleyway. He gasped for breath and cried out for help, but his breath would not come. The fourth demon motioned to the shadows behind him. From the shadows, red eyes appeared. A thing with four legs moved from the shadows. Sharp, spiked ears sat atop a narrowed canine snout. Yellow teeth appeared as the thing growled. It was joined by others and the pack of devil jackals descended on his body and soul. The last thing his physical self felt was the pain as the teeth and jaws tore out his heart. One of the demon dogs hurled the heart and the fourth demon caught it with his free hand and put it on the other pan of the scale. The heart tilted downward, much heavier than the feather.

"Well, I'm sorry, Micah. It is time for you to go to the underworld."

The scroll slipped from Micah's hands and the wind caught it, unfurling it and carrying it into the night wind. It floated into the courtyard and fell into a fire pit. It burst into flames and was no more.

CHAPTER
EIGHT

THE IMAGES FADED, and Meridian sat back in his chair. "Nice memories, huh? There is more I could give you from your shards of the Grimvox. Let's see, there was Herod. Now there's an all-American psychopathic family!" Meridian leaned forward again and his eyes lit up with excitement. "One of Herod's legal advisors whispered in Herod's ear. Want to know what he whispered?"

I tried to ignore him, but I couldn't. Knowledge was power, and the more I knew about this man and the fourth demon, the more leverage I would have. "What?"

"Herod's brother Philip, who he killed by the way, had a wife named Herodias and Herodias had a daughter. Herod was a little too perverse, and he wanted to see the daughter dance. Four whispered in his ear to promise to give Herodias anything she asked for as long as she would get her daughter to dance for him."

Meridian sat back. "You know the rest of the story. Herodias' daughter danced and Herod had to deliver the head of John the Baptist. He was growing a little too interested in John, so we had to intervene."

"You mean he was feeling convicted of his wrongdoings?" I asked.

Meridian shrugged. "Whatever. It worked. Herod forgot about John. But, when Pilate, the man he hated the most, sent Jesus to appear before him, Herod couldn't resist. Four was there standing right beside Herod again as his trusted legal advisor."

Meridian stood up. "Let's see. If we remember correctly."

————

Herod was fairly quivering with excitement. Mesha had urged Herod to dismiss Herodias so he could have time with the so-called Messiah. Herod sat on his throne, resplendent in a white robe. His beard was braided in tiny cords adorned with droplets of gold. His eyes glowed with anticipation.

The sound of approaching soldiers echoed outside his throne room. "They are really coming?" He whispered to Mesha.

"Yes, your highness. The Messiah is being brought before you."

Herod giggled and motioned to a fountain with a surrounding pool. "Perhaps he can walk on water again." He rubbed his hands in anticipation. "I should have someone executed in front of him and he can bring the creature back to life."

Mesha put a hand on his king's shoulder. "You are the king. The law permits you to do anything you choose to this blasphemer." Yes, the law, he thought. It was a powerful tool. In the hands of the religious leaders of the day, the law had become the perfect weapon. It brought strict rules for everyday living. But it also put control in the hands of the priests. It was sharper than a two-edged sword!

The guards appeared, and the Man followed in their midst. The guards stepped away, and the one known as Jesus of Nazareth stood defiantly before Herod. Herod arose, and the guards fell to their knees. Mesha followed suit but kept an eye on the proceedings.

"Will you not kneel before your king?" Herod said.

The Man was silent. His eyes were penetrating and unrelenting. Four had been absent for most of the evening and had only recently returned. Mesha was blessed to be one of Four's Legion! Mesha avoided that gaze and within, Four writhed in discomfort. What was that all about, he wondered?

Herod made many requests of the Man. Work a magic trick. Make a pomegranate plant bear fruit. Walk on water. He brought out a servant and threatened to kill him and still the Man kept his unwavering gaze on Herod. Herod finally broke his stare with the Man and returned to his throne.

"I am bored. You are not what I thought you would be." Herod waved his hand in the Man's direction.

"This is not going as you hoped, is it, your highness?" Mesha said.

"This Jesus of Nazareth is nothing like John the Baptist." Herod whispered. "But what am I to do? The priests demand his death. I've already killed one prophet, and it cost me dearly."

"Perhaps a bit of humiliation? Then send him back to Pilate?" Mesha whispered.

Herod nodded and stood up. "If this man claims to be a king, then let us dress him accordingly."

Mesha smiled and ran to a nearby wardrobe filled with robes, for Herod's vanity was such he would change robes a dozen times a day. He found a robe of maroon threads worthy of a king. He brought it forward, and Herod nodded approvingly. Mesha approached the Man and as he drew nearer, the Man's eyes shifted from Herod to him. He felt Four retreat quickly into the background and Micah stumbled. A guard caught him and Mesha shoved the robe into the guard's hands. Where was his power? Where was Four? He was weak and his heart sank under the gaze of the Man.

"Dress him in the robe." He said to the guard and Mesha fell back quickly. The guard put the robe around the shoulders of the Man. He stood there unmoving, unspeaking and the robe fairly glowed with power. Herod looked away as Mesha joined him at the throne. Four resurfaced from the depths of Mesha's mind.

"Send him back to Pilate, your highness." Mesha whispered. "Only the Roman governor has the power to order this man to be executed."

"Return him to Pilate." Herod gestured. Mesha sighed in relief as

the guard took the Man by the arm and turned him away from Herod. The guards disappeared down the hallway and silence descended into the throne room.

Herod stood up. "Get me a clean robe, Mesha. I've sweated through these clothes." The kind stripped away his robes and stood naked before Mesha. Mesha smiled because this is how Herod would appear one day in hell, naked, powerless and distraught. He turned to the wardrobe and paused as his hands fell on a white robe. His hand began to tremble and fell to his side. He blinked in shock as the entire right side of his body grew numb. He stumbled backwards and fell into the pool. Water covered his face and his arms would not move. He looked up through the water at his powerless king whose visage was eclipsed by a dozen dog shaped demons appearing out of nowhere. Behind the dogs loomed the fourth demon holding up a set of scales. "It is time to weigh your heart!" He said. Four's laughter echoed into eternity and Mesha faced his inevitable eternal fate.

"After the Son came along, I got real busy." Meridian said. He crossed his arms. "Let's see, I was at the Council of Nicea. I served on Nero's court. Loved those early heretics. I used my knowledge of the law to persuade them to question the teachings of the Son. Almost got to Paul and Peter over the whole Gentiles versus Jews thing at the Jerusalem Council." He frowned. "But too many apostles. Couldn't pull another Judas, so I moved on. Always using the law as my tool. It worked during the Crusades. It was my most powerful ally during the Inquisitions." Meridian rubbed his chin and sat forward.

"The Salem witch trials. Now that was truly enjoyable. Ah, the smell of burning flesh will never leave my memory. And I helped H. L. Mencken persuade Clarence Darrow to take on the Scopes trial." Meridian laughed. "What a windbag William Jennings Bryant was! To think he ran for president three times.

You know he died right after the trial. That was when I realized the power of modern law."

"Do I have to relive all of your failures?" I said.

Meridian froze. "Failures?" Meridian stood up. "We discovered long ago that truth is nothing when you elevate opinion to the power of absolute truth. You know you've been in this courtroom before." He returned to his desk.

I froze. "What?" I glanced around at the generic courtroom. I had no memory of this place.

Meridian stood behind his desk and seemed to shrink, to deflate. He shook his head and slumped back in his chair. He yawned and stretched his eyes. He glanced around the chamber as if awakening from a nap.

"I could trigger those memories for you. But unfortunately, Four just left for more pressing matters. He is bored with you, it would seem. He has a few powerful hosts and we are his Legion." Meridian leaned toward me again, and his eyes twinkled with mischief. "He trusts me to do his work. He knows I am loyal to the law, Steel. It is a powerful tool of almost unlimited power."

"He will return to me tonight. And once we have a brief discussion about your fate, then I will decide whether to grant Ms. Martinez's wishes and be the sole judge over your case." He shrugged. "It won't matter. I will insure you get off. We don't want you in prison. Too many operatives of the other council who will try to take you out of commission."

"Vitreomancers." I hissed. "Why make sure I get out of prison?"

Meridian pointed a finger at me. "You see, number three and I have come up with a plan for you. It will be a much smarter plan than the plans of those ineffectual triplets. We will break you, Mr. Steel. Your amnesia has protected you from harsh, debilitating secrets and we will see that your memory is restored." He leaned toward me. "And when it is, when you recall what happened right here in this courtroom, you will no longer have the desire to fight us. You will no longer have the ability to serve the other side. In fact, you will no longer have the strength to go on. It will break you. It will destroy you." Meridian leaned closer. "And we will sit back and watch as you take your own life!"

Meridian laughed and made his way back to the door of his office. "Oh, by the way, you can call the fourth demon Anubis." He turned. "He holds the scales of demonic justice. Have a blessed day." He opened the door and disappeared into his office.

CHAPTER
NINE

Switzerland

Faye Morgan leaned across Jason Birdsong and looked out the airplane window as they touched down. She could not see the runway in the darkness.

"Where are we?" Her grip tightened on his arm.

"Not sure. Somewhere in Switzerland?" Birdsong said.

"Jason, I don't like this." Faye whispered.

"I don't either. But Jonathan trusts this Max person with his life. If anyone can help Jonathan with the murder charges in Europe, it would be her."

Faye sat back as the airplane slowed. Her mind was awhirl with conflicting emotions. Since Steel's arrest on Thanksgiving Day, things had proceeded with the velocity of a tornado. Now she found herself on an international flight to Switzerland with a man she was slowly growing to care deeply about. She looked at Jason's profile, his strong, straight nose and high cheekbones. His deeply tanned skin and straight black hair were a sign of his heritage as part of the Tohono O'odham nation. The man had saved Joshua Knight's life and probably hers, too. She thought of her adopted siblings back in Dallas shopping for Christmas and getting the decorations out for the family tree. They always put the tree up the weekend after Thanksgiving, but she had been in Shreveport, Louisiana, after Jonathan Steel's arrest. And now, just days later, she and Jason were on a flight to Europe.

"What do you know about Raven's condition?" Birdsong said as the airplane came to a halt.

"Not much. Just that she has lost herself. No memories. Basically, a blank slate." She said. At least this was what little she had learned from Max's brief email requesting her help.

The airplane was a small jet they had transferred to in Paris, France, and normally held two dozen passengers. They were the only ones on board. The cockpit door opened and the co-pilot went immediately to the outer door and opened it. Frigid wind blew snow into the cabin.

"You might want to put these on." He motioned to parkas on the front row seats. "She's waiting for you." He shouted as the wind drowned out his words. He went back to the cockpit and closed the door.

Faye made her way down the aisle into the blowing snow and shrugged into the heavy parka. She handed the larger one to Birdsong. A bright pair of headlights blinded Faye as she walked carefully down the snow-covered stairs. Blowing snow tossed her hair behind her. A young man in a dark blue parka with a hood waited for them at the bottom of the stairs.

"Ms. Morgan?" He said as he examined a tablet tucked into the meager protection of his parka.

"Yes. And Jason is right behind me." Faye shouted into the wind.

The young man motioned to a nearby van. "Get inside where it will be warmer."

A sliding door opened on the side of the van, and Faye and Birdsong climbed in. The interior had been redone with a sofa against the side and back. A small table sat in the center. Faye settled onto the sofa and Birdsong sat beside her.

The young man slid the door closed and then climbed behind the wheel and drove away from the airplane. Faye looked at Birdsong and put her arm around his.

"What's next?" She said.

"Don't know." Birdsong shrugged.

The van bounced along the runway as it encountered snow drifts and then turned onto a service road. The young man behind the wheel drove the van along rows of warehouses and hangars and pulled into a narrow alley between two buildings. He glanced over his shoulder.

"Wait here." He climbed out of the van and closed the door behind him. The buffeting wind was less in the alleyway, but Faye could hear the screech as the wind funneled around the van. The door slid open, and a tall, willowy figure stepped in, sliding the door behind her.

Max wore a long, white wool coat with a hood that encircled her gray hair. She threw back the hood and slid out of the coat, revealing a long, gray evening gown. A large, jeweled dragonfly brooch held a gauzy wrap around her shoulders. Fay stared at the brooch, no doubt costing more than her entire year's salary.

"Now, let's get to it." She said. She sat across from them. "Mr. Birdsong?"

"Yes." He said.

"Ms. Morgan?" She turned her glittering gaze on Faye.

"Yes."

"Good. I have been forced to take extraordinary precautions. Inspector Goudreaux and her ilk have me in their sights, it would seem. They have practically shut down my entire operations. I convinced the local authorities to let me leave my house if I didn't leave the country. I'm sure that Inspector Goudreaux is in panic mode. She will try to track my movements. I started out this evening at an elegant dinner party but got 'lost' in the crowd."

Faye swallowed. She doubted this woman would ever get lost in a crowd. "Where are we?"

"Away from prying eyes, my dear." Max adjusted her hair as she crossed her legs. "That is why we are meeting in a van hidden between two hangars at a private airfield on the outskirts of Zurich."

"I was hoping you would clear things up." Birdsong said.

"You do want to help Jonathan Steel, correct?" Max said.

"Of course. I would do anything to help my brother." Birdsong said.

Max turned her tense gaze on Faye. "And you?"

Faye swallowed. "I was wondering why you need me."

"You went out of your way to help Joshua Knight, Ms. Morgan. You went the extra mile to accompany the young man on his trip to Austin. Might I ask why?" Max tilted her head as she waited for an answer. Light glittered from the dragonfly.

"It's what I do. I help the helpless. It's who I am." Faye said quietly. "Josh needed me."

"Good! I have another patient who needs your care." Max said.

Faye looked over at Birdsong and then back at Max. "So I've heard."

"Time is growing short. Let me explain." She pulled off gray gloves from her long, supple fingers and wiped at her eyes. "I am very tired. Normally I would be relying on Ishido for security reasons. Unfortunately, he had to rejoin a criminal organization to defeat the plans of Lucas Malson and is still trying to extricate himself safely from the Geisha." Max drew a deep breath. "Therefore, I need someone to carry on with the investigation into this supposed murder Jonathan Steel is accused of. And, to spearhead the investigation into the airplane explosion. In that respect, my students have gathered sufficient information and I have hidden that information from the likes of Inspector Goudreaux who would gladly destroy it for the purpose of imprisoning Steel."

Max paused and put a hand to her forehead. She seemed to slump for a moment and Birdsong reached toward her. She put up a hand in protest. "I'm fine, Mr. Birdsong. Just a headache from fatigue." She tried to smile. "Goudreaux will be the death of me."

Max looked at Faye. "Ms. Morgan I only told you a little about the individual knows as Raven. She was an assassin until I helped her turn her back on her former lifestyle. Unfortunately, Dr. Monarch, the very doctor who placed implants in Raven's brain managed to accidentally erase her memory. She reset Raven's mind, you might say. I have been working with Raven to restore her to adult functional status but now that my organization is under scrutiny, I have had to hide Raven from the authorities."

Max leaned forward and put a hand on Faye's hand. It was warm. "I need your help with Raven."

"How can I help?" Faye said.

"Your kindness. Your empathy. But most importantly, your professional abilities. You see, there is a memory I must recover from her. I think it can still be located somewhere in her mind. Right now, she is like an innocent child but during her retraining, she has recalled certain names and certain memories that have disturbed her because of their emotional content."

"What kind of memory are you trying to recover? And why can't this Dr. Monarch do that?"

Max's face stiffened and she sat back. "Monarch will not come within a hundred miles of Raven. That monster has done enough harm to people I care about." Max looked away and, for a moment, seemed to have something in one of her eyes. "I'm sorry for getting so emotional. Raven is like my child."

"I don't know that I have the skills Raven needs." Faye said.

"Raven needs someone with empathy and patience, Ms. Morgan. You have impressed me and I think you are the perfect person for this time in Raven's life. I believe you can gently help her recall some of her memories." Max paused. "And then, there is Margo."

Faye stiffened. "How did you know?"

"About your sister? I know how you have helped your sister with her autism and this type of help is exactly what Raven needs. Time is short and Goudreaux will not be long behind me. I must leave here in the next five minutes to make it back to the dinner party."

Faye was still reeling from the fact this woman knew about her sister. She cleared her throat. "And what memory is so important?"

"I believe Goudreaux hired Raven to kill someone. It was an off-the-books job. Raven kept a record of almost all her jobs as insurance, if you will, in case any of the ones who hired her tried to take her out. To help Jonathan, I need to find out more about this person. It gives me leverage in my effort to not only clear Jonathan Steel but myself."

"Yourself?" Birdsong said.

"Goudreaux, I fear, is part of a larger organization like the Council of Darkness, and she has set out to destroy me. Have you heard of the Vitreomancers?"

"Yes." Birdsong said at the same time Faye said, "No."

Faye looked at Birdsong. "There's more than one of these demonic organizations?"

"There are many such organizations, Ms. Morgan. And thanks to the death of Dr. Faust, there will more than likely be a new member of the Penticle who is controlled by a demon. The question will be which one of the two major councils will control that person?" Max sat back in her seat and steepled her hands.

"What is the Penticle?" Faye asked.

"A highly secretive cadre of five individuals who control most of the world's commerce. They thrive on the fact the world thinks of them as an urban legend. Until now, no member of the Penticle has ever been associated with a demon. Such opposition to the workings of God has gone on for thousands of years under many poorly and, sometimes, well-organized movements. Most of these groups act in the background, in the shadows, pulling the strings of human puppets to oppose the works of Godly men and women. But if one of these organizations was successful in putting a demonic controlled host on the Penticle, well, there would be hell on earth."

Faye leaned into Birdsong and gripped his arm more tightly. "I didn't know I was getting myself into something like this."

"I'm afraid you 'got yourself into this' the minute you walked the side of good and help Josh Knight." Max said quietly. "Your involvement in this whole affair is now a moot point. You have become an enemy of Satan, Ms. Morgan, and he will come after you and your family unless you take a stand." Max sat forward.

"'Finally, be strong in the Lord and in his mighty power. Put on the full armor of God, so that you can take your stand against the devil's schemes. For our struggle is not against flesh and blood, but against the rulers, against the authorities, against the powers of this dark world and against the spiritual forces of evil in the heavenly realms. Ephesians 6.'"

A holy intensity had entered Max's eyes. Faye felt goosebumps on her arms. Max continued.

"Yes, I memorized it. And you should as well. Ms. Morgan, we are now facing those powers and principalities of evil. This is war and you either stand and take sides or you lay aside and die spiritually from apathy. You must make the choice and I think you already have or you would not be here." She touched the dragonfly brooch. "I found this brooch in the last year when I found out my daughter had been enslaved by the eleventh demon most of her life." Max looked away and sighed. "Legend has it that dragonflies were given an extra set of wings so that angels could ride on their backs. It is said when you see this winged beauty, it's a reminder that an angel from heaven is visiting you. This brooch reminds me that I must remain on the side of the angels and not the demons."

Birdsong squeezed Faye's hand. "I see now why Jonathan trusts you. So, what now?"

Max recovered her steely repose. "For you, Jason, I have a tablet loaded with surveillance and information on the whereabouts of Reginald Drake. He is somewhere in London." She retrieved the tablet from a pocket in the side of the van's interior. "On this tablet is information on Goudreaux. I'd like your professional opinion on her. She is hiding something and I have yet to find it."

Birdsong took the iPad. "I'll get right on it. But I need to know if you can do anything to help Jonathan."

Max pointed to the tablet. "That is the best way to help him, Jason. Clear him of involvement in the airplane crash and find Drake. We know from Jonathan that the Crimson Snake is responsible for the airline disaster. Jonathan had officials convinced to look for her. But Goudreaux has resurrected the idea Jonathan was also a terrorist with a separate agenda or, at the very least, an accomplice to the Snake. After all, he has had several run ins with her since the crash. And although they were adversarial, Goudreaux has seized upon the occasions as evidence the two are in collusion."

"Crimson snake? Was she the one with the Captain at the mansion?" Faye asked. "You know the woman with the prosthetic arm?"

"Yes." Birdsong said. "That was her."

Max drew a deep breath and exhaled slowly. "She was with the Captain?"

"Who is the Captain again?" Faye said.

"Jonathan's father." Birdsong said.

"The Snake is an assassin for hire much like Raven once was, only ten times as lethal. She took down an entire airplane with over two hundred souls on board." Max said.

Faye shuddered. "What in the world have I gotten myself into?"

"Welcome to my world." Birdsong said. "I didn't want you

involved. But as Max said once you agreed to help Josh, the die was cast."

Faye felt her world crumbling around her. All her carefully built walls of protection for her family, for her heart, for her mind were now under assault by supernatural forces she had once partially believed in. Now, they were becoming very real. She felt a hand on her arm. Max had leaned across the van.

"My dear, put on the armor."

"I need to find my Bible." Faye said.

Birdsong tapped the tablet. "Looks like I have homework, too."

"My assistant will take you to my mountain compound, Ms. Morgan. It is a two-hour drive and you can settle in and rest on the way." Max looked at Birdsong. "Gamma will take you to a nearby train station. You will travel through the night to London by train."

"You could have flown me directly to London." Birdsong said.

"That would have alerted Drake. You'll take trains from here on out. Now, I must return to the party to avoid any unnecessary attention from Goudreaux." She reached into another pocket in the side of the van and retrieved two phones. "High level security. Call my operatives first and they will relay any outgoing calls."

Birdsong took the phone and Faye grabbed hers. "I need to call my parents. Christmas is coming and they will want to know where I am."

Max smiled. "Of course. Just don't tell them you're in Europe, Faye. When you begin to dial you will be connected to Omicron. She will get you a secure connection. But keep it short." She opened the door to the van. Cold air blew in along with a flurry of snow. "God be with us all."

Gamma, the driver of the van, appeared in the open door. "Mr. Birdsong, if you'll come with me, please?"

Birdsong looked at Faye and opened his mouth to say something. She shook her head and pulled him to her. She kissed him. At first, he stiffened and then relaxed. He pulled back and his eyes were moist. "Well."

"That is for good luck." She kissed him again, but gently. "That is my prayer for your safety."

Birdsong beamed. "I think I can do this, now." He touched her cheek. "Wish things were different."

Faye's heart skipped a beat and she nodded. "We are at war, Jason. Let's win this thing."

Birdsong slid out of the van and the door slid shut on the cold snow. She glanced at the phone in her hand. It was a folding phone of a make she did not recognize. It was time to call her family.

CHAPTER
TEN

LONDON, England — Hampton's Museum of the Weird

"Cold, Monty?" Jason Birdsong asked.

Dr. Montana Holmes shivered in the dark furnace room of Hampton's Museum of the Weird. Holmes wore a blue polo shirt under a tweed jacket over khaki pants. He ran his hands through his thick, dark hair and he hugged himself. "Cold and creeped out." He said. "I mean, Drake was in the basement trapped in this furnace the whole time I was working on Cephas' artifacts in the next room."

Yellow crime tape stretched around the furnace. A yellow tag with a number sat on the floor. Birdsong squatted down to inspect the tag. "This is where they found Drake's anklet. Where Jonathan took it off Drake's ankle."

"Jason, you know Jonathan didn't kill Margaret McGuire." Monty said.

Birdsong stood up and nodded to his friend. "I know. He wasn't here. He was on the transport to America. But how do we prove it, Monty?"

Birdsong stepped over the crime tape and pulled out a flashlight. He directed the beam into the interior of the furnace. He smelled body odor and excrement layered on top of old ash. "Jonathan said Hampton kept Drake a prisoner in here when he arrived."

"But Hampton was in the United States." Monty said, joining him. "Man, does that stink, or what?"

Birdsong smiled as he spied a pile of cafeteria trays in the back of the furnace. "If Hampton wasn't here, then who fed Drake?" He straightened and turned to Monty.

"Who indeed? It wasn't me. Or Cassie. We didn't know this place was down here." Monty said. "Must have been McGuire."

"Then McGuire knew Drake was here. And she worked for Hampton."

"McGuire was Drake's prison guard." Monty said. Birdsong took out his cell phone. "No signal. Let's go back to the foyer. I have an idea."

———

In the foyer of Hampton's Museum of the Weird, Birdsong ended his call and sat on the edge of the late Margaret McGuire's desk. "Our friend at the police station said the crime scene investigators never checked the furnace. They're sending a team to look at those trays. I'll bet you they find only Drake's and McGuire's fingerprints on those trays."

"How does that help, Jonathan?"

"Motive."

"Enlighten me?"

Birdsong smiled again. "If you were naked and locked in an old furnace surrounded by the ashes of the cremated humans being fed with nasty food on old trays shoved through a crack in the furnace door, would you be happy?"

"No!"

"I studied Drake's profile. He is fastidious to a fault. Sharp dresser. Clean shaven. Perfectly styled hair. It would be one thing if the person bringing him food every day was a young woman he could work his wiles on. But McGuire? She was a bit dowdy."

"That's very British of you." Monty said. "And accurate."

"I can almost hear him promising he would kill her when he was set free." Birdsong said. "Of course, that just establishes a motive. It doesn't help us exclude Jonathan."

The old elevator rumbled and screeched to a halt. Cassie walked out, rubbing her eyes. "I did not know how hard it would be to get just a simple wedding venue."

Birdsong stood up and looked back and forth between her and Monty. Cassie froze, and her eyes widened. "Jason?"

"Wait! Did you say wedding?"

Cassie slapped Monty's shoulder. "Did you tell him?"

"No, you did!" Monty rubbed his shoulder.

Birdsong swept them both up in his enormous arms and squeezed tight. "This is wonderful! Great news! I'm so happy for you guys."

"Fighting Romans in ancient Jerusalem is easier than planning a wedding." Cassie sighed. "I can't find anywhere back home to get married."

Monty put an arm around her shoulders. "We don't have to do anything fancy."

Cassie glared at him. "I'm not going to Vegas!"

"Who said anything about Vegas?" Monty dropped his arm.

"You just don't understand." Cassie said, and tears ran down her cheeks.

Monty looked helplessly at Birdsong. "Don't look to me for help, brother." Birdsong said.

Cassie wiped her cheeks. "We promised each other. That's all. We promised."

"Who promised?" Birdsong asked.

Monty drew a deep breath. "Renee?" Cassie's sister, Renee Miller, had disappeared through the Portal to another world to help the Children of the Bloodstone. She had essentially died.

Cassie tucked into him and buried her face in his chest. "Yes." She mumbled. "She would have been my maid of honor. Now my sister is gone and it just won't be the same."

Monty pulled her into him. Birdsong pointed to the doors. "I'll leave you two alone. I have an errand to run."

———

Chief Inspector Julianne Holland blew cigarette smoke and glared at Jason Birdsong. She sat behind her desk in a cramped office in the local police headquarters. Her dirty blonde hair was cut short, and she wore no makeup. Her dark eyes glittered with irritation.

"Mr. Birdsong, do you realize what a bloody pain in the rear you are?" She sucked on the cigarette again. "Sometimes I wish I had never met Max. Bloody timing, if you ask me, calling in a favor when I've got cases up to the--." She paused and blew smoke across the stack of folders on her desk.

Birdsong waved smoke away from his face. He sat across the small desk from her and tried not to cough. "Don't you have rules about smoking indoors?"

"We are not in the United States, Birdsong!" She finished the cigarette and stubbed out the glowing butt in an ashtray. "But in the spirit of showing you some professional courtesy I'll wait a few minutes before lighting my next one."

"Thanks. I'm sorry for being a nuisance. But you must admit you should have examined the interior of the furnace." He said.

Holland sat back and crossed her arms. She wore a gray jacket over a light blue blouse. A St. Christopher medal hung on a necklace around her thin neck. "Look around you, Birdsong. This office is over seventy-five years old. We don't have the funds to be up to date. I share my crime scene team with two other districts. But they are at the scene now and processing the furnace." She wiped her mouth and reached for the pack of cigarettes on the table. She glared at the pack and then dropped it.

"I was with the Tucson Police Department." Birdsong said. "I know about budget restraints. At least you didn't have to deal with the whole 'defund the police' movement."

Holland laughed and put her hand up to cover a deep, wet cough. "You must have funds to cut in the first place. Bloody bureaucrats! What did you do on the force?"

"I was a patrol officer."

Holland nodded. "Why'd you quit?"

"They fired me." Birdsong sat straighter. "Politics. I'm an indigenous Native American and there were some bad mojo that went down involving my partner. He was dirty, but they didn't want it to come out, so they shifted the blame to me when he died. Said I was incompetent." Birdsong was back in Tucson on that fateful day someone knocked on his front door.

———

Birdsong opened his front door. "Lieutenant Rodriquez?"

"Hello, Jason. Can I come in?" Rodriquez was out of uniform and dressed in a tee shirt and shorts.

"Sure." Birdsong motioned to his chair. "Have a seat."

Rodriquez carried a satchel, and he sat stiffly in the chair. "There's been a development or two."

Birdsong sat on the couch. "I was wondering when I might hear something."

"Your statement claims that the driver of the SUV shot McCall through the shoulder. Through and through, right?"

"Yeah. How is he?"

"In a minute." Rodriquez opened the satchel and pulled out a photograph. "I had the crime unit go over the area with a fine-tooth comb. We found the bullet lodged in a boulder."

Birdsong studied the photograph. "38?"

"Yeah, and it matches a gun used in a murder ten years ago."

Birdsong handed the photo back to the man. "Good. Then we have an assailant."

"Yeah, that's the problem. The assailant was McCall's old partner, Julian Grosbach. Dirty cop involved in drug trafficking across the border. He killed an informant and claimed it was self-defense. The evidence didn't match his claims, and they put him away for manslaughter. He was released from prison a month ago."

Birdsong sat back on the couch, his mind reeling. "Are you saying that McCall recognized his old partner?"

Rodriquez took another photo from the satchel and handed it over. Birdsong took one look and froze, nausea climbing from his stomach. "What happened?"

"McCall. Found him hanged in his home yesterday. Suicide note and everything. Jason, answer me some tough questions right now. I'm here on my day off. I believe McCall was dirty and had something to do with that SUV. In his suicide note, he claimed you were involved too."

Birdsong stood up and tossed the photo back to Rodriquez. "No way! Look, he tried to talk me out of following the SUV. It's all there on the dash cam."

"I listened. I agree. But, this morning, the crime team went through your locker and found this." Another photo. A clear zipper bag containing cash. Birdsong shook his head.

"I've never seen this. Ever."

"Ten grand, Jason. Now, you look me in the eye and tell me you had nothing to do with this?"

"Captain, you know me. I joined the force five years ago because of what happened to my sister. You know what kind of person I am. I'm a Christian. I'm hardworking. I'm honest. I'm loyal. I don't know where this money came from. I swear. Besides, why would I be stupid enough to hide it in my locker at the police station?"

"Well, unfortunately, that cash in the evidence locker has been misplaced. For now. I will cover for you. But I'll have to ask for your badge and your gun. As of today, you're off the force pending this investigation."

"What? Captain, you can't do this! Let me go after this SUV. Let me find Grosbach."

Rodriquez stood up and took a folder out of the satchel. "You know

I can't do that. Officially, you are no longer with the force. Now, badge. Gun."

————

Not long after that, he went with Jonathan Steel to investigate the SUV that had cost him his job and subsequently traveled back in time to ancient Jerusalem. But he couldn't tell that story to Holland. She wouldn't believe a word of it.

"So now?"

"A private investigator. I work with Jonathan Steel, the man you want for the murder of McGuire. But he couldn't have killed her. He was on a private flight back to America at the time she was murdered."

Holland pursed her lips and pulled a folder toward her. She opened the folder. "If he has an alibi, where's the bloody evidence for it?"

"It was a private flight. No tickets. No check in at the airport." Birdsong felt a tic under his right eye.

"Affidavit from the pilots?"

"They have, uh, disappeared."

"Other people on the flight?" Holland said.

"They are unavailable." Birdsong shifted uncomfortably in his seat. He did not know where Vivian was. Max had refused to tell him. And Dr. Monarch and her secrecy would prevent her from testifying that she and her two children were on the flight with Steel.

"That's bloody inconvenient, if you ask me."

Birdsong nodded. "The FBI showed up in Austin, Texas. They have a record of Jonathan Steel being at the mansion a couple of hours after the flight landed in the United States."

"I have no records from your FBI."

That's because FBI Special Agent Ross sealed them in the deal with Vivian Darbonne, Ketrick, Wulf, or whatever she finally landed on as a last name. But he couldn't tell Holland that. "They are sealed."

Holland sat forward. "Look, your partner, or boss, or whatever your mate is, had his fingerprints all over Reginald Drake's anklet. He took it off and let that murderous bugger free. That alone is a crime. Drake was a fugitive from your country, but we have an extradition agreement."

Holland stood up and took another cigarette and lit it. She inhaled deeply as she paced the small area behind her desk. "Drake is a bloody devil, if you ask me. I read his sheet. I can't believe he escaped prosecution, but he would never have gotten off with murder here. I want him. I want him badly." She paused and pulled another folder from the untidy pile on her desk. She slid it across to Birdsong. "Go ahead. Take a look at the bloody photos of that girl back in the states. He got off on a technicality about the definition of death in your bleeding heart court system. And if you take a close look, there are at least a dozen other cases I suspect him to have been involved with."

Birdsong put a hand on the folder. "I've seen the photos."

Holland paused and blew smoke toward the ceiling. She picked a piece of tobacco from her lip with her broken fingernails and pointed a finger at Birdsong. "Then, there's the knife."

"I know. A golden antique knife from Dr. Cephas Lawrence's collection. Jonathan said he picked it up as a weapon of defense when he heard someone in the furnace." Birdsong said.

"I have the deposition from his lawyer."

"And his were the only prints?" Birdsong said. "That knife was handled by Dr. Montana Holmes when he took if from Lawrence's crate. There should have been more than one set of prints."

Holland looked at him. "Are you saying that Drake wiped the fingerprints from a knife, then placed it on a table among many other weapons, knowing that Jonathan Steel would pick it up? So he could take the same knife and carefully handle it to prevent any further prints and use it to kill Margaret McGuire?"

"We're talking about Reginald Drake. You said it yourself. He's a master of misdirection. He managed to get his name cleared in what should have been a slam dunk conviction for murder. He planned all of this, Holland. He knew Jonathan would come. He was and still is always three steps ahead of us."

Holland blew some more smoke. "Doesn't matter, love. Your partner let that creature loose in my city." She leaned over the desk and put both hands on the top. "We have two murders other than McGuire that match his M.O. I know he did them. But he is in the wind and it's Jonathan Steel's fault."

"I'm sorry about that, Holland. They had Jonathan's son and coerced him to let Drake go. What would you do to save your child?"

Holland turned away. She finished her cigarette in short, deep strokes and dropped the butt on the floor. She ground it out and collapsed back into her chair. "Want to know why I'm a policeman?" She said, her gaze directed to the corner of her office. She pointed to a pink umbrella hanging on a coat rack. "That belonged to my sister. I was ten. She was nine when the traffickers took her. Do you know what a ten-year-old can do to track down her kidnapped sister? Nothing. I lost my innocence that year. I vowed I would do whatever it took to find her. I studied criminal techniques in what you call middle school. When I was in high school, as you would call it, I worked for the police. When I entered college, I took law enforcement and criminal law."

She put her hands on the table. They trembled. "By the time I had started my police training, I had amassed a huge amount of information on human trafficking. No one wanted to hear it. What would a young woman with a thirst for revenge have to contribute, eh?"

Holland looked at her hands and slowed her breathing. She picked at a broken fingernail. "I found out about the Geisha. Local criminal boss. But she was the low hanging fruit. The big boss was hiding behind smoke and mirrors. My last year in the academy, I took a week off and located the trafficking hideout. *I did that."* She glared at Birdsong with wet eyes.

"They had an old cruise ship set up off the shore in an obscure bay. Had the local small town under their control. I infiltrated that ship and found my sister, Birdsong. She was an empty shell working in the 'harem', as they called it. She went into rehab and never recovered. Died ten years ago. I was a hero. But I had worked outside the system, so they were going to drop me from the academy. When I told them I discovered the identity of the 'big' boss over the Geisha, I made a deal." Holland lifted an eyebrow. "I basically gave them an ultimatum. Let me graduate and give me a position in the force, and I wouldn't give them the evidence they needed to find the boss. They did. But they stuck me here in this hellish corner of London. Been here for fifteen years. And the boss? He slipped through their fingers like snot from your bleeding nose."

"Who was the boss?"

"Some bloody culprit called Lucas."

Birdsong frozen. "Lucas Malson?"

Holland sat up in her chair. "You know Lucas Malson?"

"Jonathan just took down his operation. Check with that other policeman, McBride, I think it was."

Holland blinked several times. "Are you telling me Jonathan Steel brought down Malson?"

"So he tells me. Rescued two of our friends from the slavers. Olivia Monarch and Vivian Darbonne. Check with McBride."

Holland stood up quickly and stormed out of the office. Birdsong watched her through the slats of the blinds on the window of her office as she stopped in the hallway outside. She talked on her cell phone, raising her voice several times. Holland came back in and slowly sat behind the desk.

"McBride confirms your story. Lucas was there, but he got away. However, McBride is a hero now because he broke up the Geisha's largest fentanyl and prostitution ring." She tapped the tabletop with her fingernails. "I don't get it. Jonathan Steel lets a known serial killer loose in my city and then turns around and almost single-handedly brings down one of the largest criminal operations of the past decade."

"I told you he was coerced." Birdsong said. "Let me ask you a question. If Reginald Drake were sitting in my chair right now and he was willing to give you the location of your sister in exchange for his freedom, what would you have done?" Birdsong held his breath. Big risk here, but he had to try it.

Holland looked at him with a venomous gaze and then averted it. She wiped her mouth and massaged her eyes. "Point well taken." She looked back at him. "Doesn't change the fact he broke the law. Even if he didn't commit the murder, at best he will be considered an accessory to murder."

Birdsong sighed. It had been worth a try. "I get it. The law is the law."

"Why are you here?" Holland asked.

"To find Drake. To force him to admit he killed Margaret McGuire. To clear Jonathan's name."

Holland nodded and sat back. She tapped her chin. "There are other charges against Steel from Switzerland. A terrorist attack on an airplane that cost the lives of over two hundred people."

"Of which he was the sole survivor?" Birdsong said. "Those kind of attacks are suicide missions. Besides, there is compelling evidence the airplane was compromised by the Crimson Snake."

Holland nodded. "I read that. Again, no evidence."

Birdsong looked around the office in thought. "Why do you owe Max a favor?"

Holland froze. She blinked a few times and sat forward. "When I was in the academy, I was approached by one of Max's operatives. Max was also looking for Lucas Malson and we shared intelligence. It was Max who located the cruise ship. She was my informant, so to speak. She said I could never divulge her involvement to anyone and that, one day, she would dial me up with a favor."

Holland looked at a photo of two young girls sitting on her desk. Had to be her and her sister. "Will you at least grant me the professional courtesy of having access to all your files on the murder?" Birdsong said.

Holland reached for another cigarette and paused. "I promised myself that when Lucas was found I would stop smoking." She looked at Birdsong. "I hate to admit it, but you've given me a shot of hope, Jason Birdsong." She picked up the package of cigarette and crushed it in her hands and dropped it into the trash can. "I'll get you access. But, if you see anything my budget deprived department has missed that will let me lay hands on Drake, you bring it to me, understand?"

"Yes ma'am." Birdsong smiled.

CHAPTER
ELEVEN

MAX'S COMPOUND

Victoria drew a wiggly red line across the blue line. She moved the felt-tipped pen through a circle and then a curve. She replaced the blue pen with a green one. More lines now, all in an intricate and woven pattern. She sat back and looked at the sketchbook page. The lines made nothing she recognized, but something about them appealed to her.

"Victoria?"

She looked up into the face of a woman with dark skin and warm brown eyes. "Yes, that is my name. So they tell me." She said.

"I'm Faye. I'm here to help you."

"Help me with what?" Victoria said.

Faye looked aside at Lucille, the aide who had been working with Victoria. She had arrived at the "Compound" the day before and had settled into an enormous suite overlooking the majestic Swiss Alps. In the valley below the Compound, a small town and a dairy farm were the closest signs of civilization. Today was her first meeting with Victoria, also known as Raven.

"Max thinks Lucille might need some help. We want you to become the best person you can become." Faye said.

Victoria nodded. "I'd like that. They say I was someone else? They say I am a new creature? What kind of creature was I before?"

Something dark crossed Faye's face, and she sat across from Victoria. Faye glanced at the sketchbook. "What are you drawing?"

"Lines. Colors. Shapes. It pleases me. It feels right." Victoria said. "But not complete."

Behind Faye, she heard Lucille roll a cart across the floor of the basement work room. Faye glanced over her shoulder. Lucille was tall and lithe with long blonde hair and pale blue eyes. The cart was covered with a sheet.

Faye stood up and met her halfway. "What is this?"

"Max said this might jog her memory." Lucille said.

Victoria watched Faye lift the sheet. "Guns? Knives? Absolutely not! We do this my way, or I walk."

Lucille tensed. "But I have been her teacher."

"Up until now." Faye turned back to Victoria. "Victoria, Max asked me to work with you for a while. I had a sister who was having trouble with her thinking and her perception of the world around her. I helped my sister, and I can help you. Will you let me?"

Victoria glanced between Faye and Lucille. Something knotted in her stomach. She frowned. "I like Lucille." She looked at Faye. "But I like you, too."

"But, Max said to try something more drastic." Lucille said. "She wants results as soon as possible."

Faye glanced at Victoria. "I'm sorry for this, Victoria." She looked at Lucille. "Max brought me here from the United States. She said I could do this my way. Please put that cart out of sight." Faye said to Lucille. Lucille's face reddened and she pushed the cart to the corner and disappeared from the room.

Faye turned back to Victoria and drew a calming breath.

"That probably made you feel uncomfortable, Victoria. But sometimes your awareness of the world around you can become jarred if something is too foreign to you. Do you understand?"

Victoria considered her words. Just days ago, they would have made no sense but now, they seemed to fill her mind with meaning. "I am beginning to understand more each day. What Lucille wanted to use to help me might have hurt me?"

Faye sat down. "Yes, but not intentionally. Max would like you to improve quickly. What is on that cart is a piece of your past you have forgotten, and I think it is too dangerous to shock your mind that way. I prefer to move slowly and deliberately. I want to help you, not hurt you."

"Lucille wants to hurt me?" Victoria said. She blinked. Maybe she wasn't understanding everything like she thought.

"Not intentionally, Victoria. You see, I have experience working with my sister who had the same kind of altered vision of the world as you. I worked with her and helped her get better. Max thinks I can do the same with you. But Lucille may not have the same experience I have developed by working with my sister. What she thinks would help might cause more harm than good. Max trusts my judgment. You'll see. If you let me help you."

Victoria drew a deep breath. The knot in her stomach seemed to settle some. "Okay. The words are not all making sense. But I would like to try."

CHAPTER
TWELVE

JONATHAN STEEL

The rest of the weekend was uneventful. The Black and Blue Angels stayed away since Muck was still recovering. On Monday morning, we were back in the prison meeting room. My mind still reeled from the revelation of Judge Meridian. How to tell Ruth? Would she believe me? The key to all of this was to find Drake, wherever he was. Ruth studied her laptop screen.

"Ruth, how did Drake get off with just house arrest?" It was Ruth who defended Drake for murder. He had been exonerated and freed because of her efforts.

Ruth glanced up at me and frowned. "What?"

"I need to know." I said.

Ruth crossed her arms, and she blinked. "I'm not overly found of talking about Drake. Why does that matter?"

"Just humor me."

Ruth drew a deep breath and sighed. "Okay. You know the jury acquitted him for the murder charge."

"Thanks to you." I said.

Ruth tensed. "Thanks for reminding me."

"Just want to put all the facts on the table. You and I are complicit in this."

Ruth's face darkened, and she looked away. "Don't shift the blame to me, Jonathan. You are the one who took off Drake's anklet."

"And you are the one who cleared his name in court. Seems like we were both manipulated by the man." I said. Drake had coaxed Ruth into using a defense that was truly unexpected and that had resulted in the man's acquittal. "Even after he was acquitted of murder, there were still serious charges against him and yet, he walked away with only surveillance."

Ruth looked back at me and clenched her jaw. "Fair enough. If I hadn't done the job I did, he would be in jail for murder."

"Ruth, you're an excellent attorney. You did the job you were supposed to do. Drake just out maneuvered you. He's a clever monster." I leaned back. "Did the same thing to me and to Hampton. He's been one step ahead of us all this time."

Ruth tapped keys on her laptop. "Okay, how did he get off? After the trial, the only charge left against him was for aggravated assault. I'm pretty sure he pulled some strings, and the judge gave him community duty with nine months of ankle surveillance."

"Who was the judge that let him off?" I asked.

"It wasn't the same judge who oversaw the trial." Ruth glanced at me, and her eyes widened. She went back to her laptop and studied the screen. She gasped. "No! It can't be!"

"Let me guess, Meridian?"

"Yes." Ruth said in a hushed whisper. "Meridian."

"Ruth, there's no such thing as coincidence." How to tell her? Should I tell her? It would be best to let her come to the conclusion on her own. "Ruth, look into Meridian. He's out to get me."

Ruth pushed the laptop aside. "Is that what your private conversation was about?"

I pursed my lips and crossed my arms. "Let's just say his interests are far from neutral. He has it in for me." My gaze locked on hers. "He's working for certain, shall we say, nefarious forces."

Ruth stiffened and stood up. She paced across the room. "No! Jonathan, we can't go that way. If you bring up demons in your trial, they'll think you are crazy. You'll lose right from the start." She paused and returned to the table leaning forward to lock her gaze on mine. "And now you want to accuse the judge who can release you of being demon possessed?"

I placed my hands on the table. "He let Drake go. This has Drake's fingerprints all over it and the demonic councils." I paused. I had to tell her. "He all but admitted such to me, Ruth. And he also said I had been in that same courtroom when I was a teenager. He all but admitted I was tried for murder. He might have been the judge who oversaw that trial."

Ruth's face paled and she collapsed into her chair. "This is real, isn't it? All this spiritual warfare crap? What have you gotten yourself into? I can't put Satan on trial."

"You put God on trial in the Miller case and you won." I said.

Ruth shook her head. "Do you know how many times I've heard the excuse 'the Devil made me do it?' There is no way we can go there. Even before a jury! And if Meridian is, well, possessed, then such a defense is pointless."

I sighed. "Okay, let's go back to the Drake angle. Let me ask you. How did Drake get out of the states with an anklet on? Shouldn't he have been stopped at the airport?"

"I can't figure that out, Jonathan." Ruth said.

"I'll tell you how." I drew a deep breath. Here we go! "He teleported."

Ruth raised an eyebrow. "Like, 'beam me up, Scotty'?"

"Ruth, powerful demons can move through other dimensions of space. They can teleport their human host across space. It takes its toll on the human host. Damages them and shortens their lifespan. But why should a demon care what it does to its host?"

"You can't expect me to believe that!" Ruth sat back.

"Check the time codes and date codes. You said his anklet mysteriously appeared in London. Did you ever check on when he was here in the states the last time? Did he kill Dr. Moshander in Shreveport then teleport to London? Check it out."

"I'm not wasting my time on a science fiction fantasy, Jonathan."

"Indulge me. Just look." I said as Lane came back into the room.

"Time for lunch, Steel." He growled. He glared at Ruth. "I'll have him back by two."

As I shuffled out of the room, Ruth blinked furiously in confusion. I had just turned her world upside down. Again.

CHAPTER
THIRTEEN

Dr. Jack Merchant studied the diplomas and certificates of achievement on the office walls of Richard Stapleton, attorney at law. His reflection stared back at him; dark hair showing gray at the temples and a pair of gold wire-framed glasses. He had lost weight in the past few weeks since coming to know Jonathan Steel. It was almost like being back in Talako, Louisiana, when he had been accused of murdering his late wife. The supernatural affairs of Jonathan Steel eclipsed the things he had been through in the past few years.

Using his legal credentials as an assistant medical examiner in Louisiana, he had contacted the district attorney's office for information on the murder fifteen years ago. It had taken two days of calling before the man agreed to see him. How strange his journey had been from a radiologist who performed a spinal tap on Joshua Knight to a member of Jonathan Steel's army against evil!

The door to the office opened and Stapleton walked in. He looked to be in his early fifties, with thinning black hair. He was a bit overweight, with bags under his eyes. He shuffled across the office and slumped in his chair. He drew a deep breath and belched.

Merchant stood up and put his hand out. "Dr. Jack Merchant."

Stapleton looked at his proffered hand as if it were a snake and belched. "Sorry. Tex-Mex will be the death of me. I'm not happy to see you, Dr. Merchant. Sit down." He ignored Merchant's hand. "You are a persistent man."

Merchant sat down. "I am, Mr. Stapleton. And I realize as Assistant District Attorney you are busy as well. But I need information that may help in the trial of a very good friend of mine."

Stapleton pursed his lips and nodded. "Jonathan Steel, you told my assistant. I know all about the man. Wanted on several federal charges. He's wanted internationally for terrorist activities and a murder in London. Not to mention a known accomplice of Reginald Drake, currently a fugitive who somehow eluded law enforcement here in the United States and showed up in London. Jonathan Steel removed the man's surveillance anklet." He leaned forward. "Tell me why I would be interested in helping you clear this man's name?"

Merchant cleared his throat. "I see you're caught up on the man."

"I am." Stapleton sat back. "Want some advice, Dr. Merchant?"

"I guess you're going to give it to me, anyway."

"Find a new friend. Now, I have a meeting on my schedule, and I don't have time to waste on scum like Jonathan Steel."

"So, you've researched the man's background?" Merchant said.

"What little there is."

"He doesn't have a record, does he?" Merchant said.

Stapleton looked away, deep in thought. "No, he doesn't."

"Isn't that odd? I mean, here is a man who is a supposed

terrorist and murderer, and he has no criminal record." Merchant tapped the table. "I've investigated everything I can on the man. The FBI gave him a new identity as Jonathan Steel. He claims to have amnesia and doesn't recall his past. There's something there, Mr. Stapleton."

Stapleton raised an eyebrow and smiled. "Are you searching for information to help the man or to satisfy your curiosity? How did you end up connected with him? Maybe I should be looking into your background?"

Merchant froze and sighed. "There was a murder in Shreveport, Louisiana recently. Dr. Moshander, a colleague of mine, killed in the most heinous way. The police and the FBI think Drake killed him." I paused, collecting my thoughts. "Look, I ended up helping Jonathan recover his son, Joshua Knight. Josh had been deliberately infected with a virus by some pretty vicious people as leverage to force Jonathan to perform certain possibly illegal actions."

"Ah, so where there is smoke, there is fire." Stapleton said.

"No, wait. Jonathan was in London on one of these missions because he was trying to help Josh. He turned the tables on the perpetrators. It's all in the FBI report from the raid on the mansion in Austin. I was helping Jonathan because Josh was one of my patients."

"I thought you were a medical examiner. Josh isn't dead."

"I am an assistant to the coroner's office, but I'm also a radiologist in private practice. My interest in forensic radiology led me to help our coroner, Dr. Francisco, solve cold cases. But I am still in private practice, and I performed some diagnostic tests on Josh when he first got sick. Look, it's a long story, but I trust Jonathan Steel with my life."

"These 'perpetrators' you talk about, drug cartel?"

Merchant drew a deep breath. Should he tell the man everything? He was desperate for help. "Okay, so Jonathan called them the 'unholy triad'. They were triplets. Doctors at a clinic in

Dallas." Merchant swallowed hard. *Here we go!* "Jonathan called them the seventh, sixth, and fifth demons."

Stapleton stiffened, and he turned a pasty shade of white. He blinked several times and his breathing quickened. "Great! I knew that would come back to haunt me." He reached over and pressed a button on his phone. "Marshall, I'm going to be a bit late for that meeting. Hold my calls for a few." Stapleton's hands trembled. "Okay, now you have gotten my interest. Go on."

Merchant studied Stapleton's features. His pupils had dilated, and a fine sweat had broken out on the man's forehead. "You know about the demons, don't you?"

Stapleton was silent. "There was a case. Maybe fourteen, fifteen years ago. A teenager accused of killing his mother. I prosecuted the case." Stapleton was sweating now and loosened his tie. "I haven't thought about it in years. I can't. I refuse to. What happened in that courtroom was," he paused and grimaced in pain. He clutched his chest. "Oh God! Not now!"

He tumbled sideways onto the floor. Merchant shot out of his chair and ran around to the far side of the desk. Stapleton was gasping for breath and clutching his chest. "Heart!" He hissed.

Merchant stabbed the button on the telephone and a voice answered. "Marshall! Call 911. Your boss is having a heart attack."

Merchant pulled Stapleton's body away from the chair and knelt beside him to feel his pulse. Thready. Weak. Erratic. Probably ventricular fibrillation. Did the courthouse have a defibrillator? Stapleton's eyes rolled back in his head and Merchant started CPR. The door to his office burst open and a young man ran in.

"Help me." Merchant said. "Mouth to mouth or chest compressions."

Marshall hesitated and then squatted beside Stapleton and began pumping on his chest. A woman appeared at the door with a container. Merchant glanced up.

"Defibrillator?"

She nodded, her face stricken. Merchant motioned for the box. "I'm a doctor. Give it."

Merchant opened the box and found a handheld respirator, and he motioned for the woman. "Put this over his mouth, tilt his head back and squeeze the bag. Now!"

She knelt beside him, and Merchant ripped open Stapleton's shirt. He slapped the defibrillator pads on the man's chest and activated the defibrillator. He looked at the monitor and sure enough, Stapleton was in ventricular fibrillation.

"Hands off. I'm shocking him." He pressed the button on the defibrillator and Stapleton's back arched. He settled down, and the monitor showed normal rhythm. Merchant nodded. "We got normal rhythm. What about 911?" It was then he heard the sirens approaching.

"On the way." Marshall said.

"Stop pumping. He's got a weak but steady pulse and he's breathing." Merchant said.

Stapleton opened his eyes and looked up at Merchant. "Yvonne Brown. Find her. She defended the teenager. She will tell you everything." He whispered.

Merchant leaned closer. "What?"

Stapleton mouthed something and Merchant pressed his ear close to the man's lips. "The third demon. It was the third demon."

The defibrillator screeched, and Stapleton was back in ventricular fibrillation. Paramedics appeared in the door and burst into the room. Merchant stood up. "V. Fib. Heart attack. I shocked him once, but he's back in V. Fib."

The lead paramedic nodded. "You are?"

"Dr. Merchant. Take over and take care of him." Merchant backed away as the team went to work on Stapleton. They never got his normal rhythm back. Twenty minutes later, he was legally dead. In his own jurisdiction, he would be the doctor to declare the man dead. Here, he was just a bystander. Merchant wandered out into the hall wiping sweat from his brow. What had happened in that courtroom that could send this man into a deadly heart attack?

"What have you gotten yourself into? Again, Jack Merchant?" He mumbled to himself.

———

Merchant glanced up at the clock. Nearly five P.M. and the archive room would soon close. He had grabbed a sandwich and coffee in the courthouse lunchroom, which did not sit well after the incident with Stapleton. He had requested access to court archives. The supervisor was an elderly African American man somewhere in his early sixties. After scrutinizing Merchant's I.D. he shook his head.

"Heard you tried to save Mr. Stapleton." He said.

"News travels fast." Merchant said. He was still shaking. "Heart attack. I was in his office when it happened."

The man shook his head sadly. "Good man. Too good for his job, if you ask me."

"Why do you say that?"

The man looked up at me and pushed a registry toward me. "Sign in. I've been here twenty years, Dr. Merchant. Stapleton was an up-and-coming attorney. He had his sights set on Congress, if you ask me. But something happened, and he settled down. You know, actually started caring for the average man. Politics went out the window."

"What happened?"

The man shrugged. "Not sure."

"Did it have anything to do with the case of a teenager accused of murdering his mother, say, about fifteen years ago?"

The man stepped back from his counter. "How do you know about that?"

"I don't. Do you know anything about it?"

The man shook his head. "Just rumors. Why?"

"I'm actually looking into that case." Merchant said.

The man pursed his lips. "Won't do you any good. Records are sealed."

Merchant placed the pen in the spine of the registry book after signing his name. "So, you do know something. You sure you don't remember anything?"

The man backed away. "Nothing. Take room 3. I'll give you access to all records, and you can see for yourself. Good luck." He then did the strangest thing. He performed the sign of the cross and disappeared into the archives.

————

That had been three hours ago. Merchant rubbed his tired eyes. Nothing. No records in the juvenile file or the adult criminal file. He had even accessed police records. Nothing. How could that be? Who had the power to completely erase all evidence of a murder from police and court records? He couldn't even find a name. Name?

Merchant hurried from the room and back to the counter. The attendant returned. "Told you. Sign out. We close in five." He pushed the registry toward Merchant.

Merchant signed his name. "Can I ask you one last question?"

"Maybe."

"Do you recall an attorney by the name of Yvonne Brown?"

The man flinched. "Where did you find that name? Was it in the records?"

"No."

He swallowed hard and nodded. "She was bright. Worked for a law firm here in town. Don't remember the name of the firm. Took on a lot of pro bono cases from what I understood. Rumor was she was out for the underdog." The man stopped. "That's all I know about her."

"Know where I can find her?"

The man shook his head. "No. Fact is, she disappeared off

the map about fifteen years ago. I had to take her off the registry at the request of Mr. Stapleton." The man took the registry back and closed it. "And we both know he won't be talking anymore. Wish I could help you, my friend." He took the registry and disappeared into the archives, turning off the light as he went.

———

Merchant sat in the reception area of the Austin Police Department the next morning holding a box of donuts. The receptionist had been frosty until he offered him a donut.

"Really?" He had said. "What am I? A walking cliche?"

"No, you're probably hungry. I hear these are the best in town." But not as good as Southern Maid donuts in Shreveport, he thought. Merchant opened the box and offered them to the man. He sat across a counter from Merchant and reached in and took one. "Let's see some I.D."

Merchant showed him his medical examiner credentials. He nodded. "Long way from home. What can I help you with?"

"I'm looking into a murder case. Fifteen years ago." Merchant said.

"Fifteen years ago? I was on the streets back then. Lots of murders under the bridge." He chewed the donut. "Not the famous bridge."

"The one with the bats?"

"That would be it." Austin was famous for a bridge under which bats lived. Every evening, it was literally a show when they streamed out from under the bridge.

"So, a homicide?"

"They accused a teenager of killing his mother. He and his mother lived in a mansion on the outskirts of town." Merchant said.

The officer froze. He frowned. "I seem to recall that. Big news. Rich lady. Weird husband. Let me think." He turned to the squad room behind him. "Hey, Gridlock, who would have handled a juvie homicide about fifteen years ago."

"Gridlock" a huge man of Latino descent strode up to the desk. He had short salt and pepper hair and a hungry gleam in his eyes.

"Who's asking?"

"The man with the donuts."

Merchant offered the donuts. "Should have gotten the empanadas." Gridlock took a donut. "To die for. My sister works in that shop." He took a bite from the donut. "He legit?"

"Yeah. Medical examiner from Louisiana."

Gridlock smiled. "Go tigers!" He finished the donut and brushed sugar from his hands. "Okay, there was Sam O'Malley but he retired that year. His partner was Corsair."

"Yeah, Corsair is retired." He turned back to Merchant. "He's a security guard at the Super Wal-Mart." He looked at a computer screen and wrote something on a business card.

"Is that his phone number?"

The man slid the card toward Merchant and opened his other hand. "Nope, Corsair's home address and my name. Corsair won't talk to just anybody. You get it in exchange for the donuts."

"Fair enough." Merchant handed over the box and picked up the card.

"Next time, empanadas." Gridlock said, licking his fingers.

———

"I can't talk about it." Corsair said. He sat on a bench on his front porch. Merchant watched as mothers strolled by pushing strollers. Joggers passed by. It was a nice area in northern Austin. Corsair was somewhere in his sixties with a heavy gray mustache and bushy hair. He wore his blue Wal-Mart security outfit. "I have to go to work in thirty minutes, so I don't have much time."

Merchant had told him about the case he was investigating. "What can you tell me?"

Corsair glanced at Merchant and his eyes filled with a haunting memory. "I signed a nondisclosure agreement."

"You're retired. What can they do to you?"

"Send me to jail. It was a pretty tight agreement and I wasn't even at the trial." He said.

Merchant drew a deep breath. So close. "Can you at least tell me why you had to sign that agreement?"

"The case and all evidence and reports were sealed."

"Under who's authority?"

Corsair looked away. "The federal government, I can tell you that much. A captain made sure everything was sealed tighter than a tick."

Merchant tensed. The Captain? Now he was getting somewhere. "What did this captain have to do with anything?"

Corsair pulled a toothpick out of his shirt pocket and worked on his front teeth. "Okay, I'll tell you this much. I wasn't the first on the scene. My partner was. It was bad." He stopped and moisture filled his eyes for a moment. "It was beyond bad. My partner left the force that day. He was pretty shook up."

"And?"

Corsair looked at Merchant. "I can't."

"You already did."

"No, I can't. Don't want to dredge up those memories."

"The perpetrator was a teenager, right? The woman's son?"

Corsair nodded, still working at his teeth with the toothpick. Merchant pushed some more. "This captain, what did he have to do with the case?"

"Boy was his son." Corsair said. "Look, no more. I got to go." He stood up and started down the stairs off his porch.

"Mr. Corsair, you have a very nice place here." Merchant followed him down the stairs.

Corsair turned and tossed the toothpick into the grass. "Normal, yes. After that case all I wanted was for the world to return to normal."

"Did it?"

He looked around at his neighborhood. "It's all a facade. Everyone just moving along as if nothing was wrong with this world. But it's a crock. They're out there. Spinning their lies and doling out evil." He looked back at Merchant. "I don't have to worry about them at Wal-Mart."

"Who are you talking about?"

Corsair paused for a moment and then looked away again. "Demons. That's what happened in that courtroom. Demons. That boy killed because of demons and I'm done talking about it." He walked around the corner of his house toward a garage. I tried to follow him.

"One more thing. Did you know a Yvonne Brown?"

Corsair froze and glanced over his shoulder. "Don't go looking for her. Or him."

"Him?"

"My partner, Sam. They both disappeared right after the trial. And if you keep pushing, you'll disappear, too." He went through the side door to his garage and slammed it shut.

CHAPTER
FOURTEEN

LONDON, England

"Agent Darbonne, when will I get the money?"

Vivian Darbonne reached across the kitchen table and retrieved the Interpol "badge" Max had given her. She used it to dispel suspicion in her job of repaying families of those assassinated by Raven. The woman did not know the badge had absolutely no force behind it. Interpol provided investigative support, expertise, and training to law enforcement worldwide and itself was not a law enforcement agency.

"I'm not an agent." She said. "Ms. Darbonne will do. The funds will be transferred to your bank account within the week."

The dowdy woman looked out the nearby window of her small, cramped house. The tiny garden held nothing but dead flower bushes and leafless trees covered with a patina of frost and slowly falling snow. "I do not know who would want to kill my son. He had so much promise. Up and coming barrister and all." She sniffed and wiped her nose with her bare hand. Her graying blonde hair was limp and hung around her plump, red face. She looked back at Vivian with tear-filled eyes. "I would say I miss him, but I don't really, love. He was a bit of a bully. There was a time I believed he got what he deserved." She motioned around her. "I mean, just look at this hovel I live in. You'd think your own son would find it in his heart to share a bit of his riches for his own mother, wouldn't you? You help your own mother, don't you, love?"

Vivian drew a deep breath and looked down at her laptop. Her mother had been a monster. She nodded. "I would if she were still alive." Her old self would have made sure the same bull that killed her father gored her mother. In her new, redeemed state, she had found it in her heart to forgive her mother. It had brought her peace.

"Oh, I'm sorry, love." She said.

Vivian tapped on her laptop. "Mrs. Cambridge, I want to share something with you. My mother was a monster. I hated her most of my life. But, not too long ago, I found forgiveness in my new relationship with Jesus Christ." She paused. That sounded so strange coming from her mouth, but it was right. It was good. It was who she was now. "I forgave my mother, and it has given me peace. Whatever deeds your son committed," Vivian paused and for a second wanted to tell the woman what her son had been doing. Yes, he was an attorney. But he was also a psychopath who channeled his desire to kill as a serial killer to being a quiet "fixer" for certain business interests. He had always made his targets seem to be victims of a vicious, mindless killer. Someone had hired Raven to stop the man from "fixing" things when he strayed outside the business model and started killing for his own amusement. She swallowed and continued. "If you can find it in your heart to forgive him, you might find some peace."

Mrs. Cambridge stared at her and then laughed. "Forgive him? Love, this money will go a long way to helping me find a way to forgive him."

Vivian slid the laptop over. "Enter your bank account number and we will transfer the money next week."

Mrs. Cambridge tapped on the laptop, her tongue protruding as she did. "There you go, love. How much am I getting?"

Vivian grimaced at the thought of giving this woman that much money. It would destroy her. But Vivian's job was fulfilling Raven's wishes to make recompense for the families of her victims. Instead of prison, she would most likely spend the next decade tracking down these individuals and giving them money. Money that very well might ruin their lives.

"One million pounds." Vivian said.

Mrs. Cambridge's mouth fell open. She blinked furiously. "I'm sorry, love, did you say one million pounds?"

"Yes."

Mrs. Cambridge whooped and clapped her hands and looked up toward the heavens. "All is forgiven, lad. All is forgiven. Christmas is here!"

Somehow Vivian doubted the depth of the woman's words or the destination of her son's soul. She closed the laptop and left the dismal home of Mrs. Cambridge, mother of the late professional serial killer Macbeth Cambridge. What had his mother expected when she named her son Macbeth? One down and so many more to go! The most difficult part of this new job was locating the victims' significant others.

Vivian's rental car was covered with a fine sheen of snow. Stuck under the wiper was a bright pink note. She grabbed it and sat behind the driver's seat, started the car, and ramped up the heat.

"Meet me at the nearest coffee shop. I'm disarmed." Vivian read. Underneath the words, a line drawing of a snake squirmed across the note. Vivian almost swore. She stared through the snow-covered windshield. "You really should just drive away, Vivian. Go back to the hotel and report to Max and get the name of the next victim's family. Don't be tempted." She closed her eyes and sat back in the seat. She knew exactly who had written that note. Curiosity got the better of her and she headed for the corner coffee shop.

———

The shop was busy and almost all tables were full. In the back corner, one table sat next to the hallway leading to the restrooms and the Crimson Snake waved to Vivian. Vivian slipped through the customers to the table.

"What are you doing here?" She said.

Snake wore a red wool sweater and a green scarf worn "Sherlock" style around her neck. Her carrot-colored hair was tucked into a red knit cap. Both hands looked normal.

"Happy Christmas, Vivian. I just wanted to have coffee with an old friend. I heard you were in town." Snake slid the other chair back from the table. "Come on. Humor me. I'm not here to hurt you."

"Or kill me?"

Snake shrugged. "Not today."

"Who are you working for now? Last time we saw you, it was the Captain."

"We?" Snake leaned forward. "Now you are a 'we'?"

"I've changed Snake. If you had stayed around at the Austin mansion and saw what we did to the triplets and their demons, you would know that I serve a new Master. And He is not of this earth." Vivian said.

Snake studied her bulky brown coat and the black sweater beneath. Her eyes roved over Vivian's shoulder length hair. "You let your hair grow since Lucas. He liked it short."

"It hasn't been that long since then, Snake. Lucas made me pin it up." Vivian said. Vivian had been a prisoner of Lucas Malson in an abandoned theme park he had converted into a drug lab and "harem". While Vivian recovered from brain damage after removing the goggles in the virtual reality world of Numinocity, Lucas had dressed her like a 1950s television mother.

"And who made sure that poor, helpless Olivia Monarch

didn't end up in the harem but was appointed to be your dresser?" Snake said. "That would be me."

"And you did that because you knew Olivia's presence would help my memory return?" Vivian snorted. "You enjoyed every moment of my misery.

"Well, I guess I had a soft spot for the girl. After all, I saved her from the burning warehouse when Thakkar's Numinocity collapsed. Would have been a waste of a good 'save' to let her die in the harems or from a hole in her gloves in the fentanyl factory." Snake said as she examined the nails on her good hand.

"Snake, the only reason Olivia ended up with me was because of answered prayers. I can't believe you went back to work for Lucas."

"Lucas was the puppet. Someone else pulled the strings." Snake said. "But now, I work for myself, Vivian." A server showed up with two cups of coffee in steaming mugs. The server sat one mug in front of Snake and the other in front of Vivian. Vivian studied the foam on the top. A brown spiral colored the foam. She looked up at Snake.

"What is this?"

"Decaf latte with skim milk, sugar free vanilla syrup, and three sweeteners. Reggie said you like it that way." Snake sipped her mug. "Did I get it wrong?"

Reggie had been Vivian's assistant until the government seized all her assets and removed her from all executive positions. "Not the coffee. The spiral."

"Ah, yes, that." Snake smiled. "Your first collaboration. The thirteenth demon, right? Whoever was possessed by the thing manifested a spiral around their right eye, right?"

Vivian stirred the foam to dissipate the spiral. "What is your game?"

"Just reminding you of your past, dear." Snake sat forward. "Now that you've found religion."

"Found forgiveness. Religion is man-made. Man always screws up what we make." Vivian said. "I should know."

"You found Jesus?"

"Jesus found me." Vivian said. For a moment, she was back in ancient Jerusalem. Jesus had looked down a long, dreary alleyway and had pierced her soul with those eyes. "You ought to try it."

"Oh, no, no, no, dear." Snake wagged her prosthetic hand. "I've done far too many horrible things to turn to Jesus. Nope, not for me. If you recall, I brought down an airplane with a couple of hundred people on it."

"225." Vivian said. "You're on my list."

Snake raised an eyebrow. "That's right! Your new job is to keep yourself from going under the jail. Track down every family member or loved one left behind by Raven's assassinations and do what? Buy their forgiveness?"

"I'm not the one they need to forgive."

Snake laughed and sipped more coffee. "Vivian, honey child, you hired Raven to kill that lawyer. What was his name? Probably forgot, haven't you? Your name is on that list, too. You're no better than me, Vivian."

"I was someone who did the hiring. You were someone who did the killing. There's a difference."

"Not much. What did your Jesus say? If you plan to kill someone, it's as bad as the deed itself?" She grinned. "I've read the Bible. Well, some of it."

Vivian drew a deep breath and sighed. "You're absolutely right. And that is my point. We are no different. Broken people are broken people. But some of us have found a way to heal some of the cracks and make this world a better place than we found it instead the other way around. I'm at peace with my past. I'm paying restitution now. And it won't be enough, Snake. Never enough." Vivian leaned across the table. "In fact, Snake, there is no amount of good deeds that will every heal your brokenness. You are incapable of that. Which is why you need a divine healer."

Snake held up her artificial hand. "Yeah? Where was the

healer when this happened to me? Where was the healer when Lucas had me as his slave?"

Vivian looked away. "I don't have all the answers." She looked back at Snake. "I'm mortal and broken. There is no way I can come up with all the answers on my own. I need someone with a broader perspective, someone who sees the bigger picture, someone who can look at me from outside the limitations of our feeble reality, someone eternal."

Snake sat quietly for a moment and sipped more coffee. "Nice speech. Or should I say sermon?"

"I'm not a priest or a preacher, Snake. I'm just a new person. The old me is gone, washed away. I like who I am now. I hated who I was before." Vivian sipped her coffee. "Do you hate yourself?"

Snake looked away and sighed. "Yes."

They sat in silence for a while. Vivian finished her coffee. "Tell me why I shouldn't call the police?" She said. "More importantly, why am I here?"

"I want to help." Snake whispered.

"What?" Vivian almost spit her coffee.

"I want to help you. Off the books. Out of sight of Goudreaux and Max. I don't have a job and I need to do something. Balance the scales." She looked up at Vivian. "Something good."

Vivian thought furiously. Could she trust Snake? The woman had killed hundreds. She was a stone-cold assassin worse than Raven ever had been. But there was one thing that might help. "You know that Jonathan Steel has been arrested for terrorism. He's being blamed for the air disaster you caused."

Snake blinked and nodded. "I know. The evidence just isn't there to convict him. Goudreaux is ignoring the facts on purpose." She leaned forward. "Something else is going on, Vivian. Something deeper. Something more insidious."

"Then confess." Vivian said. "Tell them you did it."

Snake sat back and examined her artificial hand. "I already did." She said quietly.

"What?"

"That's my point. I recorded a video confession and sent it to Goudreaux. I even called her up and made sure she got it. Know what she said? 'Don't try and help Steel. He's dead meat.' The woman ignored my confession. That's what I mean when I say something else is up here."

Vivian drew a deep breath. "Max and Goudreaux are joisting over the murder of that McGuire woman as well and the murder took place in another country. Goudreaux wants to drag Max down with Jonathan."

"I had nothing to do with the McGuire woman. It has Reginald Drake written all over it." Snake said.

"I suspected as much."

"Look, Vivian, that 'badge' of yours has no power. Interpol is not a law enforcement agency. You have no leverage against Goudreaux." Snake said.

"I know that. Goudreaux is working under Swiss credentials. But I agree with you that more is going on than can be seen on the surface. I believe her marching orders come from more, shall we say, nefarious organizations."

"Like the Council of Darkness."

"Or the Vitreomancers." Vivian said.

Snake pursed her lips. "You know they are the two big ones. But there are a lot of minor groups out there with the same end goals: chaos and destruction. True, the smaller ones think they are serving their own interests and they don't realize who they REALLY serve. But the outcome is the same."

"Goudreaux is not a small-time player. She has connections. She is working for one of the two big ones, I'm sure." Vivian decided. "Okay, you want to help Jonathan? Then bring down Goudreaux. Surely you have contacts."

Snake blinked slowly like her namesake. "What about Drake?"

"If I know Jonathan Steel, he already has someone working on that end. But this information about Goudreaux is new to me and he has no idea of your confession. Take down Goudreaux, without killing her, Snake. Remove her influence from this case. Jonathan and Max would be grateful."

"You know, my last job was to protect Jonathan while he is in jail." Snake said.

"What?"

"Hampton and Dr. Sno didn't want him to die in prison. They reached out to me to, shall I say, influence one of the prison guards." Snake looked down at her coffee. "Lane was nice. Naive, but nice. In another place and another time, maybe we could have had a chance for normalcy."

Snake sighed. "So, I hear Max took in the assassin Ishido and rehabilitated him. Gave him a new purpose. Did the same thing with Raven." She looked up at Vivian. "You get me in with Max, and I'll take down Goudreaux." Her face softened, and she blinked away moisture from one of her eyes. "Think there might be hope for me? Think I might one day find normal?"

Vivian actually smiled. She had made some progress! "There is always hope, Snake."

CHAPTER
FIFTEEN

JONATHAN STEEL

Ruth had court appearances for the rest of the week. Friday came and I would meet with her after lunch. Maybe Meridian had decided. There had been no word from Jason Birdsong. Nothing from Josh or Jack Merchant. I still waited patiently for my transfer to the federal facility. I kept to myself and avoided the BAA most of the week. By Friday morning, Muck showed up without his neck collar. He had recovered.

At lunch, I studied the stale sandwich on my tray sitting next to brown and inedible kernels of corn. A dollop of applesauce filled one of the depressions in the tray. A shadow passed over my tray and the table sagged at one side as the enormous man leaned on the edge.

A huge bruise covered most of Muck's neck. "You going to eat your sandwich?" He rasped.

"You're welcome to it." I slid the tray toward him. He placed a meaty hand on the table to stop the tray from sliding onto the floor. Applesauce slopped onto a misspelled curse word tattooed on the back of his hand. His piggy eyes widened and he drew in a deep breath. "Hope you can swallow." I said.

He took one look at his hand covered with food. Before I could react, he swung his other hand backhanded and caught me across my right eye. I fell out of my seat and rolled across the floor. The other inmates paused in their ingestion of their own goo for only a second before returning to their repasts. Muck loomed over me. He grabbed my collar and picked me up bodily. Only my toes touched the floor. Lane had indeed left me to the fate of the BBA.

"Who do you serve?" I managed to ask.

The man blinked for a few seconds and then he smiled. "He calls himself number three." He squinted. "But I can't kill you. Not yet, anyway."

"That's how you can touch me without burning." I said hoarsely. "He's not inside you right now. You're not important enough to be a host."

"Ain't nobody inside me but me." Muck blinked. It had taken a lot out of him to come up with that response.

My left hand tingled. I could barely turn my head downward to see it because of Muck's huge hands gripping my collar. My palm glowed. I looked back at Muck and smiled. "Let me give you a hand."

I shoved my palm up against his right temple. His eyes widened to normal size and his face faded away.

The floor was hard and cold beneath me. Muck seemed different now, hovering over me, and I felt his hands on my throat. I couldn't breathe and I grabbed his arms with my hands. My fingernails were painted a bright pink. The depth of anger and fear reflected in his eyes filled me with despair and hopelessness, even as I gasped for breath until his eyes filled with tears.

"Why you made me do this? I love you! You made me do this to you!" He screamed and reflected in the wet corneas of his eyes

I saw the contorted face of a woman. What was happening? I was seeing Muck's crime!

My hand fell away from his face and he dropped me. Gasping for breath I pulled myself up by the edge of the table and leaned against it. The light began to fade from my palm. Muck looked at his hands. Tears poured from his eyes.

"Why you did that? Why you brought her back? I done told everybody I'm sorry. I can't bring her back! Why you did that?" He stumbled back away from me and ran into several inmates standing behind him. He shoved them out of the way as I slumped back into my seat. The remainder of the Black and Blue Angels had gathered behind Muck. He swept them aside as if they were bowling pins.

My eye throbbed and I could feel the swelling begin. Looking down at my palm I wondered again what had just happened. My palm had brought me into the man's memories of the murder for which he was incarcerated. His anger, his fear, and yes, his regret still echoed in my mind and heart. This meant that Muck's attack on the woman had been at the directions of a demon or the event would never have been recorded. He had mentioned number three.

Looking up at the remaining BBAs I expected the next attacker to head my way. Instead, the fear and confusion in the faces of the three men standing before me told me all I needed to know. No one would ever touch me again. They did not want to relive their crimes!

———

I held the ice pack to my right eye. It was swollen shut, but I could still see Ruth clearly.

"What happened?"

"One of Meridian's buddies picked a fight with me at lunch." I said through my swollen lip. "Don't worry. He's not doing so well, either."

Ruth shook her head. "I will not stand for this, Jonathan."

"You can't control what goes on in this prison, Ruth." I put the ice pack on the table. "If I had fought back harder, my chances of getting out of here would diminish. Besides, I heal quickly. And the forces of evil will not prevail over me." I said that last with as much bravado as I could muster.

I reached across the table, rattling my manacles until my hand rested on hers. It was warm and a faint tingle passed along my arm.

"After all, I have been through, Ruth, I am convinced now, more than ever, that God is on my side. That comes with a price. I will not give into the despair of hopelessness. They may harm my body, but they cannot touch my spirit."

Ruth's gaze softened and moisture filled her eyes. "Oh, Jonathan, what you have been through!" Ruth's hand turned palm upward, and she tightened her grip. A faint blue light leaked from our grasp, and she gasped. "What is that?"

I gently pulled my hand away and held up my palm. It still glowed with a blue light. The relief from the pain was almost instantaneous when I placed it on my swollen eye. I took it away from eye and turned my palm toward her. "I have no idea. Maybe a shard of the Grimvox?"

"The what?"

"A repository, a recording of certain evil deeds. Only I think God has flipped it for me. It works for me at times when I get discouraged. It has revealed things to me."

Ruth's mouth fell open. "The swelling in your eye! It's better!"

I nodded. "Like I said, I heal quickly. Now, back to the issue at hand." A faint smile creased my lips. "Pun not intended. I will resist the devil in this place. I must trust that God will not let me come to a deadly end because the battle is just beginning. I am near the end of the Council of Darkness. Things could only get more difficult, but I will persevere."

"Nice speech." Ruth said. "You actually mean it, don't you?"

"Yes." And I did. "Look, I was out of line pushing you so hard about my mother. I don't know for a fact what happened. But I now see that I'm not like Muck out there who just tried to rearrange my brains. I'm not that guard, Lane, who let the Crimson Snake manipulate him."

"Wait? The Crimson Snake is involved?" Ruth dropped her pen on the table.

"I told you this was getting complicated. I told you we are at war. Ruth, I don't know if I really killed my mother or not. But I can tell you that the enemy will use my guilt over that possibility to distract me. Right now, we must stop Drake. I made matters worse when I took his anklet off. He killed Margaret McGuire and Dr. Moshander. Let's focus on Drake. Implicate him and you clear me. And then, I'll look into my mother's death. Fair deal?"

"Well it's about time you came to your senses. Yes, it's a deal." Ruth said.

There was a tap at the door and Ruth stood up and opened it. Detective Citronella Jones walked in. Without hesitation she rounded the table and hugged me from the side.

"What are you doing here?"

"I was the arresting officer on Drake." She sat next to Ruth. "When Ms. Martinez asked for more records on the latest disappearance of Drake, I told her I was here to help. Not get you convicted. You done a good enough job of that yourself." She placed a backpack on the table and pulled out a computer tablet and handed it to Ruth.

"It's all there. I downloaded the same information we reviewed yesterday."

"I asked Detective Jones to bring this so you could see for yourself." Ruth slid the tablet toward me. "You were right. Time stamps and GPS data show Drake traveled to Shreveport and arrived at 8 P.M. on the night of Moshander's murder. The anklet data places him at the physical location of the murder and then in a motel room for the next twenty-four hours." She pointed to a map on the screen with a blinking red cursor. It stopped blinking and faded away.

"Then he just disappears off the map at 9 P.M. the day after the murder. In looking back at this, we thought he had deactivated his anklet somehow. Spooky!" Citronella said.

"I called Detective Jones and had her check on the anklet data when you called me to look for him. I found out he was in London, right? But I never thought to check when he arrived in London. I just notified the authorities to go after him." Ruth said.

Citronella swiped the screen to the side and another screen showed. "This was the map I let Ms. Martinez see when we met to look for Drake." She pointed to a blinking red dot. "Drake was here in Hampton's museum. If we backtrack the data, he was there for a couple of days."

"Drake said he had been imprisoned in the furnace. They took his clothes so he wouldn't escape naked into the city. Like that would stop him! Someone had him captive." I said

"Exactly. He appears on this map on this date and time." Ruth looked up at me and her face was pale. Her finger shook as she pointed to the map. "His anklet shows up on the surveillance grid exactly five minutes after it disappeared from our surveillance in Shreveport."

"He teleported." I said. I froze. "Wait a minute! He had no clothes? Perhaps when you are teleported, you leave all behind? But he still had his anklet." I shook my head. "Demons! They are capricious and nasty and love chaos. They left his clothes behind but left the anklet. Without clothes and trapped in a furnace, he was the perfect bait for a trap set for me! This was all a setup."

"Say what?" Citronella leaned forward. "Teleport? Like using a transporter?"

"I didn't believe it the first time, either, Detective Jones." Ruth sat back in her chair and shook her head.

"Jonathan, what is going on?" Citronella asked.

"I told you the first time we met. I was looking for the thirteenth demon. He and his host, Rocky Braxton, killed April

Pierce. There is a Council of Darkness of twelve demons carrying out Satan's plans. I have been fighting them since the day we met." I rubbed my sore eye with my manacled hands. "We have to find him, Ruth. He killed that woman and framed me for it."

"Drake is a monster, a serial killer." Citronella said quietly. She was still processing the teleportation statement. "If he can pop in and out of anywhere at will, how do we pin these murders on him?"

"It takes its toll." I said. "He can't teleport very often. It's too hard on the human body. So there were other murders?"

"Drake is a player. Wealthy and unfettered by morality." Citronella said. "Honey child, he is Satan incarnate, if you ask me."

Ruth moved through images of the victim on her tablet. The final image appeared, a photograph of Drake. He sat in a pale green chair as if in a professional portrait. His discordant colored eyes gleamed for the camera, and his brilliant smile was electrifying. And yet, disturbing, as if the lines of his face were just a bit off kilter, almost out of alignment. On the wall behind him hung framed certificates. I froze. An icy wave poured down my neck. I grabbed the tablet and my manacles rattled on the table.

"Where did you get this photograph, Citronella?" I said.

"We pulled it from his cloud account. Why?"

I resized the photograph and zoomed in on the wall behind Drake. My blood ran cold, and my spit dried up. My hands trembled as I worked the track pad to zoom the photo even larger. One certificate had a barely legible name: Richard Pierce! Even though it was still poorly resolved, there was no doubt about the origin of the photograph. To the left of the chair, I could see red letters of some foreign, unknown language on a white wall. And just at the top of the photograph was a sock with the tip of the toes barely visible, dripping a dark red liquid onto the wall.

"Oh my God!" I shoved my hands against my mouth. Nausea gripped me. Ruth was at my side instantly.

"Jonathan? Do I need to get the guard?"

I could only shake my head, and I pointed a shaking finger at the photograph. "The wall. The letters. The blood! He was there at the beach house when Braxton killed Robert and April Pierce!"

"What?" Citronella said as she stood up and studied the tablet screen.

I turned in the chair and looked into Ruth's eyes. "Ruth, the certificate is Richard Pierce's. It's still hanging in a bedroom at my beach house. And there's a body in that photo. I know where that took place. He was there."

"Where?"

"Once the police were through with the crime scene, Ruth, I locked up the room. Never repainted it. I left it just as it was on the night they died. Drake was there!" I shuddered. "Drake was involved in the murder of Robert and April. That is Robert's toe. Those writings were on the wall. He was there before they took the body down!"

Citronella's phone warbled. She looked at the screen and answered the call.

"Hello Mosquito Whisperer."

Citronella froze and looked at the screen. She punched the speaker button.

"Let me talk to Sweetums." An unctuous voice said over the speaker.

Ruth glanced up at Steel. "It's Drake!"

"The very one. I see you accessed my photos. Can I speak to Steel?"

"I'm hanging up now." Citronella said.

"Oh, now Nella, you know I have my eyes on Mr. Steel's loved ones! If you value their lives, you won't hang up." Drake said. I motioned for the phone and Citronella slid it over. "Take me off speaker. This conversation is between us."

I did as I was told and put the phone speaker to my ear. "What do you want?"

"I'm coming back to see you, man of steel, a bit rusted though you are. In two nights, I'll meet you where that photo was taken. See you then. Oh, and if police show up, bad things will happen to those around you. I know exactly where to find Dr. Monarch. I know where to find Dr. Merchant. So don't tell anyone you're meeting me."

"I'm in prison." I said.

"Not for long. I've worked out a deal with Four." The line went dead.

Citronella snared her phone and tapped the keyboard. "Didn't register the number he called from."

"He's smart. He's got someone in here who can manipulate a cell phone."

Citronella looked up from the phone and pierced me with her fiery gaze. "Honey child, if you know where he is, you better tell me so I can put an end to all of this."

"No, I can't tell you right now." I said, and she glared at me. "Wait! Trust me." I looked at Ruth. "He said Meridian was going to release me. You will insist on an anklet so you can keep tabs on me. That way, you can follow along where I'm going. It'll give you about an hour's lag time to respond, but that way, I keep the police away long enough to deal with Drake."

"I don't know, Jonathan." Ruth said. "We want this man. I want him bad. They can put him away for good this time."

"He threatened our loved ones. I must go alone." I reached over and took her hand. "It's a good plan, Ruth. I know what I'm doing. I can incapacitate him. I can use my spiritual ability to keep him there until you guys arrive. Make sure he doesn't communicate with anyone. It's the perfect sting operation."

Ruth pulled her hand slowly away from mine. "Okay, Jonathan. I hope this will work out better than the last time I trusted you."

Citronella sighed. "The last anklet didn't last long enough. I hope this time you know what you're doing."

SIXTEEN

MY MIND WAS REELING. I couldn't get the image of Drake out of mind. That and the sight of the huge dog that sat before Meridian's desk. It was black with long, spindly legs and pointed ears that stood straight up on either side of its narrow head. The dog's ebon eyes were focused on me.

"Mr. Steel, are you listening?"

I glanced up at Judge Meridian sitting behind his desk. Ruth nudged me as we stood before him.

"Jonathan, stop daydreaming." She whispered.

"I'm not daydreaming." I said and glared at Meridian. "I'm looking at your dog."

"Anubis?" Meridian sat behind his desk. "He goes everywhere with me. Not usually into my courtrooms but today I thought I might need some protection."

"From me?" I raised my manacled wrists.

Anubis tensed and barked. I jerked at the sound. Meridian motioned to the bailiff. "Bubba, take those manacles off Mr. Steel."

Bubba gave Anubis a wide birth as he came over and unlocked the manacles on my wrists and on my ankles.

I rubbed my wrists and tried to ignore the huge dog. "Did you know?" I asked Meridian.

Meridian pulled off his huge glasses and steepled his fingers before him. "Know what?"

"About Drake and Rocky Braxton."

Meridian's eyes widened and he motioned to the bailiff. "Bubba, put the tracking anklet on Mr. Steel and then leave us alone. Take Ms. Martinez with you."

"Just a minute." Ruth said. "You made me leave the other day and I will not allow my client to be browbeaten in a session alone with you."

Meridian stood and seemed to grow in stature. Anubis growled and bared yellow teeth. I felt the wave of evil wash over me. Meridian reached beneath his desk and brought out an ancient set of scales. He plopped it on the desk. The bronze set of scales oscillated back and forth until the empty pans settled at the same level.

"Ms. Martinez, I have agreed to your request for a hearing without a jury. I am the scales of justice in this case. As you requested, I am dismissing the charges against Mr. Steel as along as he stays in the city. As you requested, I am agreeing to allow your client to leave prison with a location anklet pending his extradition to Great Britain. It seems you should be grateful for whatever 'browbeating' he took in our brief session alone. Now, I have some directives for Mr. Steel that do not affect you. If you do not cooperate, I can arrange for you to take Mr. Steel's place in prison for contempt of court."

I put a hand on Ruth's arm. "It's okay." I said as Bubba fixed the anklet around my left ankle. "I can handle Meridian."

"I know what you're thinking, Jonathan." She whispered. "Don't go after Drake on your own. This isn't about revenge. We must think about your extradition and try and stop it."

"Ms. Martinez, will you accompany me, please." Bubba said as he stood up.

Ruth reached and squeezed my hand then followed the

bailiff out of the courtroom. Meridian sighed and shrugged out of his robe. Under his robe he wore a red golf shirt with bright green holly leaves that matched his green pants. He moved gracefully down from behind his desk and sauntered across the courtroom to the double doors. The locks clicked and he turned to regard me.

"Now that we are alone, I will answer your question, Mr. Steel." He hopped over the swinging door separating the spectator's seating from the front of the courtroom and crossed to the dog. Anubis rubbed his head against Meridian's leg.

"Anubis is my comfort dog." Meridian rubbed the dog's head. Anubis' tongue came out and the dog relaxed onto the floor.

"He doesn't bring me much comfort." I said.

"Well, Mr. Steel, your discomfort comforts me." Meridian grinned and slid into a chair at the prosecution's desk. "I've known Drake for some time. Did you know I was the judge who assigned his case to a certain courtroom where I was certain he would be convicted?" Meridian sat back and propped his feet on the table. He wore golf shoes. "I did not know Ms. Martinez would be so capable. They acquitted Drake, much to my dismay. I had planned on locking that host up for the rest of his life."

"Host?"

"Back then, he hosted any number of bottom feeding demons. Vile, uncontrollable, chaotic demons. Insane demons! Now, of course, he hosts the third demon, Mr. Steel. Pay attention." He put his hands behind his head and nodded. "After his acquittal and his brief visit with you he convinced someone on the Council to allow him to become a host. Yep, three outwitted me. He's smart and crafty. Legion is what he calls himself. Copies me! He uses a host of smaller demons who are enamored by his charismatic personality to be placeholders when he moves from host to host." He smiled. "You see, Four has a Legion of hosts and Three has a Legion of lesser demons. I was hoping to take Drake off the board."

"This isn't a game." I said.

Meridian chuckled and sat forward. "Oh, but it is, Mr. Steel. One massive global game with eternal consequences."

"Why do you keep fighting a battle you've already lost." I said. "Satan is a dead man walking. I've read Revelation." Anubis growled and I tried to ignore him.

Meridian's features darkened and he stood up. "Prophecies are not always fulfilled, Mr. Steel. We can change the future."

"Wasn't that the plan with the crucifixion?" I said. "Kill God's chosen one? Did you even realize he was the God man? Didn't you see he was God in man form? You can't kill God."

"Oh, but we did. He just didn't stay dead." Meridian crossed to Anubis and took a treat out of his pocket and tossed it to the dog. Anubis snapped the snippet out of thin air and loudly crunched as he chewed. "But you are correct. The angle we used with Judas assumed Jesus was a military general to lead Israel against Roman occupation."

"If you had read the prophecies, you would have known He would be more than that." I said.

Meridian paused. "Prophecies? There was no Old Testament back then, Mr. Steel. We had the Torah and the other holy scriptures but you, your race, you men were only interested in conquest and revenge. Our hosts did not see the underlying meaning of the prophecies. We were blinded by people's hubris and self-centeredness. Something we encouraged, I must admit."

"As I said, it doesn't matter if you've already lost. Jesus Christ's crucifixion was not Satan's triumph. He was used by God to allow the greatest evil act in the the universe and it resulted in the greatest good for all mankind." I smiled. "You were conned."

Meridian froze and then looked away. For a moment something monstrous and unholy appeared surrounding the man's figure. He snapped his fingers and Anubis crossed the distance between the desk and the table in seconds. The dog hopped onto the table and thrust his snout into my face. His yellow teeth bared, Anubis growled at me. Saliva dripped from his lips. I remained absolutely still, refusing to be cowed by this demon dog. The thing's breath was hot and rancid and bore a wave of evil.

"I can send your dog to Tartarus, Meridian." I whispered.

Meridian appeared behind Anubis and chuckled. "You are weak, Steel. Let me show you why I chose this dog and his namesake. Take a look at your palm. It glows with HIS memory."

I cut my eyes down to my left palm. It began to glow and I was somewhere else.

"Pharaoh, these men represent a weak god." Bactik whispered in the man's ear. Bactik wore the ceremonial robes of priesthood. His totally black robe draped his body and his headdress bore the jackal face and ears of the god, Anubis. "I say we weigh their hearts before you let them speak."

Pharaoh's bare head gleamed in the candlelight. His heavy eye makeup was marred by sweat. He was a weak man and Bactik counted on that. Pharaoh's white and gold robes hung on his thick body and he wrung his hands.

"We cannot lose the Israelite workers." He said. "Even now they build my tomb."

"Yes!" Bactik whispered into his ear.

"But I will hear what they have to say." Pharaoh clapped his hands and two men approached his throne. One was taller and thin and carried a long staff. His salt and pepper hair hung to his shoulders. His eyes were familiar. Too familiar.

"Moses, you return to your courts." Pharaoh said. "You are not welcome here. You deserted my father, and the death sentence is still upon your head."

Moses motioned to the man next to him. He was shorter and

stockier and carried a shorter staff. "My brother, Aaron will speak for me."

Aaron nodded. "What Moses will say is that he is no longer a citizen of this pagan realm. His citizenship resides with the children of God and you will let them go."

Bactik stepped between Pharaoh and the men. "You are infidels and slaves to speak this way to the god Pharaoh. It is fitting that you should face death and then travel to my realm. There, your hearts will be weighed on the scales of truth and it will find you wanting and Ammitt will eat your souls."

Moses raised his hand. "My God is more powerful than any of your pagan gods. He will protect us, Bactik."

Bactik opened his mouth to speak and felt the hand of Pharaoh.

"I will allow it." Pharaoh said. Bactik tensed but backed away. "If they can demonstrate the power of their god."

Bactik smiled. This would work in his favor. Aaron looked at Moses and then raised his staff above his head and hurled it onto the tiles of the throne room. The wooden staff clattered to the ground. Bactik laughed.

"What is this? A show of physical prowess. I can defeat you with a dozen men with spears having more accuracy than you!" Bactik turned quickly to Pharaoh. "Master, he has tried to strike you down. Have these men executed immediately."

Something hissed and Bactik whirled. One end of the staff now bore the head of a serpent. Its glittering eyes turned toward Pharaoh as the staff's wood softened and elongated. The serpent coiled upon itself and now, the entire staff was a long, scaled snake. The thing's eyes glittered a bright green. It slithered across the floor toward Bactik.

Bactik calmed his breathing heart. "A magic trick?" He motioned to Pharaoh. "Master, you have a dozen sorcerers who can outdo this trickery." Bactik clapped his hand. From around him, a dozen men appeared carrying their own staffs.

"Show these men what true magic is like." He said.

Each sorcerer tossed their staffs onto the tiled floor. One by one, the twelve staffs took on the shape of a serpent. Each serpent was shorter and stockier than Aaron's serpent. The twelve serpents coiled and snapped at each other until the larger serpent slowly slithered in their direction.

With a quick strike, Aaron's serpent shot into the midst of the twelve serpents. They writhed, they hissed and struck at the larger serpent. One by one, the larger serpent devoured each snake from head to tail. The last serpent tried to slither away and Aaron's serpent caught it by the tail and swallowed it whole. During the entire time, Aaron's serpent never once seemed bloated or full.

Bactik stumbled back among his sorcerers. Pharaoh stood up in shock. Now, Aaron's snake studied Bactik with a wary look and then stretched out on the floor. The scales faded and it became an ordinary wooden staff. Aaron picked up the staff and held it above his head. "Our God has proven He is superior. Moses says to let our people go." The two men turned and walked out of the throne room. Pharaoh regarded his sorcerers.

"Get them out of my sight!" He shouted. Bactik ushered the sorcerers away from the throne room and into an inner chamber. The chamber was dark and lit by a few torches. Bactik stood before the sorcerers.

"You couldn't manage a simple magic trick? You are useless to me! It is time to weigh your hearts." He motioned to the four corners of the rooms. The twelve sorcerers' eyes were wide in fear and their voices raised in pleas of mercy. Bactik snapped his finger.

From out of the shadows the sound of growling echoed in the chamber. The shadows elongated and matured into four legged beasts with spiked ears. Red eyes gleamed in the darkness.

A gold set of scales materialized in Bactik's hand and he held it up. He took a white ostrich feather from within his robe. He placed it on one of the pans. "Now, all I require are your hearts."

The beasts hurled themselves from the shadows and the demon jackals merged on the sorcerers. Bactik laughed with glee.

———

The world faded around Steel and he was once again face to face with Anubis. "Get this devil dog out of my face before I sent you both to Tartarus." He roared.

Anubis froze and slowed backed away. The dog tensed and then disappeared leaving behind the odor of sulfur and brimstone. Meridian slumped for a moment and shook his head. He sat up slowly and rubbed his eyes. Meridian continued in a subdued voice.

"You may think what you saw was triumph on Moses' part. But twelve serpents were devoured by Aaron's rod. And, Mr. Steel, twelve souls harvested for my true master. It is now a game of numbers. Every soul we take from God is another blow to His ego, to His hubris. No matter how this ends, we will have claimed and rejoiced in every human soul dragged off to Tartarus."

"Four is gone, isn't he?" I said.

"Temporarily." Meridian said.

"You shouldn't have shown me that last memory." I said.

"You have recovered your spiritual strength." Meridian stood up slowly.

"Now is the time to denounce the fourth demon. Stop this evil enterprise of yours."

Meridian hurried around and up to his desk and put on his glasses. He blinked at me. "Are you insane? Better to rein in hell than serve in heaven. Isn't that one of those sayings?"

"Hell is not for reining." I said. "It is for suffering. Imagine being separated from God for all eternity."

"My master already knows all about that." Meridian said quietly. "I sense his loss, the death of his connection to God. It is tragic and painful. But then so are our lives as humans. If there is even a chance I can stay above my fellow man in hell, I will stick to my plan, Mr. Steel." He motioned to his clothing. "I love golf. I play regularly and I always win. A perk of possession. I oversee this 'evil enterprise' as you call it and I always win, Mr. Steel. I enjoy a great and wondrous existence thanks to the fourth demon."

"At the expense of others." I said.

"So what? It's every man for himself. Darwin had it right. Survival of the fittest. Well, Mr. Steel, the fittest are those with power and the fourth demon gives me great power." He sat back in his chair and looked down on me. "Look at you. At my mercy. I could have you on death row in a heartbeat. I can have you sent to a prison that makes your recent detention center look like Disneyland. Or I can grant you freedom, Mr. Steel. Which is what I am doing."

"Why?" I stood up and approached his desk.

"History lesson is over and now you have recovered your spirit." Meridian studied me for a moment. "I grow tired of the third demon and his interferences. He is too haughty, too confident. Worse, he has no grand plan. How he ascended to the rank of number three is beyond me. I want him gone. I want him taken off the board. Too chaotic."

I laughed and Meridian glared at me. "What is so funny?"

"Chaos. Isn't that the main goal of Satan? Sow chaos and confusion in the minds of humanity? Keep us stirred up and searching for answers and then misdirecting our attention back to ourselves? Making us think we are gods? Love yourself. Follow your heart. Find the inner you. Be true to you? Whatever it takes to keep our eyes off a transcendent God?"

Meridian sat silently, the muscles in his jaw flexing. He ran a hand across his face. "There can be purpose in chaos, Mr. Steel."

"Like the chaos that Drake leaves behind? Purposeless killings? He's a serial killer with the mind of madman. He is chaos."

"Which is my point about Three, Mr. Steel. You should know."

I froze. "What do you mean?"

Slowly Meridian smiled and licked his lips. "So haughty now, aren't we? Just because Four isn't here right now, you think I am powerless. Well, you will learn soon enough. If and when your memories return. Three has taken a special interest in you because of your past. Talk about chaos!" He chuckled and my face grew warm.

"There is a connection with Braxton, then?"

"Yes. How did you know?" Meridian said.

I looked away. "A photograph of Drake. When you study it, you see a wall behind him with bloody scrawling from a madman. And a foot." I looked back at Meridian. "He was there when the Pierces were killed by Rocky Braxton. And you knew it."

Meridian sat very still, and then slowly nodded. "I suspected. Drake is like a hog that goes back to his slop. Three teased him back then, seducing him with a taste of power by giving him some of his lesser demons. Drake is dangerous to us. He can't stay away from his kills. Three knows that and still uses the man, and Drake will be Three's undoing." Meridian nodded slowly. "You are the instrument of that undoing."

"What are you talking about?"

"Drake will return to the scene of the crime. He made sure you saw that photo for a reason. Am I right?"

I nodded. Meridian leaned back. "I'll give you twenty-four hours, Steel."

"For what?"

"Before I report to the authorities that your anklet shows you have left town as you are not supposed to. Twenty-four hours to meet Drake and take him out." Meridian tapped on his desk. "And I'm not talking about the man, Steel. I want Three's eternal demon rear end in Tartarus ASAP. Now get going before Ms. Martinez realizes you are gone." He stood up and stretched. "I have a game to play. A tournament to kick off this festive season. And I love my 'handicap'. Seasons Greetings, Mr. Steel."

CHAPTER
SEVENTEEN

SHREVEPORT, Louisiana

"Mama Liz, just give me another day." Josh pleaded with the video feed on the monitor. He played with the bloodstone dangling from the necklace around his neck. Since the virus had almost killed him, Josh had gained at least ten pounds and most of his strength. Faye Morgan had taken the bloodstone from him and hid it before his transportation to the Austin mansion, and she had given it back to him at Thanksgiving. Just before Jonathan Steel had been arrested! If only the bloodstone could give him some kind of magical power to find out how to free Jonathan. But since he had gotten it back, the jewel had not glowed once.

"Josh, I can't keep covering for you. The FBI has called twice today looking for you." Liz Washington's features filled with concern. "Where are you?"

"It's best you don't know, Mama Liz. Trust me. I'm trying to help Jonathan and I can't do it from the lake house with the FBI watching over my shoulder." Josh said. "Give me one more day. Please."

Liz rubbed her eyes and then looked tiredly at Josh. "If they found out what you've done, Josh, they will send you back to the foster program in Texas. You know that." She looked over her shoulder. "There's someone at the door. Probably the FBI again."

"Then tell them the truth. Tell them you don't know where I am. Let them decide I've run away from home. I don't want to get you into trouble. I know how to elude the authorities. I learned that lesson the hard way." He thought back to his fugitive status after the killers came for him at his friend's house.

"Josh, I'll do what I can. Take care. God be with you." Liz ended the call.

Josh sat back and yawned. Since Thanksgiving Day, he had been hiding in Olivia Monarch's "secret headquarters", a unit in a long term storage facility. He hadn't shaved. Using bottled water, he'd taken a "spit" bath. His clothes were the same, and he had aired them out at night while sleeping in the sleeping bag on the cot. His nights had been filled with restless sleep and recurring nightmares of the days he spent in a stupor under the influence of the "Pandora Stone". He still heard the creepy voice of the old man in a pith helmet. Who was he? What did he have to do with the Council of Darkness and Jonathan Steel? For a second, he fought to recall the strange man's words.

"There is a spiritual battle coming and you and the man known as Jonathan Steel will be at the epicenter. What you have been through so far is nothing compared to what is coming. You will lose heart. You will be discouraged. You will possibly lose your faith. I tell you all of this because you are so important to my cause and you must endure to the end." He had said. But then, he seemed to have changed his tune when he said, *"You see, there are many demonic factions in this universe. As long as you are prepared for the faction that is coming for you, I can breathe easier. After all, the enemy of my enemy is my friend."*

Unfortunately, the memories of that encounter were fading as if they had come to him from some supernatural realm. Jonathan had spoken of how his experiences in the "extra dimensional" spaces of the heavenly realms stayed with his memory for only a short period of time.

His mother had often spoken of how the human mind could not retain memories of that realm. In the basement of the church in Lakeside, while under the influence of the thirteenth demon, Josh had passed briefly through that realm. But his memories of the thirteenth demon and the death of his mother were all too real. They did not fade no matter how much he might wish they would. He could still see his mother's eyes and hear her voice as she dove over the altar and took Ketrick into the burning furnace with her. His eyes stung with unshed tears and he angrily wiped them away. He couldn't dwell on the past. He had much to do.

Josh closed the video chat window and studied the document on the computer monitor. Being here in Olivia Monarch's hiding place at a local storage warehouse would shield him from the FBI for now. But there were much smarter hackers than he in the FBI. He had maybe a few days' time.

He highlighted and copied large sections of the document on his desktop into a separate folder. A tiny red dot blinked in the menu bar. Josh froze and opened an image window on the desktop. Someone moved down the hallway outside the storage room, but the image failed to reveal anyone. He squinted at the screen and whirled as the door behind him screeched upward.

Olivia Monarch glared at him and stepped into the storage compartment and lowered the doorway. "Josh, what do you think you are doing?"

Josh relaxed. "Living off the grid." Olivia looked lovely in her long, red coat. She wore a knit cap over her short hair.

Olivia's phone chimed and she studied the screen. "Just got an alert. Local police have been notified by the FBI to find you." Beneath the coat, she wore a tee shirt with "The Child" on it and a pair of black jeans. "What have you done?"

"They came looking for me at the lake house. I told Mama Liz to tell them the truth. You weren't followed, were you?" Josh turned back to his computer monitor.

"I think I can elude any surveillance." She joined him at the desk. "You should have included me from the start, Josh. I know how to do this better than you. Remember, my family has been on the run for years." She tapped on the keyboard and hit return. "There. I just pinged another router in Bossier City. They'll go there. We're still safe here, thank you very much." Olivia grimaced and looked around at the shelves with supplies and the makeshift cot. "What is that smell?"

"I haven't emptied the bedpan, yet."

"Gross! Josh, what makes you think you can leave bedpans full of your stuff sitting around my escape room?"

Josh pointed to the document on the computer screen. "I gotta help Jonathan, Olivia. I can't do that if I'm in foster care in Texas."

Olivia glanced at a partially eaten pizza on the counter beside the computer. "The least you could do is keep the place clean."

"Yeah, and how do I do that without getting caught?"

"You do that by getting me to help in the first place." She picked up the pizza box and walked to the corner. She slid a box aside on the shelf and pulled down a metal flap in the back wall. "There's a trash bin right outside this wall and I authorized the placement of a trash chute without the owner knowing it." She slid the pizza out of sight. "But I'm not emptying your bedpan. Although, if you go to the other corner and swing the shelf out toward you, you will find a portable potty connected to the main restroom. One flush and you're good."

Josh turned and shrugged. "Fine. You thought of everything."

"I had to. Keeping safe was my mother's mantra. Now, what are you up to?"

Josh pointed to the document. "I've been researching the legal standards in Texas. Looking for loopholes in the international agreements with European countries. FBI Special Agent Ross delayed the inevitable, but there must be a way to keep Jonathan from being extradited to England."

Olivia came back and settled into the chair. "You've been busy."

"Lots of precedents have been established. If I can collect them for Jonathan's lawyer, it might help."

"I didn't know you were interested in law."

"I have to be. Now you need to leave so you will not become an accessory to the fact."

Olivia rolled her eyes and reached out to his face. She turned him so their eyes met. "Josh, I love you. You know that. Where you go, I go. What you do, I do. Good or bad. We're in this together. We've been through too much for me to walk away now."

Josh felt his heart melt, and he sat back and sighed. "Olivia, I love you, too. That's why you can't get involved."

"I was involved the first time you climbed into my car way back before Numinocity. And, if it were not for you, I would never have made peace with God." She looked away. "If only mother would come around. And Steven."

"They'll come around. You did. I did." Josh reached out and took her hand and kissed it. "Olivia, I've changed. Battling Pandora made me relive some of my most painful regrets. I had to grow out of my childish teenage hubris."

"Wow! Hubris? Such big words."

Josh nodded toward the monitor. "Legal documents. Lots of big words."

Olivia leaned into him and touched her lips to his. They kissed, and she sighed. "If only we didn't have other matters to worry about."

Josh pulled back awkwardly. "What? No, no! We can't, Olivia. Not now. I will not be distracted."

"Babe, I promise I'm not here to distract here. I was here to rescue you, but you've convinced me. We must help Jonathan." She smiled. "You had me at hubris!"

Josh took both of her hands and gazed into her eyes. He studied knit cap and the barely visible bump that covered her neural stimulator. "Before we go any farther, how are your seizures?"

Olivia looked away. She pulled her hands gently away from his. "I am still having an occasional absent seizure every day." She looked back at him, and her eyes were wet with new tears. "I don't understand why Steven's hands were healed in Numinocity and I wasn't." She shook her head. "I know I shouldn't ask these types of questions, Josh. I know there is a God and I'm willing to get to know Him. After all, now I see demons. Sometimes." She took his hands again. "I just want to be normal. Is that too much to ask?"

"No. That's not too much to ask. I don't know why God does things the way he does. The Bible says His ways are not our ways. He has an eternal perspective, and He sees the big picture we can't see. I have to believe there is a reason you weren't healed, Olivia. Maybe it is because only with your seizures can you see demons."

Olivia looked away and wiped a tear from her cheek. "You, quoting scripture to me. Josh, you've changed. I haven't heard 'Dude' or 'Bro' the entire time I've been here."

Josh touched her cheek and turned her face back toward his. "I have been reading the Bible again. It's weird. It's dense. Sometimes it is difficult to comprehend. Especially the Old Testament. But that story of Joseph resonated with me. I mean, here was a young man who was the apple of his father's eye. And his bros," Josh paused, and Olivia smiled, "There I said it. His bros got jealous and threw him in an empty cistern to die. Then sold him into slavery. And then he was taken to Egypt and took the high road and served Potifer until Potifer's wife tried to seduce him. He refused her advances, and she accused him of attempted rape. So, here was a good man doing the right thing and honoring God, who ended up in a foreign land in prison for doing the right thing."

Josh drew a deep breath. "I don't think I could still be doing the right thing. I mean, you were in a similar situation with Vivian in Lucas' compound."

"Yes, and it was horrible, Josh." Olivia had been kidnapped and taken to Lucas Malson's hideaway with its drug labs and sex slaves. Vivian Darbonne and Jonathan Steel had rescued her.

Josh nodded and pulled her hands up to his mouth and kissed them. "So, hear what I'm about to say. Joseph was in the perfect position to interpret a dream that caught the attention of Pharaoh. He interpreted Pharaoh's dream of an upcoming famine only because God revealed that meaning to him. Joseph became a powerful leader in Egypt and when his own bros came to Egypt looking for food at the start of the famine, he could have thrown them all in prison. In fact, he did for a while. But eventually he revealed himself to his brothers, and he said, 'What man intended for evil, God has used for good.'"

"Olivia, if you had not been kidnapped and taken to that compound, you would have never been there to help Vivian recover her memory. Your presence, including your ability to see demons, was the key to rescuing hundreds of human trafficking slaves. That would have never happened if you did not have seizures. I know you hate having epilepsy. I know you long for the day you will be normal. But God has used your disease for the purpose of good. And, Olivia, I must believe that someday you will find healing."

Olivia was crying now, her tears dripping onto her shirt. She pulled her hands from Josh's grip and wiped her face. She leaned into him and they touched foreheads. "Oh, Josh, thank you, thank you, for understanding."

"Hey, I'm here for you. Always." Josh said.

Olivia straightened and nodded. "I like the new, improved Josh. But please throw in an occasional bro or dude?"

Josh laughed. "Deal!"

"And that portable potty room?"

"Yes?"

"There's a shower head. Just close the door and you are in a portable shower. You need it. You need it badly, babe."

"At least I brought my toothbrush."

Olivia pointed to the computer monitor. "So, get back to what you were doing best, helping Jonathan."

Josh turned back to the computer. "Okay, so I have found a legal angle on Jonathan's status. There's an old law on the books that forbids extradition if the criminal is mentally incompetent. I need a medical examiner to certify that Jonathan is insane."

"What?"

Josh turned to her. "What did you think the first time I mentioned demons?"

Olivia nodded. "That you were crazy."

"All Jonathan needs to do is keep insisting he is fighting demons. Then we find someone with the appropriate credentials to swear an affidavit Jonathan is not mentally competent for extradition until he receives treatment."

"And who would we find that has that kind of psychiatric training and the legal authority."

Josh sighed. "That's the next step.

A message notification pinged on the computer screen. Olivia leaned forward. "Nice! You forwarded all calls to an anonymous voicemail box. Very smart. Why haven't you returned my calls?"

"I haven't returned any calls. I threw my phone away." He reached into his jacket pocket and took out a phone. "Bought one at a convenience store. I haven't used it yet." He clicked on the notification box and the recording began to play.

"Josh, I'm using a secure line established by Max. This is Dr. Jack Merchant. I need to talk to you and find out where you are. I understand you are now a fugitive, and I hope that you have reached out to your very smart girlfriend to shield yourself from scrutiny. I may have found something that would help Jonathan, but I can't get in touch with him. The prison is only allowing his attorney inside and she won't return my calls. Very frustrating. Call me on a burner phone."

CHAPTER
EIGHTEEN

WITH OLIVIA SITTING at his side, Josh activated the extra security VPN protocol and started the video chat. Dr. Jack Merchant's face appeared. He wore a cap, and a jacket zipped up to the neck and sat outside before a coffee shop. Behind him, people moved along carrying Christmas themed bags.

"Jack, where are you?"

"At a very public place, the Domain. In northern Austin. Apartments above lots of trendy shopping stores. I am outside the Starbucks. I'm using the secure phone Max gave me and I used the app to make sure I wasn't under surveillance. The more public the place, the less chance they will stop me." Merchant's gaze shifted back and forth.

"They?"

"Sorry. I'm so paranoid right now. You would not believe what I've found out."

"Tell us."

Merchant recounted all he had learned. Merchant constantly paused to glance over his shoulders.

Josh glanced at Olivia. "Well, at least we know Jonathan's flashback was an actual event. And there were demons involved."

"And they acquitted him or he would still be in jail." Olivia pointed out.

Merchant looked over his shoulder and shuddered. "It's cold out here. Kind of unusual for Austin. Josh, I don't think there is anything more I can do right now. I'm sending you names and a summary of everything I've learned."

Josh studied his screen. "Got it! Jack, go home. Spend some time with your fiancée. Get ready for Christmas. Take a breather and I'll start looking through files for some of this information." Josh said.

Jack sighed. "I think you're right. I've done all I can do."

"Dr. Merchant." Olivia said. "You've earned a rest. Come home and maybe Steven and I can meet you and Pam for dinner one night."

"What about your mom?" Merchant asked.

"She went back to London to tie up some details in her lab. She'll be home next week."

Merchant leaned into the image. "And how about you? Your demon eyes?"

Olivia smiled. "I have had no sightings since the unholy triad was taken into custody. Josh and I are working on how I can control it. You know, turn it on when I need it, and off when it gets annoying. For what it's worth, I don't see any demons around you. But my gift may not work on video footage."

"And your seizures?"

"Still have an occasional absent seizure. No better." She paused and glanced at Josh. "No worse."

"Just take care, Olivia. I'll see you next week." Merchant ended the chat. Josh started downloading the data from Merchant. He glanced at Olivia.

"Now what about school?"

"Got a doctor's excuse to study from home like we did during the pandemic. There are advantages sometimes to have a medical condition. What about you?"

Josh smiled. "You're looking at the most recent graduate from

Captain Shreve High School. I had enough credits to finish early." He frowned. "I haven't had a chance to tell Jonathan yet. And I was supposed to finish up some office work in the next two weeks at school. But I'm done with high school, Olivia."

Olivia smiled. "In that case, let's celebrate. Order pizza and I'll go get it while you look at Jack's info."

Josh was already reading the file. "Good. There are names of the attorney that represented Jonathan and a retired police officer that was first on the scene of the crime. But, Jack says they have disappeared. No record of them after the dates of the trial." Josh sat back. "But if the lawyer and the police officer disappeared and there was no record of their deaths, they may have assumed a new identity." Josh started up another program to dig into the FBI database.

"Good idea. Why don't you call Ross?"

"I'm a fugitive." Josh tapped on the keyboard and ordered to go pizza online.

"I'll call him when I get home tonight. I can use one of mom's secure phones. And, before I get back, get rid of the bedpan!" She kissed him on the cheek and left the room.

After emptying his bed pan, Josh took a quick shower in the small bathroom. It felt wonderful! He toweled off and pulled on clean clothes.

Sitting back before his computer, he searched several databases for information on an attorney named Yvonne Brown and a policeman named Sam O'Malley. Soon, Olivia returned and, after finishing pizza, he stared at the empty box.

"Nothing left." He frowned as he looked at Olivia. "Just like the results of my search for these people." He tapped the print-out. "I found nothing. Nothing, Olivia. How can that be? Lots of Yvonne Brown's but none in Austin. No record of a Yvonne Brown in the college databases or law school databases and she would have had to graduate to be a practicing attorney. No record of Sam or Samuel O'Malley on any police force or at any police academy."

Olivia stood up and paced. "Do you realize what this means?"

"What?" Josh yawned. He was growing very weary.

"Someone with powerful ties to local, state, and federal resources erased multiple records of those two people. Who would have that kind of access?" She turned and her mouth formed an "O". "Got it! The Captain! Military background. Heavy into off-the-books military operations. He would have resources to erase a person completely from the record. After all, he not only erased Jonathan's memory--"

"He erased Jonathan so that he never existed." Josh said. "Why? What happened at that trial that could possibly prompt such drastic action?"

"Merchant's summary said Stapleton's last words were 'third demon'. This is all tied to the Council of Darkness." Olivia said.

"And the Captain is on the Council." Josh said. "But he also works with the rivals, the Vitreomancers. Why?"

"Double agent? Playing both against each other?" Olivia sat down and took Josh's hand.

"Yeah, but what is his endgame? His son is accused of killing his own mother, the Captain's wife. The trial is weird, and everyone is sworn to secrecy. The attorney and a policeman disappear. Years later Jonathan has surgery by your mother to implant a device that erases his memory. Again, why? Then Jonathan is tortured by his father and dumped into the ocean to die only to wash ashore with no memories." Josh said.

"And now, Jonathan is a, what? Demon buster? Demon killer? Demon warrior? There is so much we are missing." Olivia rubbed her eyes. "Not to mention whatever happened was so frightening it caused that Mr. Stapleton to have a fatal heart attack."

"When was you last seizure?" Josh asked.

"Yesterday. Just a small one."

"And what does fatigue do to your seizures?"

She rolled her eyes. "You're not my mother. I agree I'm tired. I'm heading home, Josh."

"Got your self driving car?"

"Two blocks down the street. It is a little conspicuous. I parked by the aquarium for security reasons. They are having a big Christmas party tonight and there will be lots of policemen. I'll be safe." She kissed him on the lips. "Thanks for washing up. You were getting gamey."

CHAPTER
NINETEEN

OLIVIA WALKED the two blocks from the storage facility to the aquarium. The Shreveport Aquarium sat on the Red River and had once been an art gallery with a large, domed garden area. In the past few years, someone had converted it into an aquarium and each Christmas it hosted several parties for children and for charities. Tonight the party was for the mover and shakers in the city to officially kick off the Christmas season. Olivia paused in front of the Bally hotel, home to one of the casino riverboats on the Shreveport side of the Red River. Limousines pulled off after ejecting tuxedo and evening gown clad couples in the Aquarium's drive through. Her car was parked in the handicapped space to the left of the aquarium. A policeman stood at the entrance to the parking lot. She would have to show her I.D. even though she wasn't attending the swank party.

Olivia dug in her backpack and found her wallet. Her vision blurred, and she felt the familiar creeping sensation of a coming seizure. She stumbled back and slid onto a park bench at the side of the parking lot. Darkness overcame her, and she was gone.

Olivia blinked her eyes and squinted into the brightness of a streetlight. She sat slumped on the bench and she straightened as she glanced around her. She had been out. For how long? She pulled her phone out of her pocket and studied the screen. It had only been out for a couple of minutes. A shuddering chill passed over her as she recalled the last such seizure on the snowy streets of London. After that spell, someone had kidnapped her.

A chilly wind suddenly blew over her, and she took a deep, shuddering breath. She looked up, and they had returned.

The first time she had seen demons, Olivia had blamed her seizures. Over the past couple of weeks, she had acclimated to her new "gift" and had worked hard to learn how to control it. Now, the air filled with pulsating, gyrating forms hovering over the partygoers as they unloaded at the Aquarium. A second police officer joined the one in the parking lot. Olivia got up carefully from the bench and ducked behind a dumpster. Two of the things were attached to the men's shoulders.

She peeked around the dumpster. One officer had a crab like creature sitting atop his head. The creature had four red legs that were buried in the officer's temples. Four purple eyes on stalks wavered over the flat body of the crab creature. It waved its two other pinchers in the air at the other officer. That man had a snake-like creature wrapped around his neck. The tail descended into the officer's shirt over his heart. The head of the serpent was bright green and the tail orange. The head was flat and flared out like a cobra. It had three eyes that glowed with a blue light and two forked tongues that continually caressed the man's forehead.

The officers glanced around to make sure no one was listening.

"Heard from the boss?" Crab said.

"Yes." Cobra answered. "He's coming back to the states tonight."

"He'll be helpless for a couple of days. These humans are so weak when it comes to moving through the void."

"What's the game plan?"

"He sent a message to Steel."

Both men froze as their demons spat and coughed at the mention of that name. They regained composure and the officers began speaking again.

"What are we to do?"

"Keep looking for the boy." Cobra said. "Boss wants to take him somewhere special."

"Good! I hope he lets us have a go at him." Crab said.

"What good would that do?" Cobra hissed. "You were practically worthless in the furnace room. Ran like a rabbit when Steel showed up."

"As I recall you did, too." Crab said sheepishly.

"I didn't run." Cobra said. "It was a strategic retreat. Now, I've had some of the scum demons tell me they might have seen the boy downtown in the past few days."

"Have any idea what the boss plans are?" Crab said.

Cobra looked around at the other nearby pulsating floating demons and the ones attached to their hosts. No one was in earshot. "Well, I kind of paid a visit to Four. You know they are working together. Well, sort of, on this. Don't want to end up like the triplets."

Both men hissed and spat on the ground. Cobra continued. "I overheard Four making plans with our boss. There's something going on at that beach house where Steel lives. Some room with writing on the wall. They're going to lure Steel there."

"He's in jail."

"Not for long. Four released him with an anklet just like they did boss's host. They hope to lure him to the house." Cobra said. "Used a secret message. Some kind of photo."

"Why?"

"Don't know. I've tried to pay a visit to that room. It's protected. Guarded."

Crab shuddered. "Guarded? You mean by, one of them?"

"Yeah, one of the glowing bleeding heart ex-brothers. Only the boss can handle one of that level of, uh, goodness." Both cops spat on the ground again.

"When does this happen?" Crab asked.

"Tomorrow." Cobra said.

"Who is he going to choose as placeholders?" Crab said and there was an unmistakable tremble in his voice.

"You coward! He might choose us. After all the boss made us placeholders in London and we were there when he killed that woman."

Crab cackled and his face split in an inhuman grin. "Man, was that tasty, or what?"

Cobra hissed and the host giggled. "Best thing I've ever experienced. We might to do that again."

"With Steel?"

"Who knows. Maybe boss is finally going to end this thing!"

Cobra's radio squealed and he pulled a microphone to his lips. "Furgeson here."

"Got a squatter behind the Aquarium. Grab someone and get them off the property." A voice said.

"Ten four." Ferguson said and he widened his eyes in anticipation. "Looks like we got a live one."

"Can I hurt him?" Crab asked as they turned and walked off across the parking lot toward the dark, surging waters of Red River behind the Aquarium.

Olivia released her breath and hurried to her car. She got in and keyed in the address for home. Once she got home, she would call Josh on a secure line and tell him what she had just heard. The car pulled out of the parking lot and the floating demons parted as she moved through them. They wanted nothing to do with a child of the King.

CHAPTER
TWENTY

HAMPTON'S MUSEUM of the Weird

"I'm sorry you didn't get any help from the police." Cassie said.

Birdsong sipped coffee from a chipped cup in the old conference room on the fourth floor of Hampton's museum. "Holland, let me go through the evidence. I've spent the past few days in a dank, dark room worse than the dungeons of this place!" He sighed. "The evidence is very damaging to Jonathan. Especially the anklet. His fingerprints were on it. He let Drake go. At the very least, they will arrest him as an accomplice. And then, there's the knife."

"Knife?" Cassie said.

"From Cephas' collection. It had Jonathan's fingerprints all over it. Whoever killed McGuire left the knife. No other fingerprints." Birdsong said.

"Mine should have been on it. I remember taking that knife from one crate and placing it on the table for cataloging." Monty said.

Birdsong nodded. "Exactly. Holland said as much. A single

set of fingerprints seemed sketchy, but there it is. Evidence is evidence."

"Drake did this." Cassie said.

"Jonathan said he picked up the knife to defend himself when he heard someone in the furnace room." Birdsong said. "Or, as a weapon of convenience, Holland said."

"Jason, that was the same knife from the thirteenth demon. The same knife that killed Robert and April Pierce. The same knife used in ancient Aztec sacrifices." Monty said.

"Drake is dramatic. Jonathan said he dropped the knife and Drake picked it up and took it with him. He told all this to his lawyer, Ruth, back in the states." Birdsong said. He sipped his coffee. It was cold. "Enough of that for now. What's next for the two of you love birds?"

Monty reached over and took Cassie's hand. "Cassie and I are headed back home this morning or we would stay and help."

"This is my job, Monty. Just pray for us that something will turn up."

Monty pointed to the elevator. "One last time, dear?"

Cassie sighed. "All we need is for it to take us down slowly one last time. I never want to come back to this dreary place."

"What about Lawrence's crates?" Birdsong stood up and followed them to the old, rickety elevator.

"I shipped them back yesterday." Monty pressed the button, and the elevator groaned lie a dying whale. The door slid open, and they stepped in. The elevator dropped an inch and Cassie grabbed Monty's arm. Birdsong punched the button for the first floor. "Would we survive a four-floor drop?"

"We may be about to find out." Monty said.

The elevator made it safely to the first floor. Monty and Cassie's luggage were in the foyer. Birdsong glanced at Margaret McGuire's desk. "This is where she sat. Every day she sat behind that desk and did what?"

"Mainly gave me the stink eye." Monty said.

Birdsong studied her desk. It was clear of any documents. A

landline telephone, a blotter, a penholder. The only personal item on the desk was a framed photograph of her and Nigel Hampton. Birdsong picked it up. McGuire was short and squat next to the equally dumpy Hampton. She wore a dress and a blazer. Her hair was teased into a main of salt and pepper around her head. She wore a necklace and from it dangled a St. Christopher medal like Holland's. He put the photo back on the desk.

"Monty, our cab is here." Cassie said.

Birdsong turned back to them. "Where are you going when you get home?"

Monty grabbed their suitcases. "I'll be at the house on the lake going through Cephas' crates. Cassie is heading back to California to work on the wedding."

"And my new show." Cassie glanced at her phone. "Another possible wedding venue has fallen through." She shook her head and came to Birdsong and hugged him. "Take care, Jason."

"I will." Birdsong said as Monty shook his hand.

"Let us know if there is anything we can do to help." They rolled their luggage through the glass double doors and Birdsong followed them out into the cold, crisp air. The sky was uncharacteristically clear. Snow still lay in the shadows of the buildings along the narrow streets. The cab pulled away.

To his right was the alley where McGuire had died. He stood at the entrance of the alley and studied it. A dumpster sat about twenty feet in. The killer could have hidden behind the dumpster. A yellow crime scene tape fluttered in the chilly breeze from a pile of boxes next to the dumpster. That was where they had found her body. It was not a complicated crime. Perp hid behind the dumpster, grabbed her from behind when she walked by, slit her throat and left her on the pile of boxes.

Birdsong glanced around the streets. No CCTV coverage, they had said. Wires had been cut. Drake had covered his tracks well. Birdsong went back into the museum and called Holland.

"Birdsong here. What did you find in the furnace?"

Holland coughed. "Do you know how hard it is to quit smoking?" She coughed some more. "Makes me very irritable."

"What's new?"

"Don't bloody mess with me, Birdsong. So the trays all had McGuire's and Drake's fingerprints on them. Seems she was the one who brought him food each day."

"And kept him imprisoned." Birdsong said.

"Yeah, I get it, love. You're looking for a motive. It's there and you're right. Drake would have resented her for leaving him locked up in that nasty furnace. Doesn't help clear Steel, I'm afraid. Unless you get more, we're done." She ended the call.

Birdsong glared at the cell phone screen and shoved the phone into his back pocket. He set off down the hallway to the back stairs to the lower rooms. He had been down that hall before with the creepy dioramas and he ignored them as each one lit up at his approach. Birdsong hurried down the back stairs into the lower surgical amphitheater and through two doors to the furnace room. New yellow tape was stretched across the door to the furnace. He wiped his lips and drew a deep breath. Truth was, he was claustrophobic. But he had mastered the ability to put himself into the crime scene and he had to look inside.

The door to the old furnace was a round, gaping hole in the massive metal monster, and the hinged door had a smaller port for viewing. The lower lip was two feet off the ground and Birdsong lifted his leg carefully and climbed inside. He pulled out his flashlight and tried to control his breathing. The entire furnace couldn't have been over ten feet in length and six feet across. The floor was a metal grate that allowed ashes to fall into a removable drawer beneath the furnace. On each side, spigots poked out into the chamber by at least a foot. Gas would gush from the spigots and fill the furnace with fire.

The investigators had cleared out the cafeteria trays and gray fingerprint powder covered the walls. This had to have been a joy to process! Something grated behind him, and he whirled.

The heavy furnace door slammed shut! Birdsong rushed across the short distance to the door. A face appeared in the one-foot opening. Two different colored eyes gleamed back at him.

"Returning to the scene of the crime is a regular habit of us bad old criminals, Jason. You should have remembered that."

"Drake!" Birdsong wasted no time trying to grab the man through the small window, but Drake was too fast. He hopped away and Birdsong slammed against the door. It did not budge.

"Now you know how I felt, Mister Birdsong. Imprisoned in that furnace while little Miss McGuire slipped me her school luncheons through the lower grate there. Only you have your clothes on. And a flashlight." Drake laughed. "Imagine being in there in total darkness. No sound. No light except for when Margie paid a visit. I hated her from the first time I saw her until I realized she was more than just Margie."

"Drake, let me out of here." Birdsong screamed.

"You know, the nice thing about being possessed by a demon is the demon has access to all the old memories of its previous hosts." Drake stepped closer. "Of course, most demons are insane. Who wouldn't be after millions of years of rejection by God? But the sane ones are the ones in control. Take, for instance, my demon, number three. Calls himself Legion because he has a legion of lesser demons who are placeholders. When the big chief moves around his herd of humans, he leaves another demon or two behind to keep things moving in his desired direction."

Drake ran a hand through his hair. "Right now, the two little imps who stayed with me in that furnace are sitting quietly in the back of my mind at my beck and call."

"What's your point, Drake? Or are you going to monologue me to death?"

"Nice one!" Drake stepped closer. "As I said earlier, I have access to some of Jonathan's memories. The ones he lost. Number three was there when his mother died. Jonathan doesn't know this yet, but he suspects it. He was one of us! A tainted soul, Jason. And you threw in your lot with him. Look where it has landed you."

Drake moved to the side of the furnace out of sight of Birdsong. "I've been busy for a couple of days making sure the old gas lines were restored to this furnace." A metallic screeching sound filled the furnace. Birdsong began to gasp for air. The chamber was closing in on him. This couldn't be happening. He pulled out his phone. No signal!

Drake reappeared holding a wrench in his gloved hand. "I just loosened the valves a little. It will take a while for the gas to trickle down here through the old, rotting pipes. In fact, gas will leak all over this building. Hasn't used gas for decades so when it all goes up?" He made a whooshing sound and threw the wrench aside as he pushed his hands up into the air. "A fiery inferno!"

"Drake, don't do this." Birdsong was panting, hyperventilating.

"Oh, I'm going to do it, Birdsong. By the time they dig through the rubble, your body will be nothing but ashes and soot. Even your cell phone will be incinerated. No one will ever know what happened to you. Except for your partner, Jonathan Steel. He will know because I will make sure and tell him." Drake pulled back the base of his glove and glanced at his watch. "In fact, good old number three will be here any minute to take me back to the states. All my stuff will still be at the Hoskins. Can't move through other dimensions with inanimate objects. And I'll be out of commission for a few hours, but I plan on meeting up with Jonathan Steel. I know exactly where he will be going. He'll show up like a fly in the spider's web."

Drake turned to go and paused. "Oh, and I lit a candle upstairs in memory of dear, departed Margie. It will take an hour or so, but the gas will reach the candle and then we'll have a proper and fitting testimonial to the former host of the third demon."

"What?" Birdsong gasped.

"Margie was one of his hosts. Kept an eye on that Vitreomancer Hampton. But number three promised me he would give me a place on the Council if I would take out McGuire and incriminate Steel. Piece of cake. Easy peasy." Drake stopped and looked around him. "Oh, he's here. I have an old friend to meet. Ta ta!"

Drake disappeared from sight leaving behind his clothes and shoes. His watch hovered in the air for a split second before falling onto his empty socks.

JONATHAN STEEL

"Jonathan! Where are you going?" Ruth said over the phone speaker.

Rain pounded the windshield of my car. I was somewhere east of Baton Rouge on Interstate 12. I left Dallas in the darkness of the morning hours hoping to make the eleven-hour drive and arrive at the beach house before dusk. "I'm heading to the beach house." I said over the sound of thunder.

"You're not supposed to leave Dallas." Ruth's voice bounced around the cabin of my truck.

"Meridian gave me twenty-four hours, Ruth."

She sighed. "Jonathan, I just got off the phone with Interpol. They are demanding your extradition in three days."

"I'll be back by then."

"But your anklet will alert the authorities you've left town. That will not look good." She paused. "Wait! What do you mean Meridian gave you twenty-four hours?"

"He said he would wait that long before reporting I had left the Dallas area. That was yesterday afternoon. I wanted to leave immediately, but I knew you would find out."

"I don't understand what is going on with you, Jonathan." She pleaded.

"Meridian is in league with the fourth demon, Ruth. He's playing games with the third demon and all our lives are wrapped up in it. He wants Drake taken out." I said.

"What? You can't kill Drake?"

"Not Drake, but his demon." I said. The rain had not abated, and I tried to concentrate on the barely visible interstate before me. "This is spiritual warfare, Ruth. It has pulled me in since the day we met. Grace Pennington let me see a mask that confirmed the thirteenth demon was alive and well. I tracked it down and, before I could stop it, Josh's mother sacrificed her life to save her son. Those are the kind of stakes in this game they are playing. People get hurt. People die. And souls are dragged off to hell, Ruth."

With a sudden break in the rain, I drove into sunlight. I squinted at the sudden brightness.

"I'm so sorry, Jonathan. I looked Drake in the face. He stalked me in a parking garage after he orchestrated the death of a total stranger. He used me in that courtroom to walk free of murder charges. I have to live with that, and the only way I can make amends is to see he is thrown under the jail. You jeopardize that path, Jonathan, when you march off on one of your spiritual vendettas."

I glanced at my intense turquoise eyes in the rearview mirror. Outside, the surrounding light was a glowing yellow green, that eerie glow before the coming storm. Behind me, the storm clouds from which I had just emerged barreled onward toward the east.

In the sudden silence, I listened to the wipers squeak against the now dry windshield and turned them off. Travelers around me once again raced their velocity up to 80 miles per hour on the dry road. The storm was behind me but moving my way. "Ruth, I have no choice. Reluctantly, I have come to realize this is my mission in life. Until the last demon on the Council of Darkness is neutralized, this is what I must do."

"Even if it costs you the guardianship of your son?" She said quietly.

"Josh will be an adult soon. He knows what is at stake. We've talked about this. After what he just went through at the hands of the unholy triad and Nigel Hampton, he is just as willing as I am to do the right thing needed to stop these creatures."

Ruth sighed. "I will see what I can do to delay the extradition hearing. But hurry back, Jonathan. And bring Drake with you." She paused. "Did you hear me?"

"I'm no bounty hunter." I said.

"If what you say is true, Drake will still be vulnerable once you send his demon packing. Subdue him and bring him to the authorities here. That will go a long way to proving he killed that woman in London and not you. Don't let me down, Jonathan."

"I'll try my best." I said and the line went dead. No matter what lay ahead, I was going to stop Drake and the third demon!

———

Three hours later, I reached Perdido Key and the beach house. Clouds had rolled in from the gulf as the storm caught up with me from the west. I parked the car and studied the back door of my home. So much had happened here. Bad things. Evil things. But also good things. Raindrops dappled the windshield, and I hurried through the coming storm to the back entry.

I unlocked the back door and stepped into the stale darkness. It had been weeks since I had last set foot in the beach house. I flipped on the light in the kitchen and shivered. A cold, rainy day on the beach could be miserable and the interior was freezing. A change to the thermostats brought welcome heat.

Standing at the living room doors, I looked out over the beach. I had put the furniture on the deck up against the house for storage. The empty deck was shiny with the falling rain. The surf pounded upon the white sands. Black seaweed covered the normally glistening sand. I glanced at a clock on the wall.

Once I crossed state lines, my anklet should have alerted the authorities. My twenty four hours was officially up and I was sure Meridian had alerted the authorities. The third demon should be here soon. The authorities would also know once my anklet established my current location. They would be here in a couple of hours. I went back to the kitchen and opened a corner drawer and dug into the back beneath the silverware. My fingers touched the key chain, and I pulled it out.

I crossed the living room and started up the stairs. The locked bedroom was on the second level and looked out over the beach. Lightning flashed through the windows on the stairway. I paused in front of the door and touched the padlock. For a second, I heard their voices; her voice crying out in pain. My mouth dried up and my pulse raced. It had been at Christmas time when Braxton came. I had just confronted Ross in a house down the beach from the big beach house.

———

I stepped out onto the deck and looked toward the condo. The lights within were blazing, and I caught the strains of music coming from the open doors of the first-level balcony. I did not hear Christmas carols. Instead I heard a scream. Heart thundering, I leaped over the deck railing and sprinted toward the condo.

I hurried up the outside stairs into the den and stepped into chaos. The tree was toppled over, and the balls and ornaments were thrown carelessly around the room. The furniture had been overturned. April and Richard were nowhere to be found. I turned off the stereo. Silence descended, eerie and disquieting.

The kitchen and downstairs bedrooms were empty. A large stairway led up to the second and third levels. I bounded up the stairs and burst into the guest bedroom on the second floor.

Richard had been nailed to the wall. His arms were outstretched, and his legs were spread apart, making him look like some bizarre Christmas star. Nails protruded from his wrists and arms, and blood ran down the walls like red tinsel. A nail protruded from the right side of his forehead. His eyes were closed, but his chest still moved. A nail gun from the toolshed lay on the bed. Bizarre writing in his blood covered the wall around him.

I felt the world shift, spinning out of control, and felt something ill-defined build within him. The past few months of domesticity fell away like the dead skin of a molting snake, and I realized this was what I was meant for. For some reason I did not feel shock or nausea at the sight of Richard nailed to the wall. Instead, a hot center of rage stoked itself in my gut, flowed outward into my arms, my legs, my mind. I yearned to call out for April, but my instincts prevailed, and I paused and examined the hallway for clues.

Bloody footprints led up the stairs to the third floor. I leaned against the wall and smeared wetness against my back. More of Richard's blood. Slowly I inched my way up the stairs, and then I heard the voice.

"Oh, man of steel, where are you?" The voice echoed down the stairs, eerily familiar. It was Braxton! "I came looking for you and found your playmates. I've had so much fun. Too bad you weren't here to protect them."

I knew he was trying to taunt him out into the open. I resisted the urge to hurtle up the stairs. The voice came from the third-floor master bedroom, a large room with a huge wraparound balcony overlooking the ocean. I quietly eased back down the stairs and out Richard's bedroom to the balcony on the second floor.

Outside, a fine mist of rain had begun to fall, and I found the railing slippery as I stepped up onto it to reach the railing on the third floor. Slowly I pulled himself up to the third-floor balcony. Through the glass doors I saw a shadow move across the bedroom ceiling toward the inner door. Braxton had moved to the inside stairs. I slipped across the balcony and stopped beside the glass door. Glancing in, I saw April tied down to a trunk at the foot of the bed. Her head was slumped, but her chest moved.

I slipped in through the door and hurried over to untie April. She stirred, and her eyes widened in fear.

"He came for you, Jonathan," she whispered hoarsely. "You've got to get out of here. He's demon-possessed." I recoiled at the words.

"I know. Somehow we are connected, and this confrontation should not have involved you," I said as I untied April. "Quiet. We're getting out of here," I said, and Braxton hurtled into the room, moving through the air in an unnatural flip to land on my back. We fell and rolled out onto the balcony into a pounding rain. Braxton's arm tightened around my chin, and lightning glinted on metal as he raised a knife. I rolled forward, using Braxton's weight against him to flip him over and away from me. Braxton struggled to his feet as blood and rain dripped from his bare chest. He wore a pair of combat fatigue pants and boots—just like in my flashback. The swirling tattoo pulsed around his right eye.

"Look familiar, sonny? Do I remind you of your daddy? They told me all about you and the Captain. Me and my buddy, the thirteenth demon, will kill you and then offer your little girlfriend as a sacrifice to the master."

Braxton plunged the knife toward my heart, and I slid beneath it. I struck out with my fist and crushed Braxton's throat even as I diverted the knife's trajectory. Braxton struggled away from me toward the open door into the bedroom, gasping for breath through a crushed windpipe. He stopped and arched his head back. As lightning splattered the balcony with strobe-like shadows, I watched the bruised, crushed tissues return to their normal shape with supernatural speed. Braxton laughed and suddenly lurched as April struck him over the head with a fireplace poker. She hurried to me and into my arms.

April turned away from me to face the balcony, and suddenly, Braxton was there, blood pouring from a cut in his head. The golden knife arched through lightning and plunged into her chest. I screamed, and fury took me. I had never felt anything like it. It was a righteous anger, a holy rage filled with as much supernatural power as Braxton had. I lay April on the floor and reached out to grab Braxton by the throat. Braxton encircled me with his legs and squeezed. The air left my lungs, and my eyes began to fill with pinpoints of light. Without my surge of supernatural power, I would have been crushed. But I had enough strength to lurch across the balcony and backward against the railing. It cracked, and we plummeted through the rain-filled air.

I bounced against the second-floor railing, and it shattered and the spindles showered beneath us onto the outside deck. One stubby spindle speared through my sweater, and I came to a halt, hanging from the second-floor balcony. Braxton continued on and crashed through the lower decking to the sand below. As I spun on the torn sweater, I saw one of the spindles protruding through Braxton's chest. For a moment something hideous moved behind Braxton's open eyes, and then the life left him. The spiral tattoo faded away.

I reached above me and grabbed the edge of the balcony and pulled myself up onto the second floor. My sweater tore away in shreds as I ripped away from the broken spindle. I crashed through the glass door into the second-floor bedroom and hurried up the inside stairs. Outside on the balcony April lay on her side, and I pulled the knife from her chest. I tossed it aside and held her. Rain splashed on her face and cascaded down onto the deck. She opened her eyes and studied me.

"Don't let them win, Jonathan. Braxton said you were their enemy. That you would stop them if you didn't die." She coughed, and blood stained the corners of her mouth.

"Don't!" I wiped at the blood. "Help is coming."

April's eyes filled with tears. "Promise me you'll fight them, Jonathan. Don't let them win. I told my father the demons were real, and he didn't believe me. Promise me."

I blinked back tears. "Don't talk like this, April." She reached up and touched my face.

"Just promise me."

"I promise, April. Don't talk. The ambulance is coming."

April smiled, blood on her lips. "I'm sorry I wasted the time we could have had together. Remember, I've always loved you." She died in my arms. I was still holding her, my tears mixing with the rain when Franklin Ross and the local police walked onto the deck.

———

The memories took me and shook me to my core. Since that night I had not changed the bedroom where Richard had been killed. I kept it locked. With a shaking hand, I placed the key in the padlock and unlocked the door.

Slowly, I pushed it open and stood on the threshold. The air was musty, but there was an unmistakable metallic odor. Old blood. I had forbidden the crime scene cleaners from cleaning the room. Rocky Braxton had nailed Robert Pierce to the wall to my right in a gruesome parody of a crucifixion. Now, I knew Drake had somehow been here before they removed the body. Was he here during the deed? Had he been Braxton's accomplice?

Churning rain clouds obscured the evening sun, and the room was only dimly lit from the windows along the wall closest to the beach. I stepped into the tainted room and fought my racing heart.

Something moved along the left-hand wall. A man stepped forward, and I gasped.

"Jonathan?"

"Drake?" I hissed.

The man stepped into the meager light. He was tall and well built in a white long sleeve tee shirt and blue jeans. He had shoulder length white hair surrounding a youthful face. His eyes almost gleamed in the light.

"No. I am a friend, Jonathan." He said quietly.

"Who are you?"

"A messenger." He said again and then I felt it. A wave of warmth, comfort, reassurance. My pulse slowed.

"An angel." I said.

"That is what you call us." The man moved closer. "I am Alphus."

"What are you doing here?"

"Waiting for you."

"How did you know I was coming?"

"I have been waiting since the death of your friend Richard." Alphus said. "It is time."

"Time for what?"

Alphus pointed to the wall. I turned and regarded the wall for the first time since I had locked the door. After Braxton had killed Richard Pierce, he had used the man's blood to scrawl illegible gibberish on the wall. The arcane letters covered most of the wall except for a void shaped like a man with outstretched arms. For a moment, I recalled my visit to this room in the virtual reality world of Numinocity. The wall had been identical except for a brief appearance of the crucified Jesus. And a strange, surreal visit from two of my dead friends, Cephas and Theo. Even now, the memories of that encounter were strained and uneven.

"We knew one day you would come to this room." Alphus was beside me.

"What do the letters mean?"

A finger touched my left hand and it throbbed. My palm began to glow. Alphus took my wrist and held my hand, palm out toward the wall. The pale, blue light illuminated the letters. The writing moved in and out of focus and then congealed into legibility.

"The words are in Aramaic." Alphus said. "Now, with the spiritual gift of language, you can read them."

"You are mine. You belong to me." I began to read out loud. "I have had you in the past and I will have you again or everything you love will die. I will return for you someday." One single letter at the bottom twisted into a numeral. The number three.

"Three?" I looked at Alphus. "As in the third demon?"

"Yes." Alphus said.

Before I could speak, I heard the back door open letting in the sound of rain and thunder. I glanced over my shoulder. "Who is that?"

Alphus moved between me and the door. "It is the enemy. They have found you."

"What?"

A dark figure appeared in the doorway. He stepped into the light and his glistening eyes cast forth two different color irises. "Hello my friend." Reginald Drake said. "We return to the scene of the crime."

Alphus reached out and took my arm. "It's time to go, Jonathan. Don't hold your breath." The world twisted around me, and I was nowhere and everywhere and somewhere and I was not and I was and I would be and I could not be.

I moved through darkness, punctuated by flashes of light. Flash and there stood my father in his Army uniform. His intense gaze focused on me as I passed him by, and he mumbled something. "I'll teach you, boy!"

Flash and Clay glared at me with blood running from the cut on his forehead. "Bro, you left me to die."

Flash and April looked up from the knife in her chest. "Why didn't you come sooner?"

Flash and Claire stood in front of the flames from the basement furnace. "You could have died in my place and let me spend my remaining time with my son."

Flash and Raven was falling and spiraling as she looked at me. "You abandoned me to death."

Flash and Cephas glanced over his shoulder as he plummeted through the open iris of the portal into the blackness of space. "There was another way." He said.

Flash and Theo looked up from an open scroll. He wore a dark robe, and short, gray hair covered his head. "You left me in the past, brother. But it turned out for the good. All things turn out for the good."

Reality reasserted itself and I fell forward onto rock and dirt. I hit the ground hard, and the air left my lungs. Nausea gripped me and I vomited and retched and gasped for breath as pain wracked my entire body. I was naked and cold and hot at the same time. My clothes were gone. My anklet was gone. I fell over and tried to focus on what lay above me. The sky was black and filled with thousands of stars, and the air was frigid. I shivered uncontrollably. Alphus leaned over me. "Sorry for that. I had to get you out of there."

"You teleported me?" I rasped and the back of my throat burned with acid.

"Yes, JJ." Someone else said. The light from my palm glowed as I lifted it toward Alphus and the other person who had spoken. The woman stepped into the light. She was probably in her early fiftys with salt and pepper hair that hung down to her shoulders. She wore a heavy coat and carried a quilt. "I'm sorry for that but we had to hurry. I was hoping Alphus would bring you by simply flying here." The woman placed the quilt over my shivering body. "We'll get you into the cabin and get you warmed up."

"Who are you?"

She knelt over my face and the light from my palm reflected from eyes. "You don't remember me, but I was your attorney when you were accused of murdering your mother. I've been in hiding since then and it's time you know the truth."

The night sky burned with stars around her face, and I fell into darkness.

CHAPTER
TWENTY-TWO

JOSH SPLASHED through rain puddles as he pulled his motorcycle into the parking space outside the beach house. Once Olivia had told him of Drake's plan, he had tried to call Jonathan. No answer. He even called Ruth, but she was evasive. Didn't want to get him into trouble and suggested he go home to Elizabeth Washington. Josh surveyed the mostly empty driveway. It was here that Cassie had returned the very motorcycle he sat on. That seemed like an eternity ago. A voice crackled in his earpiece.

"I'm here, Olivia. I made it through the storm, but it's right behind me." He said through the Bluetooth connection. He had left early in the morning and, eight hours later, reached Perdido Key. "Two cars are in the driveway, both rentals. Jonathan is here."

"And maybe someone else? Just be careful, babe." She said. "Don't hang up. I want to keep an ear on you."

"Wish you were here to look for any demons." Josh said. Thunder rattled around him. "I'm going to go inside no matter what and try to dry off. I'm freezing." He took off his helmet and made sure the earpiece stayed in place. Icy rain soaked his hair and his scalp and he killed the motorcycle engine and pushed it up next to the cars. He hurried up the back stairs and noticed the back door was open. "The door is open. It has to be Jonathan." He stepped into the kitchen and wiped rain from his hair and face. He unzipped his coat and shook water onto the floor. If Uncle Cephas were here, he would not approve!

"Don't call out. I have a bad feeling about this, Josh." Olivia said. "Just keep quiet for now."

"Okay." He whispered. He heard someone move up the stairs. He shrugged out of his coat and hung it on a chair at the island bar. His pants were waterproof, but still his legs were numb from the chilly rain. He glanced at the thermostat. Someone who knew the house had turned it on. Jonathan had to be here.

He started up the stairs and froze at the sight of the mysterious bedroom. The door was unlocked and open. Jonathan had forbidden him from ever entering that bedroom for any reason. And now an open door invited him into the secrets of this bedroom.

Josh heard a whispering voice. A bright light burst forth from the door, temporarily blinding him, and he slumped back against the wall. He rubbed his eyes and tried to focus on the door. Darkness had fallen again. He heard cursing. Loud, very expressive cursing, and then someone talking. Beneath the folds of his leather jacket, nestled against his heart, he felt the blood-stone shard heat up. It pulsated with his every heartbeat. The stone had been dormant since the encounter with the demons in Austin. Now, it had come to life and that could only mean evil was nearby!

"Olivia, can you hear that?" He whispered. "That is NOT Jonathan!"

"Yeah. I'm going to record it." She said in his ear.

"Now what? You idiot. You let him get away. Yeah, what was I supposed to do? Tackle one of them? You should have grabbed him and then we both would have been teleported with him, you moron." A man's voice changed back and forth in timbre and quality, but it was obvious the voices were coming from one man.

Josh moved quietly up the stairs and over to the open doorway. He glanced in and drew a deep breath at the sight of the blood covered wall.

"Beautiful, don't you think? A work of art." A voice said from behind the door.

Josh whirled, and the door to the bedroom closed, revealing a man standing in the shadows. "Well, well, well. What have we here? You must be Joshua Knight."

Josh hurried toward the door but a metallic clicking outside came through the wood. "Don't even try. I had them close the padlock again. We're locked in. Together."

Josh backed away toward the blood covered wall. "Where is Jonathan?"

The man stepped into the waning sunlight from outside. Josh gasped at the sight of the man's two different colored eyes. "Now that, Josh, is the question you must answer for me. Where is Jonathan Steel?"

"I thought he was here." Josh said.

The man bent over and held up a pile of clothes. "Jonathan was right here until one those wretched do gooders took him away." Drake moved closer holding out Jonathan's clothes before him. "They teleported him and you are going to tell me where."

Josh shook his head. "I'm not telling you anything. Drake, right? Serial killer? Loser? What was your name? Sylvester Doofus?"

"Reginald Drake, the one and only!" Drake bowed and when he straightened his lips twisted in a grimace. "I'm not a loser, Josh. I think I just won the jackpot. After all, I'm here with the person most important to Jonathan Steel. You are in my control which means Jonathan will do whatever I ask of him. After all, he freed me from my anklet to save your life."

Josh nodded, his mind racing for options. "Yeah, he told me. He shouldn't have done that."

"Oh, but he did." Drake moved closer. "That makes him my accomplice, Josh. And he is my partner in crime."

"What do you mean your partner in crime?"

"The murder in London." Drake shrugged. "True, I was the one who killed her. Never could stop bragging about those deeds. Gives me a thrill to see your reaction."

"Jonathan wasn't there. He was on an airplane to America." Josh said.

"True. A private, unregistered flight and we made sure the pilots won't talk. The authorities will never discover I killed that woman and framed your father." Drake said and then pointed a finger at Josh. "But I would never have been free to do that if he hadn't taken off my anklet to save you. So, in a way, you both are accomplices to the crime."

"I knew Jonathan didn't kill that woman." Josh said. "He's not a murderer."

Drake paused and laughed. "Oh, but he is. You don't know his past like I do." He gestured to the wall behind Josh with his free hand. "Right up there is where Robert Pierce died. He would still be alive if it weren't for Jonathan Steel being in his life."

"How do you know about that?" Josh said. "Rocky Braxton killed them."

"He was a lowdown, amateur. Lacked finesse." Drake smiled and whirled around with his arms outstretched. "It was my idea to do the crucifixion scene. You must paint a picture. Creates a shock effect." Drake stopped spinning and tilted his head. "I did shock you, didn't I?"

"Yes. So you were, what, directing Braxton by phone or something? Because as impressive as this is, there just seems to be something lacking." Josh said and crossed his arms.

Drake's lips twisted in disgust. "Braxton was an idiot. I was here. Rocky Braxton was just my student." Drake paused and blinked. "Well, technically, we were both students of Robert Ketrick, but I was far more advanced than Braxton." He raised an eyebrow. "Braxton had his demon and Ketrick promised me a powerful demon. Instead, I got these two idiotic demons. But, in time, the third demon came to me and now we are more powerful than the thirteenth demon who couldn't even inspire Braxton to do that."

Drake moved to the wall and pointed to a cluster of four letters. "That is from the account written by Luke and it says 'No, he is mine. I want him.' And these four letters? That is the phrase 'for eternity'." He gestured to the wall. "The writing was my idea, and I used the fractured memory of my lesser demons at the time. They recalled some of the spoken words of, well, of Him." Drake shuddered. "This is the original language, Aramaic."

"I don't believe you." Josh said. He had to keep the man talking.

Drake turned his back on the wall. "How do you think one man could put Pierce up that high on the wall and nail him to the studs? It took both of us. Jonathan should have figured that out long ago."

Drake stepped closer and dropped the clothes in front of Josh. "Now, my boss, number Three, by the way is away for the moment, and he has given me a couple of low life demons so I don't have that much power, but I can still kill you a dozen different ways."

Josh swallowed and thought back to the man in the pith helmet when he was under the influence of his dreams. Once again, his bloodstone pulsed. He was on the right track. "But what of the real boss?"

Drake paused. "What?"

"He came to me in my dreams. He told me all about you and your partners in evil. He has plans for me, Drake. You kill me and you risk that old man coming after you." Josh said as forcefully as he could.

Drake raised an eyebrow. "Old man?"

"Grandfatherly figure. Pith helmet. Turquoise eyes. Ring any bells?" Josh moved toward Drake. Drake stepped back. "You know who I'm talking about, don't you? What's wrong? Afraid of him?"

Drake blinked. "I'm not afraid of anyone. I'm a host to the third demon. He calls himself Legion. Well, Four claims to have used the name first. He has little imagination. He just copied Three! Four has a legion of hosts and Three has a legion of demons. That way, he keeps us all in the loop on his plans."

"Except when it comes to the old man." Josh said.

Drake frowned. "Why would he come to you?"

Josh's pulsed quickened. This might work. "I must be important to him. To his plan. In fact, he all but told me I was. What has he told you?" Josh said and then his eyes opened wide. "Wait a minute? He hasn't talked to you, has he? You're not that important. Certainly not as important as I am. Tell me, did the old man tell you to kill that woman in London? Or did Three?"

Drake backed away and held up a hand. "I am important, Josh. I even met with the Captain and asked to be put on the Council. And, yes, Three and I worked together to kill that woman. And the third demon and I will serve on the council."

"Assuming he stays in you long enough. Sounds like he wanders around a bit."

"All part of our plan." Drake tried to sound convincing, but his voice had dropped in volume. The bloodstone pulsed again against Josh's chest.

Josh's foot hit something on the floor. He glanced down at Jonathan's anklet. Taking a corner of Jonathan's shirt, he picked up the anklet without touching the band. "Well, look here. Jonathan's anklet is off." He pointed to the pile of clothing. "When you are teleported, do your clothes and any attached object remain behind?" With each pulsation of the bloodstone, clarity came. Dr. Merchant thought Drake had killed his colleague, Dr. Moshander. But then Drake had appeared in

London on the same day and Jonathan had released him from his anklet. Was it possible? Had Drake teleported from Shreveport, Louisiana, to London? It made sense. But, the anklet had stayed with Drake and he had been naked and unarmed while imprisoned in some old, abandoned furnace according to Jonathan. Was it possible during teleportation, anything inorganic stayed behind?

Josh smiled and tossed the anklet to Drake, and he caught it. He glared at it like it was a hot potato. "Tell me, Drake. Jonathan said your clothes were left behind when you teleported to the abandoned furnace. If you were teleported to London, why didn't your anklet stay in the states? Why did your demon leave it on you?"

Drake glared at the anklet. He opened his mouth to answer and then closed it. Josh laughed. "You don't know, do you? Did Three bring you to London? Or was it one of Hampton's buddies? One of the Vitreomancers?"

Drake seemed speechless. Josh reached out with Jonathan's shirt covering his hand and snatched the anklet from Drake's grasp. He held up the anklet. "Don't you see? You're just a pitiful pawn in a cosmic game of chess. They set you up just like they set up Jonathan. They left your anklet on so you would be primed to do whatever they wanted. You said Three comes and goes. When was the last time he was in charge of you?"

Drake's face twisted in defiance. "I call the shots! I caught his attention, and he chose me! He came to me after I did what he told me. After I killed her and after I made Jonathan take off the anklet so his fingerprints would be on it." Drake licked his lips and nodded his head. "And, the knife. Oh, that was so clever of me. Lay out the knife that Braxton used to kill April Pierce where Steel would see it and pick it up. I wiped all the fingerprints off first so only his would be on the knife. When he dropped it, I had the perfect murder weapon with no one's prints but his. Don't you see?"

"So, you think you're clever?"

"I am more than clever, little boy. When Jonathan dropped that knife he was holding, I knew instantly I was going to kill someone with it. It was so pretty. It had carved out so many hearts! And, if I was careful, oh so careful, I wouldn't smudge Jonathan's fingerprints and he would take the blame. The third demon saw all of this. I am important to Three. I am Three's primary host, don't you see?"

"Let me talk to him." Josh said.

"What?"

"Let me talk to Three. If you are so important, summon him here. Let's see what he has to say about all of this." Josh paused. He thought of something else. "Bring me Three and I'll tell him all about the old man in the pith helmet."

Drake froze and glanced around the room. "It doesn't work like that."

"How did you get back to the states from London, Drake." Josh stepped closer. "Did they teleport you again? Did they send you here to meet with Jonathan after they realized he was coming to the beach house? I know they are listening. They have ears everywhere."

"This was my idea, kiddo! I suggested coming back to the scene of the crime. When Jonathan accessed that photograph of me standing right over there at the foot of the kill, I knew he couldn't resist it. And, I made sure that the Fourth demon, who is beneath me, I might add, let him go with nothing more than an anklet. Now, who's clever?"

Josh nodded, and another idea surfaced. "If they agreed to your clever plan and let you come here, why haven't they taken you away now that Jonathan's anklet is activated?"

Drake's face paled, and he glanced at the locked door. "What?"

"You know they're coming. FBI, probably. Or at least the locals. The minute Jonathan disappeared, the anklet alerted them."

Drake ran to the locked door and waved his hand. He

grabbed the handle, and the door did not budge. He waved his hand again.

"Lost your power?" Josh asked.

Drake glanced over his shoulder and, for the first time, Josh saw fear there. "The place holder demons are gone! Just gone! The little buggers!" He whispered as he patted his chest and grabbed his head. "Where are you? Get back to me. Now!"

Shouting echoed in the hallway and Josh lifted his voice. "We're in here. He has me as a hostage." He shouted.

Drake moved toward him. "I'll kill you where you stand, boy! I don't need a weapon."

Josh tossed the anklet into Drake's face, and Drake stumbled back. He touched his ear again. "Did you get all of that, Olivia?"

"I recorded the whole thing." Olivia said into his earpiece.

Drake froze, and the door behind him exploded inward. Josh flattened against the wall as figures streamed into the room with flashlights mounted on rifles and pistols. Josh raised his hands.

"Thank God you're here. He was going to kill me."

Drake started toward Josh and light lanced from the electrodes of a Tazer that connected with Drake's neck and his back. He stiffened and fell forward into the pile of Jonathan Steel's clothes. Josh put his hands behind his head and fell to his knees.

"I'm Jonathan Steel's son, Joshua Knight. Don't shoot." The bloodstone grew cold beneath his shirt.

CHAPTER
TWENTY-THREE

Switzerland
Dairy Farm

The woman was acutely aware she was in danger. She stood at the door and her heart raced in anticipation. It was just this level of danger that attracted her to the man in the room. That and his power, his charisma. She adjusted her hair and knocked on the farmhouse door.

"What is it?"

She opened the door slowly and stepped into the living room. A leather couch sat between her and the fireplace. The warm, wooden walls smelled of cedar. The man sat on the couch facing the fireplace. At the end of the couch sat a table covered with two computer monitors.

"I am here to report." She said quietly.

He motioned with a hand, and she approached the couch. He stood up and walked over to the fireplace and stood in the shadows. She could not see that face, those eyes lost in darkness, but his dark jacket and black shirt fit his youthful body perfectly.

"Drake has been arrested in Pensacola, Florida. It seems he

met Jonathan Steel in his beach house." She said quietly. Yes, he would like this news.

"Don't you think I know that? Three abandoned Drake and left placeholders with him. Those unreliable, weakling demons!" He snapped. "But that is not the news, is it?"

"No, sir. It seems Jonathan Steel was teleported by the other forces to an unknown location. His anklet was left behind." She said, her heart now pounding with fear instead of admiration.

"Four was clumsy! He thought putting an anklet on Steel would allow him to keep track of him. No, this is a trap for Three. Four is trying to take Three down. And my plans are getting jinxed in the process." He stepped closer. "What of the other matter?"

"Faye Morgan has made little progress with Victoria. Faye will not allow more forceful intervention." She said.

The man stepped into the light. His eyes glittered brightly. "And you think you can do it better? You've been totally worthless to me so far."

"I can still intervene. I am convinced Victoria would revert to Raven the minute we put a gun in her hands." She said.

"And then she would kill everyone and escape. I want her alive. I want her memories."

He stepped around the couch and closed the distance between them. Her face warmed as she felt the heat radiate from his body. She wanted to luxuriate in it, bathe in it! His hands came up, and he took her by the shoulders. Her heart raced!

"Good work. You've been a faithful partner." Suddenly, his grip tightened and she gasped in pain. He released her and one hand slid into his jacket and came out with a gleaming, golden knife. "Isn't this beautiful? Do you recognize it?"

She rubbed her arms. "No."

"Drake used that knife in London." He whispered. "Want to know how I got it?"

She nodded. "Yes."

"I took it from the evidence room in London. Popped right in and then right out. Don't worry. I'll put it back when I'm done with it. I just wanted to hold it. It has such a long history." He held the knife up for her to study the hilt. "This knife was forged in the Aztec empire. It was used in human sacrifices by the priests who served the thirteenth demon. It found its way into the hands of a man who was present when Jonathan Steel was born! Imagine that!"

He tossed the knife and caught the hilt in his hand. "Such awe-inspiring irony that the very knife that killed so many and was owned by Ketrick would one day be Jonathan Steel's undoing. Now you see why I had to have it. To hold it. To hold his future in my hands. Yes, the third demon did me a favor in this one respect only. The man is clever. His demon not so. You are privileged to feel it's sting."

The man lifted her arm and turned the inside of her forearm toward him. "Roll up your sleeve."

Her heart raced and she began to take deep breaths as she rolled her sleeve up exposing her forearm. The touch of his hand was hot and tingling.

"Are you strong? Are you willing to take on my work?" He said.

"Yes." She whispered.

The knife point touched her skin and the pain lanced up her arm. She bit her tongue to keep from screaming. He carved the letters "J" and "S" into her skin. He raised the arm up to his lips and kissed the bloody carving. The touch of his lips was like electricity. She felt warmth on her lips. She had bitten her lips and her tongue.

When he pulled away, his lips were covered with her blood. He leaned into her and let his lips brush hers. Their eyes met, his so bright and filled with an unearthly power. She did not close her eyes but stared into the man's soul. But something hideous and foreign moved in the dark pupils of his eyes and she pulled away. She tasted copper.

"Now you belong to me. You are mine. You will go to the

compound, and you will get rid of this Faye. I put you there to bring back Raven and you will reassert your authority. Do you understand?"

"Yes." She said. "I will do anything for you."

"Of course you will." He lifted the knife and blood dripped from the tip, "Even die if need be."

"Yes!" She said. And she would. He moved back to the couch and slid the knife into an inner pocket of his jacket. "I have to be about finding Jonathan Steel. You may go, Lucille."

Lucille backed slowly to the door and the shadows deepened around her. They writhed and moved and susurrated with vile whispers. Fear grew within her but she kept it a bay with her absolute devotion to the man with the turquoise eyes.

CHAPTER
TWENTY-FOUR

JONATHAN STEEL

I gasped and sat up. The surrounding air was warm and filled with the fragrance of bacon and baked bread. A small bedroom with cedar planking on the walls surrounded me. I rubbed grit from my eyes. When I had materialized, I had been naked. Now, sitting on this small bed, I saw someone had dressed me in a gray sweatshirt and sweatpants with wool socks. I reached down to my ankle. The anklet was gone! When I tried to stand up, dizziness gripped me, and I stumbled up against the nearby wall.

The door to the bedroom opened and an older man peeked in. He wore a pair of khaki pants and a flannel shirt. His white hair was draped carefully in a comb-over, and his intense brown eyes sparkled.

"Good. You're awake. I was getting worried. Let me help you to the breakfast table."

I blinked in confusion. "Where? Who?"

The man took me by the arm. "Come on, and we'll explain everything." He led me out of the bedroom and down a long hallway into a kitchen. The roof extended up into a tall peak, an A-frame house. An open living room lay beyond and to one side a funnel shaped flue hung over a circular fireplace. A dining table sat in an alcove to the left of the small kitchen. The front wall of the living room was all windows reaching up to the peak of the A-framed house. Beyond the windows a snow-covered landscape stretched away toward snow-capped mountains in bright, morning sunshine.

The woman who had leaned over me stood at the kitchen counter spooning scrambled eggs onto three plates. "I know you're hungry. Going through the void messes with your mind and your body. The sooner you eat, the sooner you'll get back to normal."

She was shorter than me and wore a long-sleeved tee shirt and jeans. She had pulled her salt and pepper hair back into a bun on the back of her head. A chopstick held it in place. Her face was lean and ageless. The man steered me toward the table and I sat groggily. "Looks like your clothes fit you fine. We've had them ready for you for a long time."

"What is going on?" I mumbled.

The woman sat a plate of eggs, bacon, and biscuits in front of me. Her bright green eyes reflected the smile on her face. "Eat. Now. Drink the orange juice. You need the vitamin C." The man retrieved a plate of food from the counter and sat across from me. The woman took her plate and a steaming cup of coffee and sat to my right. "I take it you still don't like coffee?"

I opened my mouth to reply, and my stomach growled. She pointed to the plate. "No explanation until you eat."

I reluctantly took a bite of the eggs and for a moment felt nauseous but managed to swallow them. It was then the hunger hit me. I was ravenous and I wolfed down the eggs and crunched down the bacon. The man pushed a jar toward me.

"Homemade huckleberry jam for the biscuits. You need the sugar."

I lathered the flaky biscuits with butter and covered them

with the jam. The strange, all consuming hunger took me by storm. Almost in a haze I finished the plate and downed the orange juice. I sat back and blinked as normalcy returned.

"What just happened?" I said.

"The void. I told you it messes with your mind and body. The body takes over because it needs sustenance to make the repairs. Especially your body. You needed the energy to repair all the damage from passing through the void." The woman said as she ate some eggs. She sipped at her coffee.

"I think I will have coffee." I said needing something to clear my mind and chase away the cobwebs. "Alphus took me through this void?"

The man nodded and retrieved a mug of black coffee from the coffee pot and sat it in front of me. He pointed to two containers on the table as he sat down. "Cream and sugar. Alphus and his brothers have the ability to move through inter-dimensional space. The void. I've only done it once. That was enough for me."

I looked at the woman. "And you?"

She averted her gaze staring into emptiness. "Too many times. I had no choice. I had to escape."

"Escape?"

She placed her fork on the edge of her plate. "It's a long story and it's time you heard it."

"You know me?"

Her green eyes turned toward me. "Yes. I know everything about you, JJ. I was there. I was your lawyer when you were arrested for killing your mother. Sam was the investigating detective who helped clear you."

My heart raced and I stood up. My chair tumbled backwards and fell to the floor. "Tell me. Now!"

The woman shook her head. "You're not ready."

My face warmed and the old fury built. "Don't tell me I'm not ready. Do you know what I have been through? No memories except for a flashback of holding my mother's dead body?"

Sam stood up slowly. "You don't understand, son. After you've eaten for the first time out of the void it will hit you."

"What will hit me?" I shouted. And then it did. Dizziness took me and I fell backwards over the chair. The world spun above me and all I saw was growing darkness until I was gone.

———

I awoke to the sharp pain of frigid air entering my lungs. I coughed and tried to stand up. A hand pushed me down.

"Hold on there, young man."

My vision cleared, and I looked out over the snow-covered hills leading upward into tall mountain peaks. The fragrance of evergreens filled the air. A fine snow fell just a few feet away from me. The morning sun was gone behind gray snow clouds. I looked around at the front porch of the A-frame. Sam sat next to me, bundled in a parka.

"We tried to tell you." He said.

"I passed out." I sat in a rocking chair with a hand stitched quilt covering my chest and legs.

"Passage through the void does that to you. After you eat, all the blood shunts to your body and away from your brain. That's how they were able to subdue Drake after he teleported and put him in that furnace."

I shook my head. "How do you know that?"

Sam shrugged. "She told me." He pointed over his shoulder toward the house. "Learned it from Alphus, I guess. Now, let my detective brain kick in for a second. You arrived buck naked without your anklet, right? How did Drake's anklet stay with him? They wanted it to. It was all a setup for you and for Drake."

"I had concluded as much." I said hoarsely. "How long?"

"You've been out a couple of hours. You're going to hurt from falling over the chair. But you'll heal quickly, according to Sharon."

"Sharon?"

He smiled. "Sharon Barker. Name ring a bell?"

I shook my head. "Why are we out here? It's cold." My breath streamed from my nostrils and my mouth.

"Sharon thought the cold air would revive you. She was right. As always." He looked out over the snow. "I prefer to think it is the snow, the hills, the mountains. The air is a little thin for my old lungs, but I got used to it. If I had known I would live this long, I would have taken better care of myself. Too bad we'll be moving again soon."

"Moving?"

Sam nodded. "Have to stay one step ahead of them."

"Them?"

Sam turned his gaze toward me. "Sharon will explain. If you're up to it, we'll go back inside."

I wrapped the quilt around me and followed Sam into the living room. "Sharon" had placed three comfortable chairs around the fireplace. She sat in one and motioned for me to sit next to her. Our two chairs faced each other. I kept the quilt around me as I sat in the chair.

"JJ, do you want something to drink? I suggest a sports water to replenish your electrolytes." She said.

"Sure." I mumbled and shivered beneath the quilt despite the warmth from the fireplace. "How long do these side effects last?"

"A few days. At least for normal people. You'll come around quicker." Sam brought me a bottle of sports water and I sipped the liquid. "It's room temperature."

"Cold water will give you esophageal spasms." Sharon said.

"Let me guess. From passing through the void." I said.

Sam smiled and settled into the other chair. "Are you going to tell him about the quilt?"

I glanced down at the quilt. "What about it?"

Sharon smiled. "Your mother made it. They wouldn't let you have it in prison. Your father kept it from you. I made sure it didn't get lost after." She paused. "Well, after the debacle in the courtroom and the fight you had afterward."

"Fight?"

"With the third demon." Sam said.

I gasped and almost choked on another swallow of water. "It's true? I was possessed?"

Sharon nodded. "Yes."

I felt the cold grow even deeper beneath my mother's quilt. I had to know. "Did I kill my mother?"

Sharon drew a deep breath. "Why don't I start from the beginning? You told Ruth you had a memory of holding your mother's body."

I grit my teeth. "I want answers, Sharon. How did you know what I told Ruth?"

"I have my sources." She said tersely. "JJ, you must let me tell it my way. I've been waiting for years to find you and tell you. Years. Let's not rush it. Please."

I glanced at Sam and then back at Sharon. "Fair enough. I had a flashback. I was with Clay on the bluff with my new car and I accidentally pushed him off the hood and he hit his head." I drew a deep breath. "Then my mother called. I left Clay behind. I had to get to mother."

I felt a hand on my knee and did not realize Sharon had leaned forward. "JJ, Clay was fine. He didn't die, okay. Now, go on."

I drew a deep breath. Clay was fine? I hadn't killed my best friend? "Well, I hit a guardrail. Passed out. Woke up later and came home. The doors were open. No one was around. I went to the library and through the double doors and down the spiral stairs and found her." I swallowed hard. "She was dead. That's what the flashbacks revealed to me."

"Okay, calm down." Sharon still gripped my knee. "I need to know something. Have you found the photo journal?"

I glanced up at her. "What?"

"Your grandfather's photo journal?" Her eyes burned intensely.

"Yes. It was at the house when the FBI raided it the week before Thanksgiving. But Hampton took it and disappeared through those doors. They stayed locked. I couldn't open them." I said. "Josh was okay. We made it home for Thanksgiving."

Sharon sat back and looked into the fire. "You need to understand something, JJ. Sam and I have been moving and hiding for years from forces that want to find you and destroy you." She looked back at me. "Do you want to know why?"

"Yes." I said as my mouth grew dry.

"Because you are not Jonathan Steel. You are Jude Josiah Stone. And, if you had gone by that name for the past few years, you would be dead by now."

I flinched at the sound of the name. I mulled it around in my mind. "What?"

"You went by JJ Stone." Sam said.

I shook my head. "I don't feel anything when I hear that name."

"It's because of the conditioning. Your father was a master at it." Sharon said.

I grit my teeth and my fists clenched. "Yes, how well I know. I remember the torture in the boat before he threw me into the ocean to die."

Sharon sat forward and glanced at Sam. "You think he was trying to kill you?"

"Yes."

"Oh, no, JJ. Everything your father has done was to protect you. If they knew who you really were and had found you, then you would have been dead long ago." Sharon said.

"Or worse." Sam said.

I glanced at them both. "No! He operated on my brain! He made me forget."

"For your own protection. He made you someone else other than his son." Sharon said.

I leaned back in the chair. "No, this can't be!"

"Look, let me tell you my story. Once you hear it, you will understand. Time is running short and we have to get you up to speed." She paused. "Before he finds you."

"He?"

"The real person everyone thinks they want. You see, they want you because they think you are him. But you're not him, and your father changed your identity and erased your memory so they would look for the other person and ignore you. It has worked for years, but at a great cost to you. Once I explain, you'll understand everything, JJ."

My world spun out of control filling my mind with confusion. I rubbed my eyes. "Fine. Tell me your way. I'm listening."

"My real name is Yvonne Brown." Sharon said. "Not Sharon. I have had to change it for my own protection."

I glanced at Sam. "And you?"

"Still Sam. They aren't interested in me." He said.

I glanced back at "Sharon" and pulled the quilt back up over my chest. For some reason my insides were cold again. "Okay, Yvonne. It's time for me to learn about my past."

PART 2 — THE TRIAL OF JJ STONE

Then the Lord said to Cain, "Where is your brother Abel?"

"I don't know," he replied. "Am I my brother's keeper?"

The Lord said, "What have you done? Listen! Your brother's blood cries out to me from the ground. Now you are under a curse and driven from the ground, which opened its mouth to receive your brother's blood from your hand. When you work the ground, it will no longer yield its crops for you. You will be a restless wanderer on the earth."

Genesis 4:9-12

CHAPTER
TWENTY-FIVE

THE STONE MANSION — Austin, Texas

Yvonne Brown wiped sweat from her forehead and tilted her sunglasses up on the top of her short hair. The house was not really a house. It was more of a mansion with the most bizarre appearance. Bushes carved into the shape of animals decorated a garden surrounded by the driveway. And the doorway and front of the mansion looked like a face with an open mouth! She shivered despite the heat. It was supposed to reach a hundred today in Austin, even though it was only late spring. Yep. The shivering had nothing to do with the weather. If what they said had happened inside was true, the mansion fit the crime.

Detective Dale Corsair put his hands on his hips and stared at her from behind his mirrored sunglasses. "Well, you wanted to see. What are you waiting for?"

Yvonne glared at him. "I'm taking it in."

"Gruesome isn't it? Kind of makes you think fricking zombies will come through that door." Corsair snapped his gum and massaged his heavy mustache. "Okay, look, Ms. Black."

"Brown."

"Whatever! You know I don't have all day."

"They promised me access to the crime scene." Yvonne said.

"Look, my partner is waiting at the bar with two cold mugs of beer." Corsair glanced at his watch. "It's after my shift already. So, we gotta hurry, little missy."

Yvonne stiffened. "Little missy? Really?"

Corsair just leered at her. "Yeah, little missy. Small. Petite. And a bleeding heart to go with it all."

Yvonne drew a deep breath. She had heard it all before. But that wasn't the only reason the name drove fear into her heart. She hid it well. "Everyone deserves a fair trial, detective."

"Even that freak? Wait until you see what he did." Corsair turned back to his cruiser and retrieved a folder. "When we get down there, I'll show you the crime photos. Hope you brought a barf bag. Now come on." He led her across the wide driveway and up the stairs into the mouth of the mansion. They passed through the dank foyer and into a large living area. Three people stood at the fireplace.

"The servants." Corsair pointed at them. "I asked them to stay out of the library."

Yvonne itched to talk to the servants, but that could wait for another time. "I'll meet with them later. Crime scene?" She nodded toward the library doors.

Two heavy wooden doors opened outward from an enormous library. Rows of books filled the shelves. Plush leather sofas and chairs sat in the center of the room. But the most striking feature was a second set of huge double doors on the wall to her left. Corsair paused at the threshold. "Last chance, little missy. The scene hasn't been cleaned yet. But don't worry. They have removed all the body parts for evidence."

Corsair walked through the open doors into darkness. Yvonne paused and drew a deep breath. She had to do this. She had no choice. "I'm coming."

The interior of the room beyond was hewn out of rock. In the center of the room a wrought iron spiral staircase led downward into a dark shaft carved from rock. Corsair took a small flashlight from his hip pocket and directed its cone of light down the stairs.

"Electricity was shut off to the room below. Your client used candles for illumination. Scented candles. Pina colada." Corsair said and an unmistakable hesitation came over him.

Yvonne reached out and snagged the flashlight from the man's hand and started down the staircase. "Then have a pina colada for me at the bar."

Corsair hurried after her. Their footsteps echoed against the stone as they descended. Corsair was quiet as Yvonne landed on the bottom step. She directed the light ahead of her to the 'altar'. The crime scene investigators had given that name to it. The smell of blood filled the cool, dank air. Bile rose in her throat, and she coughed.

"Yeah, it stinks. He wrote some kind of weird letters with her blood on those doors." Corsair whispered, pointing to the five stone doors spaced evenly around the chamber. Five doors. Five walls carved from the rock. A pentagram. Yvonne fought down the fear and revulsion. This is what she had to do. She had to see. She had to know. "Where do those doors lead to?"

"Don't know. Couldn't open them." Corsair stepped past her and handed her the folder of photos. "I'll show you the layout of the remains."

Yvonne turned her back on the five-sided altar and placed the folder on a step of the stairway. She opened the folder and illuminated the first photo with the flashlight.

The sight of the first picture drove the air out of her lungs. JJ's mother had been beautiful in life, reddish blonde hair now stained with fine droplets of blood. Close-up pictures of her face showed a startling blue that defied the absence of life, the blue she had seen in the boy's eyes.

Wounds covered her chest and abdomen. Yvonne's hand strayed to her own stomach, feeling the ridges of the scars underneath, the hardness of the muscles she had worked on every day. This woman had not lived to heal and form scars. But Yvonne had. Something wet splattered on the picture. Yvonne wiped the tear away before Corsair could see it. She felt him hovering close to her, and she suppressed the urge to take him down.

"She was spread out on this stone fixture we call the altar like a sacrifice. Go ahead. Check out all the photos." Corsair went back to the altar.

Yvonne closed her eyes and closed the folder. For a moment, she was back in the basement with the smell of her own blood. The smell of *him*. She put her hand to her mouth and suppressed the scream. If she started, she would never stop. Her client was not HIM! She drew a deeper breath and reached inside to her safeguards to block out the odors, the feelings, the pain. Calling upon those safeguards, her control returned. She opened her eyes and turned toward Corsair. His face was pale in the flashlight beam.

"Okay, let's go over everything in detail. You were the first to arrive?"

Corsair raised an eyebrow. "No. I was late getting here. My, uh, partner was the first to get here. And, well, he couldn't take it, so he turned everything over to me and left."

"Left? I need to talk to him. Where did he go? Back to the precinct?"

Corsair shook his head and averted his gaze. "No. He left. The department. He was only nine months from retirement. He walked up those stairs and out the door and never came back to the precinct. I processed the scene. The uniform already had your client in custody and taken him up to the library. That's where I first saw him." Corsair walked toward me. "But my partner says he found the boy sitting right here on the altar with his mother's head in his lap. It was the only part of her that was, well, untouched."

Yvonne nodded and laid the folder on a step. "I need to talk to your ex-partner. And the servants."

"Fine with me. Good luck finding him. And you'll have to work out the interviews with the servants on your own. I'm heading to the bar. I need a drink. Lots of drinks."

Corsair glanced once at the altar and then hurried up the spiral staircase. She calmed her breathing and closed her eyes, seeking the quiet center of her very being. She was alive. The woman was not. She had been lucky. The woman had not. With the folder of photos in her hand, she circled the room slowly, pausing before each of the five doors. Each door was a massive stone door placed in a threshold carved from the rock. The doors bore no handles or indication as to how to open them. Did these doors slide aside or open on hidden hinges. Were they doors at all?

Yvonne studied the dark smeared letters written in the woman's blood. What did they mean? Or were they letters at all? Maybe just the insane ravings of a mad man! Like the one who had tried to carve letters in her own stomach. She pushed those memories away.

Yvonne moved to the walls between the doorways. Blood splatter had dotted the stone walls. She stopped. Between two of the doors was a segment of stone with no splatter.

Yvonne directed the flashlight along the wall. The void was small, but something had blocked the splatter. What? She turned and looked back at the altar. The floor was a mess of clotted blood and smears from the footprints of the crime techs.

She backed away from the wall and placed the folder on one of the steps. She looked for the photos of the floor around the altar until she saw it. The floor at the foot of the wall with the void had a definite pool of dark blood. She squinted and put the flashlight closer to the photo. There! Three circular voids in the pool. She needed to talk to the crime investigators.

Yvonne slowly closed the folder on the grisly photos with trembling hands. She slowly made her way up the stairs to the library. One of the servants stood in the open library doorway.

"I understand you would like to talk to us?" The older gentleman said. He held out his hand. "Malcolm Hobbs."

Yvonne shook his hand. "Yvonne Brown. Thanks for talking to me. Where were you the day of the murder?"

"Mrs. Stone had given us the day off." Hobbs looked away and ran a hand through his thinning gray hair. "If I had stayed, she would still be alive."

"You can't know that." Yvonne said.

Hobbs looked back at her and his eyes filled with tears. "I knew something wasn't right. Mrs. Stone was so agitated after she received a phone call. I tried to inquire if there was anything I could do to help her. She said, 'Only if you can teleport my husband from the jungles of the Amazon.' Then she told us to take the rest of the day off."

"Mr. Stone wasn't home?"

"Captain Stone was on some kind of military mission. Very secret. South America, I understood. So, we left. But there was a somewhat strange request she made of me before I left." Hobbs said.

"What was that?"

"To put out some tea cakes and make some tea." Hobbs stepped closer to her. "Mrs. Stone evidently was expecting a visitor. And she wouldn't have done that for her son. JJ's mother would not have gone to such trouble. Mrs. Stone was expecting a visitor."

Yvonne nodded. "Did you tell this to the police?"

"The never asked. Once they realized we weren't here, they lost interest. We're used to it. We are just lowly servants. No one understands the servants are the ones who hear and see all."

Yvonne took a card from her pocket. "My card. Call me if you think of anything else that might help. Once I get into this case, I will need to understand Mr. Stone a little better and I would value your insight."

Hobbs nodded. "I will help as much as possible. JJ was a troubled young man, but he is not a murderer."

CHAPTER
TWENTY-SIX

YVONNE BROWN SIPPED her cappuccino and tapped on her laptop keyboard. She had to understand the precedents of trying a juvenile as an adult. JJ Stone was only fifteen and yet there was a strong possibility they would try him as an adult because of the heinous nature of the crime. A shadow passed over her and the fragrance of cologne engulfed her. Very familiar cologne. She closed her eyes and sighed.

"Not now, Richard." She said to the man standing behind her. He moved around the table and sat across from her.

"Yvonne Brown. So good to see you." Richard Stapleton smiled his thousand-watt smile and rested his manicured hands on the table. His hair was perfect. His skin was perfect. And, of course, his teeth were perfect.

Yvonne opened her eyes and glared at him. "What are you doing here?"

"I heard about your case. Pro Bono, right? I mean, who in their right mind would take on the defense of a teenager monster?" He leaned back in his chair and adjusted his tie. It was as perfect as his three-piece suit. Yvonne's head hurt from thinking the word "perfect" over and over.

"Yes, it is a pro bono case." Yvonne said, averting her eyes back to the laptop. "And when you were with our firm, you defended lots of monsters."

"You know, the district attorney has decided to try him as an adult." Stapleton said. With far too much delight.

Yvonne slammed the laptop closed. "What? I haven't even filed anything yet."

"You haven't met with the client yet?" Stapleton motioned to an attendant. "Decaf mocha latte with light foam and no cinnamon."

"I'm gathering my facts." Yvonne said.

Stapleton nodded and pursed his lips. "Yvonne, I know you. Pretty well. You're scared of meeting the man."

"He's a boy." Yvonne said tersely.

"In the eyes of the court, he's a man. And you are afraid to sit across the table from him and realize he is an un-defendable fiend." Stapleton sat back as his coffee arrived. He handed a twenty-dollar bill to the attendant. "Keep the change." He sipped the coffee and grimaced. "I asked for light foam. You never get what you want, do you?" He tilted his head as he studied her. "Like this case for you. Come on, Yvonne. Admit it. You never take on the hard cases. Everyone you have ever defended has been obviously innocent. A ball lobbed right into center court." He leaned toward her. "Problem is, you can't even return a lob. Don't take this case."

Yvonne's heart raced and her eyes narrowed. "Why are you suddenly concerned about my welfare?"

Stapleton drank some more coffee and frowned. "Because I'm the prosecuting attorney on the case."

Yvonne gasped and looked away. This was bad. Terrible. She looked back at him. "What happened to conflict of interest?"

"I would hardly classify a bad romance as a conflict of interest."

"We were engaged!" Yvonne said. "Engaged, Richard. But

you couldn't keep your eyes off the other junior partners. How old is Richard, Jr. now?"

Stapleton's face reddened. "I have set up a trust fund for him and his name is not Richard."

Yvonne raised an eyebrow. "Do you even know his name? Do you even remember *her* name?"

Stapleton tugged at his collar. "It cost me my position with the firm, Yvonne. That was punishment enough."

Yvonne reached across the table and flipped his tie out of his suit. "No, it was the best thing that happened to you. Richard you were born for political office. Joining the D.A.'s office was inevitable. Your sleaze quotient was too high for pro bono work."

"Oh, yeah?" Stapleton nudged his coffee cup and spilled the foamy liquid on the tabletop. "I was the apple of Steurman's eye, Yvonne. He was grooming me for a top full partner position. Everything was going my way until we got engaged."

Yvonne snorted. "So now this is all my fault? Oh, grow up Richard."

"Grow up?" A malignant gleam filled his eye. "You are the one nursing a grudge the size of Everest. Still involved in those ring fights? You can't hide your scars anymore. I may have messed up once, but I'm not screwed up on the inside like you are."

Yvonne's eyes watered. "How dare you? You know what I went through."

"Yeah, kidnapped and held hostage by a serial killer. Lucky to be alive, yeah. You told me a dozen times. That's your problem, Yvonne. Anytime things get rough, you play the victim card. You identify with this teenage murderer because he's just like the lover that cut you up."

Yvonne vaulted up from the table, grabbed the latte and splashed it in Stapleton's face. Stapleton fell back in his chair and tumbled to the floor. His cursing filled the air.

"I'll see you in court, mister prosecutor." Yvonne grabbed her laptop and stomped out the door.

"You know, that's the real reason I called off the wedding." He screamed as the door closed. "You're damaged goods!"

CHAPTER
TWENTY-SEVEN

JJ STONE, at age 15, stood almost six feet tall, gangly with thin but sinewy muscles. He shuffled into the juvenile prison conference room, heavily manacled. The guard pointed to a chair.

"Sit and I'll secure you."

JJ looked at Yvonne with intense turquoise eyes. His ginger hair was cut almost to the scalp. He sat in the chair and the guard locked his chains to the floor and to a metal ring in the middle of the table. He slammed his elbow into JJ's temple as he stood up from the floor. JJ jerked and groaned in pain.

"Sorry about that." The guard snickered and glared at Yvonne. "You going to defend this creep?"

"We're all innocent until proven guilty." She said with little conviction.

The guard chuckled. "They all say that. Good luck. If he attacks, you just scream, and I'll be right outside the door." He slammed the door behind him, and JJ flinched. He looked at her with those intense eyes.

"Who are you?"

"Your attorney. Yvonne Brown."

"Did my father hire you?" JJ said quietly.

"No one can get in touch with your father." Yvonne placed the folder of photos before her and opened her laptop. "He is still deep in the Amazon on some kind of mission."

"Black ops." JJ said.

"I am your court appointed attorney." Yvonne said.

"What about the funeral? Who's handling that?"

Yvonne froze. "I don't know."

"My mother deserves a good funeral." He said.

"I agree. I'll check on that for you." Yvonne opened a document on the laptop. "I need to ask you some questions if I'm going to defend you."

"No need. I'm guilty." JJ said.

Yvonne stopped typing. "Now just a minute."

"I can tell you, can't I? Attorney client privilege. I deserve to go to jail."

Yvonne swallowed. "The judge has approved of you being tried as an adult, JJ. That means if you are convicted, you could get the death penalty."

"I deserve it." JJ said, and he stiffened, as if proud of his admission.

"Where's the knife?" Yvonne said.

"What?"

"The knife you killed your mother with."

"In evidence, I assume."

Yvonne pulled a photo from the folder. She slid it over. The photo showed a golden knife with the image of a hummingbird carved into the hilt. "This knife?"

"Yes." JJ said and looked away. A tear trickled down his cheek.

"Where did you find this knife? It's not your ordinary knife."

JJ drew a deep breath. "I don't remember."

Yvonne opened more documents on her laptop. She had obtained some court records that showed JJ had been arrested for some minor misdemeanors and had undergone professional counseling. She studied one document.

"JJ, have you been in trouble in the last few months?"

JJ looked back at her and his face twisted in anguish. "Yes. I do things and don't remember. I wake up and something bad has happened. That's why I must have killed my mother."

Yvonne looked away as a memory surfaced. The man leaning over her with the box cutter. She had pushed that from her memory and for some reason, it now surfaced. She fought to clear her mind. She looked back at JJ.

"Are you saying you killed your mother, but you don't remember it?"

"Yes." JJ said and his voice caught. He tried to put a hand to his mouth to stifle a sob, and the manacles clanked as his hand froze in midair.

Yvonne looked back at the document and read silently. Something wasn't right. Every incident listed in the summary of the counseling had been minor. Some were violent like starting, or rather, finishing a fight at school when JJ had defended a friend. A friend.

"Who is your best friend?" She looked back at JJ.

JJ tried to wipe tears from his cheeks. "Clay. I probably killed him, too."

Yvonne typed in the name Clay and searched the court documents supplied to her. She studied a medical record. "Says here he was found on a bluff with a blow to the temple. Unconscious but only suffered a minor concussion. Want to tell me about that?"

"So, nothing has happened for two weeks?" Clay asked.

"Just the new car." He slapped the hood of the car they sat on.

JJ looked out over the river far below them flowing through valley. Opulent homes had been built along the lower reaches of the river side. Some were almost as big as his 'manor'.

For his last day at school, his father had bought him the car. It was small and efficient, a blue convertible with a hybrid engine. His excitement at receiving the car was subdued with the news that he would soon be sent off to a boarding school. He would need the car. That was why his father had given it to him. Not because he had finished the tenth grade and was now old enough to drive. From their conversations at the dinner table, he realized his father had not yet mentioned the boarding school to his mother. What was he going to do?

Right now, he didn't care about the future because for weeks he had not had a single absent spell. His father had taken the journal and put it in a safe in the library. The voice was still there in the back of his mind but rather subdued. JJ had driven Clay to the park along the ridge of the valley overlooking the river. How was he going to tell his friend he probably wouldn't be back in the fall?

"That's really cool. I mean, my dad never bought me anything new like this." Clay leaned back on the hood and rested his head against the windshield. "If I had a car like this then Amy would pay attention to me for sure."

"Amy would still think you're a loser." JJ said and laughed. But the laughter died away with the realization he had to tell his best friend he was leaving in the fall.

"Hey, what's eating you? New car, dude. You should be chilled!" Clay punched him in the shoulder.

"My dad wants to send me away to a boarding school in the fall." There, he had said it out loud and his good mood faded quickly.

"That sucks!" Clay hit the hood. "There's no way you're going off to a boarding school."

"It's because of my blackouts."

Clay sighed and slid off the hood. He paced in front of the car. "We've got to come up with a plan. You can't go. You're the only friend I have."

JJ sighed. "My dad says I'm under too much strain. He thinks I might be having some kind of multiple personality thing going on."

Clay stopped and laughed. "That's crazy. You don't have one personality much less multiple."

JJ smiled. "Nice try. Something is going on. I wake up and lose *time and something bad has happened. I mean people say they've seen me doing these things. What if it's true?"*

Clay leaned against the hood. "Bro, it hasn't happened in weeks, right? I mean, don't you have to be seriously screwed up as a child to do that?"

"My dad thinks it's my mother's fault."

"Oh, yeah, they always blame the mother. Look at me. My dad bailed when I was nine. My mother raised me and I'm perfectly normal. We all know your mom is the coolest mom around. And she's hot."

JJ slapped Clay on the arm and frowned. "This isn't funny. I mean, what if I hurt someone I care about while I'm having one of these blackouts?"

Clay slid back up onto the hood next to him. He gazed out at the afternoon sun settling lower on the horizon. "If you had multiple personalities, then sooner or later you will hurt someone who is standing in your way. At least, that happens in the movies. Who is standing in the way of your, you know, other self?"

JJ glanced at his best friend and shrugged. "I don't know."

"Look, you said that your dad is sending you to a boarding school. Maybe your alter ego wants to take him out."

"That can't happen. He's gone on another of his oversea trips and isn't supposed to be back until July."

"OK, I know this is twisted, but what if your evil side wants to take out your mother?"

JJ shivered and looked out over the city. The thought had crossed his mind. "That makes no sense."

"Sure, it does. Your dad said that she was the reason you are the way you are. See, your evil side wants to get her out of the way and then he can take over."

JJ shoved Clay with all his might and his friend slid over the side of the hood. "Cut it out! Don't say that about my mother, dude!"

Clay tumbled to the ground. There was a profound silence, and JJ slid off the hood and walked around the car. Clay lay on his side, his head at an odd angle. Blood was pooling across a rock at the top of Clay's head.

"Clay?" He squatted beside his friend. He lifted his head off the rock. A cut leaked blood onto the ground. Clay's eyes fluttered open, and he groaned. Inside the car, his cell phone rang. He grabbed the phone.

"Hello?"

Heavy breathing came over the speaker. "Son, is that you?" It was his mother. "Listen, don't speak. I'm in trouble. Come home now. I think someone may be in the house." She whispered. The line went dead.

JJ looked at the phone and started the car engine. He tore out of the gravel and dirt on the side of the mountain road and headed down the mountain. While he was driving, he realized he had a phone to call the police. He reached for it and had to lean all the way over to the passenger seat to reach it. The car swerved with his effort, and he straightened up as a huge, hairpin curve came into view. He slammed on the brakes and the car spun on the asphalt, slipping sideways toward the guardrail that separated him from a deadly drop. There was a tremendous impact, breaking glass, the sound of metal on metal and his head thudded against the steering wheel. Blackness came as he remembered leaving his best friend on the side of the road.

JJ sniffed and wiped his nose. Glittering tears filled his turquoise eyes. "The next thing I know, I'm waking up in my car."

When he awoke, it was pitch black. He sat up in the driver's seat of the car. It sat in the driveway of his home, just outside the garage. He blinked in confusion. The night sky was above, cool and filled with stars. What had happened? He had been sliding toward the edge of the road and then there had been a crash.

JJ stumbled out of the car and examined the passenger side. The fender and door were caved in and scraped, probably by the guardrail. But the car was still drivable. Then, he noticed the blood on his hands.

He studied the blood and recalled Clay. He had left him on the side of the room with a blow to the head and he had to call for help.

Wait! His mother had called. Someone was in the house! He started toward the front door and felt a sharp pain in his heel. He glanced down. He was barefoot. What had happened to his shoes? It was then he noticed the bloody footprints. They led down the steps from his open front door and toward his car. He raised up his foot. It was covered with blood.

He ran up the stairs and through the foyer. "Mom! Mom! Where are you?"

JJ glanced around. More bloody footprints led back into the house.

The library doors were open. Bloody handprints covered the doorknob. Bloody footprints led into the library. He hurried in and followed the prints across the floor. The black doors were open!

JJ stopped in shock, his mind reeling, his heart racing. The black doors were open! The bloody footprints led inside. He calmed his racing heart and his breathing and hurried through the doors. The inner chamber was carved from the mountain. In the center of the chamber a spiral staircase descended into darkness.

JJ slowly made his way down the stone stairs into a creeping cold that permeated his bones. Far below him, the stairs descended into a fine mist. From the depths of the stairs, he heard a moan of pain. He hurried into the mist and stumbled down the stairs.

A pale green light from flickering candles filled the chamber at the base of the stairs. The room was hewn out of the raw rock that was the foundation of the manor. In the center of the chamber was a low platform of smooth rock. Draped across the stone was the body of his mother.

He hurried through the mist and slipped in blood. He looked around the chamber. There was blood everywhere. He gasped, his heart racing. He knelt beside his mother's head. Fine spackles of blood splattered her white skin. A huge golden knife protruded from her lower chest. He grabbed it and pulled it out of his mother's chest.

"Oh, my God!" He sobbed. "Mother, who did this?"

Her eyes flickered open, bright jade green. She tried to smile, and blood appeared on her lips. "I love you, little man. I love you."

The life faded from her eyes. "Who did this?" He screamed. He was still crying when the first policeman appeared at the bottom of the stairs.

Yvonne sat back at the end of the story and crossed her arms. There were some discrepancies in his story. He had not mentioned the five doorways. He hadn't mentioned the letters written with his mother's blood. Maybe he was confused? Had he suffered a mild concussion from the car crash? He must have if he did not remember driving to the house.

"So, when you found your mother, she wasn't dead?"

"Yes. I think I must have stabbed her and ran back up to the car to leave and then sort of woke up from one of my absent spells." JJ moaned and put his head down on the table top.

Yvonne shuffled through the photos again and tried to ignore the bright eyes of JJ's dead mother. She did her best to keep them from his sight.

"Are those photos of the crime scene?" JJ looked up.

"Yes."

"I don't have to see them. I lived them." He said quietly.

Yvonne paused and looked at the pattern of blood on the floor in one of the photos. "When you woke up in the car and came to see your mother, were you wearing shoes?"

JJ blinked. "What? No. I was barefoot. I don't know why. I had been wearing sandals."

Yvonne sifted through documents until she came to the crime scene report of the contents of JJ's car. "The crime scene investigators found your sandals in the floor of your car. No blood."

"What does that mean?"

Yvonne slid a photo across the room. JJ gasped at the sight of blood. He swallowed hard. Yvonne pointed to a yellow crime scene tag. "See that. Footprints. Bare footprints. Yours."

"You see what I mean? I did it."

Yvonne slid another photo across the tabletop, and her heart rate picked up. "What is that?" She tapped the photo.

"Another footprint?"

"Of a shoe. In the blood. If you were barefoot, then where are the shoes?"

JJ blinked in confusion. "Those are flat sole tennis shoes. I don't wear those types of shoes. I wear running shoes."

"Exactly. JJ, what size shoes to you wear?"

"Ten."

Yvonne turned back to the laptop. "Says here in the report the size of those shoes is eleven. Not enough of a difference, I'm afraid."

JJ was breathing hard, his fist clenched. "I don't wear those type of shoes. I don't even own shoes like that." He turned his turquoise eyes on Yvonne. "I didn't do this! I didn't kill my mother, did I?"

Yvonne put the photo back in the folder and, for the first time, felt a shimmer of hope. "I looked through the list of items recovered at your house. No tennis shoes, JJ. Someone else was in the room before you got there."

JJ erupted out of his chair. His fists clenched, and the manacles tightened around his wrists and ankles. "It wasn't me! That means there was someone else! Who! We gotta find out who!"

Her breath quickened, and she put her hand up to calm him down. "Just calm down, JJ."

His eyes widened and glowed with hatred and anger. His body became tense and rigid, his muscles bulging. "I'm not to blame. There is someone else. Someone else. I don't think, I know there was someone else!" He screamed, his face contorting, his eyes bulging. He pushed the chair away, and it clattered across the room. He seemed to grow in stature, muscles enlarging. His face twisted into a mask of hideous rage and his eyes took on a reddish hint.

"I'm the one, can't you see? I'm the one that did it, not that wimp, JJ! You want to meet the real power, then say hello to number three, little missy." His voice had grown in volume, coarsening.

Yvonne fell back, her chair tumbling. Her legs twisted, and she slumped to the floor, the photos cascading around her. With the sound of metal screeching, JJ ripped the manacles from the floor and leaped up onto the table, squatting on the edge like some loathsome gargoyle. Spittle dripped from his leering lips, and he laughed. "My precious little Yvonne. I want to play with you. Come to Poppa."

The voice! It was him. The scars pulsed in her abdomen. The memories returned, searing and paralyzing. "Why did you call me that?"

"Because you are my little missy." JJ said. "I was there with him. I was the one who made him carve his initials in your belly. After all, you belonged to him." The chains between his wrists snapped like dried spaghetti, and JJ hopped off the table and squatted over Yvonne. "What did he say? You belong to me, little missy? What do you think those letters on the five doors say? Huh?"

Yvonne screamed and rolled out of his way. The door flung open, and the guard ran into the room. JJ turned and hissed at the guard, springing across the open space with unnatural power. He landed on the guard and pummeled him with his fists. Yvonne kept screaming and two more guards came into the room, drawing their nightsticks. One pulled a Tazer from his belt and fired it at JJ's hulking figure. The boy convulsed as the wires sent electricity into his body and he tumbled off the first guard. He jerked on the floor until his body became motionless. His face slackened, and the fire left his eyes. He looked up at Yvonne.

"What happened? How did I get on the floor?" He mumbled through partially paralyzed lips.

CHAPTER
TWENTY-EIGHT

"CAPTAIN O'MALLEY?" Yvonne said as the door opened.

O'Malley wore a tank top and khaki shorts. He was stooped over, his body thick and muscled. Iron gray hair covered most of his head in a comb-over and he glared at her with deep brown eyes. He had not shaved in several days.

"If you're a Jehovah's Witness, I'm not interested."

"Wait!" She put out her hand to keep him from slamming the door. "I'm Yvonne Brown. An attorney representing JJ Stone. I need to talk to you."

He froze, his eyes filling with hatred. "Why should I help you defend him?"

Because of what she saw this morning at prison, she wanted to say. Yvonne swallowed down the echo of the panic she had felt in the room with JJ. "Because you saw something at the crime scene that made you leave your job."

O'Malley didn't move, his eyes drifting to focus somewhere else. "You can come in for a few minutes. Then, you've got to go. I've some fishing to do."

Detective Corsair had given her O'Malley's address, a house on the water of Lake Pflugerville, east of Austin. It was a modest lake known for fishing and some water sports. Brown followed him into a two-story house. Dirty clothes lay scattered around the small living room and uncleaned dishes sat on a small dining table just beyond the couch in an alcove that looked out over the lake. O'Malley brushed a pile of clothes from the couch onto the floor.

"Have a seat. I'd offer you something to drink, but all I have is liquor." He crossed to a small fireplace, and he leaned against the brick mantle. "What makes you think I would help you defend that perp?"

Yvonne sat gingerly on the couch and tried to ignore the odor of dirty clothes. "Just a hunch. A man of your experience doesn't just walk away from a crime scene like that. What did you see that made you walk?"

"That's none of your business!"

"Would you rather answer that question on the stand?" Yvonne tightened her stomach muscles and felt the scars roll on her skin. She had to be tough with this guy.

O'Malley's eyes narrowed. "You're pretty bright for a woman lawyer."

"And you're pretty sexist."

O'Malley actually smiled and shook his head. "Why are you defending this boy, Ms. Brown?"

"That's none of your business." She said.

"Ah, I hit a nerve. You tell me your dirty little secret and I'll tell you mine." O'Malley picked up a glass filled with amber liquid and brushed a pile of newspapers from a chair. He collapsed into the chair and sipped his drink.

"Fair enough. I must defend JJ Stone in order to keep my job." She said. At least it was partly true.

"Well, that's much better. Your motives are more than altruistic." O'Malley downed the rest of his glass. "Junior partner trying to work her way into partnership, right?"

"Yes." Yvonne tried to hide her doubts. Even if she won this case, it would probably not be enough. "Truth is, Captain O'Malley, I have a weakness for taking on cases where I know the victim is innocent. I don't like to take on the cases where I am certain they are guilty. I was forced to take this pro bono case or leave the firm to prove I'm willing to do whatever my bosses tell me to do."

"Well, this case certainly doesn't fit one of your innocent cases, does it?" O'Malley said.

Yvonne nodded. "I know." She looked down at her satchel resting on her lap. "Maybe I don't belong at this law firm. But I am determined to show them I will do the best job I can, no matter what." She looked up at him and the image of JJ's wild antics in the conference room played in her head. "I saw something in JJ that makes me think underneath it all he might be innocent. I'm betting you saw something, too."

O'Malley froze and placed the glass slowly on the table beside him. He pursed his lips and then rubbed his eyes. He looked around the room and seemed to see it all for the first time. "I've let this thing get my goat." He pointed a finger at her. "You saw something? Unusual?"

"You first." Yvonne said and she tried not to hold her breath. O'Malley nodded.

"Okay. Fine, then. When I got the call, I should have sent one of the uniforms. But I was covering the desk that day for Sergeant Smith. He had to take his wife out for lunch for their anniversary. We got a 911 call saying there was blood everywhere and then they hung up. When I looked up the address, I decided to check it out on my own. You don't know how many crank calls we get about that mansion. Kids dare each other to sneak up and bang on the door. 911 operators stopped taking calls from there and would forward it to one of the desk cops. That's how I ended up getting the call and loading up in my car to head out to the mansion. I figured it was a hot day but would be a pleasant drive into the foothills. I had planned on grabbing a coffee and pastry on the way back."

O'Malley sat back and his eyes focused on an unseen memory. "I found the front door open. I went in after not hearing any reply. No one home. I had been in that house many times on such calls but had never seen the library doors open. That's when I saw the trail of bloody footprints. I immediately called for backup and should have gone back out to the cruiser. But what if someone was still alive?"

O'Malley paused and swallowed. "The bloody footprints led into the library and across to those pitch black, wooden double doors. I used my flashlight and saw a room carved into the mountain and a set of stairs leading down a shaft. That's when I heard the crying and moaning. Down at the bottom of those stairs."

O'Malley sat forward and fidgeted with his hands. "When I got to the bottom of the stairs, I noticed the glow from a dozen or so candles and the smell. Blood. Excrement. It smelled like a slaughterhouse."

O'Malley stood up and paced, rubbing his face with his hands. "I've seen nothing like that. Even in Afghanistan. Letters written with the person's blood. A flat stone like an altar with her body on it. And there he was. Sitting on the stone, his mother's head in his lap, crying like a baby. Blood all over him."

O'Malley paused and looked at his hand. "He was holding that golden dagger in his right hand with his arm hanging down by his side. I drew my weapon and pointed it at the boy and told him to drop the dagger."

O'Malley froze, and his hands shook. The room had grown still and the air thick. O'Malley stood as still as a statue. "Are you a religious woman?" he said.

Yvonne flinched. She had not expected that question. "Yes. Well, sort of. I have a conscience. That's what got me in trouble at the firm."

O'Malley nodded and moved back to sit in the chair. "I'm a back slidden Baptist. Stopped going to church when I got tired of seeing little girls turned into prostitutes and teenage boys killed by meth." O'Malley looked at her, his eyes filled with sadness. "Evil is winning, Ms. Brown. Where's God if evil is winning?"

Yvonne shook her head and kept silent as the images of the man in the basement tried to haunt her mind.

"I felt evil in that room. You could have cut it with a knife."

"What happened, Captain O'Malley?"

"I'm not Captain anymore. I've lost the battle. I'm only 49 but I've got 25 years with the force. I'm calling it quits and going fishing. Fish aren't evil."

Yvonne stood up and made her way around the couch. She passed the crusted dishes of half-eaten food and liquor-stained glasses. She stood in front of him and lifted her blouse. His eyes widened at the sight of the scars.

"What happened to you?"

"Evil." she said. She dropped the blouse. "Captain."

He looked up at her, and his entire demeanor changed. "Sam. Call me Sam."

Yvonne nodded and sat on the floor in front of him. "Ever hear of the Bottom Feeder serial killer?"

O'Malley straightened. "Over in Houston?"

"I was one of his victims. I was the one who killed the animal."

O'Malley took a deep breath. He leaned forward. "Then you know evil when you see it."

"Yes. What happened in that room, Sam?"

O'Malley looked out over her head. "I spoke to the devil, Ms. Brown. That boy didn't kill his mother. The devil did." O'Malley stared at her, his red rimmed eyes betraying the raw emotion within. He got up, stepped around Yvonne and went into the kitchen. "I need coffee."

"Why?"

"For the hangover. If I'm going to tell you my story, I need my mind to be sharp as possible." Yvonne heard him moving around in the kitchen and she turned and leaned her back against the sofa next to the chair.

O'Malley came back in the living room, mug of steaming

coffee in his hand. He sat and sipped at the brew. "Okay. I'm just about ready."

"You said you spoke to the devil?"

O'Malley studied the swirling clouds of steam coming from his mug. "Yeah, so to speak."

"Tell me about it."

He looked up at once from the coffee and he paled. He cleared his throat and told me his story.

CHAPTER
TWENTY-NINE

HAMPTON MANSION
Austin, Texas

"Drop the knife!" Sam screamed.

Blood covered everything, and O'Malley stood motionless with his gun trained on the boy. The teenager held the woman's head in his lap. Curiously, her face was the only part of her body not covered with blood. The boy's face twisted in sorrow as he cried. His bright turquoise eyes streamed with tears. He looked like a little boy in his blood-stained tee shirt and shorts, his bare feet trailing through the bloodstains on the stone floor. The golden knife fell from his hand and splashed as it hit the puddle of blood.

"Momma's dead! Why did this happen? She's dead!"

O'Malley let his gun fall to his side. The boy posed no threat. Not now. He had already spent his destructive energy. "Just take it easy, son. Help is on the way."

"He killed her! You've got to stop him! He did this."

O'Malley glanced around the room at the other five doors. No one else was in sight. "I don't see anybody else, son."

"Don't call me son! You're not my father!" The boy screamed.

"Sorry. Just calm down."

"Calm down! How can I calm down? She's dead. Look what he did to her. Look!"

"Who?" O'Malley asked.

The boy suddenly became motionless, his face growing slack. A strange light seemed to glow from his eyes, a reddish hue mirroring the blood-tinged room. He seemed to slump, hunching downward, and an insidious grin played across his lips. He laughed.

O'Malley felt the hair stand on his arm when he heard the guttural laughter. The boy had transformed, his eyes bulging, his face twisted into a loathsome grin.

"He's talking about me. I'm the one that caused this. But he doesn't know it, do you, my pretty?" The boy's hand came up, and he stroked his own blood matted hair. "We had to stop him. Now. Before he gets out of hand. Don't you see?"

O'Malley took a step back and felt the cold spiral staircase bite into his spine. Sweat trickled down his face. "What are you talking about?"

"Let's just say number three is on the scene. I had to intervene. The rest of us were letting things get out of hand. This little puppy is a threat, and he had to be stopped. Now. You wouldn't understand these things, mortal one. You're just a bag of blood and bile and poop. We're the immortal ones. We control your destiny and your horrid world."

O'Malley tried to make sense of the ravings. He had the distinct impression he was talking to someone else. "Who are you?"

"I told you. Number three. I had to leave for some unfinished business, but it'll still be waiting for me once we get this cleared up. Don't worry. I'll be right here with my pretty until we claim his soul."

O'Malley felt the world tilt, saw the face of other criminals, heard the laughter he had always considered insanity. But was it insanity? Here before him was evil incarnate. "Why are you telling me this?"

"Remember Garcia?"

O'Malley felt the gun slip from his fingers. Raymond Garcia. Heroin dealer and child molester. The alleyway had been dark, and he had cornered Garcia after chasing him from a murder scene. Garcia had become an animal. He remembered the glint in the man's eye, the set of his jaw as he pulled his gun to fire at O'Malley. O'Malley had taken a bullet to his right shoulder and had missed Garcia with his shot. He fell to the sticky pavement of the backstreet alley. Garcia had crouched over him, something hideous and monstrous in his eyes.

"Hey, O'Malley, baby. Thought you had me, didn't you? Well, I got me some friends now and you ain't never gonna stop me. Want to meet one of them?" And then, Garcia's face had twisted, become inhuman and O'Malley, lying in his own blood just seconds away from death, stared into the face of evil. Before Garcia could speak, a red blossom of blood spurted from his forehead, and he tumbled back onto the pavement. O'Malley's partner had arrived just in time.

"What about Garcia?" O'Malley whispered.

"He was one of mine. One of my legion. A lesser one at that, but still useful. He was about to claim your putrid little soul when your partner took away one of our finest tools. Poor Garcia. He curses you even now in hell."

O'Malley felt his breath quicken, felt the room spin. "How did you know about Garcia?"

The laughter came again, hoarse and inhuman. "Because I am Legion. I and my bottom dwelling demon slaves keep a host of mortals dancing at the ends of their puppet strings. But I've said enough. Thought I'd just blow your mind a little bit. Push you over the edge. See you in hell."

The boy's face slackened, and he fell back onto the altar beside his dead mother. His eyes closed in unconsciousness. O'Malley stood motionless, tremors overtaking him, eyes leaking tears listening to a moan that came from somewhere only to realize it was himself. He crumpled onto the floor, blood soaking through his pants, his life irrevocably changed. O'Malley left his gun stuck in clotting blood and climbed up the spiral staircase and out of the mansion. He started up the cruiser and drove back to the precinct.

Ignoring the stares from his buddies, he trudged through the brightly lit rooms and out the back door to his truck. He started the vehicle and drove away from the police station, never to return.

———

Yvonne watched the pain fill O'Malley's eyes as he finished the rest of the coffee. He wiped moisture from his eyes and looked down at her still sitting on the nasty carpet.

"Just nine months until retirement and I lost it, Ms. Brown. I lost the edge, and I can't go back. He took it from me."

"JJ?"

O'Malley looked back at me, his eyes clearing of the alcohol. "No, that spawn of hell."

"So, you think there's what? A demon inside of Jonathan?"

O'Malley remained silent, turning his attention to the surrounding room. "No one could have known what Garcia said. I told no one what he said to me. He was going to kill me when Corsair saved my life. I never even told my partner what Garcia said. How could that teenage boy know such a thing? Unless something told him."

I chose my words carefully. "If something inside of Jonathan caused him to murder his mother then it is not his fault."

O'Malley leaned back in his chair and rubbed his stubbled chin. "Yeah, that's the problem. I always thought the criminals I brought to justice were products of bad homes, bad genes, abuse, you name it. And then along comes Garcia and now, this kid, to prove to me those people weren't just a product of bad homes. They were a product of the influence of evil."

"Sin." I said.

O'Malley chuckled. "Sinners in the hands of an angry God. Yeah, I grew up in the church, Ms. Brown. Hellfire and brimstone. I ran away from it as soon as I could get out on my own, only to find out it was real to begin with. Maybe they were right, after all."

"Captain, I am a Christian. I go to church. Sometimes. I've always believed there was an absolute right and wrong. I believe there is a God and there is a Satan. But, when that thing spoke to me yesterday, I was just as shocked as you. I guess we never expect to face evil face to face."

"It spoke to you?"

"Yes."

"Ms. Brown, you can't fight the devil and win."

"Yes, you can. If JJ Stone didn't kill his mother, if some entity in control forced him to kill, then we have a choice. We must stop that thing." Yvonne said.

O'Malley regained some life and then laughed. "You're going to put the devil on trial?"

"No, we are."

"We?"

"You're going to help me. I need someone with investigative skills. You're not with the force anymore. You can help track down this thing and where it came from."

O'Malley's mouth fell open. "You're out of your mind."

Yvonne gestured to the messy room. "No. You're out of your mind. This isn't your life, is it? If you want to get your life back, you have no other choice."

CHAPTER
THIRTY

YVONNE GLANCED AT HER WATCH. She had so much
to do and sitting in her boss's office waiting for a reprimand that
would change nothing was a colossal waste of time. The door to
Zelda Tseng's office opened, and she walked in. Zelda was tall
with perfectly feathered black hair framing an exotic face. Her
Asian heritage was faint, but it gave her a mysterious flair that
she took advantage of. Now, however, her eyes filled with fire
and her frown marred her almost perfect features.

"Yvonne." She said quietly and then settled behind her desk.
"First, how are you? I understand your client attacked you."

"He tried, but never laid a hand on me."

"Good. I'm taking you off the case."

"What? No!" Yvonne said.

Zelda shook her head. "This case has too many negative
vibes, Yvonne. It's pro bono and I can appeal to the judge to
assign a new attorney. I assigned you to this case. I wanted you
to confront a truly guilty client who was caught red-handed.
There will be another such case with less negative optics."

Yvonne sat forward. "Ms. Tseng, please don't take me off this
case. This kid is innocent. You let the judge assign a lesser
attorney and they will throw him to the wolves."

"That is no longer your concern, Yvonne." She slid a folder across the desk. "This is your next case. One that is right down your alley and fits your style. I'll give you a brief reprieve before once again throwing you to the wolves."

Yvonne looked at the folder like it was a roach. "Ms. Tseng, please do not take me off this case. I have found out information that will establish this young man's innocence. I can prove it."

Zelda steepled her hands. "You have also retained a retired policeman as an investigator. How were you planning on paying for him?"

"He is doing this for free. He was the first officer on the scene."

"How can anyone seeing that crime scene believe the boy is innocent?"

"And, if he is, how can we allow the real murderer to get away with this?" Yvonne said.

"My decision is final." Zelda said.

Yvonne's heart raced and her hand resting on her lap touched the scars on her abdominal wall. She sat up straight. "This isn't about me, is it? You know the boy claims to be possessed by a demon. Like you said, this is bad optics for the firm. We win, we become the attorneys to the occult. We lose and we condemn a mentally challenged teenager to prison for life."

"I see you understand, Yvonne." Zelda said.

Yvonne's face warmed. She was back in the basement again, tied down, helpless unless he gave in to the kidnapper's demands. She couldn't let it happen again! "Then, I quit. I will take on JJ Stone's case on my own."

Zelda stood up quickly. "Yvonne, no one quits this firm."

"Richard Stapleton did and joined the D.A.'s office. Let's be honest, Ms. Tseng, my future here was questionable anyway. You assigned me this case so I would lose, and you would have a reason to let me go." Yvonne stood slowly. "In fact, the reason you are taking me off this case is because of the negative publicity it will bring this firm. If I was successful in clearing a young man for such a heinous crime, the blowback would be devastating. I understand. Thank you for the opportunity to serve this firm and learn what I could. I'll clear out my office and be out of your hair, Zelda."

Zelda's face reddened. "Fine! The partners had already decided to let you go at the end of the year."

Yvonne drew a deep breath. "Can I ask why?"

"Yvonne, you consistently have limited yourself to the underdogs, the good guys. Your conscience gets in the way of your performance."

"And it is bad to have a conscience?"

"If it keeps you from being a full partner in this firm, yes." Zelda moved around the desk to the door to her office. "Yvonne, it's just one big game. The bad guys may win a battle now and then, but they usually lose the war. They self-destruct. I just make sure we benefit from their problems along the way."

Yvonne studied her intense eyes. "And what of the innocent people who get hurt by the 'bad guys'?"

"If they're gullible enough to fall for what they peddle, then that's too bad. They learn a valuable lesson."

Yvonne nodded. "Tell that to Wendy Peters, Zelda. She was only six years old when one of our clients destroyed her life. Six years old! How can a six-year-old learn a lesson from that?"

Zelda stiffened and reached for the door handle. "Well, her parents certainly learned. So, not all our cases work out for the best. I don't know that ahead of time." She opened the door. "Yvonne, your problem is your moral convictions. Get over the 'good versus evil' mind set. It's all relative. Change your point of view and what's bad can become good. I will give you some parting advice. Plea for life in prison and use the insanity plea. Your client has multiple personalities."

Yvonne flinched. "How do you know that?"

"Because I have already done my homework, Yvonne. It's why I asked you to move on from this case. It's a no-win situation."

"I don't think Jonathan has multiple personalities." Yvonne paused, preparing to relish the reaction she was about to get. "I think Jonathan is demon possessed."

Zelda's eyebrows arched, and she smiled. "So you claim."

"There is precedent to the case. I checked it out just before I came in here. If I can show a reasonable doubt with the jury."

"You are kidding, right?"

"You said I have moral convictions. Well, my 'religious' side thinks JJ may be demon possessed. Captain O'Malley said he spoke to the devil when he got to the crime scene."

"O'Malley? The alcoholic dead head?"

Yvonne stopped, a chill running down my spine. "What?"

Zelda sighed and went back to her desk and retrieved another folder. She handed it to Yvonne. "Might as well give you this. It's another reason to take you off the case since you insist on using that loser. Check out that info before you go a step further down your self-defeating path. Let's just say his upcoming retirement wasn't elective. It was mandatory."

Yvonne glanced at the folder. Dared she open it? Zelda moved back to her door.

"Yvonne, you don't have a chance in, pardon the pun, hell in getting that boy off unless you claim temporary insanity. Talk to his shrink. And, put your conscience on the shelf."

Yvonne glanced at her one last time. "At least I have a soul." She rushed out of her office.

TWO GUARDS BROUGHT JJ into the conference room. Both guards carried Tazers. JJ's eye was swollen, and his hobble came not from his manacles. He sat down in the chair and groaned.

"What happened to you?"

JJ glanced over his shoulder at one guard. "They straightened me out."

Yvonne glared at the guard. "I'll report you to the warden."

"Knock yourself out." The guard laughed and the two of them left the room.

Yvonne pulled her laptop out of her satchel along with a folder. She drew a deep breath and calmed her racing heart. The boy sitting before her housed a demonic presence. "JJ, do you remember what happened the last time I was in this room?"

JJ nodded. "The guards told me. Told me some demon took over. I think it killed my mother."

Yvonne tapped on the keyboard. "Will it show up again today?"

JJ shrugged. "I do not know. Now I understand what has been happening to me for the past few months. Every blackout I had, I thought, was because of a multiple personality problem. Now I know it was this demon taking over."

Yvonne studied the boy's face, waiting for any sign of the approaching demonic storm. "I don't want to stir him up, JJ. But I want to put this demon on trial, not you."

JJ's turquoise eyes widened. "What?"

"It wasn't you fault if a demon took over. That's how it works, right? You do things and you never remember what you did. That means you weren't in the driver's seat." Yvonne said.

JJ looked away and swallowed hard. "I guess so. I have thought little about it. Never believed in all that devil stuff. Until now."

"JJ, where did this demon come from?"

JJ leaned his head down and rubbed his swollen eye with an extended finger. "It all started with my grandfather's journal."

"Journal?"

"I found it in the garage. My grandfather was an adventurer. Traveled all over the world. He had a journal with his photographs and one day, in the garage, I knocked over a box and there it was." JJ looked up at me. "When I touched it, I heard something. A voice. I started looking through the photos and it wasn't long before the voice became clearer." JJ picked at his fingernails. "I started acting differently. At least that is what my teachers said. And my friend, Clay." He looked up at me. "Why can't Clay visit?"

Yvonne froze and tried to think about how to answer the question. "He doesn't want to visit you, JJ."

JJ drew a deep, shuddering breath and nodded. "Can't blame him. I almost killed him."

"Say nothing like that in the courtroom, JJ. You can't talk about how you treated your best friend or any girlfriends." Yvonne said.

"I had a girlfriend for a while, but I treated her wrong. And then there was Mercedes." JJ frowned. "A one-night stand. At least, that is what it seemed like. I remember nothing. That was the night I threw the journal into the woods. I thought it was gone for good. Not long ago, one of my relatives, Nigel Hampton, showed up with the journal and left it for me in the library. But my father took it and hid it from me."

"Speaking of your father." Yvonne said. "He finally responded to the police. He is on his way back home. He should be here tomorrow."

JJ tensed. "I don't want to see him. I don't want him anywhere near me."

Yvonne raised an eyebrow. "Why?"

"Because you would have to defend him for murder. He's going to kill me." JJ said. "My father knew something was wrong with me. He never trusted me and he was going to send me off to a boarding school."

"JJ, I might need him to testify in court in support of his son."

"Well, forget that happening, Ms. Brown. I'm sure he is in favor of the death penalty." JJ said.

Yvonne made some notes in her notebook to call and talk to Captain Stone. Maybe putting him on the stand was the wrong move. And now, this photo journal? If JJ's father had taken the journal, he would be the only one who could help her find it.

"Am I going to die, Ms. Brown?" JJ asked.

She glanced up from her laptop. "I will do my best to clear you, JJ. If what you say is true, you are innocent."

For a moment, the boy's eyes seemed to glow and Brown drew in a deep breath. The glow faded. "Can you kill a demon? Because if you can, I will not sleep until it is destroyed!"

YVONNE ARRANGED a meeting with Captain Stone in a coffee shop down the street from the juvenile detention center. When she arrived, the man was waiting impatiently for her, tapping his hand on the table where he sat. He wore a camouflage uniform. His hair was ginger and gray and he was short and twitchy, like he was wound up way too tight. When he saw Yvonne, he stood up quickly from the table. His eyes were turquoise, like his son. "You're late."

"Sorry, Captain Stone. Austin traffic is notoriously terrible, especially on MoPac." Yvonne placed her satchel on the table and slid into a seat across the table from the Captain.

"Then you take that into consideration, and you start earlier." He sat down. "I don't like the fact my son's attorney is sloppy."

Yvonne froze, and her pulsed quickened. "If you want someone else to take on your son's case, then take it up with him. He wants me as his attorney." She didn't mention she had quit her job to defend his son. She pulled out her laptop. "And I want to represent him. I believe he is innocent."

Captain Stone stared at her silently. "Did he tell you why he killed my wife?"

Yvonne tilted her head. Time to be just as direct. "No, he said the demon inside of him made him kill your wife."

Whatever reaction Yvonne was expecting, the Captain surprised her. "The third demon, right?"

Yvonne opened her mouth and then closed it. "How did you know?"

"The journal. I'm sure he told you about my father's journal. My grandfather told stories for years about demons." The captain seemed to relax a bit. He had a cup of coffee in front of him and he picked it up and drank deeply.

"What does this have to do with JJ?" Yvonne said.

"My wife and I were having difficulty getting pregnant. My father handed me some kind of stone from the Amazon where he claims to have met demons. He said it would help." The captain paused and drank more coffee. "He said the third demon would make sure I was successful. I never thought to ask him where the other two demons were. A stone would help us have a child? What next? Bury a baby doll in the backyard? The man was insane! Which is where JJ gets it from."

Yvonne raised an eyebrow. "This entire conversation was something I never imagined coming from you."

"Imagined?" The Captain snickered. "My father had quite the imagination. No, my father was not mentally stable. There are more tales I could tell you that would curl your hair and leave you sleepless at night. I have spent years trying to undo his vile deeds." The captain looked away and wiped at his eyes.

"When JJ found that journal, I was worried he would find out about these demons. It doesn't surprise me he blames a demon for this." He looked back at her. "The truth is, JJ's psychologist has diagnosed JJ with multiple personality disorder. There is no demon."

Yvonne sat back and crossed her arms. "No wonder JJ is so messed up between you and his grandfather." She pushed her laptop aside and sat forward. "JJ transformed the other day. He took on another personality, all right. But he told me things no one could have known. Captain Stone, a serial killer kidnapped and tortured me. I, well, I escaped and left him for dead. What transpired between us was never recorded in detail. Your son told me details about my captivity no living person could know. Want to know how he knew?" Yvonne tapped the tabletop. "According to the demon's own words, he was there when I was tortured. He said he was the third demon, and his name was Legion."

"Like in the Bible?" The Captain said quietly.

"What?"

"The story where a demon possessed man was healed by Christ. The man said his name was Legion because he harbored a legion of demons." The Captain looked away. "Just a story, Ms. Brown. Another one of my father's stories."

"No, this demon claimed he used one of his legion to, well, control my captor. That is the only way this third demon could have known those details. And he told me this through your son. Now, how could JJ know these details?"

The Captain stood up. "I don't know, Ms. Brown. Maybe someone in prison knows more about your captor than you know. Maybe he set my son up. All I know is that there are no demons. There is no supernatural influence in this world." He pulled a Meerschaum pipe from his pocket and tapped it in the palm of his hand.

"Sounds to me like JJ has the perfect attorney, after all. One as crazy as he is. The reason I don't want you to be sloppy is not because I want my son exonerated. It's because he deserves a decent defense so when he is convicted, he won't stand a chance for a mistrial. He killed the love of my life and he deserves to die." He turned and stormed out of the coffee shop.

JONATHAN STEEL

A log settled in the fireplace, and the grating sound startled me. I jerked in surprise and my mind reeled under the story Yvonne had told. Yvonne drank some water from a bottle, and I stood up. My legs trembled and my hands shook. "I need some time to process what you've told me already. It's almost midnight."

Yvonne nodded. "I agree. I'm getting tired and I could use some rest."

"Not to mention that you're going to feel it if you don't sleep." Sam stood up.

"I don't know if I can sleep." I said. But I was feeling it. My thoughts were muddled, and trying to process what I had just heard was taking its toll on me. "I will say that everything I've heard so far has not triggered any new memories."

"And the third demon?" Yvonne stood up slowly. "Any memories of it?"

The memory of the fight in the alleyway when I was a teenager shimmered in my muddled mind. Had that been the third demon? "No new ones." I nodded to the couch. "Do I try to bed down here?"

"No. You can go back to the guest bedroom where you were earlier." Sam motioned down the hall, past the kitchen. "Yvonne's bedroom is upstairs and mine is across the hall from you."

I looked back and forth between them. I guess my unspoken question was obvious.

"I'm almost old enough to be Yvonne's father." Sam said.

Yvonne nodded. "We're friends, JJ. Just friends united against this evil enterprise. We've been together for almost sixteen years, most of that on the run."

"It seems like yesterday to me." Sam said. "But that shouldn't surprise someone my age. An old friend once told me life is like a roll of toilet paper."

I smiled. "Crappy, huh?"

Sam laughed. "No. The closer you get to the end, the faster it unrolls. Good night, all."

Yvonne put a hand on Sam's arm as he passed by her. "We are safe, right?"

"I'll check the sensors before I go to sleep."

"Sensors?" I asked.

"There's only one road up to the house. Anyone turns off the main highway it activates an alarm. It takes ten minutes to drive up the mountain. Not much time to react, but we will have a fair warning. Good night all." Sam made his way down the hallway and disappeared into the bedroom.

I walked over to Yvonne. "I need to know who is coming after you."

Yvonne seemed to deflate. "I'll tell you more tomorrow." She put a hand on my chest. "I can't tell you how relieved I will be to tell you the truth. Before now, there were too many demons to contend with, but you have single-handedly decimated the Council of Darkness, and their power and influence are waning quickly." She looked down at her hand and a tear trickled down her cheek. "JJ, you need to understand that until a few weeks ago, you were an anonymous nobody." She looked up at me. "But when your face went viral after the disaster in Switzerland, the forces aligned against you had a person they could target. They are coming after you and your family now."

I drew a deep breath and guilt gripped my heart. "I was afraid of as much. The unholy triad were far too aggressive. Normally they fly under the radar." I looked into her moist eyes. "I will stop them, Yvonne. And I will stop whoever is coming after us. I promise."

"And you always keep your promise, I know." Yvonne smiled weakly. "Get some sleep." She patted my chest and wiped tears from her face. She crossed the living room to a set of spiral stairs leading up to the second level and her bedroom.

I studied the dying embers in the fireplace then went down the hallway to my bedroom. I undressed and slid underneath the blanket made by my mother. The cool darkness of the bedroom enveloped me. I pulled the quilt up to my nose and inhaled. Was that a faint scent of her perfume? No, mostly musty cloth.

I sat up and pushed the quilt off me. Did I really want these memories? I had no recall of the presence of the third demon inside me. No memories of the encounter in the conference room. I studied the palm of my left hand. The faint blue glow illuminated the quilt. If these shards of the Grimvox held memories of past demonic events, would memories of my encounter with the third demon be there?

I extended the index finger of my right hand and held it above my glowing palm. Did I want this? Or, should I wait and hear their side of the story. I had to know. I touched my palm.

The air was rich with body odor and stale urine. I blinked and realized I sat in a jail cell. The cell was not too different from my cell at Rockwall. I looked around at the concrete walls. Night had drenched my cell and the hallway outside in shadows. From a shadow in the corner, he appeared.

The man was almost my height. His ginger hair was standing on end and he wore a prison jumpsuit identical to mine. I looked down at my body. I was fifteen and thin and hard muscled. I looked back at the man as he stepped into the faint blue light from my palm. His turquoise eyes glittered with malice.

"Hello JJ." He said in a voice that was far too familiar.

"Who are you?"

A surprised look came over his face, and he pointed to his chest. "Me? I'm you." Then he giggled. "And, not you." He sat on the cot beside me. The odor of hot coals and sewage drifted off him. He patted my knee. "It's time we got to know each other a little better. They're going to take me away from you and JJ, you do NOT want that."

I looked into his eyes, MY eyes, and shivered. "You're the demon, aren't you?"

He shrugged. "Well, sort of. Where do I stop and you begin? We're in this together." He rubbed his hands together. "Now, there's a good chance you could have the death penalty if they find you guilty. You need to be prepared for that eventuality."

My heart raced and sweat broke out on my forehead. I scooted away from the man to the end of the cot. "Did I kill my mother?"

The man titled his head back and forth. "Well, yes. And, no." He glanced at me. "You have a magnificent gift."

"What?"

"Your anger. Your fury. It makes you very powerful." He leaned toward me and licked his lips. "And potentially deadly." He laughed again.

I gasped for breath. "I killed her, didn't I?"

"Frankly, JJ, you don't have that much potential. You have too much of your mother in you and not enough of your father." He stood up and paced. "Now, if I had to guess, you could have killed her if properly motivated. Unfortunately, the motivation you've had recently, thanks to your grandfather's photo album, hasn't been quite enough." He paused and his eyes gleamed. "That's where I came in. I took over

and gave you the needed push to be the person you should become. Violent. Angry. Powerful!" He smiled and his teeth gleamed in the meager light of my cell. "JJ, I am what you must become. I am your future. Look at me! Don't you want this power? You'll never make it out of that courtroom without me!"

I studied his glaring face, his glittering eyes. There was something off about him, something not quite right. He was me. And, yet NOT me. I stood up and stepped toward him. "But, you are NOT me. If you had to make me do those things then I'm not YOU. You're a demon, aren't you? Sent by Satan to destroy my life." I paused as the realization washed over me. "To destroy my family." A flicker of hope burned within me and I almost smiled.

"If what you say is true, then I did not kill my mother." I reached out and poked him in the chest. "You did! And if you did, then there's hope for me."

The man's face twisted and he suddenly roared. The roar echoed around the cell and out into the hallway. I put my hands over my ears until he stopped. His chest heaved with each labored breath and he glared at me with evil filled eyes. "Hope? JJ, there is no hope for you. You are damned and you don't know it. You are a dead man walking and we will claim your soul before this is done. We will take care of your little legal team and keep them distracted and we will see you at the executioner's table."

I stepped back. "Distraction? Wait, that means they are on the right track! That means I have hope, after all." I smiled.

The man's hands tightened into fists. "Well, we shall see about that. We can take some of the pawns off the board, JJ. Without the help of Yvonne Brown and Sam O'Malley, you will be prosecuted. We already have the judge in our pockets so think about that! And see if you can possibly hold on to hope!"

The man stepped back into the shadows and disappeared. I collapsed onto the cot. What was about to happen to Yvonne and Sam? They were in trouble!

———

The scene faded and I found myself once again in my bed, covered with my mother's quilt. My heart raced. I had been in that cell with a manifestation of the third demon. I stood up and wiped sweat from my forehead. I had to work this out. I pulled on my clothes and stepped out into the hallway.

Heavy parkas hung on pegs by the back door. I shrugged into one and went out the back door. The air was beyond frigid, burning my lungs as I breathed in the crisp, night air tainted with the fragrance of evergreens. A porch stretched across the back of the house. The snow had stopped falling and the night sky had cleared.

Where was I? What part of the world was I in? I walked down the stairs of the deck. A pathway led into the trees. Towering above me was another mountain peak. I followed the path into the quiet trees with the only sound the chuffing of my shoes in the fresh snow. Eventually I came to a clearing. A single fir tree stood in the center of the clearing not much taller than me. A bench sat in front of it.

I brushed the snow from the bench and my hands were numbed by the snow. The cold seeped into my bottom as I sat on the bench. I turned and lay across the bench and looked up into the deep, infinite sky. The stars were of startling clarity. I made out the north star so I was in the northern hemisphere.

"God, I know I have let you down." I whispered. My breath formed a cloud that hovered over my body. "I won't make any deals. I've tried that before. It's time I fully understand where I am in this battle. I give myself to you fully, completely. You have watched over and guarded me despite my anger and my hubris. You have delivered me from the hands of the enemy time and time again. I tried to do things my way with the unholy triad, and it almost backfired. I should have listened to you. I have no idea what tomorrow will bring. I do not know who or what my father is. But right now, you are the only Father I know who has been faithful to me."

I raised my hands toward the stars. "I give myself to you

fully. I surrender. Take all of me. Use all of me. And I know that you will protect my family. It's time to finish this. It is time to face the enemy and remind him he is already defeated, the walking dead."

My cheeks stung as the tears literally froze in the frigid air. A flash of light split the stars and streaked across the heavens, a falling star that left its glowing trail across the brilliant sky. It blinked out of existence as the tail of light faded. Was this my fate? To glow with the light and power of my Father only to fade and die? If so, I was willing and ready to accept my fate. Whoever or whatever was coming after me, I was now ready.

CHAPTER
THIRTY-FOUR

LONDON, England
Hampton's Museum of the Weird

Jason Birdsong fought for control. Already he could smell the faint odor of gas. Were the walls closer? Sweat drenched his clothes. If he could just push the sides of the furnace away! Keep them from closing in!

He closed his eyes and imagined he was in the wide open countryside of Tucson. Towering cacti. Rolling hills. The drive up the mountain until the cacti transitioned to evergreens and the hot air cooled and snow covered the mountainside. He saw the eyes of his Hu'lu, his grandmother, and imagined her hunched over the stove at the retirement center. He recalled the fragrance of her cooking. In his mind she looked at him with those powerful eyes.

"You can do this, my son." She whispered.

Birdsong opened his eyes and coughed. Already a faint whisper came from the spigots. He had to get out of here. But how? The furnace door was dogged with an iron crosspiece. He hurled himself against the door. It did not give. He used the flashlight to look all around the chamber. Nothing! No way out! The flashlight slipped out of his sweaty hands and bounced on his foot. It fell through the grate into the darkness beneath.

Birdsong fell to his knees. The gas would be lighter than air. It would gather around the top of the furnace and, hopefully, the top of the museum. The candle would be on the first floor. He had time.

He couldn't get his hand through the opening in the grate. The flashlight sunk into soot and ash, and darkness descended on him. He pounded the grate in desperation and heard the sound of metal on metal.

Could it be? He grabbed the grate and pulled. It lifted in a three foot by two-foot section. The grate was removable! He put it aside and slid through the opening, barely squeezing his shoulders into the space beneath the other grates. He knelt in the nasty miasma of soot, ashes, and who knew what else from Reginald Drake? He found his flashlight and wiped the grimy goo from the lens. The underside of the furnace was a drawer holding the removable ashes. Could he push it open?

He grabbed the strut between the grate plates and lay down in the goo. He placed his feet against the side wall and pushed. Nothing. No movement. He coughed again as gas filled the furnace. He twisted one hundred eight degrees and pushed against the other wall. It budged. Barely, but it budged.

"God, help me with this." He prayed. He pushed again with all his might and felt the entire "drawer" in the bottom of the furnace move beneath him. He shifted his grip closer to the edge and pushed some more until he felt the far edge of the drawer opening. He slid through the wet ashes until he breathed fresh air and felt a gap above him. He used the flashlight and found he had about a two foot opening between the edge of the drawer and the side of the furnace. Enough? It would have to be.

Birdsong squeezed himself upward on his side. His chest caught between the lip of the drawer and the furnace and he couldn't breath. Claustrophobia again! Not now! He panted, inhaling more gas and more soot until his chest slid past the furnace and he lurched up onto his side. He rolled out of the drawer and hopped to his feet. He ran through the surgical suites and up the stairs to the first floor. He coughed as more gas filled the air and more soot clogged his nose. He slid into the foyer and stopped at McGuire's desk. No candle! He heard a whoosh far above him and fire and broken glass cascaded outside the front door. Drake had lied. He had lit a candle higher so the museum would burn quicker. He glanced once at the photo of McGuire and something tickled at the back of his mind. He grabbed the photo and hurtled through the front door. Fire gushed out of the windows upstairs and he knew that when the flames reached the critical mass of gas in the center of the museum, it would explode.

He was halfway across the street when the top of the museum exploded upwards. The concussion threw him through the front window of the establishment across the street. More explosions shook the earth and the windows in the office around him shattered. He crawled across the floor of the office to a back hallway and stumbled upward, running down the hallway as more explosions filled the night.

———

Chief Inspector Holland stepped through the curtain at the emergency room and glared at Birdsong. "You don't know when to stop, do you?"

"I was just doing what you allowed me to do, Holland." Birdsong said. The doctor was putting staples into a cut on the side of his head.

Holland looked up and down his clothes. "What have you been wallowing in, love?"

"The bottom of Drake's furnace. He trapped me in the furnace and then opened up the gas valves for the building. I managed to crawl out just in time before the building exploded. He also admitted to me that he killed McGuire."

"Well, if we ever catch the man, we'll put you on the stand so you might can clear your partner. Where is Drake?"

Birdsong winced as the last staple went in. "You wouldn't believe it, but he went back to the states."

"Great! Out of my jurisdiction."

A glint of light reflected off her necklace and Birdsong stiffened. "Over there. On the table with my things."

Holland turned and picked up the framed photo. "This? What about it?"

"She's wearing a medal like yours. Did she have it on her when she was killed?"

Holland's forehead wrinkled in thought. "I don't remember it being mentioned in her things. Why?"

"It's worthless to a thief. But Drake is a serial killer. He keeps souvenirs. He might have taken that medal to commemorate his kill."

"How does that help us?" Holland said.

Birdsong hoped he was right about this. "Let's just say that when he went back to the states, he left everything behind. He said he'd be back for them at the Hoskins? What is that?"

Holland smiled. "You've got to be kidding, love! The Hoskins is a five-star private hotel on the outskirts of London. Only club members are allowed."

"Well, Drake must have joined the club. If you hurry before he sends for his stuff I wager you'll find that medal in his room. With his fingerprints all over it as well as McGuire's."

Holland nodded. "If you weren't covered with incinerated people, love, I'd kiss you."

PENSACOLA, Florida

FBI Agent Franklin Ross entered the interrogation room and put a folder on the metal table. He wore his every present red tie over a rumpled white shirt under a rumpled black coat. Ross was rumpled! He sat in the chair opposite Josh Knight and rubbed his eyes.

"I'm tired, Josh. Very, very tired." His intense gaze bored into Josh's skull. "I'm tired of you. I'm tired of Jonathan Steel. I'm tired of demons. I just want to retire to an island somewhere and drink myself into a stupor. Do you have any idea what Jonathan did to my case against Dr. Faust? And then, Faust died, murdered by an unknown assassin? Two years of work down the drain. And you know who started the process that led to Faust dying? Your father!"

Josh sat quietly and let the man vent. Fact was, he didn't care about Ross and his problems. He only cared about Jonathan. What had happened to him? He had been in that room and then all that was left of him were his clothes and his anklet.

"Did Jonathan take off his anklet?" Josh asked.

Ross froze and blinked furiously. "Did you hear a word I said?"

"You needed to vent. Fine. Now, let's get to it." Josh said.

Ross sat back and crossed his arms. "Well, someone has matured."

"I've been through a lot, Ross. I don't have time for games. I need to know how Jonathan took off his anklet."

Ross opened the folder and studied the inside. "We don't know. It wasn't disarmed. No blood. No lubricant. He didn't slide it off his ankle. He didn't cut off his foot to remove it. If he had opened it and re-closed it, we would have known. Bottom line. We do not know."

"His clothes, his anklet. It was as if he had just disappeared." Josh said.

"What are you suggesting?"

"How did Drake get to London?"

Ross sat forward and put his hands on the table. "Josh, I'm the one asking the questions. Not you. Where is Jonathan Steel?"

"I do not know. When I found out he was coming to the beach house, I followed on my motorcycle." Josh said.

"And how did you know he was coming to the beach house?" Ross said.

"You're not going to like it. From a demon." Josh said.

Ross sighed and closed his eyes in exasperation. "I was hoping it was because you dug around where you weren't supposed to. You disappeared for a few days and we also noted some rather suspicious activity on our website. You hacked our server, didn't you? Found out they had released Steel."

"Why would I admit to such a thing?" Josh said. "That is a federal offense. You can't arrest me for eavesdropping on a demon."

Ross put his face in his hands and groaned. "He'll be the death of me."

"You were tracking him?" Josh said. "Right? So, I'm not the one who lost him. You are."

Ross's face reddened, and he sputtered. "What is this?"

"Ross, Jonathan is in trouble. Drake knew he was there. Drake was tracking him, too." Josh put his cell phone on the table. "I recorded my entire conversation with Drake. He admitted he killed that woman in London. Not Jonathan. He said he was in league with the third demon. Somehow, Jonathan knew he was there and disappeared. The reason I asked about Drake in London is that, just like Drake, they teleported Jonathan."

Ross drew a deep breath and nodded. "Okay, okay. Are we really going to go there?" He closed the folder and stood up. He crossed to the corner of the room to the video camera and jerked the cable from the wall. Sparks flew. He came back to the door and opened it a crack. "Don't bother me." He slammed the door on the hallway and locked it. He sat down at the table again.

"My gut hurts, Josh. My head hurts. My blood pressure is through the roof. I eat antacids like candy. So, I'm tired of playing games." He intertwined his fingers and sat forward over the table. "So, fine. You're not a kid anymore. So let's talk about this. Drake was in Shreveport one moment, and literally five minutes later, his anklet appears in London. At first we thought he used some kind of hacking to switch his anklet identity number to another anklet. But, when we found his anklet in the basement of Hampton's Museum, it was the same anklet. No evidence of tampering." He opened his mouth to speak and then closed it. "Okay, I'll bite. So what is this about teleportation?"

"Powerful demons can move their human hosts through inter-dimensional space to another location. It takes its toll on the host so they can't do it that often." Josh said.

Ross nodded and his forehead wrinkled in thought. "Are you telling me a demon teleported Drake to London? And then what? A demon teleported Jonathan from the beach house?"

"Jonathan would never let a demon teleport him." Josh said.

"Just like he wouldn't let a demon talk him into stealing Raven's dossier? Or do the bidding of three demons?" Ross said.

"You know Jonathan. He turned the tables on those demons. He wouldn't let it happen again." Josh leaned forward. "If demons can teleport, so can angels."

Ross rolled his eyes. "Now angels?"

Josh slapped the table. "Ross, wake up? How much have you seen? You know these demons exist. And they are fallen angels. If they exist, then the good ones do too. I know. Dude helped me out when I had the virus."

"Dude?"

"My guardian angel."

"Of course!"

"Bottom line is, I've met some angels. This explains Jonathan's disappearance. An angel took Jonathan from that room right after he read whatever was on that wall. Somehow, when a person is taken, all the inorganic stuff is left behind. Clothes. Anklet."

"Then how did Drake keep his anklet?" Ross actually smiled. "Huh? I have you there."

"Because they set Drake up! They wanted Jonathan to be able to track him. Wherever Jonathan is now, the angels don't want anyone to find him."

Ross sighed. "Okay, point taken. Back to the writing on the wall. Why hasn't anyone talked about that?"

"Jonathan said he never cleaned the wall. Whatever was up there was put there by Braxton and Drake admitted he was Braxton's accomplice. He was in that room." Josh took his phone and brought up an image. "I sent the writing to Olivia. She was able to locate an ancient language. Aramaic. The language spoken by Jesus. Want to know what the writing says?"

Ross's demeanor changed. "Yes."

"You are mine. You belong to me." I read out loud. "I have had you in the past and I will have you again or everything you love will die. I will return for you someday. And look at the number beneath it. The number three." Josh sat back. "The third demon's fingerprints are all over this, Ross. Jonathan is knee deep in the next demonic battle. And this time, he has an angel on his side. You need to give him some time. With this recording of Drake's guilt, you can have the case against Jonathan dismissed in Europe. You can drop the FBI charges. If you do this, Ross, you free Jonathan to do what he is called to do and defeat the Council of Darkness' next demon. And take down Drake in the process. Are you willing to do that?"

Ross stood up and paced, crossing his arms over his chest. He paused at the wall and then pounded a fist against the cinder block wall. He turned abruptly and leaned into Josh. "Fine! I'll need a copy of that recording and an affidavit you heard Drake say all of this. For now, Drake is in custody."

"You'll need to keep an eye on him. Right before your team arrived, he was powerless. The third demon left him. He explained that the third demon uses a dozen or so other minor hosts who do whatever he tells them to do. He may have abandoned Drake and if so, Drake will not be able to teleport. Even so, don't be surprised if he disappears from his holding cell."

Josh stood up. "I need something else. I need you to contact Judge Bolton and tell him I'm working with the FBI so I won't have to go into the foster program in Texas. Otherwise, I'm useless and I have tools at my disposal that are somewhat outside the law. You can use that, Ross."

Ross ran his hands through his hair. He loosened his tie. "Okay, you can stay at the beach house for now. I'll post an agent outside to keep an eye on you. I don't want you taking any unnecessary chances. And when you find Jonathan, you will let me know immediately or this deal is off."

"Actually, I need to go back to Shreveport to the lake house." Josh said.

Ross froze. "How did you get to the beach house?"

"Motorcycle. Frankly, my butt hurts."

"Too bad."

"Do you really want me to waste another 8 hours driving back to Shreveport? I can leave the motorcycle here and you can get me a flight out of Pensacola today." He held up his cell phone. "One leaves in an hour. Just guarantee you'll reimburse me."

"You have this all figured out, don't you?" Ross said.

"I don't have time to go back to the beach house. You have the keys."

"What keys?" Ross said.

"To the rental car. I need someone to take Jonathan's rental car from the beach house to the airport and drop it off. I can come back for the motorcycle later."

Ross pulled out a small notebook. "Of course. Whatever you want, Josh." He scribbled on the notepad sheet with a stubby pencil. He held up the notepad.

"Special Agent Ross, that is anatomically impossible!" Josh said. "Such language you're using to a minor. I might have to file a complaint."

Ross's face turned red. He snapped the notebook closed and shoved it into an inside pocket of his jacket. "Just find Steel."

"I will. I'll text you the audio file."

Ross nodded and unlocked the door. He turned and stared at Josh. "You realize throughout this entire conversation, you've never said bro?"

Josh shrugged. "Sorry, bro. If it will make you more comfortable thinking I'm a brainless teenager, I'll try to throw some in from now on. Now, dude, can I get a ride to the airport?"

ZURICH, Switzerland

Inspector Goudreaux glanced at her watch. Inspector Swarsin was late. She had gotten the secure email at her office that Swarsin had pinpointed the location of Max's rogue operation on the outskirts of Zurich. The man was a reluctant ally, totally unaware of her true motives. But such men, who did not think women belonged in her position, were easy to dupe. Swarsin had refused to send her information digitally and insisted she meet him in person at the Zurich train station. She blinked as one of her contacts shifted. She had to get some new ones! Walking through the cold air to the train station had dried one of her eyes.

The outside of the station was a two story, ancient building with arched windows and an imposing arched entry beneath statues. The station first opened in 1847, but the current main hall, Haupthalle, was where passengers once circulated in the original 1871 train shed and where the tracks & platforms were until 1933. Haupthalle now housed the main gathering area for travelers with the ticket office, a mini-market. Escalators led to the lower levels, where shops and luggage lockers could be found.

A small coffee and snack shop with canvas umbrellas over small tables sat in one corner of the Haupthalle. The umbrellas were superfluous in the huge two-story open area, but gave customers a sense of intimacy in the face of the loud, chaotic crowds that surged through the Haupthalle.

Goudreaux sat at a table sipping hot tea and glanced once again at her watch. Where was Swarsin? She had already stepped out on a limb taking the initiative to neutralize Steel. Sno thought Steel was an asset. But Goudreaux knew once Steel finished with the Council, he would come after her comrades, the Vitreomancers. Best to take him out now! Patience was NOT one of her virtues.

Something cold touched the back of her neck and her hand went instantly to her nape. A small, round, cool metal disc was attached to her skin. Suddenly, paralysis moved from her neck down and her hand fell into her lap.

"If you move, you die." A voice said behind her. The Crimson Snake moved into her vision and sat at the table. She wore a long, gray wool coat over jeans and a sweater. Snake had tucked her red hair into a beige knit cap that hugged the edges of her face. She wore black gloves over her hands. Huge polarized sunglasses hid her eyes. "I just placed a small explosive disc on your neck. Won't hurt me, but if it goes off, it severs your medulla oblongata, and you stop breathing. You die. It also contains a short-lived paralytic."

Goudreaux's face warmed with anger. "Snake!" She managed to hiss.

"Swarsin isn't coming. The email was from me. We need to talk."

"I have nothing to say to you." Goudreaux slurred.

"I believe we have a lot to discuss. I gave you my confession, and you ignored it." Snake motioned to a server. "Earl Grey tea, hot with three packets of sugar, please."

The server nodded and moved away. Snake looked around her. "I thought meeting here in the wide-open space would guarantee my safety." She reached over with her artificial hand and snagged Goudreaux's phone. "How do you like my outfit?" She held the phone up to Goudreaux's face to gain access. She started tapping on the screen as she spoke.

Goudreaux remained silent, fuming, as the server placed a mug of tea in front of Snake. She opened her coat to expose her sweater. "As you can see, I'm wearing one of those dreadful Christmas sweaters." She motioned to her white sweater and the three reindeer dancing across her chest. The reindeer wore red and green dresses and were doing the can-can.

A muscle twitched at the corner of Goudreaux's eye. Snake smiled. "Happy Christmas. You know this is my favorite time of the year. Everyone is in good spirits. Snow. Red and green everywhere. I lost my arm on Christmas Eve. Best present I ever received." Snake shrugged. "Well, it was until Master gave me a fake one and freed me from Lucas. I would never have realized what a beast Lucas was if I hadn't lost my arm."

Snake leaned forward as she sipped more tea and glanced around her. "In fact, Goudreaux, I've discovered the wonderful motivating power of pain." She snapped the fingers of her artificial hand and Goudreaux trembled as her lungs refused to expand. She tried to open her mouth but could not. Sweat broke out on her forehead.

Snake sipped more tea. She grimaced. "Not enough sugar." She motioned to the server and asked for two more packets. Goudreaux continued to tremble, and a quiet moan came from her throat. The server glanced once at Goudreaux.

"Don't worry about her. Her blood sugar is falling." Snake held up the sugar. "This will help." As the server turned away Snake smiled and poured the sugar into her tea. She snapped her fingers again. Goudreaux's gasp was audible as she sucked air into her lungs.

"It's really bad when you can't scream. Screaming seems to

help with the pain, doesn't it? One snap of my fingers and you can speak. Another snap and you will stop everything, including breathing."

"What do you want?" Goudreaux managed through her trembling lips.

"Just to have tea with a friend." Snake sipped more tea and leaned back. The sweat trickled down Goudreaux's cheek. "Now, I want to know why you ignored my confession. It's that simple. What is it with your vendetta against Max? And Jonathan Steel? Everything you have done was to set them up instead of me. Why? Do your superiors know about my confession? If they did, they wouldn't authorize you going after Max and Steel." Snake snapped her fingers twice in quick succession and Goudreaux almost collapsed as the paralysis left her face but remained from the neck down. She gasped for breath and glared at Snake.

"I will kill you!"

"Oh, no!" Snake put a hand across the dancing reindeer. "Are you threatening my life, Inspector Goudreaux?"

"I will hunt you down and gut you." Goudreaux managed through clenched teeth.

Snake shook her head. "I don't think so. You see, I'm about to disappear for a long time and you won't be able to find me. My video confession that I sent you has now shown up in the hands of every law enforcement agency in Europe. In a few brief hours, they will wonder why Inspector Goudreaux ignored a confession to the worst aircraft disaster in Swiss history and instead continued to target someone else. They will want to know why you and I had a leisurely tea time together. In short, I have compromised you, Inspector Goudreaux. The case against Jonathan Steel and Max will be dropped, and your personal vendetta will end. Along with your career."

Snake stood up and tossed some cash on the table. "Public places have cameras everywhere." She leaned down to the level of Goudreaux's ear as she removed the disc from her neck. "By the time the police get here, the paralytic will have worn off. They won't find it in your system. Everything that has transpired will seem as if you planned it. After all you did. That email is now changed on all servers to one that came from me, not Swarsin. You see, sweetie, you can't talk your way out of this one." She pulled back to look deep into Goudreaux's eyes. "One of your contacts is slipping, you white eyed ghoul. And for what I am about to say you'll have no choice but to play along."

Snake stood up and pulled a USB drive from her pants and place it on the table. "My good friend, here are the records of that cash transfer you arranged when you hired me to take out the aircraft just to remind you what you owe me. I have done the job for you, but you never transferred the money. That is why on this day, I am betraying you." She leaned in once again. "That little lie will send you under the jail, sweetie." She kissed her on the cheek and finished her tea.

"Happy Christmas!" She kicked her legs up. "Ooo, la, la!" Snake walked away from the table while Goudreaux felt the world crash around her.

CHAPTER
THIRTY-SEVEN

Dr. Elizabeth Washington drank her tea and stared out over the lake at the setting sun. The sky was clear of rain clouds and the coming cold seeped into her very bones. She stood on the dock that reached out over the gray waters of Cross Lake and felt its gentle motion from the waves set off by a passing boat. She glanced at her watch again and tried to suppress her anxiety. When would he be here?

In the distance, she heard an approaching car, and she smiled. Josh was coming home. After his plane touched down, the FBI had insisted on a policeman driving him to the house for safety reasons. She would have been glad to pick him up. Actually, she was surprised Josh had somehow eluded arrest and relocation to the foster program in Dallas. The boy was clever. She had to give him that.

Liz tossed her cold tea into the lake and made her way back to the lake house. By the time she passed through the patio doors and across the living room to the kitchen, the sound of the car had died and a shadow passed over the window in the kitchen door.

Josh opened the door and stepped into the kitchen. The first time she had seen Josh, his hair had been dyed black, and he had multiple facial piercings. His eyes had filled with mischief and anger. He had been through so much since then and the young man who looked into her eyes now was no longer a rebellious teenager searching for significance.

Josh ran a hand through his reddish blonde hair, so much like his late mother's hair. Liz gasped at the memory of the missionary house in what seemed like ages ago.

———

Claire stumbled through the dark interior of the missionary house until she found a light switch. Pale light illuminated the walls, and she located the thermostat. The hot, musty air was stifling. The central air conditioning unit thrummed on as she turned the thermostat down. She was about to take her bags down the hall to one of the bedrooms when the front door opened and Steel stepped in off of the front porch. His face bore the same stern expression of disapproval as before. Josh pushed in behind him and surveyed the dwelling.

"Where's Opie?" He pulled off his black T-shirt and exposed a white tank top. He tossed the shirt on a nearby chair and collapsed on the couch. "Dude! Sure is hot in here."

Claire sniffed. She placed her hands on her hips and glared at her son. "Josh, you stink."

"I know." He wore a smug look. "If you had told me about this little field trip earlier, I would have had time to shower."

"I told you last night." She felt uneasy and glanced at Steel. "Josh, there is a bathroom down the hall with a fully functional shower. Hit it."

Josh ignored her and raised his arms and crossed his hands behind his head. "I would rather compete with the mildew."

"If you're smart," Steel said, "you'll do as your mother said and go

take a shower." There was an unmistakable quality of authority in his voice, Claire noticed.

Josh glared at Steel and then shrugged. "Whatever, bro." He got up and went back toward the bathroom. Claire tensed as Josh passed her, expecting the usual outburst. Instead she heard the sound of a shower running. She exhaled and leaned against the wall. Advantage Steel.

———

Josh had matured so much since the first time she met him. Josh pulled off his black leather jacket and hung it on a chair at the kitchen table. He blinked moisture from his eyes.

"Mama Liz." He groaned.

She opened her arms and he came to her. "It's okay, Josh. Mama Liz is here. It's okay."

Josh stiffened as he pulled away. "I don't know where Jonathan is." He said hoarsely.

Liz motioned to the living room. "Come sit down and tell me everything."

Josh did. Liz tried to piece together the story. "So between the FBI and the local authorities, you're no longer in trouble?" Liz asked.

"Ross said he would take care of everything in exchange for the recorded comments from Drake. The dude will challenge it in court, I'm sure. But it was enough to arrest his butt and throw him under the jail. That is if he doesn't try and teleport out again!" Josh shivered. "I'm cold and soaking wet. I need a hot shower."

"And maybe a warm fire in the fireplace." Liz stood up from the couch and walked over to the fireplace. Above the mantel, her lion stick hung two pegs. Dr. Holmes had placed it there. She had missed it! Something tingled in her hands. She paused. An awful feeling of oppression and doom came over her and she stepped back away from the fireplace.

"Mama Liz?" Josh stood up and hurried to her side.

"I just had the worst feeling." She studied the lion stick. She rubbed her eyes beneath her glasses. "Not about Jonathan, Josh. About my lion stick."

Josh put an arm around her. "Then leave it be. I'll go take that shower."

"I'll make us some dinner. I cooked a roast yesterday and I'll warm it up." She felt Josh leave her side and her eyes were locked on the lion stick. For a moment, it seemed to move, to writhe in agony as if it were alive! She stepped back again and put a hand to her mouth.

"Hello?"

Liz jerked in surprise and whirled. Olivia Monarch stood in the kitchen. "Anyone home?"

Liz glanced over her shoulder once more at the lion stick and hurried into the kitchen. One more for dinner! "Olivia! Come in."

Olivia shrugged out of her coat. "Hello, Dr. Washington."

"Now, honey, I told you when we met to call me Liz. Josh is in the shower and I'm about to heat up pot roast, potatoes, and carrots if you're hungry."

Olivia smiled. "I'm just glad Josh made it back safely."

"How did you get here?"

"My self-driving car." Olivia hung her coat on a chair. "Can I help with dinner?"

"Absolutely." Liz turned once more toward the living room. The lion stick hung innocently and motionless above the fireplace. "Absolutely."

———

Josh's hair was still wet when he joined them in the kitchen. He wore a tee shirt and sweatpants. When he saw Olivia, he hugged her and they kissed. Liz raised an eyebrow and shook her head.

"Young love!"

Josh looked up from Olivia. "We've been through a lot, Mama Liz."

"I know. Sit. Eat. Relax."

After dinner Olivia and Josh sat on the couch before the fireplace. Liz sat in a chair to the side and ignored her lion stick. "So, what is next?"

"We have to find Jonathan." Josh said. "But before we start on that, there is something I must do."

He stood up and took down the lion stick with one quick motion. Liz gasped and stood up. "What are you doing?"

"You told me this stick was given to you by an African chieftain who asked you to marry him." Josh said.

"That is true. I've had it for years. I use it in the wild to keep snakes at bay." She smiled at Olivia. "Better a snake attack my stick than me. I left it here accidentally and it's been hanging above the mantel ever since. I'm too old to go into the bush anymore."

Josh held it out to Liz. "I want you to keep this with you all the time. We are in danger and if the lion stick is by your chair or by your bed, you can whack anyone who tries to hurt you. I imagine you can handle it better than a gun."

Liz studied the lion stick and gingerly took it from Josh's grasp. It had been her companion for years and she couldn't understand why she was so hesitant. It felt warm in her hand. The smooth wood slid easily through her palm. She planted the lion stick on the floor and it made a solid thump.

The air around them suddenly thickened and a figure appeared before the fireplace. Liz raised the lion stick before her. Josh collapsed on the couch and cradled Olivia. The figure solidified into a tall man in green scrubs.

"Dude!" Josh said. He jumped up from the couch and Dude put out a restraining hand.

"Do not touch me, Josh. I had to come here quickly and I am not quite substantial yet." He looked at Liz. "You may lower your staff."

Liz blinked. No one had ever called her stick a staff. "You must be the famous Dude, Josh's guardian angel." She lowered her stick.

Olivia smiled. "That may be why I saw no demons around this house."

"This house is protected." Dude said. "This is what I have been permitted to tell Josh and his family. You will be safe as long as you stay in this house."

"But I have to find Jonathan." Josh said.

Dude nodded. "Another reason I was sent. Jonathan is safe with another of our kind, Alphus. You must trust God that all is working out for the good. Now, I must go." And as quickly as he appeared, Dude faded from sight.

Josh glanced at Liz and then at Olivia. "I guess we're under house arrest."

CHAPTER
THIRTY-EIGHT

SHREVEPORT, Louisiana

Dr. Jack Merchant settled into his chair before his radiology monitors. The sensation was strange. He had been away for over a week during Josh's ordeal and then the past few days in Austin, Texas. He was fortunate to have a practice that allowed him to take a week off at a time. But his time away from his practice had cost him several days he "owed" to his partners. When he had been in practice in Talako, Louisiana, his partners had readily agreed to trade out days and weeks. Since he had taken the job in Shreveport with the large radiology group, there was less camaraderie. Fortunately, he was at the one satellite hospital where he was alone for the day. No one to ask awkward questions.

The door to his office opened. "Jack?"

He stood up as his fiancée, Pam, closed the door behind her. He smiled, and she kissed him.

"Can't let anyone see you fraternizing with a hospital employee." She said as she combed his hair with her fingers. "Jack, where have you been?"

"Helping out Jonathan Steel. You remember, the father of the kid who had that virus?"

"Yeah, you went to Dallas to find out more about that virus. Then, after Thanksgiving dinner, you said you had to go to Austin for a few days."

"More medical examiner business." Jack told the truth.

"Does this have more to do with Jonathan Steel and his son?"

Jack sighed. "Yes, Pam. He needs my help. He was falsely accused of murder and I was doing what I could to help him out."

Pam nodded. "Kind of like what you went through a few years ago?"

Jack nodded. When he was in practice in Talako, Louisiana, he had been accused of killing his wife. A series of events had culminated in him joining the medical examiner's office part time as a forensic radiologist. "Yes, Pam. I understand what he's going through."

Pam kissed him on the cheek. "You see, this is one of the reasons I love you, Jack. You are willing to help your friends. You care. You're compassionate." She straightened his white coat and smiled.

"I love you, too." His cell phone rang. Pam stepped away and closed the door behind her as she left.

"Merchant." He said as he answered the call.

"Jack, this is Sam." Dr. Sam Francisco was the local medical examiner who had moved from the Talako area to Shreveport a few months before. She had talked him into switching practices so he could join her as the forensic radiology consultant in the medical examiner's office.

"Hey, Sam."

"Welcome back." Sam said cheerily. "And Merry Christmas. Just so you'll know, I've already dyed my hair."

"Green or red?" Sam was notorious for celebrating holidays with great gusto. And her entire appearance.

"Green." Sam chuckled. "Just wanted to give you a heads up. You're two weeks behind on cold case reviews and I have MRIs on two fresh cases I need you to review. Oh, and that FBI agent was asking for you and is coming to your office today."

Merchant sighed and rubbed his eyes behind his glasses. He was already tired from his travels and now Ross was coming? Did he want to ask about Josh? What would he say? "Thanks, Sam. I'll be by this evening to catch up on those cases."

"Great! Wear that blinking reindeer sweater I gave you last Christmas. Get in the spirit." She laughed once more and ended the call. Someone knocked on his office door.

"Come in."

The door opened and FBI Special Agent Franklin Ross stepped into his office. He wore a heavy beige overcoat over a rumpled white shirt and red tie. His hair was a mess and his eyes were hidden behind sunglasses.

"We keep our offices dark so we can read our images better." Merchant said.

Ross pulled off his sunglasses and blinked. "You're telling me. Got another chair?"

I motioned to the other chair in my small office. "Have a seat. You look like something the cat dragged in."

Ross sighed and plopped into the chair. "Jonathan Steel. What can I say? I just flew in from Pensacola on an Air Force transport to Barksdale. Hitched a ride. Had a little visitor with me."

Merchant stiffened. "Josh Knight?"

Ross raised an eyebrow. "That clever boy talked me into letting him fly commercial. No, I'm talking about Reginald Drake."

Merchant sat forward. "Drake?"

"Arrested for the murder of Margaret McGuire in London. Josh managed to record a confession by Drake on his phone. Won't hold up in court, but now Jonathan Steel is cleared of the charges as of an hour ago. Of course, he's still in trouble for disappearing and leaving his anklet behind."

"Disappearing?"

"From his beach house. Not sure how, but I'm certain it involves demons."

Merchant sat back and smiled. "Angels can teleport humans, too."

"Oh, really? An angel a day keeps the devil away?"

Merchant shrugged. "I don't know that for sure, Ross. But I've seen a lot lately that blew my mind. I'm a man of faith but I've never really appreciated the whole spectrum of spiritual, I guess you would call it, warfare before I met Jonathan Steel."

Ross was silent and fidgeted with his sunglasses. "Yeah, me, too. Anyway, I wanted to touch base with you while I have a few hours before taking Drake on to Dallas for his arraignment. I know that Josh talked to you while he was, uh, hiding from the authorities." Ross sat forward and an uncomfortable look crossed his face. "Much as I hate to admit it, he's in the clear. No charges filed after what he did to help us out." Ross pointed at Merchant. "And you're clear, too."

"What?"

"Accessory, right? You knew Josh was eluding us. You could have turned him in and yet you protected him."

"He's been through a lot lately. Almost died thanks to Nigel Hampton and his virus."

Ross stood up. "Yeah, Hampton has disappeared. He's on the most wanted list now and no one has seen hide nor hair of him. I can't focus on the man right now with Drake in my possession."

"Why hasn't Drake teleported again?"

"You should see him. In the last few hours, he has gone to hell in a hand basket. Sweaty, nauseated, weak. I think this tele-portation thing is catching up with him."

"I hear it's hard on the host of a demon. I wonder if his demon has abandoned him?"

"For now, it would seem so. He's angry and keeps screaming

out for 'number three' to come back." Ross leaned toward me. "I wonder if he hears his victims screaming out for help when he does the same thing? Probably not. The man is a psychopath. Well, good day, doctor."

Ross donned his sunglasses and walked out of Merchant's office.

CHAPTER
THIRTY-NINE

JONATHAN STEEL

I woke up to the smell of bacon. Again. My stomach growled. I was starving. I sat up on the edge of the bed and rubbed sleep from my eyes. After coming back inside from the bench, I had fallen into a restless sleep. My watch revealed it was ten o'clock in the morning. I went into the bathroom and stayed in the shower until the hot water turned cold. I paused in front of the mirror and wiped away the steam. During my time working for the triad, I lost some weight. Dark circles cupped my eyes. My eyes! Bright turquoise, like father's. I inherited my ginger hair from my mother, but my eyes came from him. I looked into my eyes, trying my best to penetrate the wall around my lost memories. I had been possessed by the third demon? During that time, I couldn't remember a moment of my past until the brief memory when I had touched the shards of the Grimvox imbedded in my palm. Josh came to mind. He remembered the time he was possessed by the thirteenth demon. I had never appreciated what that meant until now. Gratefully, the mirror had fogged over again until the only thing I could see was my relentless gaze.

I found a clean set of jeans and a flannel shirt in a drawer, along with underwear and wool socks. Water dripped from my hair and ran down my neck while I dressed. Yvonne and Sam sat at the table eating breakfast when I came into the dining area.

Sam pointed to the kitchen. "Eggs, bacon and cinnamon rolls are on the stove. If you want coffee, I brewed a pot."

"We need it." Yvonne said. "Did you sleep at all?"

"Yes." I made myself a plate of food and looked at the coffeepot. For as long as I could remember, I had refused coffee. It made me irritable. That irritability was gone. There was a growing calmness, a sense of tranquility inside my soul and my mind. Or maybe it was just the peace of surrendering everything to the inevitable, the realization that I was in God's hands and not my own. Surrendering had been the most difficult thing I had ever done. At least that I could remember! I poured a mug of coffee and moved to the table.

Sam watched as I wolfed down my food. It was good. It was filling. It was comforting. I sipped the black coffee and the bitter taste burned down my throat. The caffeine kicked in and my thoughts sharpened. I glanced at Sam. A troubled look was on his face.

"What's wrong?"

Sam swallowed his food. "It's probably nothing. Someone pulled off the road last night. About three A.M. But they just turned around and went back the way they came. Someone got lost. That's all."

"You can't tell me where we are, can you?" I said.

"It's best for now." Sam said.

"Well, we are in the mountains, of course. They don't look like the Rockies. Could be in Canada or Europe." I sipped more coffee. "How would someone find us?"

"Like I said. I think the car was just turning around." Sam said.

Yvonne finished her coffee. "Just to be sure, let's send out one of the automated drones."

"One of us will have to monitor the surveillance." Sam said.

"I'll take the first round while you fill JJ in on the attack."

"Attack?" I said.

Sam nodded. "Remember, when they realized we had a chance of acquitting you? They came after us. They haven't stopped looking since then."

Yvonne stood up and started toward the spiral staircase. "I'll be in the situation room monitoring the drone. You tell him the story and then we will switch out."

Who were "they", I wondered? Maybe I was about to find out.

CHAPTER
FORTY

SAM O'MALLEY'S House

A thunderstorm rolled along the horizon as Yvonne pulled up to O'Malley's house. They were supposed to have met for lunch to complete her approach to defense. The trial would begin the next day. She knocked on the front door and waited. No answer. Maybe he was in the back. Fishing? She hoped not.

Yvonne made her way around the side of the house to a gate that opened onto a spacious backyard extending to the edge of the lake. A dock ran out into the water. A cedar deck snugged up against the back of the house and at a patio table, Sam O'Malley sat with his head resting on the table.

Yvonne hurried up the steps to the deck. "Sam!"

Sam sat up abruptly and tried to focus his eyes. Sleep left his hair awry and his eyes puffy. He blinked red-rimmed eyes and tried to focus on Yvonne.

"Sam, you told me you had stopped drinking." Yvonne shouted.

Sam put his hands over his ears. "I did. Don't shout."

"We were supposed to meet for lunch." Yvonne pulled a chair away from the table and sat down.

Sam looked at his watch. He rubbed his red eyes. "I was up until 4 this morning finishing up on some of that research you asked me about. I came out here to drink a cup of coffee and wake up and instead fell asleep."

Yvonne raised an eyebrow. "Just coffee?"

Sam pushed an empty mug across the tabletop. "Smell for yourself."

Yvonne glanced at the mug. "Okay, I believe you."

"Why wouldn't you?" Sam said, and he closed his eyes. "Wait! What did you find out about me?"

Yvonne pointed to the mug. "That your retirement wasn't voluntary, like you said."

Sam looked away and sighed. "Remember that story about Garcia?" He looked back at her with red-rimmed eyes.

"Yes."

"Lots of repercussions from that one. Turns out one of the squad was on the same payroll as Garcia and in order to divert attention during the investigation into his death, Internal Affairs went after me. Claimed I had botched the arrest because I had been drinking."

"Had you?"

Sam nodded and crossed his arms. "Poker game. Lasted until midnight. I got word about Garcia around two. I still had alcohol in my system. We had been tracking Garcia for weeks. When I found out where his drug rendezvous would be, I couldn't let someone else make the collar. I was off duty, but I went after him." He leaned forward and rested his arms on the table. "Spent three months in court ordered rehab, but I knew the writing was on the wall. I accepted the early retirement. My plan was to find out who shafted me and take them out once I got off the force."

"Sorry I doubted you." Yvonne said. "You said you were doing research?"

Sam sat up and nodded. "Ever heard of Dr. Cephas Lawrence?"

"No, should I?"

"Or a man named Max?"

Yvonne glanced at her watch. "I've met a few men named Max. What is so special about your 'Max'? Or, your 'Cephas'?"

"Dr. Lawrence has a website dedicated to exploring evil. I went to the site, and he mentioned something about twelve demons on some kind of dark council." Sam cleared his throat and sat up straighter. "Lawrence claims that according to legend, Satan chose his twelve most powerful demons to form a council to offset the work of the twelve apostles."

"Most powerful? That doesn't sound good."

"It gets worse. The higher the number, the less power they have. Meaning," Sam said.

"Meaning number three is the third most powerful demon of the twelve." Yvonne sighed. "Great. If it's true."

"There's more. This Max is legendary. Just whispers on the web about him looking for the eleventh demon. Seems it killed someone he loved. I curated several sites that mentioned his name and one, in particular, said Max had collected the names of demons." Sam said.

"And?"

"According to Lawrence, if you know the demon's name, you can control it. Cast it out. Send it back to hell. Something like that." Sam sat up.

"How does this help us in the courtroom?" Yvonne asked.

"If you can find out Three's real name, you put JJ on the stand and then call out the demon for everyone to see." Sam said. "Case closed."

Could that work? An alarm went off from Sam's pocket. He pulled out his cell phone and studied it. He stood up quickly and looked over his shoulder at his house. "Yvonne! Move. Now. To the dock."

"What?" Yvonne said as Sam grabbed her arm and pulled her

up painfully from the chair. "Someone just broke through the front door. Get to the dock. Now. I have a boat down there."

Yvonne hurried down the stairs toward the dock when something hit her hard from the side. She fell across a pathway filled with shredded rubber tires. Her instincts kicked in and she rolled off the pathway just as the figure thudded a knife into the pathway.

The man wore a totally black sweatshirt and pants and a ski mask to hide his face. He whirled toward her, wielding the knife, and slashed it at her mid-section. Yvonne moved back quickly and tensed her muscles. The man paused. Where was Sam? She heard him grunt behind her. She couldn't take her eyes off her assailant. He lunged at her with the knife, and she feinted, drawing him to her left and then shifted mid stance to swing about on one leg and kick him in the kidneys. The man grunted and fell to his knees. She spun around once more and kicked him under the chin. He flipped backwards and fell onto his face. She jerked the knife from the man's hand and turned to check on Sam.

Sam stood over another man now unconscious on the pathway. Blood ran from his nose and a cut on his head. Sam glanced back toward the house. "The dock. Now."

Yvonne ran down the path and onto the dock. Sam caught up with her, breathing hard. He shoved her into the lake, and she fell headfirst into the freezing cold water. She came up sputtering.

"What did you do that for?"

"Under the dock. Hide."

Yvonne glanced under the dock. The water line was up to the lower edge of the timber siding, but there was scant room beneath the center of the dock. "Why?"

"Trust me. Go!"

Yvonne dove into the cold water and surfaced beneath the dock. She had about eight inches of space, just enough room to keep her nose above the waterline. She heard footsteps coming down the pathway and the unmistakable "chuff" of a silenced gun. Sam ran down the dock toward the small boathouse at the end. She heard more footsteps as someone ran up onto the dock. She peered through the cracks between the timbers above her and three men dressed in black ran toward the end of the dock.

The unmistakable rumble of a boat motor echoed along the water, and she heard a boat roar off toward the lake. She prayed Sam would escape. Then, more chuffing and the sudden explosion caused her to inhale water. She stifled her cough and peered through the opening just above the water. Sam's boat had gone up in a ball of flame out on the lake.

A hand came up around her mouth and she tried to whirl and bring up the knife. A voice whispered in her ear.

"It's me, Sam. Don't move."

Yvonne fought the urge to cough, and her eyes watered as she turned to face Sam. Blood ran down his face into the water. The footsteps approached, and the three men paused at their end of the dock. She glanced up through the cracks. One man slid his mask up, exposing ginger hair and bright, turquoise eyes.

"Dead?"

"Yes." Another of the men said.

"Then there'll be no trial tomorrow. Go get the other two and let's go before the police arrive."

The men disappeared across the lawn and in the distance, sirens grew in volume. Sam pointed to the water. "Let's get out of here."

———

It took two hours to take their statements and when the crime scene investigators showed up it was growing cooler outside. Yvonne shivered in her wet clothes underneath a useless blanket. Sam wore an old, faded house coat.

They sat on the deck while the police moved in and out of the living room and across them back yard. "I really loved that boat." He said.

"You saved our lives, Sam. Thank you." Yvonne said. She watched the nearest investigator head out toward the dock. She glanced over her shoulder and then back at Sam. "Did you see that one man's face?"

"No." Sam said.

"He looked like JJ."

Sam froze and pulled his house coat tighter. "What?"

"He seemed to be the leader, Sam." Yvonne said.

"Coincidence? I don't think so. We know it's not JJ. Does JJ have any relatives?" Sam said.

"None." Yvonne said through trembling lips. "Sam, that means there is someone out there who looks like JJ.

"That means someone could have seen this man and mistaken him for JJ." Sam said.

"He wants JJ to take the fall. He came after the two of us! Which means he thinks I can get an acquittal for JJ." Yvonne said. "If this man is so worried about JJ going free, then there must be some evidence that could absolve JJ. The evidence is out there, Sam. We just have to find it."

"Will this let you delay the trial tomorrow?" Sam said.

"I doubt it. Stapleton would think this was a delaying tactic on my part. We press on with my plan. Did you talk to the servants at JJ's house?" Yvonne asked.

"Hobbs called this morning and said he remembered something. He wouldn't tell me over the phone. I don't know that it will help. The man is desperate to say anything to get JJ off." Sam said.

Yvonne watched as the investigators converged on the front of the house. They were about to leave. "Why don't you meet with him in the morning? I won't need you for opening remarks."

A policeman looked around the corner of his house. "Hey, O'Malley, we're out of here."

"Thanks, Bill." Sam stood up. "Let's go inside and get something hot to drink and you can warm up."

Yvonne shook her head. "I'll just head home for a hot shower. I have my opening statement to review. If you think of anything new, call me tonight." She cast one last look at the smoke still hovering over Sam's boat. The lake patrol boat was hauling the remnants of Sam's boat toward his dock. "Looks like you have another official you need to talk to."

Sam swore. "They are very protective of the environment. I'll probably have to pay a fine."

CHAPTER
FORTY-ONE

THE COURTROOM WAS PACKED when Yvonne met JJ at her table. Stapleton and his young, very beautiful assistant sat at their table. Stapleton wore a flawlessly tailored suit and a maroon tie. He winked at her.

A bailiff appeared from behind the judge's desk and had everyone stand. "The Honorable Judge Matthew Meridian presiding." He announced.

A huge, long legged black dog appeared from the doorway of the judge's office. The dog's ears were tall and thin as railroad spikes. It moved with restless energy on a long leash, and behind the dog, Judge Meridian emerged. He was tall and lanky, with salt and pepper hair above a cadaverous face. He wore large, black round lensed glasses. The members of the gallery murmured, and the jury looked back and forth at each other in dismay.

Meridian led the dog to the front of this desk and snapped his fingers. The dog reclined at the base of his huge desk. Meridian unsnapped the leash and then returned to the back of his desk and ascended to his chair. He sat almost ten feet in the air and peered out over the courtroom. He tapped his gavel.

"Quiet! Anubis is my comfort dog and you do not want to

upset me. If you upset me, you upset Anubis. I would not advise against it." He said.

Yvonne swallowed. She had heard Meridian was eccentric, but this was absurd. Meridian tapped his gavel again and studied her through his large glasses. "Is there a problem, Ms. Brown?"

JJ squirmed in his chair and she put a calming hand on his shoulder. She stood up. "No, sir! It's just rather unconventional to have a dog in the courtroom."

Meridian shrugged. "I'm very unconventional, Ms. Brown. If you object to the presence of a comfort animal, I suggest you leave and find your client different representation." He smiled. "I would think you might welcome the comfort of such a large animal after what you went through yesterday. You could have used a little protection from what I understand."

Stapleton stood up. "Your honor, I would like to request we do not discuss this matter in front of the jury."

"You would like to request?" Meridian stood up and seemed to tower even higher over them. He turned to the jury. "I will address the jury. It seems that some hoodlums accosted Ms. Brown and her investigator, Sam O'Malley yesterday. If you might have heard of these events then you should know they have no bearing on today's proceedings. In no way should you allow such events to sway your sympathy in any particular direction. Especially toward the defense. Do I make myself clear?"

No one answered from the jury section. Meridian snapped his fingers. Anubis jumped to his feet, faced the jury, and barked once. Yvonne flinched, just as did every person in the jury. The foreman stood up, a heavy-set man in his mid-forties. He wiped sweat from his brow. "We understand, your honor."

Meridian snapped his fingers again and Anubis returned to his restful repose before the desk. Meridian placed his long arms on the desk and leaned toward the courtroom. "Now, let's get on with it, shall we? I have a golf game this afternoon."

———

Jonathan Steel

"Wait a minute!" I interrupted Sam. "Meridian was my judge?"

"Yes." He said.

"He's the same judge who is presiding over my case now."

"We know." Sam said. "Does he still have Anubis?"

"He has a dog like the one you describe named Anubis. But it's been years. That dog should be dead." I said.

"It's only been fifteen years, JJ." Sam said. "But I think we can truly say that Anubis is not an ordinary dog."

"I would agree on that point."

"I need the restroom, JJ. I'll be back." Sam got up from the table and disappeared down the hallway. I got up from the table and put another log on the fire, then settled into a chair and tried to wrap my brain around this revelation. Someone looked like me? Had I been framed? Even so, that didn't change the fact I had been possessed by the third demon.

Sam came back from the bathroom and poured himself another cup of coffee. "Need more java?" He asked.

"No."

Sam settled in the chair next to mine. "Yvonne did a good job on her opening statement. But it made little difference after the prosecution presented its case. The photos were devastating. Stapleton hired his own psychologist who analyzed your records and pegged you with a personality disorder and a sociopathic tendency. He essentially neutralized any argument for the mental incompetence angle. Things were looking pretty bad when Stapleton put your best friend on the stand."

"Clay?" I sat forward.

"Yeah. His testimony was damaging."

"What did he say?" I heard footsteps coming down the stairs.

"Sam, your turn. Nothing so far on the drones." Yvonne went

to the kitchen and placed water in a kettle and placed it on the stove.

"Clay was mad, JJ." she said over her shoulder. "He wanted to make you look bad. Claimed you thought he was after your girlfriend. When I got the chance to cross-examine, he admitted hitting his head when he slid off your car was an accident. I got him to admit he was still your best friend, but the damage was done."

The kettle whistled, and Yvonne poured water into a teapot and placed it on a tray. She retrieved a cup from the cabinet and placed it on a tray next to the teapot. She grabbed a squeeze bottle of honey and brought the tray and placed it on a small table next to the fireplace chair. "Need some herbal tea. Too much caffeine makes my migraines worse." She said and Sam climbed up the stairs.

Yvonne ran her hands through her hair and took a red pair of reading glasses from her shirt pocket. She put them on and grabbed a tablet from a nearby lamp table. She studied the screen and then handed the tablet to me. "You can read the transcript if you want."

I studied the words on the screen. "My father's testimony?"

Yvonne sat forward. "Stapleton put him on the stand. You don't need to read that if you don't want to. It'll be pretty painful, JJ."

"I have to read it. Yvonne, as painful as you think this might be, something in these stories, these words, might trigger a memory. So far, everything you've told me sounds like it happened to a stranger. I don't recall any of this except for the moments before and after I found my mother's body."

Yvonne poured herself some tea and added honey. "I'll be right here if you have any questions. I'm not going anywhere."

————

Trial Transcript

Testimony of Captain Saul Stone

STAPLETON: Captain Stone, is your son in the courtroom?

STONE: Of course, he is. He's sitting at the defense table.

STAPLETON: Where was JJ born?

STONE: In Mexico. My wife was investigating an archeological dig. She was writing a paper on the findings. She gave birth to JJ while we were there.

STAPLETON: And then you moved back to Austin, Texas?

STONE: Yes, almost immediately. We moved into the mansion, and that is where JJ grew up.

STAPLETON: This mansion, did it belong to you?

STONE: Technically, no. It belonged to my uncle, Dr. Nigel Hampton. My father designed the mansion and Nigel funded its construction. My father asked me to move in after JJ was born. After my father died, we stayed on even though the mansion remained in Uncle Nigel's name.

STAPLETON: It's a rather strange mansion, wouldn't you say? A bit creepy?

STONE: My father had an obsession with a lost tribe of indigenous peoples he discovered in the Amazon. He designed the house to remind him of those people. To the uninformed, I guess it would appear unusual. I never thought that much about it.

BROWN: Objection, your honor. Where is this going?

MERIDIAN: Mr. Stapleton, I wondered about that myself.

STAPLETON: Your honor, I would like to establish the environment in which the plaintiff grew up. I believe it will establish his state of mind not only at the time of the murder, but for many years before.

MERIDIAN: I will allow it then. Proceed.

STAPLETON: Captain Stone, what can you tell us about the chamber off the library?

STONE: I really know little about its purpose. My father

never told me. It has always remained a mystery and was locked after my father's death.

STAPLETON: How did your father die?

STONE: He took his own life.

STAPLETON: In the chamber at the bottom of the spiral staircase, correct?

STONE: Yes.

STAPLETON: The same chamber in which your son murdered your wife.

BROWN: Objection, your honor.

MERIDIAN: Overruled. Proceed Mr. Stapleton.

BROWN: But, your honor!

MERIDIAN: Ms. Brown, one more interruption and I will find you in contempt.

STONE: I know where you're headed with this. JJ was young when his grandfather died, and JJ has always been fascinated with what lay behind those locked doors. For some reason, the doors were locked, and we had never been able to open them.

STAPLETON: Captain Stone, the doors were open on the day of your wife's death. Do you have any idea how the doors were unlocked?

STONE: There was an incident that took place right before I left the country for my latest assignment. Uncle Nigel showed up for the first time in years. He had my father's photo journal that chronicled my father's journeys in South America. Turns out JJ had located the journal a few months before and never told me. And somehow JJ lost the journal not long after he found it. Uncle Nigel came across the journal at a garage sale.

JJ: How could I have told you about the journal? You were never at home!

MERIDIAN: Mr. Stone, you will not speak out of turn in my courtroom. The jury will disregard that outburst.

· · ·

Note: Mr. Stone continued to speak and was escorted from the courtroom. Judge Meridian reconvened after an hour's break. Mr. Stone returned to his place at the defendant's table for the duration of the questioning.

STAPLETON: Captain Stone, before the break you said your son had found your father's journal. And you also said your uncle wanted it? Can you clear this up for us?

STONE: My father exhibited unusual behavior after returning from his last trip to the Amazon. He was obsessed with his journal, pouring over the photographs and spending long hours in the library talking to himself. We tried to get him to seek professional help, and he refused. It wasn't long after that he took his own life. I regret not being more aggressive with my father. He should have been hospitalized. I have to live with that guilt. I took the journal and placed it in a box with some of my father's other possessions and lost track of the box. As I said, JJ found it. I believe he became fascinated with my father's photographs and his obsessions. I'm not a psychiatrist, but common sense would tell me that his fascination with his mentally unstable grandfather's journal pushed him over the edge into mental instability that ended up with my dead wife. He either hid it or lost it and my uncle found it afterwards.

BROWN: Objection, your honor. Captain Stone is not a health care professional.

MERIDIAN: Sustained, Ms. Brown. The jury will disregard the comments about Mr. Stone's mental condition.

STAPLETON: No further questions, your honor but I reserve the right for rebuttal.

MERIDIAN: Ms. Brown.

BROWN: Captain Stone, first let me offer my condolences for your loss.

STONE: If you were really sorry, you would have had my son plead guilty to avoid the death penalty.

MERIDIAN: Captain Stone, refrain from these comments. Just answer the questions or I will hold you in contempt.

STONE: Sorry, your honor.

BROWN: Captain, you say your son exhibited unusual mental behavior after he found the photo journal, correct?

STONE: Yes.

BROWN: How did you draw this conclusion since you were in another country when this happened?

STONE: I returned just a few weeks before my wife's death. JJ was different. Aggressive. Angry. And Christine, that's my wife, told me JJ had been seeing a counselor. When she told me JJ had been involved in several incidents bordering on criminality, I realized my son was not acting like he normally did.

BROWN: I see. Did he show these same signs of abnormal behavior before he found the journal?

STONE: Not really. He was a passive individual. Very quiet. Didn't want to take part in sports. Wouldn't go to the gun range with me. Read a lot of books.

BROWN: Did that upset you?

STONE: Did what upset me?

BROWN: The fact he wasn't fitting your image of Captain Stone's son?

STAPLETON: Objection, your honor.

BROWN: I withdraw the question. Captain Stone, I understand that when you discovered your son's new, more aggressive behavior, you made a decision about his future schooling.

STONE: Yes, I decided it would be best to send him away to a boarding school.

BROWN: Could you tell me why you thought this would help your son?

STONE: More discipline. More boundaries he couldn't cross.

BROWN: Who was responsible for those boundaries, as you call them, before he found the journal?

STONE: What do you mean?

BROWN: Is it fair to say that since you were out of the

country so much that your wife was the primary person responsible for disciplining your son?

STONE: Don't you dare sully my wife's name!

MERIDIAN: Captain Stone, you will refrain from these outbursts.

STONE: My wife was a wonderful, loving person. Kind. Compassionate.

BROWN: And those were qualities you did not want your son to have?

STAPLETON: Objection, your honor, please. Where is this line of questioning going?

BROWN: Your honor, I am trying my best to determine who had the most influence on the mindset of JJ Stone prior to his mother's death. Since Captain Stone admits he was often absent, then it would be reasonable to assume his wife was the primary influence in their son's life.

MERIDIAN: I will allow you to continue. But do so with caution.

BROWN: Captain Stone, did your son love his mother?

STONE: Yes. Of course he did.

BROWN: Could you conjecture how your son, raised mostly by a loving, kind, compassionate mother, as you have admitted, could find motivation to murder his own mother?

STAPLETON: Objection, your honor.

BROWN: I withdraw the question, your honor. No further questions.

STAPLETON: Captain Stone, I have just one question. Did you see a change in your son's behavior in a more dangerous direction after he discovered his grandfather's journal so much so that you had to resort to sending him away to a boarding school for everyone's safety, including your wife's?

STONE: Yes. I thought it best he was no longer in the mansion while I was away.

CHAPTER
FORTY-TWO

MOUNTAIN PEAK

The bitter cold seeped into the man's chest and abdomen as he lay quietly in the snow-filled crack between two boulders. Accustomed to waiting, he felt anxiety for the first time in months. Two objectives now vied for his attention. Lucille had not communicated in two days. He had no idea what had transpired in the compound below. This had forced him to leave the warmth of the farmhouse for this frigid mountain wilderness. He would make Lucille pay! He had already returned the golden knife to the evidence room or he would use it to do more than carve his initials in her arm!

And, to make matters more frustrating, the most important target still eluded his grasp. Recently, events had moved him closer to his aim. The face of "Jonathan Steel" appearing on a television broadcast from Switzerland revealed a man who had hidden in shadows for years.

The man had waited years for this moment in time. One person more powerful than he had held him back. The man chafed under the relentless secrecy and subversion. He was a man of action! Once, he had encountered Steel in just such a secretive operation. Then, the man had gone by the code name Sawbones, and he had hidden his identity behind contacts and makeup. He had even faked his death to throw off suspicion of his identity. The fact he had failed to secure one of the Children of the Bloodstone had cost him plenty from his boss in retribution for his weakness.

He lifted digital powered binoculars to his eyes and studied the compound nestled in the snow-covered valley. A few people dressed as ordinary men and women seemed to loiter outside the building. But their regimented comings and goings tagged them as guards. The building itself appeared to be some kind of monstrous architectural experiment in steel and concrete. Only a genuine artist would appreciate the building's attempt to blend in with the gray and black rocks of the Alps and the dirty snow around its base. Already, he had decided how to breach the entry point. His men would take care of the guards.

The man tensed as the front door opened and two people walked out into the gray light of a cloudy day. One woman was small and thin and wore a blue full length lab coat. She lit up a cigarette and then took the arm of the woman beside her. The other woman was taller and wore a one-piece jumpsuit. Her short hair hung about her face. She looked very different from the last time they had met face to face. That was long before her "death" in the caverns under Transylvania and her subsequent plastic surgery. But she could not change her eyes. He zoomed in on her eyes. They were empty and unfocused. They had erased her mind just as he had heard. Could she recover her memories? He hoped so, for his entire future depended on it. In view of Lucille's failure, he would resort to certain methods at his disposal. They were most likely be near fatal, but the woman only had to live long enough to reveal one precious memory.

The man lowered his binoculars and breathed the woman's name. "Raven." For a moment, a stray ray of sunshine broke through the clouds and illuminated his face. His turquoise eyes gleamed in the sunlight. His radio crackled in his earpiece.

"What?" He whispered.

"We may have a lead on the duo." The voice said.

The man sighed in frustration. This was the first order distraction that divided his attention. "I've heard that before. Where?"

"You will not believe this, boss. Just over the ridge from the compound."

The man's eyes widened in excitement, and he glanced up at the towering peaks of the Alps above the compound. "You're kidding! If I believed in God, I would say, He was smiling down on me today. Send out a recon drone."

The man smiled through cold, cracked lips. If this was true, and JJ Stone was with the duo, he could take out two targets in one day. It could all end. Finally! Assuming the lawyer and her toady were on the other side of the ridge! If so, it would divide his men and resources. He had to be sure. And if JJ wasn't with them, then where was "Jonathan Steel"? He sat back against the ice-covered rock and tapped a gloved finger against his right temple.

Think! How could he locate Steel? He glanced once again at the distant figures of Lucille and Raven. If only Monarch had not erased Raven's memory in an attempt to neutralize the woman's implant. The man's eyes widened. Implant? Of course! Why hadn't he thought of that before? He picked up the radio.

"I have a quick errand to run. I'll be back in a flash." And smiling broadly, he disappeared leaving behind a puff of snow.

CHAPTER
FORTY-THREE

LONDON, England

Dr. Monarch closed out the last window on the desktop of her computer monitor and leaned back. She had now successfully archived all the data and sent it into the cloud. Steven and Olivia were safely back in the states. True, Jonathan Steel was in a bit of trouble, but she had to think of her children first. She stood up and paced around her laboratory. Over the past few days, she had paid some very reliable people to come and discretely move her equipment to a storage facility on the outskirts of London. All that remained of the move were a couple of lockers with combination locks she had used to secure her precious goggles. She would finally allow the 'for sale' sign out front to serve for something other than a decoy for her hidden lab. With Steven back safe and sound and the truth behind her husband's death discovered, there was little reason to be secretive.

Granted, she would still be cautious. There were other surgeries she had to answer for than those requested by the Captain. But no one had the reach, the power, the abilities of the Captain. She stood in front of the Faraday cage in which Dr. Holmes had talked to her about Numinocity. It had helped to save everyone's lives, including Steven's.

Without her security computer running, she never heard the silent alarm tripped by the intruder upstairs. In retrospect, she should have at least brought the system over into her tablet. But she heard footsteps coming down the stairs. She froze and ran to the remaining computer. She swore and looked around for a weapon. Nothing. The only remaining items were the Faraday cage and the monitor in front of her hooked to the last computer in the server room. She woke the computer and started the program to erase everything.

She ran to the Faraday cage, stepped inside and closed the door to the phone booth sized chamber. The walls were made of a fine mesh of black metal, and anyone coming into the lab could see her. But it was the only place to hide, in plain sight.

A figure in black emerged from the stairwell. He wore a black, long sleeve shirt, pants, gloves and a ski mask. His hand gripped a pistol with a silencer. Oddly enough, he had melting snow on his shoulders but it was not snowing outside.

The man paused just inside the door and looked around the lab. He crossed to the counters and walked along them, running a gloved finger along the burnished metal. He stopped before the only remaining monitor and tapped on the keyboard. Nothing happened. The man shrugged and, aiming the pistol at the monitor, blew it to pieces with one shot from the gun.

Monarch shoved her hand into her mouth to stifle a scream. The man moved to the back of the lab into the supply closets. He came back out and climbed up onto the counter nearest to Monarch and crossed his legs. He placed the pistol on the counter and pulled off the ski mask.

Long ginger hair stood on end with static electricity. Bright turquoise eyes gleamed in the meager light. He smiled. "I know you're here. Come out."

Monarch's heart raced. Why would Jonathan have a pistol? Why would he shoot her monitor? These were not the actions of the man she knew, and, yes, trust. She smiled as she remembered the bracelet and finger glove she carried in her lab coat. She slid her hand into her pocket and pushed her hand into the bracelet and finger pods. In the dogsled hut on the mountain, she had brushed Steel's forehead and activated his implant, plunging him into amnesiac unconsciousness. Whatever was going on with Steel, she could stop him with one touch.

She opened the Faraday cage and stepped out. The man smiled as he saw her. "Hiding in plain sight? Smart. If you had moved, I would have seen you." He hopped off the counter and walked over to her. The man's eyes were bright, but his face wasn't quite right. Monarch frowned.

"Why are you here, Jonathan? I thought you had been imprisoned."

"I'm not who you think I am."

Monarch pulled her hand from her lab coat pocket and shoved her fingertips across the man's forehead. He stood there, his gaze shifting up to his forehead. He grabbed her hand in a supernaturally powerful grip. Monarch tried to fight him, and he put the pistol barrel up against the side of her head.

"That won't work on me, Dr. Monarch. I'm not Jonathan Steel. You see, you never operated on me. No one controls me."

He tilted his head in a small spasm and looked to his right. "You don't control me, right? We have a bargain." He spoke to empty air, and then his gaze came back to her. "Sorry, my demon gets testy at times."

"Demon? Which one?"

He grimaced. "Well, I would like to be number one, but JJ has always stood in my way keeping me from proving myself. So I have to settle for number two. Now, I need something from you. I need to find JJ."

"JJ? You mean Jonathan? He's in a jail in Texas."

"Was in jail. Seems Meridian gave him freedom with an anklet and he went back to that stupid beach house."

He looked again to his right. "I told you Four couldn't be trusted. He is having too much fun wielding his power."

The man looked back at her. "Humans! Absolute power corrupts absolutely and then it all bleeds over into the minds of the demons in charge. Now, JJ was at the beach house and I was about to get number two to teleport me to the beach house, but then JJ just disappeared. You see, we were tracking his anklet, and it went dead and, no JJ. He just, poof, disappeared, leaving his anklet behind."

The man glanced again to his right. "I know! One of those light loving brothers of ours."

The man glanced at the shattered computer monitor. "Now I checked your server room. You've erased everything. All I wanted was the frequency of his implant. You see I can track it just like Olivia used her implant to talk to you." He pulled her closer. Tiny flecks of red were scattered in the turquoise of his eyes. "I'm sure you know it by memory."

"I can't keep that kind of information in my head, you fool." She said.

The man pulled back and pressed the barrel harder against her head. "I know where your kids are, Monarch. I have resources and we can make them wish they had never left Numinocity behind."

Her eyes widened, and he grinned. "Yes, I was there, too. I had a little conversation with JJ about his dead mother. I wanted him to feel the guilt of her death. And it worked and he was arrested for his homicidal nature."

"And you don't have one?" Monarch said. Still her heart pounded with the fear for her children. All she had to do was give him the numbers. She knew them. Her memory was always far too good for her own good. Steel or Steven? Steel or Olivia?

"I can't trust you. I don't know who you are or what you're after. Your word is worthless." She said.

The man's face twisted into a rigor of hatred and anger and then his eyes focused on her bracelet. "Just a minute. This little toy of yours was specifically designed to interact with JJ's implant, wasn't it?"

Panic filled her eyes. "No. It works with anyone I've conditioned."

The man laughed. "You don't lie very well." He pushed her back up against the door to the Faraday cage and leaned his body into hers, pinning her against the metal. His free hand slid along her wrist and jerked the bracelet and the fingertips from her hand. He unlocked the door and put the barrel in the middle of her forehead.

"Get into the cage. Now!"

Monarch slid through the opening and he shut the door on her. Her looked around and found a lock and chain from one of the lockers. He put the chain through the handle slot on the door and closed the padlock. He spun the dial and then, holding the padlock away from himself, shot the center of the padlock. Monarch screamed at the chuff of the pistol. The man tried to pull the lock open. It wouldn't budge.

He dropped it and smiled at her. "I'm giving you a chance to live, Monarch. Don't think I don't have mercy. Number two here wants you dead." He leaned into the metal of the cage and his eyes opened wide. "They really want your soul."

He looked to the right again. "Be patient! No one will be here for a couple of days. She'll be dead by then and you can have her." He retrieved his ski mask and pulled it over his face. He held up the bracelet. "Now, it's time JJ and I had a reunion." And then, he disappeared from sight.

CHAPTER
FORTY-FOUR

JONATHAN STEEL

Dropping the tablet on the table beside me, I stood up and walked over to the windows at the front of the living room. My heart burned with the impact of my father's words. The man had hated me! I suspected as much. After all, would a loving father allow experimental surgery on his son's brain? Yvonne put her hand on my back and she stepped up beside me.

"I know it's a bit much to digest. Did it trigger any memories?"

"I had a flashback to the visit from Hampton bringing back the journal. The return of the journal probably sealed my fate." I looked into her eyes. "Every flashback about the journal comes with memories of voices whispering in my mind. The third demon was moving in for the kill, Yvonne. Every blackout had to be a time when he took over my mind." I reached out and took her by the shoulders. "I must know before we go any further. Did I kill my mother?"

Yvonne smiled. "Not exactly."

I closed my eyes. "That's not an answer."

"JJ, you need to ease into this. Look how devastating reading your father's testimony was. Be patient and you will understand." She turned me back toward the fireplace. "I must tell you about your mother's funeral. It took place during a three-day recess after the prosecution rested."

———

Yvonne Brown
  Hyde Park Baptist Church

People filled the sanctuary of the church to capacity. Yvonne wormed her way down the side aisle and found some room to scrunch in beside an elderly lady. Despite her protestations, JJ had not been allowed to attend his mother's funeral. He had begged her to get him out, but she had been unsuccessful. Yvonne agreed to come and represent him.

How long had it been since she had been to church? Last Easter? Or was it Christmas? Truth was, since escaping death, she had concentrated on overcoming the cursed serial killer who had imprisoned her. The training and the cage fighting helped. Still the anger and the fury remained. She shook her head. She wasn't mad at the killer. No, she had tried to overcome the memory of killing the beast. And relishing every second of his death. For that she loathed herself. Sitting here in this sanctuary just reminded her how hard it would be to forgive the man. Or, to forgive herself.

Christine Stone had been a faithful church member, as evidenced by the crowd gathered at her funeral. Would as many people show up at hers? Probably not many. Maybe Sam. Certainly not Richard Stapleton, unless it was to gloat.

Listening to the organ music, Yvonne craned her neck to see the front of the sanctuary. The casket was closed, understandably. One man sat alone in the family section. He turned toward her, and his unmistakable blue eyes gleamed even from this distance. Captain Stone wore his military uniform.

Yvonne listened as the voices droned on, praising Christine Stone, obviously a saint on Earth. Tears flowed as testimonials abounded. Through it all, Captain Stone sat unmoved on the front pew. She filed out through the back doors with everyone else and waited patiently by the limousine as Stone came out. A funeral attendant motioned to the car and Stone paused to study her with his intense eyes.

"What are you doing here?"

"Representing your son. They wouldn't let him come to his mother's funeral." Yvonne said.

His face bore no emotion, although a muscle flinched below his right eye. "You are not welcome, and neither is my son."

Stone disappeared into the limousine. Yvonne leaned up against the brick wall and watched the funeral procession drive away, bearing the body of a beautiful woman married to a monster.

"He's not the friendliest guy in the world, is he?"

Yvonne turned. The man wore a rumpled, oversized gray suit. His bare scalp gleamed in the afternoon sunshine after the passing of the rain. He smiled at me.

"Kevin Turner. Youth pastor."

"Yvonne Brown. Attorney at law. I'm defending JJ Stone."

Something gelled behind Kevin's gray eyes. He smiled. "Would you like to go and have some coffee with me?"

She needed something stronger, but she couldn't count on getting that with a youth pastor. "Sure."

———

The tiny café named Crossroads sat at the intersection just behind the church. Run by a couple of ex-missionaries, it catered to Christian teenagers and young singles. During the day, the café served sandwiches and flavored coffees while contemporary

Christian music played in the background. As they sat at their table, a television in the corner showed the latest skirmish in the Middle East.

"Quite a mess, isn't it?" Kevin asked, after ordering them both coffee.

"Yeah. Seems like the world is coming to an end."

"Oh, it is. But, not now. Too many prophecies have yet to be fulfilled."

Yvonne glanced at him and realized he was serious. "Are you talking about the end of the world?"

"Wars and rumors of wars. Revelation. Armageddon. Someday, you'll get thrilled or get grilled." He laughed, a high-pitched sound that made her smile. "But not today."

Their coffee arrived and Yvonne drank hers black. Vanilla cinnamon, the menu had called it. Excellent! "Why did you want to ask me for coffee?"

Kevin's smile faded. "I want to help JJ. I've been trying to reach him for the past three months."

Yvonne smiled. Maybe she had found a gold mine of information. "Do you think he killed his mother?"

Kevin shook his head and sipped at his coffee. "No. JJ worshipped his mother and if anything, would have protected her from harm. I guess you know about his father?"

"Other than what he said on the stand. I got the distinct impression he and JJ have little to do with each other."

Kevin leaned back as the waitress delivered a sandwich. He waited until she was out of earshot. "One night a few months ago when the Captain was back home from one of his military assignments, JJ showed up at my house at midnight. I opened the door and he stood there, face covered with blood and his clothes torn. He had been in a fight with his father and his father had won. He threw JJ out of the house."

"Why didn't JJ call the police?"

"According to JJ, Stone has connections. He's pretty much hands off to the police because of his government connections.

JJ was only trying to protect his mother from his abusive father."

Yvonne took a bite of her sandwich and chewed as she thought. "Sounds like the two of them had issues."

Kevin had finished his sandwich and wiped at his mouth with a napkin. "Let's just say the Captain and his wife were headed for separation according to JJ. I really don't know how they stayed together this long."

"Is there another woman?" She was grasping for straws.

Kevin grew still, and he looked around the room as if expecting someone to overhear. "Even if there was, Captain Stone would make sure no one found out."

Her mind churned with possibilities. Captain Stone could have a perfect motive for killing his wife if he was having an affair, and she discovered it. The problem was that Stone had been in the Amazon region when the murder occurred.

"The night JJ came to your house, did he act strangely?"

Kevin's brow knitted in thought. "Strangely? No more than usual for a teenager just beaten up by his abusive father."

"Does JJ have a bad temper?"

Kevin's face blanched and he averted his gaze to his coffee mug. "Yes. I think he inherited a violent nature from his father. It is the demon he will have to live with for the rest of his life."

"Speaking of demon," Yvonne began. "I think JJ may be demon possessed."

Kevin's gaze jerked up from the mug and he stared at her. He blinked once and leaned back in his chair. "That was a statement I never expected to hear. Why do you think that?"

"I spoke to the demon. Right before JJ attacked me in the jail conference room."

Kevin's face blanched. "Oh my God! This is bad!"

"Then you think it's a possibility?"

"Ms. Brown, I have been a minister for ten years. I've worked with young people the entire time. I've seen kid after kid I thought was demon possessed. But most of the time it was drugs. The last time I tried to talk to JJ, I felt something. I have a spirit of discernment for the presence of evil. I knew something had changed about JJ. I felt the evil surrounding him. But I never wanted to consider a demon."

"Consider it. Please." Yvonne reached out and touched his hand. "JJ needs spiritual support, and they don't teach you how to deal with demons in law school."

Kevin pulled his hand away from mine. His gaze met mine. "You don't understand. Until now, I have refused to believe JJ killed his mother. But if he is demon possessed, then he could have done it. He's guilty and there's not a court in this land who would admit the murder was the demon's fault."

"SERGEANT SMITH, can you identify the photograph labeled state's exhibit 15A?"

Smith took the photograph from Yvonne and squinted at it. "Yeah. It's a photograph of the floor of the chamber in which the deceased was found."

"In the detailed analysis of this photograph, the crime scene investigator's report mentions footprints. Could you point out the footprints for the jury? You can use the overhead projection unit so that the jury can follow along with you." Yvonne said.

Smith left the witness chair and sidestepped Anubis. He paused before an overhead projector unit. He placed the photo under the light, and it appeared on a projection screen. Using his pen, he pointed to the red smudges on the photograph. "Here you see one set of prints leading toward the altar. And, here, the same identical set of prints leading away from the body."

"And you found the same identical set of prints leading down the hallway and out the front door?" Yvonne said.

Smith looked up at her, the bright light shining on his face. "Yes."

"Sergeant Smith, the report also identifies the prints as

belonging to a commercially available brand of running shoes size 11. Is that correct?"

"Yes."

"And, according to the final report, which you signed out on, there was only one set of footprints, correct?"

"Well, no. There was another set of bare footprints." Smith said.

Yvonne walked across to the projector, her eyes never wavering from Smith's, and handed him a second set of photographs. "Would you identify the bare footprints in the photograph?"

Smith squinted into the bright light of the projector and then pointed to an area near the altar. "Right here."

"Now, Sergeant Smith, the investigative report describes these prints differently than the shoe prints." She said, turning to glanced at the jury. "Would you explain in layman's terms to our jury the significance of these differences?"

Smith smiled, realizing she had given him free rein to show off his forensic knowledge. "Of course. We found the shoe prints throughout the chamber. Sometimes, blood had outlined the prints and left a bare spot on the floor. This would show the perpetrator was wearing the shoes during the actual deed and the blood pooled around his shoes while he was stationary."

"Creating a negative print?"

"Yes. Now, the bare footprints are all positive prints. The perpetrator walked through the blood and created positive prints. They did not leave a void in the blood." Smith said.

"So, there were no negative prints of the bare feet?"

"No. Which shouldn't be surprising." Good. He was taking the bait.

"Why, Sergeant Smith?" Yvonne turned and faced the jury.

Smith puffed up his chest. "Because the perp left the crime scene, discarded his shoes and then returned bare footed to create an illusion he found his murdered mother."

"I would imagine that is a clever ploy to throw you off the trail." Yvonne gave the jury her best smile.

"You're right, little lady." Smith said.

Yvonne resisted the urge to retaliate for the remark. She had to remain calm and in control. "Sergeant Smith, according to this report, the bare footprint is what shoe size?" Yvonne pointed to the folder of evidence still sitting on the railing in front of the witness stand.

Smith beamed. "Size 10. Not surprising, since the foot is smaller than the shoe size."

"Thank you, Sergeant Smith. I don't think I have any more questions."

Smith nodded and started toward his seat. Yvonne let him get to the railing behind the attorney's tables.

"Ooops! I forgot something, Sergeant Smith. Would you return to the witness stand? I have one little bitty question to ask." Yvonne said. Behind her, Anubis growled, and she tried to ignore the hound from hell.

Smith froze and turned to glare at me. "Okay, little lady." He returned to the stand. Yvonne walked up to him, her eyes on the projector screen. "What are those three little dots on the screen?"

Smith squinted at the projector screen. "Dots?"

She walked over and pointed to three small bare spots in the blood at the far corner of the chamber. "These spots. Actually, they are not spots. They are voids."

Smith looked helplessly at Stapleton and then back at the screen.

"Objection, your honor." Stapleton stood up. He fumbled for more to say and finally said. "The defense is asking for a professional opinion."

"Overruled." Judge Meridian interrupted him. "The Sergeant has demonstrated he has sufficient knowledge of forensics. Please answer the question."

Smith shook his head and studied the screen again. "I'm not sure."

"You mentioned the negative prints of the shoes, Sergeant. These three circular indentations appear to be negative prints also. Would you conclude they were made during the murder?"

Smith rubbed his jaw and glanced once again at Stapleton. Stapleton avoided his gaze. "If they're negative prints, I would agree."

"So, there was something in this position on the floor that was removed after the murder." Yvonne came back to the witness stand and thumbed through the evidence folder. "And yet, the crime investigation report mentions no such object in this position."

"You're right. There wasn't anything there."

"Your honor, I have a report from a second crime investigative unit used by the FBI which also went over the same evidence as the police department. The defense would like to submit it as Exhibit #12B."

Yvonne handed a manila folder to the bailiff who took it to the judge. Meridian rifled through the papers hurriedly. "I see the coroner is on the list of experts. I will allow the report to be submitted."

"Objection, your honor." Stapleton stood. "May I approach the bench?"

"Counsel may approach the bench."

Yvonne joined Stapleton as they approached the front of Meridian's desk. They both paused a foot away from Anubis. The dog growled softly at them.

"Easy Anubis." Meridian said. "Let them be." Anubis placed his head on his outstretched legs and yawned.

"Your honor, this is highly irregular." Stapleton said, his eyes riveted on the dog. "The defense did not inform me of a second analysis. I move the evidence is not allowed."

Yvonne opened the folder she held in her hand and pulled out a sheet of paper and handed it to Stapleton. "Your honor, the prosecutor now holds an affidavit signed by a law clerk working for his firm documenting she received the report three days ago."

Stapleton glanced down at the signature. "But we fired Betty. I mean, she quit the same day." He glanced over his shoulder. Yvonne wondered if Betty was the now absent attractive woman who had been at Stapleton's side on the first day. The table was conspicuously empty.

"Perhaps she misplaced the report." Yvonne took the letter back from him. "Maybe you should take better care of your, ahem, employees."

Stapleton's face took on the unhealthy glow as his blood pressure skyrocketed. Judge Meridian intervened. "I will allow submission of this evidence. Mr. Stapleton, I suggest you contact your office and see if you have a copy of this material."

Stapleton sputtered and stomped off to his table. Yvonne took the envelope and its contents from the judge and handed it to Sergeant Smith. Expecting the inevitable objection, she turned to address the prosecution.

"I expect Mr. Stapleton will object to this line of questioning, so I will not ask the witness to analyze all the data in the envelope. I would like to state that all the evidence in the report agrees with the crime investigation report except for one thing."

Stapleton raised an eyebrow. "I will allow you to question without objection so long as you do not require the witness to draw a conclusion outside his area of expertise."

Yvonne turned back to Smith. "Sergeant, if you will look on page 42 you will find the photograph we currently see up on the projector."

Smith sifted through the pages until he arrived at the photograph. "Yes, it is the same photograph."

"And the circular negative prints?"

"They're right here labeled 15A."

"Would you read the paragraph under the photograph labeled figure 15A."

Smith squinted and read. "The three circular negative prints appear to be made by an object with three legs standing in a stationary position during the murder. Such an object would have to be elevated at least three to four feet based on the lack of disturbance of the blood spatter pattern noted on the wall behind the object. Based on this analysis, the three negative prints were most like made by a three-legged object such as an easel or a camera tripod." Smith looked up at Yvonne, his face clearly betraying the analytical nature. "A tripod?"

"Sergeant Smith, I have a copy of a list of all objects found at the crime scene. Did you locate a tripod?" She tapped the evidence folder on the railing.

"No. We found no tripod." Smith shrugged.

"Easel?"

"No easel."

Yvonne took the list from him and studied it. "Interesting, Sergeant Smith. Where could it be? Perhaps with the shoes you also failed to find at the crime scene."

"Objection." Stapleton rocketed to his feet.

"Sustained." Judge Meridian's gavel pounded his desk.

"Your honor, I have no further questions." Yvonne said as she turned back toward JJ and smiled. The prosecution's star forensic witness had just created doubt in the minds of the jury.

FORTY-SIX

SAM SAT ACROSS FROM YVONNE, chowing down a hamburger. Yvonne's stomach rolled with nerves. She had taken a chance with Smith, and it had worked.

"What were you trying to prove?" Sam said with a full mouth.

"I found out about the tripod when I reviewed the FBI file, Sam. What was a tripod doing in that chamber? Was the murderer videoing the murder? And if so, where is the tripod? Where is the camera? Where are the shoes?"

"I don't know." Sam said.

"Exactly!" I nodded. "That is what I wanted the jury's reaction to be. Doubt. I had to sow some seeds of doubt." She sat back and picked up her ham sandwich and nibbled at the stale bread. So much for courthouse food. "Sam, we must figure this out. The coroner says the body was still warm. Time of death within an hour of when you showed up on the scene. Now that is plenty of time for JJ to kill his mother, video it, take the tripod and camera back upstairs, then take off his shoes and go back down into the chamber to create the illusion he stumbled onto her body." She sipped my water. "JJ says he got a call from his mother earlier in the afternoon. Analysis of his cell phone shows that to be true. Time passed because of the wreck and when he woke up, he drove to the house and found his mother."

Sam dropped his burger and slapped himself on the forehead. "The wreck! The car! It was brand new. Yvonne, what if it has one of those GPS locators? And the cell phone! It's one of those new ones with GPS! We can prove where JJ was just prior to his mother's death." Sam stood up and nodded. "You may just have saved the boy's life."

"Unless it proves us wrong, Sam. Then I may just have driven the final nail in his coffin."

"I'll get on the car and the phone." He paused before turning away. "Oh, one more thing. I found the gardener. Hobbs told me about her. Yvonne, she was there. She saw something but I haven't been able to talk to her. She's supposed to be in the courtroom this afternoon."

Yvonne stood up and shook her head. "No! I have nothing else this afternoon. I need to interview her first."

Sam stopped and belched. "Look, Yvonne, I spoke to her briefly and I believe she saw someone else come out of the house. I put her on the witness list and was going to brief you, but this development with the GPS is too important. You're going to have to trust my instincts. I feel good about her. Now, I gotta go. I have a connection at the precinct that can get us that information."

Sam hurried out of the courthouse cafe and Yvonne sat back in her chair. A potential witness of unknown quality. Stapleton would eat her alive unless Yvonne could prep her. Problem was, she had no other witnesses other than JJ. Maybe if she hurried to the courtroom now, the gardener might show up. She froze. Who was she looking for? Sam had said 'she' but hadn't given her the name!

Yvonne paused in the hallway outside the courtroom and leaned against the marble walls. Above the entry door to the courtroom was an inscription, the Ten Commandments. There had been lots of controversy in the past couple of years about separation of church and state over such displays in public courthouses. But, for now this brought home some comfort. She wasn't in this alone. JJ wasn't in this alone. JJ had Kevin on his side. And Kevin had God on his side. She bowed her head and put her hands against her mouth.

"God." Yvonne whispered. "I'm so sorry I haven't come to you sooner. I need wisdom. I need guidance. If JJ is truly the victim of demonic forces, then he needs all the help you can give. And so do I. Please help us."

"Miss Brown?"

Yvonne looked up and Hobbs stood near the doorway to the courtroom with a short, dumpy woman in green coveralls. The woman had her hair pulled up in a scarf and she wore black rimmed heavy glasses. A pair of gloves hung from her pocket.

"Hobbs?"

"I was bringing Glorietta up here for Captain Sam to speak to. But I can't find him."

Yvonne felt tears in her eyes. "It's okay. Glorietta? What a beautiful name."

Glorietta shrugged. "My momma like it. Named me after a church retreat."

"Mr. Hobbs, thank you so much." Yvonne shook his hand and looked around for a quiet corner. A bench beneath a nearby window was empty. "Glorietta, I'm Yvonne Brown, JJ's attorney. Can we talk for a few minutes? Do you think you can tell the jury what you saw that afternoon?"

Glorietta glanced at Hobbs and the man patted her arm. "It will help Master JJ."

She nodded. "I'd do anything to help that poor boy."

Yvonne's heart sang with joy!

———

"Mrs. Tuttle, would you tell the jury what you do for a living?" Yvonne smiled at Glorietta.

"Well, sure. I am a gardener working at the mansion where JJ lives. Been there most of my life. My father was the former gardener and now he is a nursing home. I took over about fifteen years ago. I maintain the topiaries."

"Topiaries?" Yvonne asked.

"The elder Dr. Stone, JJ's grandfather, loved his exotic animals and commissioned my father to carve plants into the shape of animals." Glorietta nodded and rubbed her hands. "I ran after my father day after day while he kept the gardens. When he retired, I took over maintaining the gardens and the topiaries. I have a staff of four other gardeners, but no one works on the topiaries but me."

Yvonne loved every word Glorietta uttered. She glanced at the jury. Some of them were smiling. "Mrs. Tuttle,"

"Call me Glorietta, dear." She said. She had warmed up to Yvonne.

"Glorietta, where were you the day Mrs. Stone died?"

Glorietta's smile faded and she looked down at her hands. Her lips quivered. "It's not right what happened to her. If the Captain had paid the kind of attention to her and JJ that he did to his precious missions, she would still be here."

"Objection." Stapleton said.

Yvonne raised a hand. "Your honor, I will speak to Mrs. Tuttle about this." Yvonne turned to her. "Glorietta, the judge over there doesn't like it when you say things that aren't related to my questions. Can you help JJ but sticking to answers and nothing else?"

Glorietta looked past her at JJ sitting quietly at the table. She glanced at Anubis and the dog actually dropped his ears and looked away. "I will."

Yvonne held a folder in her hands and tapped the top page. "You were interviewed by the police?"

"No, dear. The police didn't speak to any of us."

"Us, meaning the servants and employees?" Yvonne prompted.

"Objection, your honor." Stapleton stood up. "How can this witness possibly know who was interviewed by the police?"

"Because Mr. Hobbs insisted Mrs. Stone wanted us to take the afternoon off." Glorietta said. "They never spoke to us."

Meridian tapped his gavel. "Mrs. Tuttle, the prosecution, has made a good point. The police could have interviewed any of you, after that gathering in the library."

"May I approach the bench, your honor?" Yvonne said.

"Why don't both of you join the party?" He sighed.

Yvonne picked up a pile of papers on her way to the judge's desk. "Your honor, the police report states that no one was present at the time of the murder. I personally arrived the next day and all of the staff were gathered in the library and Mr. Hobbs said none of the servants were in the house at the time of the murder."

Yvonne stood on tiptoes to reach the desk and handed the papers to Meridian. "Your honor, if you check the list of potential witnesses interviewed by the police, you will see that none of the servants were interviewed because they were not present at the time of the murder."

Yvonne looked over at the jury and felt Stapleton's gaze bore into the side of her face. The expressions on their faces told it all. Attacking Glorietta was damaging the prosecution's case. If Stapleton went after her, it was definitely in JJ's favor.

"Your honor," Stapleton glared at Yvonne. "If no one was present then there would be no need to question the servants. I don't understand where the defense is going with this line of questioning."

"If the prosecution will be patient, I will show that there was, indeed, someone present at the time of the murder." Yvonne said.

"Objection overruled." Meridian said. He leaned toward Yvonne. "But keep your witness under control, Ms. Brown."

Yvonne nodded and returned to the witness stand. Stapleton huffed off to his table. Yvonne smiled at Glorietta.

"Where were you on the afternoon of that day?"

"Like I said, I was supposed to take the rest of the day off at Mrs. Stone's insistence. But I had to trim the topiaries, or they would bloom overnight and ruin the illusion. It was only going to take about an hour, so I came back around two o'clock. I was working in the middle of the largest topiary grouping when I heard someone come out of the house."

"Now, Glorietta how do you know what time it was?"

"The topiary. In the center of the driveway. It's five bushes carved into the shape of the two lions on either side of some museum in London. And three bushes form parliament with Big Ben. Very impressive, if I do say so myself. I was down behind the Parliament topiary making sure the timer was set for the Big Ben topiary. Dr. Hampton had insisted the clock face in the topiary of Big Ben was set on London time. Precisely. I had checked my watch to make sure the clock setting was correct. I remember looking down at the clock just as someone came out of the house because Big Ben did not toll."

"Did not toll?"

"You know." Glorietta did a rather impressive imitation of Big Ben sounding out the hour. "Bong! Bong! Bong!"

Laughter passed through the spectators and Meridian tapped his gavel. "No laughter! Quiet!"

The spectators quieted and Yvonne nodded for Glorietta to continued.

"The clock and my watch were correct, but the clock face motor had come loose. That's how I knew it was right at 3 o'clock."

"Now, Glorietta, you told me all the servants, except you, had left for the day?" Yvonne said.

"Yes, dear. They had."

"So, who came out of the house?"

"JJ."

Yvonne tried not to panic. She was so glad she had talked over all of this with her in the hallway. "JJ Stone?"

"Yes." Murmurs filled the courtroom, and Judge Meridian rapped his gavel. After admonishing the crowd, the ruckus died down.

"Glorietta, are you sure it was JJ Stone?"

"Oh, yes ma'am. He stopped and looked right at Big Ben. I think he heard something in the bushes. But I was afraid to say anything to him."

"Why?"

"He was acting very strange. He had on red gloves and red shoes. And this huge black coat. And it wasn't cold that day. He just got into that car and drove off."

"He drove off in a car?" Yvonne said. Careful now. Word things carefully, she thought. "What kind of car?"

Glorietta shrugged. "One of those funny foreign convertibles. Had the top down. I guess that's why he wore that big, heavy coat."

Yvonne leaned forward. "Glorietta, was this car the brand-new car Captain Stone had given to his son?"

"Oh no. This car was much nicer than the one the Captain bought for JJ. Which puzzled me. Why was JJ driving off in another car? It was strange. Real strange."

"Was it right after that the police arrived?"

"Oh, no. It wasn't five minutes before another car pulled up. Front side was all banged up and who should get out but JJ?"

"Wait, a minute." Yvonne gave her best perplexed look as she glanced at the jury. "You just said JJ drove off in a fancy convertible only to return not five minutes later in the car given to him by his father."

"Yes ma'am. Strange, like I said. I mean, that convertible disappeared at the end of the driveway, turning right, and almost immediately, the other car comes from the left and turns into the driveway and pulls around in front of the topiary. Out hops JJ. Only he's not wearing the black coat. He's not even wearing shoes, and he ran into the house. It was then I knew something wasn't right. How could JJ have changed clothes that quickly? How did he hop from one moving car to another? I wish I knew how he did it."

Yvonne tried not to smile. "Let's move on. Glorietta, did you call the police?"

"No! I just sat there trying to figure things out and maybe about fifteen minutes passed, and a cruiser pulled up. A policeman got out and went into the house. I was going to say something to him, but I knew he wouldn't believe me."

"Glorietta, you didn't call 911?"

"No, why should I?"

Yvonne turned to study the jury. "The police report says someone called 911 from a cell phone and told them a murder had taken place."

"It wasn't me." Glorietta said.

Yvonne nodded at the jury. "It wasn't a member of the jury."

"Objection." Stapleton stood up.

"Ms. Brown, please refrain from frivolous statements." Meridian said.

"I'm sorry, your honor. But despite all the prosecution's evidence, we have yet to identify the 911 caller. We know it sounded like a man. I know Mr. Stapleton is objecting to this line of questioning, but you have just heard from Glorietta that she was the only person at the mansion. Who found the body? Who called 911?"

"May we approach the bench?" Stapleton said.

"I guess so, Mr. Stapleton. Ms. Brown has raised a good point."

Yvonne ignored Anubis and almost shouted with triumph. Another shot across Stapleton's 'airtight' case. She joined Stapleton at the judge' desk.

"I allowed you to bring this surprise witness to the stand, Yvonne." Stapleton said. "You know I can shred her testimony in a heartbeat. Who called 911 is immaterial in the face of the overwhelming evidence that JJ Stone killed his mother. You want to continue to prolong this farce?"

Judge Meridian tapped his gavel lightly. He sat forward and for a moment, he averted his gaze to the side as if he were listening to a silent voice. He rubbed his chin and looked down at them both. "After consideration, Mr. Stapleton, Ms. Brown has a valid point. You never established the identity of the caller. That may be a moot point, but she has every right to capitalize on your sloppiness. Frankly, you have taken this case for granted. You are thinking it is a slam dunk and for that reason, you've been lazy, Mr. Stapleton. You will have ample opportunity to cast doubt on Mr. Tuttle's testimony during cross-examination. It shouldn't be that hard. Even a second-year law student could do that."

Stapleton's face turned red. He glared at Yvonne. "Very well, your honor. I will look forward to destroying Mrs. Tuttle."

"So will the jury." Yvonne said quietly.

Stapleton stormed off to his table and Yvonne walked slowly to her table. She was winning for the moment. But the sweet, eccentric Glorietta would be no match for Stapleton. She paused at the table. JJ sat quietly in his seat, his eyes downcast. Was she missing something? Could this boy have managed to switch cars that quickly?

Yvonne drew a sharp breath and whirled to face the witness box. "Glorietta, it is very important you understand the question I am about to ask you."

Glorietta blinked her large eyes behind her glasses. "So far, I've understood every question."

Yvonne moved toward the witness stand. "You were brought up to the courthouse right before coming in here for your testimony by Mr. Hobbs, the head of the servants at the mansion, right?"

"Yes, I was."

"Have you talked to anyone in attendance at the early sessions of this trial? Specifically, where were you prior to noon this morning?"

"I was working on the topiaries. Mr. Hobbs pulled me out of

the topiaries and hurried me up here. I didn't even have time to wash my hands and change my clothes. I must seem a mess, but this is who I am, Ms. Brown."

Yvonne smiled. "Then you have no idea about the specifics of the evidence collected from Mrs. Stone's murder?"

Glorietta's face grew pale. "I couldn't face it, even if someone tried to tell me. I wouldn't even talk to the other servants about it." She put a grimy hand up to her mouth and stifled a sob. "I loved Mrs. Stone. She was the kindest person in the world."

Yvonne took her time crossing to Stapleton's table to retrieve a tissue from a box. She had one on her table but wanted to draw attention to Stapleton. His glare was all she needed to see. The man was loading up his ammunition for cross examination. And when he went after Glorietta, the jury would see him as the fiend and her as the victim.

Yvonne handed the tissue to Glorietta and waited patiently for her to gather her wits. She finally calmed down and blew her nose into the tissue. Some in the crowd snickered until Meridian rapped his gavel for silence.

Yvonne put a hand on Glorietta's hand. "Glorietta, I know this is painful, but I need to ask you one more question about the man in the black coat. When he came out of the house, was he carrying anything?"

Mrs. Tuttle's eyebrows knitted together and she pushed her glasses back up. "You know, now that I recall he was carrying what looked like one of those tripods all folded up with a video camera on it. He put it in the back of the convertible right before he looked over at Big Ben."

My breath came quickly, now. "Glorietta, how do you account for the fact you saw JJ twice?"

Glorietta shrugged. "I'm a simple person, Ms. Brown. I work with plants. There are weeds that look just like a healthy plant. But if you don't recognize them as weeds, they will choke out the plant you're trying to grow. I know weeds when I see them.

The only conclusion I can reach is that first boy wasn't JJ. He just looked like him."

"Objection!" Stapleton rocketed to his feet. "Opinion, your honor. Not fact."

Anubis jumped to his feet and barked loudly. Meridian snapped his fingers and Anubis froze. "Relax, Anubis. I'm in no danger. Unlike Ms. Brown." He turned to the jury. "The jury will disregard Glorietta's last statement."

Mrs. Tuttle craned her neck and pointed to JJ. "Well I will say it another way. He looked just like JJ Stone. Or, if it wasn't him it was his twin."

CHAPTER
FORTY-SEVEN

JONATHAN STEEL

"Just a minute!" I sat up in the chair. "Glorietta saw someone who looked like me?"

Yvonne nodded. "The man on the dock had similar color eyes and hair. Was about the same age. What if someone was trying to frame you by passing themselves off as you? That was our working theory."

I stood up and paced across the room. Outside, the sky was a dull, leaden gray and snow fell again. I glanced at the clock. It was afternoon. "I need to think about this. If there is someone out there who is passing themselves off as me, it would explain a lot."

Yvonne moved into the kitchen. "I'll put out some sandwich stuff for lunch. Listen to me while I work." She took luncheon meat from the refrigerator, along with a head of lettuce and a tomato. Yvonne retrieved the yellow mustard and mayonnaise and placed them on the counter. She rinsed the lettuce and tomato under running water and took a knife from a butcher block.

"Let's review the evidence against you. I didn't go into detail because the prosecution had an open and shut case." Yvonne pulled a cutting board from a drawer under the cabinet. The knife chunked into the wood as she sliced the tomato. "Your fingerprints were the only ones found on the altar and your mother's body." Chunk! "And, of course, the knife. You pulled it from your mother's chest." Chunk, chunk! "Flesh under her fingernails revealed DNA with a 97% match to yours. Of course, DNA testing wasn't as good as it is today, so the match was within reasonable limits. We protested that and the judge agreed to throw out the DNA evidence." Chunk! "But the jury had already heard it and I can tell you they can't truly disregard what they have heard."

Yvonne arranged the tomato slices on the cutting board and tore off pieces of lettuce. "JJ, look in the fridge drawer for some sliced cheese."

I wanted to scream. I wanted to hit something. Instead, I got the cheese from the fridge and slammed it down next to the cutting board. "I need to know something. Now! Was this 'golden' knife the same knife used by Ketrick?"

Yvonne paused, her knife poised to cut more tomato. She placed the knife on the cutting board. "I don't know, JJ. I never put my hands on the knife, to be honest. I never considered the knife would have some special meaning." She sighed. "In fact, there were a lot of details about this murder that had significant meanings. We only saw that in retrospect. This was a well-organized murder, JJ. This Council of Darkness we knew nothing about at the time, had an agenda to take you out."

"Why?" I pounded the counter. "That is the question I can never get a clear answer to. Why was I targeted? Why the third demon?" My face warmed, and I fought to control the fury within me.

Yvonne pulled a loaf of wheat bread from the cabinet above the sink along with three plates. The loaf of bread wasn't sliced. "There's bottled water in the fridge. Or lemonade. No liquor.

Sam insists." I took bottled water from the refrigerator. I put one bottle against my hot cheek.

Yvonne placed the loaf of bread next to the luncheon meat and cut slices from the loaf. "Go ahead and make a sandwich. Eat. You're still not completely over the teleportation."

I started assembling a sandwich when my stomach growled. "How long does that take?"

"About three days. Of course, for you only a couple of days."

I froze. "There you said it again. I'm different. Why?"

Yvonne waved a finger in the air. "Oh, no! Not yet! I must take you there gently, JJ. Trust me." She made a sandwich and motioned to the table. "Sit. Eat." She went to the foot of the stairs bearing a plate with two sandwiches and a bottled water. "Sam, lunch is ready."

Sam hurried down the spiral staircase and picked up his lunch. "Still nothing. Which is good." He went back upstairs.

"Yvonne, where are we?" I sat at the table. "Europe, right?"

"Okay, we are in Switzerland. In a chalet in the mountains. Ironically, it belongs to your friend, Max. She does not know we are using it. I arranged it through one of her proteges."

I nodded. "Then I feel better about being here. Max's safe houses would be much safer than anyone else's. So I'll be quiet and let you finish." I ate my sandwich. "Continue with the evidence."

Yvonne sat at the table. "The psychological report of your possible sociopathic tendencies didn't help. Neither did your counselor's records about a possible multiple personality disorder."

"I'm pretty sure that was the demon." I couldn't believe I was saying that about myself.

"Of course, you were covered with your mother's blood. Your footprints were in the altar chamber. Sam discovered you holding the knife over your mother's body." Yvonne nibbled at her sandwich. "But we turned the tables on the prosecution. The GPS data on your phone and your car established both were two miles away at the time of your mother's murder. Your sandals were in the car. The tripod, video camera, black coat, and running shoes were never found, not to mention the convertible."

"Stapleton tried his best to challenge Glorietta's account of the two cars appearing almost simultaneously. She never wavered. We introduced the GPS data the next day, but there were enough holes in the timeline to allow you not to be present at the actual location. After all, you could have left the car and phone, ran to the house, committed murder, drove off in the other car, ditched the tripod and the shoes and then drove the wrecked car up for Glorietta to see. It would be a tight timeline, but it was possible. Not probable, but possible. In our favor was the lack of time to get rid of the convertible and evidence. Sam had some friends from the force search nearby. Nothing. The Mansion is the only house for a couple of miles along that highway. Where would you have hidden the car? They arrested you right after the police arrived. You didn't have time to hide the car. Anyway, Glorietta was believable, but anyone could reason she was mistaken about how much time passed between the two cars leaving and coming."

I finished my sandwich and looked across the living room to the front windows. The snow was falling heavily obscuring the view of the distant mountains. What would that mean for the drones?

"Yvonne, there was something else going on. After all someone tried to kill you and Sam. Any other attempts on your life?"

"No." Yvonne finished half of her sandwich and drank some water. "Sam's friends at the police arranged around the clock surveillance. Whoever tried the first time didn't try again. But that attempt made me realize we were on to something. Just what, we didn't know."

"My father was pretty adamant about stopping you from successfully defending me." I said.

Yvonne sat back. "Your father has many resources now that he did not have then. He had been out of the country for weeks. We tried to find any evidence he had hired mercenaries or old military buddies, but nothing jumped out at us. Back then, he was nearly helpless compared to now. Besides, the case was a slam dunk. Interfering with us wouldn't change the outcome." She sat forward and her gaze bored into mine. "You need to understand something, JJ. What I am about to tell you will show you more about your father's motives today than at any time in your relationship. What happened in that courtroom on the last day of testimony changed your father forever. It made him the man he is today."

I drank more water. "Then, by all means, get on with it."

"I will. But first, I must tell you more about the third demon."

CHAPTER
FORTY-EIGHT

Kevin's eyes were rimmed in black. Yvonne found him in the far corner of an old library building on the campus of U. T. Austin, surrounded by piles of ancient books. He glanced up at her and yawned.

"Kevin, I have little time. Tomorrow morning, I have to wrap up JJ's defense, and so far, it doesn't look good. I hope you aren't wasting my time." She said as she sat at the table.

"Well, it took me a few days, but I found something that I think will help." He smiled. "Some of these books are almost two hundred years old. We're lucky the university archived them."

They were in the library's basement, in a far corner, past a hallway filled with hulking sealed crates of antiquities. Yvonne glanced around her, expecting ghosts and ghouls to pop out of the spider web covered shelves. "How long have you been down here?"

Kevin glanced at his watch. "Twelve hours today. But I've got the goods." He pulled a huge tome across the table toward him.

"This is a copy of the 'Lexicon of Death'. Every heard of the Necronomicon?"

"No."

"Well, it's a famous book of arcane, satanic knowledge. No one knows who wrote the Necronomicon. But a rival who was trying to make a name for himself wrote this book." Kevin tapped his copy of the "Lexicon of Death". Fading leather covered the ancient tome.

"Count D'Arbon from France purchased an estate near San Antonio on the river. He built a sort of black magic retreat for wizards and witches, and practitioners of magic. While over-seeing his magic 'university', he wrote this book. In isolation from the eastern coast, the witch trials never threatened him. But in 1791, shortly after the United States became a nation, and the Constitution was adopted, he realized his estate was in danger from religious institutions. Seems he had 'kidnapped' young men and women from nearby villages and used them as guinea pigs for his arcane experiments."

Kevin slid the book away from him. "I can feel the evil emanating from this book. The things he did to his victims are unspeakable." Kevin wiped sweat from his bare scalp. His lips quivered. "Yvonne, D'Arbon had raised up twelve practitioners of his black arts. Each 'professor' oversaw a 'house' of this university. When D'Arbon saw the threats growing, he realized he had to leave the United States. He dispersed his professors all over the world but kept them as members of his council of evil."

Kevin retrieved the book and drew a deep breath as he opened it. He turned the pages until he located a diagram. He turned the book so Yvonne could see a twelve-pointed star on the page containing Roman numerals like a clock. "Each number on this star represents one of the professors. Now, look at this caption. 'The Councils of the Twelve Demons'."

Yvonne felt a chill. "Twelve demons?"

"One for each of the disciples. I found one obscure reference to the twelve demons. When Christ picked his twelve disciples,

Satan called together his twelve most powerful demons and assigned one to each disciple."

"Wait a minute. I've never read this in the Bible."

"True. I'm going on conjectural and historical evidence. And look at this."

A rough hand drawn image in the center of the page showed a man in a black apron bent over a body on a table. The man was holding something in his hand with a long needle, which was in the man's eye. "What is this?"

"Occlumency." Kevin tapped the image of the man. "The theory went like this: what a person saw when they died was stored in the eye. This image portrays the practitioner extracting the vitreous humor from the eye of a dead man. But according to legend, it wasn't to see what the dead man saw when he died, but to see what the dead can visualize in the afterlife. This group of ghouls called themselves Vitreomancers. And they have a rival council to the Council of the Twelve Demons."

"Competition?" Yvonne said.

"Yeah, Satan loves pitting his own against each other. Like putting two pit bulls in a ring to see who will emerge the stronger. He doesn't care if one dies. Survival of the fittest." Kevin turned the book toward him. "Two groups of demonically powered ancient people bent on serving Satan. This third demon could belong to either of these councils."

"What does this have to do with JJ?"

"JJ spoke to you in the demon's voice, and he called himself?"

"Number three! That's right! The third demon." Yvonne sat back and tried to erase the image of the Vitreomancer from her memory.

"Yvonne, I think one of the twelve demons is inside Jonathan."

She glanced at my watch. "How does this help us?"

Kevin turned the pages of the book. "According to these writings, a demon can be controlled if you know its name. Jesus asked the demons their name and called them by name to cast them out. If we can learn the name of the third demon, we can command it to leave Jonathan."

"Why not find a priest and have him just cast it out?"

Kevin sighed. "I'm not sure any one of us is powerful enough. The entire business of dealing with demons is complicated, even for an exorcist. Scripture only gives some hints on how to deal with demons. The person driving it out would have to be almost spiritually perfect."

"That leaves me out." Yvonne said.

Kevin grew silent and slowly closed the book. "If you want to deal with the demon inside of JJ, you'll have to clean up your soul, make peace with God."

A chill settled over her. She didn't know which scared her most, the demons or the prospect of 'cleaning up her soul'. The serial killer's face appeared in her mind. She had wanted nothing more than to kill the man! And she had! How could she make peace with God with such murderous intent still in her heart? "That may be more difficult than you think."

Kevin nodded. "I know about your past. I did some research about you. Found out about the serial killer who kidnapped you."

Yvonne's face flushed and her hand went unconsciously to the scars on her abdomen. "He carved his initials into my skin. I cut them out. Left a huge set of scars."

"There will be no scars in heaven." Kevin said. "Except for the scars of Jesus."

Yvonne looked away in anger. "If you're going to tell me I need to forgive that monster, forget it." She glanced back at Kevin and a red haze settled around her vision. "I gutted him as soon as I got my hands on his knife. After he died, I spent months in rehab. I became a cage fighter. Want to know how many women, and some men, I defeated? Over a dozen. I beat the crap out of them, and I had to be pulled off of their unconscious bodies."

"Did it help?"

Yvonne tried to calm her breathing. "At the time, yes."

"And, now?"

"That man once told me he would make me like him. He almost did." Yvonne whispered. "The last person I defeated almost died. I found out she was a single mom trying to make money so she could get her kids back from foster care."

Yvonne looked away. "I went to see her in the hospital. She thanked me." Yvonne looked at Kevin. "She thanked me for almost killing her. She didn't press charges. No one did in those illegal games. Child protection thought she had been mugged while trying to buy groceries for her kids, who were supposed to come spend the weekend with her. The child protection agent had pity on her and gave her a second chance. Once she got out of the hospital, her kids were coming home. Kevin, she forgave me. So I channeled the anger and the destructive desires into something more constructive and I began to help the helpless. I take on the cases of the truly innocent people. Of course, that attitude cost me my job."

"All because she forgave you." Kevin said.

Yvonne glared at him. "This third demon claims to have influenced my serial killer. It knew things only he would have known, and the man is dead. I hope he is burning in hell. It would almost be worth it to be damned myself so I could go there and watch him burn!" Yvonne sat back and only then felt the tears running down her cheeks. "How can I possibly forgive him?"

"You can't. But God can. That's the key to understanding this spiritual realm of which I speak. God is bigger and filled with more love and mercy than you and I can ever muster. Only God can forgive anyone who asks. And who would want to follow a God who didn't? I'm glad I'm not God. I have my own specters that haunt me at night. I have a list a mile long of those who I have yet to forgive. Yvonne, claim forgiveness. You must be forgiven before you can forgive. And right now, JJ needs us. JJ is in the grip of a demon, and we have to find a way to loosen that grip and save that boy."

Yvonne angrily wiped the tears from her face. Could she ever find a way to forgive? She recalled JJ's horror-filled eyes when he realized a demon possessed him. Such desperation. The boy was crying out for help. "I'll work on it, Kevin. Now, how do we learn the demon's name?"

Kevin smiled. "I don't believe in coincidences. Yvonne, I believe God orchestrates reality in such a way that when we need it, the resources are there for us to use to complete the work God has for us. The problem for us humans is in pausing long enough from the distractions of this life to actually recognize when God is inviting us to be a part of His work."

"Nice sermon." Yvonne said.

"Oh, it's not original. I got that from Dr. Lawrence's writing." Kevin had a leather satchel on the tabletop and he pulled a flyer from within. He slid it over toward Yvonne. It was for a lecture by a Dr. Cephas Lawrence on "Demonology in the 21st Century." The lecture would take place in just two hours. "I already called his assistant and had her tell him we have some questions about demons. He's agreed to have dinner with us before the lecture." Kevin glanced at his watch. "In ten minutes at Kerbey Lane Cafe. He wants pancakes! If we leave right now, we won't be late."

"Pancakes? Here we are talking about cosmic evil and the man wants pancakes?"

"Ground yourself in simplicity, Yvonne. Jesus met with everyone over a meal. There's something to be said for breaking bread together." Kevin said.

Yvonne grabbed her cell phone. "Let me get Sam to meet us there. This may be the break we need."

FORTY-NINE

DR. CEPHAS LAWRENCE smacked his mustache covered lips as he studied the pancakes before him. "The best and healthiest pancakes in the Western Hemisphere." He said. He looked like Albert Einstein, with wild salt and pepper hair and a heavy mustache. He dug into his pancakes with glee.

"Dr. Lawrence, my name is Yvonne Brown, and I have a client who needs your help. Kevin has told me you know a lot about demons."

Lawrence looked up from his pancakes and for a moment, something sad and desperate filled his eyes. "Unfortunately, I lost someone I love to the activity of a demon. I have dedicated the rest of my life to studying evil and its corporate structure. Tonight, I will talk about the Ark of the Demon Rose, an ancient artifact filled with talismans reportedly giving someone control over demonic forces."

Yvonne glanced at Sam, whose skepticism was on high alert. "I don't suppose you have this Ark. We could use it."

Lawrence glanced at Sam and went back to his pancakes. "I have not located it. Yet. But, I will."

Kevin put a hand on my arm. "Dr. Lawrence, there is a young

man accused of murder and he claims to be possessed by a demon calling himself 'the third demon'."

Lawrence froze, and he slowly sat up from his pancakes. "Did you say number three?"

"Yes, the third demon." Yvonne said.

Lawrence dropped his fork and retrieved his napkin. He dabbed syrup from his lip and stood up quickly. "I thank you for the meal, but I must be going."

"Wait! Don't leave!"

Lawrence massaged his mustache. "Young lady, I will have nothing to do with any demon who claims to be numerically linked to the Council of Darkness. I have already lost too much."

"But I thought you were looking for these demons?" Sam said.

"I am looking for a way to control them. You would be insane to deal with a demon without a tool that gives you an upper hand. Take your young friend to a priest for exorcism. I have attempted many and have been unsuccessful." He paused, and the sorrow returned. "And one of those failures cost a young woman her life."

"Dr. Lawrence, Christ compels you to help us." Kevin said. "I don't believe in coincidences. It is no coincidence you are here in town on the very day we need your help with this demon. If Ms. Brown learns more about this 'third' demon, she will be able to defend this young man against a charge of murdering his own mother."

Lawrence froze. He looked at Yvonne, then at Sam. "Just a minute. Is this the murder case I've seen in the news? A woman viciously killed by her own son?"

"He didn't do it, Dr. Lawrence." Yvonne said. "There is some thing else involved. Someone tried to kill me and Sam to keep us from defending this young man. There are forces here we don't understand. We were hoping you would."

Lawrence sat in his chair again and crossed his arms. "I don't have time to meet with your client. I leave after my lecture tonight, driving to Dallas for a lecture tomorrow morning at 8 A.M."

Kevin cast Yvonne a hopeful look. "Then if you could tell us the third demon's name, that might help."

Lawrence chuckled. "My son, if I knew the demons' names, I would not be traveling around the country learning all I can from these universities about evil." He played with his mustache and then sat forward. "There is a legendary source that you might tackle. A person, really. Again, mostly legend. I spoke to him once, and he refused to help me. In fact, he was downright arrogant and adversarial. He conducts research similar to mine only in Europe." Lawrence fished his cell phone from his shirt pocket and studied the screen. He turned it toward us. "You can reach Max at this number. He may or may not answer. Leave a message and maybe, just maybe, he might have some information for you."

"Kevin learned something about this Max." Yvonne copied the number down on the folder in front of her.

"Probably very little. He is an enigma wrapped up in a mystery." Dr. Lawrence returned his phone to his pocket. He wiped again at his mustache and motioned to a server. "Can I get these to go, please?" She took the plate and Lawrence looked once again at Yvonne.

"No guarantee. He may not call you back." Lawrence took one more drink from his coffee. The server returned with a cardboard container. "Now, I really must be going to prepare for my lecture." He paused and looked at Kevin. "You had me when you said what you did."

"What did I say?"

"My motto. There are no such things as coincidences. May God go with you and this young man." He stood up and walked out of the restaurant.

———

Yvonne had just fallen asleep when her cell phone rang. She sat up in bed and glanced at the clock. It was just after midnight. She had called the number for Max right after dinner and had gotten only a beep showing it was recording her voice. There was a synopsis of what she needed and barely had said 'third demon' when the recording ended and the call did, too. She fumbled for her cell phone. The caller I.D. said 'unavailable', but she answered it anyway.

"Yvonne Brown." A tremulous male voice said.

"Yes."

"I am Max. I have been researching your case for the past three hours. A member of the Council of Darkness possesses your client. I would like to have more information on your client's situation, but I understand from my sources that tomorrow is your last day in court."

Yvonne's heart raced, and she sat up in her bed. "Yes, that is true. I wish we had more time, but JJ doesn't."

"Ms. Brown, have you identified the words formed by the letters written in the victim's blood?"

She froze. "No! I never thought about them. No one can identify what they mean so far."

"The letters are Aramaic. They are taken from quotes from the Gospels of Luke and Matthew." The voice said.

"What do they say?"

"Paraphrasing: You belong to me. For Eternity." The voice said. "And there is a cluster of letters that spell out a name, Ms. Brown. It is the name for Satan."

I swallowed hard, and chills ran down my spine. "What?"

"Names are important. Names are powerful." The voice said. "I am texting you a name. It is the name of the third demon. If using that name works, I expect to hear from you after the trial. You have indispensable information I need. And if you are in contact with Dr. Cephas Lawrence, my advice is to stay away from him and never contact him again. The man is beyond dangerous." The line went dead.

Jonathan Steel

"Wait!" I said. "You met with Cephas and talked to Max?"

Yvonne sipped at some hot tea. "Yes. This was long before you met either of them, JJ. And we did not know the significance of those two individuals."

I stood up and walked over to the fireplace. A chill came over me. "My entire life, these 'coincidences', as Cephas calls them, have circled and circled around me." I turned my back to the fire. "And those words? Yvonne, the words written in blood on the wall in the beach house by Braxton were the exact same phrases."

Yvonne's mouth fell open. "What?"

"And Drake all but confirmed he was there with Braxton and helped him kill Richard Pierce and hang him on the wall. That means the third demon has been in my life over and over! Am I just a puppet?" I clenched my fists in anger. "I have been manipulated my entire life! By my father! By my grandfather! By Nigel Hampton!" I pounded my fist against the metal flue above the fireplace. The sound echoed to the roof. "And, by the third demon."

"JJ, please calm down." Yvonne stood up slowly. "You're not a puppet. Can't you see? Everything that has happened is because you have chosen to always pursue good." She came over to me and took my fist in her hand. "You have made your choice, JJ. You chose always to pursue the good in this world, to do good things. When we choose that path, evil will always try to stop us."

I turned to look into her green eyes. "I wish I could believe that."

"JJ, these coincidences aren't there because someone is manipulating you. They are part of a plan, yes. But the timing is perfect. His timing is perfect. Can't you see that even when you were in jail and possessed by a demon, God moved people into place to surround you, to protect. Yes, Dr. Lawrence and Max were there because we needed their expertise. But they were there because YOU needed it! It was because of them we could find a victory in the face of certain defeat."

I drew a deep breath and blew it out, relaxing my fists. "I just get so tired of fighting, Yvonne. I am weary. A normal life is what I want. I almost had it with April, and then the thirteenth demon charged into my life and ruined it all."

"And the thirteenth demon is where?" She said.

I almost smiled. "In Tartarus."

"Along with, let's see, twelve, eleven, ten, nine, eight, seven, six, and five. Manipulated or not, Steel, you have won many victories in the Lord's name. You have taken powerful demons off the field of battle." She reached up and touched my cheek. "And, JJ, it all started back then with your first encounter with the third demon. Once you hear everything, you will understand. The battles are concluding. You are nearing the end of this skirmish with the enemy. You must stand firm and strong. Will you?"

"Yes." I said.

"Now, I will tell you what happened when I put you on the stand. Sit. Relax. Our story is almost over."

I eased back into my chair and tried to calm my racing heart.

CHAPTER
FIFTY

THE COURTROOM WAS PACKED. As Yvonne met JJ at the table and waited for the bailiff to remove his manacles, Sam leaned forward from the galley.

"Look over your right shoulder. Second row from the back."

Yvonne turned slowly and glanced over her shoulder. She ran her gaze down the row until she saw the man he was talking about. He wore a knit cap over his hair and a pair of black rimmed glasses. But it was the black coat that set him apart from the rest of the people. It would reach 80 outside and the man should have already been sweltering. His gaze met hers. He lowered his glasses and his intense turquoise eyes gleamed. He winked and put the glasses back up.

"It's him." Yvonne said. What was he doing here?

At that moment, the bailiff called for all to rise. Yvonne turned quickly as Judge Meridian assumed his position at the bench and Anubis ambled to his place at the foot of the desk and lay down. When she turned back, the man in the black coat was gone. She motioned to Sam, and he nodded.

"I'll talk to the policeman outside. We'll find the creep."

Meridian went through the motions of continuing their case, and he nodded toward Yvonne. "Counselor?"

"I'd like to call JJ Stone to the stand."

JJ stood up slowly and his eyes spoke volumes. She patted his hand. "You'll do just fine, JJ. Just follow my lead and answer all the questions honestly."

JJ nodded and at the table behind him she saw the glint in Stapleton's eye. The man could not wait to cross-examine JJ. Yvonne was hoping he would be surprised by the end of JJ's testimony.

"JJ, you've told the jury all about what you remember the Saturday morning when your mother died. Do you recall Captain O'Malley coming into the chamber?" Yvonne asked. JJ swallowed and glanced over at the jury. When he looked back at Yvonne, she smiled and nodded. "I know you're nervous, JJ. Take your time and answer the question when you're ready."

"Vaguely. I remember crying with mother's head in my lap and then I passed out right after he came into the room." JJ's voice trembled, and he wiped sweat from his upper lip. "Uh, when we spoke the other day, Captain O'Malley said my voice sounded strange, which is something I don't remember."

"Objection, your honor. The witness is relaying unsubstantiated evidence. If the defense wants to introduce this conversation, the defense needs to put Captain O'Malley on the stand." Stapleton said.

"Sustained. Ms. Brown?" Meridian glared at her.

"Sorry, your honor. JJ is just nervous. I would request the jury disregard that comment, and I promise, if we explore this any further, I will ask Captain O'Malley to be sworn in. However, I ask that you allow the jury to hear testimony based on this transcript from JJ's deposition." Yvonne retrieved a sheaf of papers from her table. "I would like to introduce these into evidence, and I have a copy for the prosecution. My questions are taken directly from Mr. Stone's deposition."

The bailiff took a copy to the judge and handed a second copy to Stapleton, who stood up. "Your honor, I would like to have time to look over this deposition."

"Your honor." Yvonne said. "The defense grants the prosecution permission for any length of extended cross-examination following JJ's testimony. If he desires more time to look at the deposition in the interim, I'm okay with a recess."

Stapleton studied her with a suspicious gaze. "No. Go ahead, Yvonne. But I will come back to your client. Rest assured."

"I would expect nothing less." Yvonne cast one last gaze over the spectators. Sam was nowhere to be seen, most likely outside with the police. But the man in the black coat suddenly sat up from a crouched position in the back row. The person sitting next to him cast a wary look in his direction, as if the man had appeared out of thin air. He had never left the courtroom! There was no way to alert Sam. Yvonne turned back to JJ and, after taking a deep breath, asked, "Do you believe you are demon possessed?"

Anubis jumped to his feet and barked loudly. Yvonne jerked at the sound of the barking and tried to calm her racing heart. The crowd erupted in murmuring, and Stapleton shot to his feet. "Objection!" He shouted.

Judge Meridian stood up and walked down from his desk. He calmly walked over to Anubis and grabbed the dog by the snout, holding his mouth shut. Anubis writhed under the judge's grip and his eyes widened in fear. Anubis tucked his tail and sat down. Meridian glared at the dog.

"One more outburst from you and I'll have you put to sleep!" He said loudly with a voice that carried above the uproar. Meridian still held the dog's mouth closed and he turned to Yvonne. He smiled at her and then looked over at Stapleton.

"You realize I was talking to the dog, right?" A strange, high-pitched laugh followed and strange gleam filled his eyes. He motioned to Stapleton and then to Yvonne.

"Counselors, approach the bench."

Yvonne joined Stapleton in front of Meridian. Anubis whined in pain and Meridian ignored it. He leaned toward Yvonne.

"I love this little charade, Ms. Brown. Just love it." He said and almost chuckled again. "Mr. Stapleton, I want to see how this plays out. For now, keep you trap shut like Anubis if you know what is good for you. No more objections until the defense is finished and then you can tear into Mr. Stone with abandon." He motioned toward their tables. "Now, shoo! Go back to your tables."

Yvonne backed slowly away from the weird scene before her. What was Meridian doing? She glanced at Stapleton and saw naked confusion cross the man's features. Meridian leaned down toward Anubis and said something unintelligible. The dog's eyes widened again in fear and seemed to collapse in on itself. Meridian released the dog's snout and held his hand toward the bailiff.

"Bubba! Get me a wipe."

Bubba hurried into the judge's office and returned with a wet tissue. Meridian cleaned off his hand and went back behind his desk. He stood over the desk and surveyed the courtroom. He cleared his throat. He reached beneath his desk and took out an antique set of scales. He set the scales on the front right-hand corner of his desk. "I am the voice of justice. I am here to see the scales are even. No more objections. No more outbursts. We are here to weigh Mr. Stone's conscience on the scales. We are here to weigh his heart. Carry on, Ms. Brown." He said.

Yvonne glanced once at Anubis. The dog was whining softly, his ears down and his eyes turned toward Meridian. A strange stillness fell over the courtroom. The smell of fear permeated the air. Yvonne returned to her position in the drama that was unfolding in the courtroom. She paused before JJ. "I asked you if you felt like a demon possessed you."

A light murmur arose, and the gavel fell. So did silence. JJ wore a pained look and his turquoise eyes filled with fear. Yvonne nodded encouragingly.

"I don't know. I've been feeling strange lately. I've had memory lapses in the last few months." JJ paused, looking down at his hands. "I would wake up with a hangover and I don't drink. When your father drinks and beats you regularly, you don't touch the stuff."

More murmuring from the audience. Yvonne glanced over her shoulder and spied Captain Stone sitting in the third row. His face was red with anger. The gavel fell again.

"Bubba, would you lock the back doors please?" Meridian said. He stood up and seemed to tower over everyone. His intense dark eyes were magnified by his huge glasses. "Now, listen to me carefully. If there are any more outbursts from the spectators, I will hold the entire lot of you in contempt of court and I will immediately incarcerate you." Silence descended. She heard the locks click in place on the doors. Yvonne swallowed hard and turned back to JJ. Meridian, nodded and sat back down. "Proceed."

Yvonne tried to calm her racing heart. This was it! "JJ, I would like to talk to the third demon now."

A gasp came from behind her, and Stapleton shouted and he rocketed to his feet. "Objection."

Judge Meridian pounded his gavel, and his eyes filled with fire. He pointed his gavel at Stapleton. "What were my instructions? No objections! Do I need to send for a muzzle? You will have a turn at the boy. Anubis! Go baby sit Mr. Stapleton."

Anubis jumped up from the floor and bounded over to Stapleton's table. He hopped up onto the table and sat on his haunches. He pointed his snout at Stapleton. Stapleton wanted to shout, to protest, but the soft growling of this beast quieted him. He glanced at Yvonne helplessly and sat down in his chair.

Something wasn't quite right with the judge. His recent actions would more than justify a mistrial. However, the doors were locked, and Yvonne doubted making such a request would be granted. Meridian looked at her and almost smiled.

"Perhaps you could inform the court why you have made this rather strange request." He said.

Yvonne nodded and tried to regain her composure. "Very well. It is the prosecution's contention that Mr. Stone is psychotic or at the very least, pretending to be. The line of questioning I wish to pursue could validate the prosecution's case. I can't imagine why he would object."

Stapleton's eyes locked on Anubis. "I, uh, withdraw my objection."

"JJ," Yvonne turned back to the witness stand. "I want to speak to the third demon."

JJ looked at her, his face filling with sorrow and sadness. "I don't want to be possessed. I don't want to have a demon in me. Don't make me do this."

Her heart broke, and she felt tears form in her eyes. Almost, she faltered, but she found the strength to press on. "In the name of Jesus Christ, I command you to speak to me."

JJ's face twisted and suddenly he changed, hulking forward, eyes hooded and lips turning up into a sneer. "You called?" His voice became hoarse. An audible gasp came from the jury.

Meridian rapped his gavel and snapped his fingers. Meridian slapped the top of his desk. "Come on, boy!"

Anubis leaped off Stapleton's table and landed on the judge's desk. He stood at attention, legs straight, ears alert, and eyes pointed at the crowd. Meridian pointed his gavel at the spectators and the jury. "I will keep an eye on the counselors. And the jury!" He pointed his gavel at the jury. "No further outbursts while we enjoy this circus."

Yvonne tried to ignore the "circus" and stared straight into JJ's red-rimmed eyes. "Am I addressing the third demon?" She asked. His gaze penetrated to her very soul. Suddenly, her heart pounded with fear. No! She could not be afraid.

"Yes, little missy. You like being called that, don't you? Isn't that what your lover used to call you? 'Come with me, little missy. Let me show you something special, little missy. Down, down in my basement dungeon. I have a special place just for you.'" JJ spewed the filth at her and she couldn't breath. She was in the basement again, panicking, pleading for mercy as she heard his footsteps in the hallway outside the locked door of her dungeon chamber.

"No! Don't bring that up. That's all in the past." She felt the tears stinging her cheeks and suddenly JJ's face softened and a battle for control played across his face and the third demon won. The twisted face returned.

"My little host doesn't like for me to remind you of your past. He doesn't want me to hurt you."

"Oh, go ahead and tell little missy the truth." Meridian said. Anubis barked once.

Yvonne glanced in horror at Meridian and fought for control, feeling the world spin around her. What was happening with the judge? He was playing along with the third demon!

"Little missy", the kidnapper had called her when he had done those things to her. She had locked all that away in her memory vault, protecting her from feeling what she had felt then. The defendant's table cut into her back. Yvonne leaned against the edge of the table and looked once at Stapleton. Surprisingly, she saw sympathy there. He looked away, and she said a prayer. She glanced at Meridian. How had he known about that name, little missy? The man's smile was a leering sham, his teeth glowing white against his red lips, his dark eyes magnified by those glasses. Meridian rubbed Anubis roughly, stroking the animal's back.

"Go ahead, little missy." He touched the scales and the empty pans gyrated up and down. "The scales of justice are waiting. Do we need to weigh your heart?"

Yvonne closed her eyes from the insanity around her. She had beaten the serial killer. She had taken the man's knife from him. She pushed the painful memory away and pushed away from her table as her strength returned. The enemy controlled through guilt, Kevin had said. She turned and looked at Kevin sitting just two seats away. His eyes were closed in prayer. Yvonne closed her eyes and pushed the monster in her memory back into his dungeon, and slammed the door.

She opened her eyes and fixed her gaze on JJ. "The past has no hold on me anymore. We will not speak of it again. You're wasting your time. I want to ask you about the murder of Christine Stone."

Silence descended over the courtroom and all she could hear was Anubis' rapid panting. JJ's face remained twisted and deformed. She saw something flash in his eyes – irritation or mischief?

"What do you want to know?"

"Who killed Christine Stone?"

JJ lifted an eyebrow and picked at his teeth with his finger. "This puny little human sure didn't. He's got potential with his violent temper, but he's not capable of murder. He loved her too much. But for now, he is my meat puppet and eventually I will turn him into a proper killer."

A low murmur passed over the courtroom. Stapleton stood up.

"This is ludicrous, Yvonne. Of course he's going to blame someone else." He stammered, casting a fearful eye toward Meridian and Anubis. Before Meridian could raise his gavel, JJ spoke.

"Would you sit down and be quiet? You make me so tired! You wouldn't be sitting here today if it wasn't for my buddies."

Stapleton fell silent, an amazed look on his face. "What?"

"Let's see." JJ tapped a finger to his forehead in thought. "About ten years ago, you were in your second year of law school. Remember that pretty young thing you sullied up to? What was her name? Oh yeah, Tarnisha. Tops in your class. But, not so popular. But you knew how to cultivate a relationship with her, didn't you? You found out about her favorite hobby and learned how to play bridge so you could get close to her. You whispered sweet nothings in her ear and convinced her to help you cheat on the final exam. Remember?"

Stapleton's face paled. "How could you know that?"

"Because we were right there encouraging you. Me and my

legion. I am the master and they are the servants. So many lesser demons who need my precious guidance. They're more like place holders, you might say. I get things started and make room for the tenants. They settle in and keep my work going, don't you see? Then I can move on to fertile ground." JJ leaned forward and put a hand aside his mouth so only Yvonne could hear. "Unlike number four over there in your judge. Only thinks he has a legion of meat puppets instead of a legion of lesser demons. Moves around. Not as effective as I am. Now step aside. I'm not finished with Mr. Stapleton."

Yvonne glanced over at Judge Meridian. His smile had faded and anger filled his eyes. He pushed Anubis from the desk and the dog deftly landed on his paws. "What did you say?"

"I'm not talking to you right now. I'm talking to Mr. Prosecutor." JJ continued. "Remember the night after the final exam when Tarnisha came running into your arms? Remember, Richey? They had caught her hacking the server to alter you grades. They were going to expel her from law school. She didn't rat on you because you told her you loved her so. You wined and dined her and convinced her to take the fall, and you would pull some strings to get her back into law school the next year. Only, you forgot all about her, didn't you?"

Stapleton looked helplessly at Yvonne. "No one should have known that!"

"We're the ones that talked you into that little move. Do you know what became of Tarnisha?"

"No." Stapleton whispered.

"Her soul belongs to us. A year after that night, she took an overdose and died alone in her ratty little apartment. She loved you to the end." JJ sat back and grinned and rapidly clapped his hands. "May I be the first to congratulate you on a job well done? You still have lots of potential. After I'm done with JJ, maybe you and I can make a deal."

Stapleton contracted in on himself, his pain written all over his face. "I didn't know."

"Oh, and, Betty? That pretty little thing that was by your side the first day? I know why you fired her. Who is going to pay for the baby? Certainly not its father." Stapleton put his face in his hands in dismay. Yvonne thought she heard sobbing. She turned back to JJ and drew a calming breath. The third demon was cocky.

"Is that what you did to Mrs. Stone's actual killer? Promised him the world and then coerced him into killing Christine Stone?"

JJ's gaze jerked in her direction. "Little missy, I didn't need to do anything. Jeremiah already belongs to us. He has since the day he was born and his father gave him over to us. He serves the master. And serves him well." JJ giggled. "Or for JJ's sake, I should say OUR father."

What? Yvonne turned and looked out over the audience. Captain Stone was frozen, paralyzed with anger and confusion. She glanced at the back row. The man in the black coat had removed his cap, his coat, and his glasses. His eyes gleamed with fire. His ginger hair stood on end with static electricity. Had JJ said *his* father? That would mean "Jeremiah" was JJ's brother?

Yvonne turned around and glared at JJ. "You possessed another man who is, what, JJ's brother?"

JJ shrugged. "Jeremiah's the stronger of the two. JJ is just a wimp. Good thing we're not identical twins."

Yvonne looked back at Kevin. Kevin, the youth pastor sharing God's word with JJ. Kevin trying his best to turn JJ away from an evil lifestyle. Yvonne turned back to JJ. "JJ was going to church, wasn't he? Listening to the Gospel. But, you had to do something to stop that, didn't you? What was the tool? The photo journal? Were you in the journal? That was it, wasn't it? And you had to stop JJ from becoming a Christian. If he had, he would become a spiritual warrior and that worried you, didn't it?"

JJ looked worried for a moment, and then the smug look returned. He sat back and crossed his arms. "The old yin and yang. Good and evil. Two sides of the coin, yes. And there were certain prophecies about him. We decided not to take a chance. And the connections with his father, the good Captain, helped us gain access. It was easy to frame the pretty boy. That is, me." He tapped his chest. "And you know what is so perfect? Everything I am saying will be dismissed as insanity. It will do JJ no good. He will die under the executioner's hand."

Yvonne stepped closer to him. "Did Jeremiah try and kill me and Sam O'Malley?"

JJ's eyes narrowed and he studied me. "I thought we had you. Where did you go? I thought you were in the boat and then you show up in court the next day. Never could trust meat puppets and their cockroach demons. Worthless."

"How could you, JJ Stone, have tried to kill us when you were in prison? I saw the eyes of the man behind it all. It wasn't you." She stepped closer and breathed a silent prayer. "Azzuzabel, I command you."

JJ's head snapped up and his eyes glowed with red fire. "What did you say?"

"I called you by name, Azzuzabel. I command you to leave JJ Stone."

JJ slowly stood up from the witness chair. His eyes glowed brightly, and a shadow darkened on the wall behind him. The shadow deepened until it seemed to penetrate the substance of the wall and became a huge, hulking humanoid figure of pale green and dappled pink scales. From his chest, abdomen, and legs, heads formed, each more terrifying than the other. Bat heads, snake heads, crocodile heads, and some that defied characterization. The main face was deformed, with the eyes on different levels and dark green hair hung to its shoulders. Fibrous wings unfurled behind it and beat at the surrounding air. The head formed into a porcine sphere with blunted snout and stained tusks. A purple tongue descended like a snake and caressed JJ's head.

The putrid odor of rot and death poured over Yvonne, and

she coughed, and fought back nausea. It grew in stature and leaned over JJ's still figure until it towered over Yvonne, an unholy creature made of seething, pulsating flesh. His voice echoed off the walls. "Who are you to command me?"

The crowd erupted in screams behind Yvonne. Judge Meridian slammed his gavel. "Disorder." He laughed. "I will have some disorder." Anubis began barking. People streamed from their seats toward the doors. They would not open!

JJ and the third demon moved in sync, gesturing with the right hoof, and the gavel flew out of the judge's grasp to shatter against the far wall. "I don't need your help, so sit back and let me have my moment." The bailiff looked around in fear and ran toward JJ.

JJ looked at him and flicked a hoof. Bubba stiffened as if suddenly paralyzed and then fell like a log to the floor. JJ turned to the crowd and his voice boomed over their heads. From its pulsating flesh, balls of writhing worms shot across the room and hovered near the ceiling. "If you worms do not sit down, I will let my worms eat your brains!" The crowd fell into almost silent whimpering.

Meridian snapped his fingers. Anubis ran toward the witness box and jumped. JJ ducked, but the form of the third demon remained standing above him. Anubis struck the pulsating flesh of the third demon's abdomen. The flesh dimpled, then opened into a huge maw and swallowed the dog. Worms gushed from the maw before it closed. JJ straightened, and the demon's voice returned. "That was futile, number four." He snorted, then looked down at Yvonne."I asked you a question, little missy. Who are you to command me?"

Yvonne prayed and fought for control. "Azzuzabel, I know your name, and that gives me power over you. I give you a choice. You can leave JJ and go back to your master, Jeremiah, the actual killer." She pointed to the man in the back row. "Or you can join your companions in hell. And don't take long to decide. There are no herd of pigs to go into."

JJ and the towering demon froze. "Look, let's make a deal. I give you Jeremiah Stone lock, stock, and barrel and you let me go."

"No, Azzuzabel. I command you and you will do as I say. Make your choice or I will make it for you." She opened the door to the memory of the serial killer. Yvonne felt the knife in her hand, the knife he had inadvertently left in the room. Her heart raced as she invited him into the room. As he leaned over her, she smelled his breath. She recalled plunging the knife into the creature's heart and his hot blood flowing across her. She remembered twisting the knife and shoving it deeper into the thing's heart. The shock in the man's eyes brought a smile to her eyes as she watched the life bleed out of the serial killer's eyes in her memories of that moment. She was no longer afraid. "And my name is Yvonne Brown, not little missy!"

"You will not speak to me like this!" The third demon waved his arms above his head and wind swirled around the chamber, papers dancing in the air like they were in the center of a tornado. The wind tugged at Yvonne and hurled her back against the prosecution's table. Above them, the worms burst forth from their orbs and rained down on the people.

Yvonne leaned into the wind. "Azzuzabel, spawn of hell and third demon of the council of darkness, I, Yvonne Brown, a child of God though sometimes fallen and broken but ultimately forgiven by the shed blood of Jesus Christ, command you to come out of JJ Stone."

JJ convulsed and fell back against the chair. The figure of the third demon separated itself from JJ and stepped forward. The thing leaned over Yvonne and its glowing, piggish eyes focused on her. But instead of haughtiness, the eyes betrayed fear. The gaping maw opened and cold, dead air flowed over her. A voice that did not belong in her space-time dimensions thundered in her ears. "I choose Jeremiah."

"Then begone and leave this place." Yvonne shouted.

The demon figure collapsed into a sphere of writhing worms

and shot across the suddenly still air. The man in the back row chair stood up and opened his arms.

"Come to Poppa!" He roared. The thing thudded into his chest and he jerked and shook his head as if awakening from a long nap. Worms from all over the courtroom streamed through the air and entered the man's open mouth. He swallowed them and burped. He smiled and hopped down from the bench. He moved toward Captain Stone and people parted like the Red Sea.

"Well, daddy, we tried. Looks like you're going to have a lot of explaining to do."

Stone lurched back. "Judge, bailiff, anybody stop him. Arrest him!"

Meridian motioned toward the doors. They burst open and O'Malley burst in with a dozen officers behind him. Jeremiah froze and saluted his father.

"We'll have a reunion later, Pop. I gotta go." And he blinked out of sight. Just disappeared, leaving behind a popping sound.

PART 3 — LEGIONS

"When an impure spirit comes out of a person, it goes through arid places seeking rest and does not find it.

Then it says, 'I will return to the house I left.' When it arrives, it finds the house unoccupied, swept clean and put in order.

Then it goes and takes with it seven other spirits more wicked than itself, and they go in and live there.

And the final condition of that person is worse than the first. That is how it will be with this wicked generation."

Matthew 12:43-45

CHAPTER
FIFTY-ONE

JONATHAN STEEL

Sam's shout interrupted Yvonne. "Up here. Now!" Sam said from the top of the stairs.

I bolted up from the chair, desperately trying to digest the flood of information. I had a brother! So many puzzle pieces fell into place.

Yvonne hurried across the room and I followed her as we climbed the stairs. On one side of the second floor was her bedroom, and across a short hallway was another room. I entered and blinked in the darkness. Computer monitors sat against the wall along with a table covered with various types of equipment. Sam motioned to a monitor.

"Two SUVs have been passing back and forth along the road. I lost them in the snowstorm and then thought to check out a rest stop ten miles up the road. Look." He sat down before a laptop and tapped on the keys. The image on a large, wall mounted monitor showed blowing snow and then cleared. The drone had moved out of the blowing snow into the shelter of what appeared to be a false bell tower atop the restroom at the rest stop.

"Thank God for tasteless architecture." Sam said. The image zoomed in on the SUVs. One SUV sat immediately next to the other, and the drone was looking down the narrow strip between them. The window on one SUV rolled down and, visible through the open window, was a man with ginger hair and mirrored sunglasses. "It's him. They're here!"

"Who is he?" I said.

"Who do you think?" Sam growled. The window closed, and the SUV pulled out of the rest stop. But instead of coming toward the road up the mountain, it went in the opposite direction. "Now, where are you going?" Sam whispered.

"What is it?" Yvonne asked.

"He's taking half the cars and going in the opposite direction." Sam glanced at her.

"Why?"

"He could be heading to the compound?" Sam said. "Maybe he suspects the compound belongs to Max." Sam said. "Maybe he thinks we would go there if trapped. He's flanking us."

"Wait. Max has a compound nearby?"

"On the other side of the ridge. We don't know what goes on there but it's associated with this safe house." Yvonne said.

"And now, Jeremiah is heading there to flank us?" I said.

Yvonne ignored me. "We stick to the plan, Sam. Time to go. You know what to do."

Sam nodded and keyed in a sequence into the laptop. The monitors began shutting down and the smell of ozone filled the room. "We need to get out of here. The corrosives will take out the SSDs and fry the RAM." Sam motioned toward the door. "We only keep the laptop." He slammed it closed.

"I'll get the gear." Yvonne ran out of the room and into her bedroom.

I paused in the hallway as the odor of ozone crept under the closed door of the surveillance room. In the past, I had been able to mobilize quickly and react to any given dangerous situation. But now my brain was a whirlwind of confusion. "What now?"

"You can't teleport. Too soon." Sam said.

"How did they find us?"

Sam shrugged. "I don't know. We've been here for a year. Nothing! The day after you show up, they show up."

"But I was naked. My anklet was left behind. Nothing left on me they could track." I said, and then it hit me. I slapped my head. "Raven!"

"What?" Sam said. "Whatever it is, make it fast. They'll be here in twenty minutes. I've set off some booby traps that will slow them down, but that won't stop them. What about Raven?"

"Her implants! Dr. Monarch tried to inactivate her implants. A new version of mine." My mind was reeling. "When Olivia thought her mother had died on the airplane crash, she told Josh she had a connection with her mother through her epilepsy implants. Monarch created Olivia's implant from the template for our implants. Could they have tracked me here with my implant?"

"Why now? Why not earlier?"

I sighed. "You said it earlier. My face was all over the news. They didn't know where to look or who to look for. You said they thought I was dead. They started looking for me. And if they are tracking my implant, then Monarch has been compromised. She may even be dead. She's the only one who could have given them the technical specifications of my implant."

Sam froze as Yvonne came out of her bedroom with three large backpacks. "I heard all of that, and if that is so, there's no way you can elude them."

"Not unless we inactivate my implant. Monarch tried that with Raven and erased her mind." I said.

Yvonne looked at me and grimaced. "So it can be inactivated. But we can't erase your mind. You are too important."

There it was again. A hint of something bigger, something

lurking in the background. I paced along the corridor. "We have to split up. They want me, not the two of you."

Yvonne grabbed my arm. "Oh, no! Not now. You can't go it alone. Not now. You're too close to shutting down the council. They are desperate."

Sam pushed me toward the stairs. "We'll talk on the way to the tunnel."

"Tunnel?" I said as I hurried down the stairs. Sam pushed beyond me and motioned to the hallway. "In the back. Tool shed? There's an escape tunnel underneath that leads into the mountain, an old mine. We have a vehicle hidden at the other end."

I paused and looked at the remnants of lunch on the island. I smiled. "A Faraday cage. In Monarch's lab, she put our cell phones in a Faraday cage."

Yvonne shrugged into her parka. "We don't have one lying about."

I pointed to the bread on the counter. "But do you have foil?"

Yvonne froze and then smiled. "You're kidding?" She laughed. "No, you're brilliant. A foil cap might block the implant long enough to get to the tunnel. Once we get into the tunnel and to the vehicle, maybe the mountain itself will block the signal."

Sam had put his parka on. "Well, go get the foil and hurry." He held his cell phone with an image on it. "They've reached the turnoff and are headed up the mountain."

"It will take them longer in this snow." Yvonne said. She pulled a box of aluminum foil from a drawer and pulled out a long sheet. I grabbed the sheet and began to wrap my head. It was the strangest thing I had ever done. I put as much of the foil around my head from the forehead up and from the crown down to the nape of my neck. Sam handed me a knit cap.

"Put that over it to hold it tight. We got to go."

"If they are headed for the compound, we have to warn Max." I said.

Yvonne paused and her eyes filled with mirth. "You really think Max needs help? She's way ahead of them. And us."

I pulled the knit cap over my head and realized the downside was I could hardly hear. After I put on my parka, Yvonne and Sam led the way out the back door and across the back porch. The snow was so heavy I couldn't see over five feet before me.

We went down the same path I had followed last night. Sam turned off the path to the right and up a short set of stone stairs to a small storage shed. He slid the door open, and we hurried inside. The shed was empty except for a snowmobile. Sam started up the snowmobile and drove it backwards through another sliding door and onto another pathway. He turned the snowmobile around and tapped on the control panel. He got off the snowmobile, and it started down the path on its own.

"One of our diversions. It will follow markers on the path down the mountain. They'll go after it for a while." He said.

"Like the boat at your house." I said.

He nodded and motioned us to the side of the shed. He flipped a light switch on the wall and a motor ground as a door in the floor opened upward. Beneath the door yawned a dark emptiness with a ladder visible at the nearest edge.

"Follow me." Yvonne started down the ladder, and I followed her into a freezing rocky tunnel. About ten feet down, we reached a level floor to the chamber. Sam followed behind us and flipped another switch on the ladder. The door closed above us and blinding darkness surrounded us.

Yvonne fired up her flashlight. "You closed the door?"

"Left the back door open. Turning off that switch will kill the door motor. It will take an hour to cut through that floor. Let's move." Sam turned on his flashlight and headed off down the tunnel.

Yvonne put a hand on my chest. "You can remove your foil hat now."

"I don't know." I said. "I may have created a new trend in men's fashion." Gratefully, I pulled the knit cap from over the foil. I peeled the sweaty foil from my wet head and tossed it into the darkness.

We moved in silence through the dusty, frigid air, our breath streaming out in clouds. It took about twenty minutes before the tunnel began a gradual upward climb. Old timbers appeared in the shadowy darkness and beneath the rubble and dirt, mine train tracks emerged.

We reached the end of the tunnel and it opened into a larger chamber. Underneath a tarp sat a vehicle. Sam removed the tarp, revealing an old truck. Yvonne went past the truck to what appeared to be a garage door. She found a panel beside the door and activated a small monitor. She studied the image.

"Sam, got any signal from the drones yet?" She said as the pale light illuminated her face.

"Not yet. We are on the other side of the ridge from the house. I'm sure the computers are fried by now." He pulled out his cell phone. "I sent one drone to the driveway outside this door. I should get a signal from it on my phone." Sam studied his cell phone. "Storm is still raging, which gives us some cover. Got the drone signal, but I can't see much. Looks like it is about one hundred yards down the lumber road. No hostiles so far from that direction."

"Where do we go from here?" I asked.

"There's a lumber road that goes back down the ridge into the valley. Problem is, the road is barely passible, and it leads deeper into the mountains, away from the town. If they come after us, we could get stranded." Yvonne said as she studied the monitor by the door. "It's clear right outside the door." She glanced at me over her shoulder. "If we wait a few more hours, Alphus can teleport you away."

"What about you and Sam?"

"You said it, JJ." Sam leaned up against the truck. "They're after you. Not us."

"And if I teleport, they'll know I'm not with you anymore." I nodded. "I know we don't want to separate. But it's the best plan we got. Hopefully, they'll leave you alone."

Sam tapped on his cell phone. "Therefore, my friend, it is time to seal the tunnel." A muffled explosion echoed down the tunnel behind us. The ground shook. "Sealed the tunnel at the other end."

"Do they know about this exit?"

Yvonne turned away from the monitor and rubbed her hands together for warmth. "Hope not. Can't be sure."

"There is the other tunnel." Sam said.

Yvonne froze. "That may be why they're going to the compound."

"There is another tunnel?" I asked.

"Leads down to the compound. Left over from World War II. We don't even know if its passible. They probably think it could be an escape route leading to the compound from the house."

"Then go. Now." I said. "Take the truck and get out of here. I'll stay behind. They'll think I'm with you for now and the longer we wait, the sooner they will find us. If you're gone, they won't bother with the tunnels. I can stay here until Alphus can teleport me and we can rendezvous."

Yvonne put a chilly hand on mine. "Oh, JJ, I don't want to leave you."

"He's right, Yvonne." Sam said. "Of course, there is another option."

I looked at Sam. "What?"

Sam lifted the edge of a tarp on the back of the truck. He took out a black equipment case and set it on the ground. He unlatched the locks and lifted the lid. Inside was a metal device with wires and a dial.

"No, Sam." Yvonne said. "I know what you're thinking and we can't take the chance."

"What is this?" I asked.

"An EMP generator. Electromagnetic pulse. Sends out an EMP for about one mile. Fries all electronic equipment. Shuts down drones and surveillance equipment and erases all SSDs. I was supposed to move it to the house so we could use it in case of an attack, but I never saw the need."

"If we use this, it will shut down the hostile's digital equipment? That would buy us some time." I patted the truck. "That's why you have an old truck. No digital equipment."

"Nope. Just a carburetor and manifold. But there is a problem." Sam looked at me. He tapped my forehead. "Your implant. It's digital. The EMP might fry it."

"And kill JJ in the process." Yvonne said. "We cannot use it, Sam."

"Wait!" I was thinking furiously. "If it neutralizes my implant, that might bring back my memories."

"Or erase your mind." Yvonne stepped in front of me. She took my face in her and turned my gaze toward hers. "We can't take that chance."

I looked over her shoulder at Sam. "You said it has a radius of a mile? This road outside the door, how far away does it lead?"

"About five miles down to the only road into the valley." Sam said.

"Then let's stick to the plan. I stay here in the tunnels until Alphus can relocate me. You take the truck down the road and once they start following you, wait until you've passed at least a mile from here and use the EMP. That gives you an edge, a chance to get away." I looked back at Yvonne. "It's a good plan, Yvonne. Alphus can take me somewhere far enough away where they can't possibly get to me in time."

"Where?"

"Monarch's lab in London. Her kids came back to the states for school but she stayed behind to clear up some things. Jeremiah must have gotten the implant information from her, so she is in danger. She may be dead. I have to know. And, she has a Faraday cage in her lab. I can have Alphus teleport me into the cage until I can find out what is happening. That will keep them from tracking me." I stepped back and motioned to the truck. "Now go. While you can. Open the door and start down the road."

Sam put a hand on my shoulder. "Son, I'm not a hundred percent sure the radius is only a mile. And if they are moving in on Max's compound, it may neutralize her defenses."

"Let's hope the ridge protects Max's compound. It's the only option we have and I'm willing to take the risk it might affect me." I looked back down the tunnel. "I can hide in the other tunnel."

Sam nodded. "A hundred feet back down the tunnel is the side tunnel leading to the compound. Follow it about a hundred yards and there is a cave that was converted into a sort of office." Sam reached down into the truck and pulled out another case. "C4 and detonators. Set two of the bricks at the opening of that tunnel and when you get to the office, detonate them. That will seal you into the tunnel."

"Wait? What if they come up from the compound through the tunnel, assuming it's passable? JJ will be trapped!" Yvonne said.

"I'll have Alphus, Yvonne. He can get me out of there before they come up the tunnel."

Yvonne looked at me and tears ran down her cheeks. "Where is Alphus now? He can only intervene if God allows him."

"Yvonne, I have faith that God is watching over us. There are no coincidences, right? Cephas was my mentor. I loved the man like the father I never really had. He was right, and I must have faith that God will take care of all of us." I pulled her to me and hugged her. She gently pushed away and pointed to my backpack with the laptop.

"When you teleport, that will be left behind. We can't let them get it. All three backpacks have laptops and hard drives." She said. "The EMP will erase ours. That's not a problem as I have backups to the backups in the cloud. But you will be immune to the EMP."

"Why are you telling me this?"

"You'll have to use one of the C4 bricks to destroy the back-pack right as you teleport. It will be tricky." She said.

I pulled off the backpack. "Then take it with you."

"I can't." Yvonne looked away and then glanced at Sam. He nodded. "JJ, you haven't heard everything yet. On the laptop there is a video interview with your father filmed right after the trial. It's imperative you know the rest of the story. You have an hour or so before you can safely teleport. Go to that office. Seal the compound end of the tunnel. That will buy you time. Watch the interview. You have to. If you don't, you'll never understand why what is happening now is happening." She put a hand on my chest. "Go. Now. Time is wasting for us to get away."

I sniffed and hugged her one last time. "This video will give me answers?"

"Yes." She said.

Sam grabbed me by the shoulders and pulled me into a bear hug. "We'll be in touch, son. We've been in worse scrapes before. God be with you. Now go down the tunnel and take care."

I pulled away from Sam and, casting one last look at Yvonne Brown, ran down the tunnel into darkness.

CHAPTER
FIFTY-TWO

JONATHAN STEEL

I found the side tunnel and put the explosives at the entrance. Further down the tunnel, around a sharp bend, I found the "office" Sam had spoken of. I was far enough away from the main tunnel now. I pressed the button on the detonator and heard the distant explosions. It was closer than the first explosion and dirt showered down from the roof of the "office". A tunnel leading out of the office was dark and cold. I walked a few dozen yards down the tunnel. It was completely blocked by a cave in. No need to use the explosives. I would save all the C4 for the laptop. Both ends of the tunnel on either side of the office were sealed. I was trapped. If Alphus didn't come for me, I would suffocate.

The walls of the "office" were carved from the mountain. Sitting against one wall were two tables covered with old, dusty folders. An old analog computer monitor sat beside an old computer tower. Placing the flashlight on the computer tower gave me enough light to see. I brushed dirt off a creaky desk chair and set up the laptop on the table. It only took a few minutes to find the folder labeled "videos". There were so many files. I was tempted to open all of them. All my answers were right here at my fingertips, but I had only a few hours before Alphus would take me away.

"Lord, I know you've got a plan. I trust you will send Alphus to me when it is time. Watch over Sam and Yvonne, your good and faithful servants." My words echoed gently in the room.

"Okay, so we find the video of the interview." It took some time, but I found a video icon labeled "Post trial interview Captain Stone". That would be the one Yvonne wanted me to see. I took a deep breath and opened the file. The video played.

The first image showed Yvonne and Sam sitting at a table. They were both younger. Yvonne sat before a keyboard. Sam nodded and stood up.

"I told you I knew how to edit videos." Sam said. "One of my hobbies. I'll let you take it from here." He moved out of the frame.

"JJ, I've put together several videos. Some are directly from your father. Others were from a hidden camera we discovered in Meridian's office. Sam helped me put them together in as close to a chronological order as possible. If you are seeing this without us present, then something has happened to me and to Sam. Be prepared. What you are about to learn will shock you." Yvonne frowned. "It shocked us. This is Video #1."

The image faded into another video. The point of view was from above and directed down toward the front of a large wooden desk.

———

Meridian's Office

Yvonne looked around Judge Meridian's office at his many framed certificates and photos with famous politicians. The man was an up-and-coming well-known judge who had been consulted on many cases outside his jurisdiction. He had influence. He also had a demon, she had concluded. She was still shaking from the trial debacle. Sam stood in the office's corner, looking out the window. The door opened and Judge Meridian and Captain Stone came in.

"You'll be glad to know that every person in that courtroom is being taken to a holding cell. Including Stapleton." Meridian said as he sat behind his desk. "They will be sworn to secrecy and sign an agreement that if they ever reveal what happened in that courtroom, they will go to jail for the rest of their lives."

"That's pretty harsh." Yvonne said.

Meridian steepled his hands as he leaned back in his plush chair. "It was that, or I call in a cadre of demons and erase their memories."

Sam turned. "Which one are you?"

"Number four." Meridian said. "Well, sometimes. He moves around among a dozen of us. How do you think I got where I am today?" Meridian gestured to the photos around the room. In each, Meridian's smiling face was captured with those of senators, representatives, and even presidents. "Now JJ is safely tucked away in a holding cell. My bailiff, who is not a member of my little legion, by the way, is watching over him while we conclude this trial. We have taken the jury into seclusion, and they will render the verdict that I determine. Question is, what do we do now?" Meridian turned to the Captain. "Want to tell them your story, Stone?"

Stone sat in a chair beneath the window and Sam stepped away from him. "Yeah, Captain, there seems to be a lot here we don't even begin to understand."

Stone looked at Meridian. "I need you to leave the room."

Meridian laughed "Oh no, I won't be doing that. I finally have you where I want you. The information you are going to share is vital to members of the Council of Darkness that were not privy to thirteen's plans."

Yvonne's mind was reeling. "Four? Thirteen? How many of them are you?"

"Twelve on the council." Stone said. "One outlier who is the most powerful of them all. That's why Satan excluded him from the council. He's uncontrollable."

A muscle twitched beneath Meridian's eye. "And you made a deal with him, Stone. I want to hear all of it."

"First, release my son to a neutral party. I don't want him anywhere near this courthouse or your minions." Stone said.

Yvonne glanced at Sam. "Kevin, the youth pastor. He'd be safe with Kevin. He's a Christian."

Meridian sniffed. "I don't like that option, but I will agree." He picked up his phone and spoke to the bailiff. He nodded and hung up. "Kevin is in a holding room. The bailiff will take JJ to him when you're done."

Yvonne held up her cell phone. "I'd like to confirm that."

"Sure." Meridian said.

Yvonne called Kevin and put the phone on speaker. "Hello?" He said.

"Kevin, are you okay?"

"After what I just saw, I'm shaking in my boots, but God is good. They told me they will bring JJ to me." He said.

"Take him to your church. Captain Stone will be by later to pick him up." Yvonne said.

"So, it's over?" Kevin asked.

"I think it's just beginning." Yvonne said and she hung up and looked at Captain. "Satisfied?"

He nodded and looked at Meridian. "Second, I will tell Ms. Brown and Captain O'Malley, but I will not tell you. You will leave this room now."

Meridian laughed. "And why would I do that?"

The Captain looked at Yvonne with those intense, turquoise eyes. "We both know that phenomenon that occur from extra-dimensional sources cannot be adequately retained by most people's minds. Those of us accustomed to dealing with these metaphysical phenomena have a better retention. Most of those people in the courtroom will forget in time. Now, because Ms. Brown knows your name, she will use it if you do not agree to my terms. I'm giving you one chance or we speak your name."

Yvonne tensed. She had been so excited to get the text from Max. She made a mental note to have Max tell her Four's name. "That's right." She said confidently.

Meridian sat forward. "I don't like it, Stone."

Stone nodded. "I'll make you a deal. You can have me. I will be one of your hosts from now on. I'll join your legion. You can take my soul in exchange for my son's. But only Yvonne and Sam will know the whole story."

"Now that's a deal I can't resist." Meridian stood up and nodded. "Once number four gets a hold of your soul, you'll tell me everything, anyway. I think I'm coming out on the good end of this deal."

Meridian glanced once at his photographs. "Just remember who you're dealing with, Stone. The fourth demon's Legion is very powerful." He left the office. Stone sat in the judge's chair and motioned to two chairs in front of the desk. Yvonne and Sam sat down.

"The reason I am telling the two of you my story is because what happened today changes everything for me." He said.

"I don't care where you send your soul." Sam said. "JJ is screwed up because of you."

"You are absolutely right." Stone said. "I'll start with JJ's birth. Christine went into labor in Mexico. JJ was born without any problems. Except the thirteenth demon was there. I learned this, well, from a reliable source. This happened that night."

———

Night had fallen, and the courtyard was lit with many torches by the time Robert Ketrick arrived at the museum hacienda. Servants were bustling around the courtyard and up and down the stairs to the second-floor entrance of the house. Bobby hurried into the main courtyard. The air was hot and muggy and smelled of antiseptic and sweat. A scream echoed down from the second floor. Bobby stopped a short woman hurrying by with a pan of water.

"Maria, what is happening?"

Maria's eyes were wide with fear. "It is the mistress of the house. She is having the baby."

Bobby watched her hurry away and looked up at the balcony. The Captain stood there, minus his hat. His shirt was soaked with sweat. "Bobby! Good, you're back. Watch for Dr. Santiago. I was hoping we could get back to the States, but Christine is in labor."

Another scream cut through the air, and Bobby flinched.

"Am I interrupting something?"

Bobby turned, and the pale man covered with tattoos stood in the open archway leading into the courtyard. "No. My teacher is having her baby. She may be in trouble."

Bobby watched the man's face flush with crimson. For a second, a smile played across his lips. Bobby studied the man's red eyes and felt a shiver course over him. For a second, he felt a sense of dread at the man's presence.

"Bobby, who is this gentleman?" The Captain was suddenly behind him. Bobby whirled. The Captain held a bloody blanket to his chest. The head of a baby lolled against his bloody chest.

"Is that your baby?" Bobby asked.

The Captain looked down at the child and blinked. "Yes."

Bobby leaned forward and watched the newborn child squirm in his father's grasp. For a fleeting second, the baby's eyes flew open, and the startling color of turquoise gleamed in the torchlight. The Captain looked over Bobby's shoulder.

"I asked you who that man was. He's not Doctor Santiago."

"Just someone I met at the dig."

The tattooed man smiled and exposed his white teeth and red gums. "My name is Lucas."

The Captain was silent for a moment, and his greenish- blue eyes *stayed riveted on the tattooed man. "I don't want you to have anything to do with him, Bobby."*

Bobby nodded. "Of course, Captain. I'll show him out." Above them, another scream pierced the night. The Captain grabbed Bobby's arm and turned him back. He thrust the baby into his arms.

"Here. Hold him until Consuela comes for him. My wife needs me."

The Captain hurried away and disappeared up the stairs.

"What a beautiful child." Lucas smiled.

"I think you need to go," Bobby said. He glanced at the squirming baby in his arms.

"I will go. In a moment. But first, I must tell you more about the child you hold in your hands." Lucas leaned forward, and a finger strayed toward the baby. He paused just before touching the baby's forehead. "Your destiny and his are connected. But it would seem that destiny may have given you an unprecedented opportunity." Lucas walked across the courtyard to the fountain. "Come. Follow me."

Bobby glanced at the baby and hurried after the man. "What are you talking about?"

Lucas sat on the edge of the fountain. "Pick the baby up by the leg."

Bobby frowned. "Why?"

"Trust me."

Bobby blinked as something swelled within him, a heat that burned its way to his fingertips. He reached down and took the baby's right leg in his hand and gently lifted the baby into the air. The baby's blanket fluttered to the ground.

"Good. Now lift him up in the air." Lucas's voice grew hoarse.

Bobby lifted the naked baby until his face was level with his, his arms and left leg dangling. The baby ceased his squirming, and for a second, his eyes flickered open as if to study Bobby.

"Now, drop him in the water."

Bobby looked at him. "In the fountain?"

"Yes. One quick release, and your future will be secure. Just like you dropped the scorpion."

Bobby blinked. That morning, he had dropped a scorpion on

Consuela, the girl he hated so much. He could still remember her screams. "How did you know?"

Lucas stood drew very close, and his eyes gleamed in the scant light. "I know everything about you, Robert. It is a matter of record that your mother committed suicide. But the truth is, you were playing with the gun and it accidentally went off and she died. You wanted the gun to kill your father. He's the one who deserved to die, right?"

Bobby trembled, and his grip weakened on the baby's leg. "No one knows that."

"I told you I have had an eye on you for some time. And now, if you listen carefully to my advice, I will complete your training."

Bobby felt the heat intensify and felt his mind blur. An inexorable force seized his mind, and he lifted the baby higher as he reached over the edge of the fountain.

"Good. Now, just relax your grip. One simple movement, and your adversary is gone. And all you have to do is blame it on Consuela."

"Son of the devil! What are you doing?" Bobby whirled, and Consuela appeared out of the darkness. Huge, red welts covered her face from the scorpion stings. She snared the baby from Bobby's grasp and pulled him to her chest.

The Captain appeared on the upper level. "What is happening?"

Consuela retrieved the blanket and wrapped it around the baby. "Bobby was going to drown the baby."

The Captain glared down at Bobby. "Is this true?"

"I don't know, sir. I just lost my mind, I guess." Bobby fumbled for words. He watched the man's face redden with anger.

The Captain glanced at Lucas. "Take your friend and get off my property. Now."

"But sir!"

"Now. Pack up your things, and have your friend drop you off at the airport. You can catch the first flight out in the morning. I don't want you around my son another moment." He motioned to Consuela, and she hurried up the stairs.

"You have failed your first test, Bobby," Lucas whispered.

Bobby flinched when he heard the name. He studied the man's features hidden in shadows. "What have you done to me?"

"I have done nothing. You have done this to yourself. Every choice you have ever made has led to this moment. Come. I'll take you to the airport. When you get home, you can begin the completion of this plan. Soon you will be eighteen, and you can finish the business you started with your father. And then, you will inherit his company and his riches."

Bobby looked at the hacienda he had once called home. Down that hallway was the woman who had been the closest thing he had to a mother. "What about the baby?"

Lucas shrugged. "He will try to stop you some day. And when that day comes, you must kill him."

———

"When I went back upstairs, Christine was having more contractions. We didn't know it, but there was a second child." He said.

"How could you not know that?" Yvonne asked.

"Dr. Santiago lied to us. He manipulated us the entire time." The Captain said. "Right before the second child was born, Christine started bleeding. Gushing blood! The midwife said she had a placental separation. The second child was born and Christine was bleeding to death. We called for an ambulance. It was all chaos and confusion." The Captain paused as emotion took away his voice. He paused and composed himself.

"In the aftermath, Christine barely survived. The second boy did not survive. On that day, I was told JJ had a fraternal twin who died because of the placental separation." The Captain wiped tears from his cheeks angrily. "I never told Christine. Why would she have to know something like that?"

"You didn't tell her she had two children and one of them died?" Yvonne said. "How could you?"

The Captain glared at her. "You don't know what we went

through to have children. It would have broken her to know. I did not know the child really survived until today." The Captain looked back at his Meerschaum pipe in his hand.

"Two faces on my pipe and two children in this world. I should have known. One a demon and one an angel." He sighed. "There were forces involved in the pregnancy. People who owed their allegiance to the Council of Darkness." He whispered. "It was how we got pregnant. I can only conclude that Jeremiah was not dead, and they took him for their own purposes. They will want JJ."

"Why?"

The Captain looked over at Yvonne. "JJ is special. Very special. He has certain traits that the Council would like to get its hand on. That is why he has to disappear. I have to make it as if he no longer exists. And then, they will go after his brother instead."

The Captain nodded and massaged his chin. "Yes! From now on, I have to be hands on with my son. I must teach him how to protect himself, how to hide himself, for there are forces now activated that could kill him."

The Captain paused and wiped at his eyes. "Or, worse. Dissect him. I'm not a religious man, but I think JJ is safer with his youth pastor than with me for the short term. But as soon as I can wrap my head around these recent events, I will start training him."

"Training him in what?" Yvonne asked.

"Self-defense. Using a gun. Hiding in plain sight. The forces that led to my wife's death are now targeting him. And you. You will have to disappear after you hear what I have to say. I will make sure the court documents are sealed. No one must ever know what happened in that courtroom. Most of the random people in the courtroom can be controlled. I will make sure the government monitors them for any leaks and move accordingly to stop them." Stone said.

"You have that kind of power?" Sam said.

"I have those kind of resources, Captain O'Malley. Once you hear my story, you won't be able to go into hiding quickly enough."

———

The video faded into an image of Yvonne again. "That was the first part of your father's story. We found out Meridian had a hidden camera to record any conversations in his office. That is where we got this video. Now, if you'll look for the video labeled, 'The Captain's Story', you can hear the rest of what your father had to say."

CHAPTER
FIFTY-THREE

JONATHAN STEEL

I sat in the frigid air of the cave, my mind reeling from what I had just heard. I stared at the last frame of the video. Like my father, I had relived that flashback of Robert Ketrick's in the lake house on our first encounter.

Was my father telling me the truth? I started looking at the other video files on the laptop.

"It is time to take you." A voice said from the shadows in the cave's corner. I stood up as Alphus walked into the meager cone of light from my flashlight.

"What is happening to Sam and Yvonne?"

"I do not know." Alphus said. "But I sense something."

Another tremor shook the walls, and dirt fell on the table and the laptop. The screen wavered and flickered. I felt the first waves of something tickling at the base of my skull.

"The EMP?" I said through numb lips.

"Yes." Alphus said. "I am sorry. I cannot stop it."

I glanced once at the video file labeled "The Captain's Story" and then the pulse hit me like a ton of bricks. The laptop screen filled with gibberish. I wish I had kept the foil cap. But I doubted it would have prevented what was coming.

My head exploded, and I fell to the ground, screaming in agony. It felt like rivers of lava pouring through my brain. Lights exploded in my vision! Sounds warbled in my ears. Nausea hit me hard, and I emptied my stomach. Awful odors assailed my senses. I screamed, and I screamed until my throat was raw. My heart pounded and slowed until all was a whirlpool of pain. Now the pain was slowing, throbbing in my head until all stopped. All stopped. My heart quit beating.

I floated upward toward the ceiling of the tunnel. I looked down at my body lying on the cold ground. Where was Alphus? Something pulled me upwards, and I moved through the rock like it was nothing more than dense fog. I was in the air now with snow swirling all about me. As I ascended, I saw men huddled around their motionless vehicles. The EMP had rendered their drones and weapons useless. As I floated higher, I saw the old truck tearing over a ridge, its engine unfazed by the EMP. Even higher, and I glimpsed the compound on the other side of the ridge. SUVs surrounded the entrance and figures moved about in a military stance. The compound was under attack!

The snow whirled around me, enclosing me in a dense, frigid cocoon, and I hurtled down a long, dark corridor toward a light. I burst into bright sunlight with colors I had never experienced. Warmth melted the snow, and I landed gently on iridescent grass. I smelled cotton candy and vanilla and fragrances I did not know existed. A shadow passed over me and I looked up into the face of a woman with long, dark hair and luminous eyes.

"April?" April Pierce smiled at me and motioned for someone. Another woman appeared and her warm face and ginger hair was lit by a fringe of light. She smiled and, for a moment I thought it might be my mother. I looked into the eyes of someone else.

"Claire?"

April and Claire stepped back, and my mother appeared. She smiled at me, and her eyes glowed with life and love. She held out her hands but not in a welcoming gesture, but as if to stop me from coming closer.

"My dear, you are undone but not done." She said softly and the sound of her voice warmed my heart. Tears trickled down my cheek. "There is more ahead for you. This is only the beginning."

"What are you telling me?" I tried to stand up and as I did two white membranes wrapped around me shutting off my view of this place. I turned and looked into the eyes of Alphus. "No! I want to see more!"

Alphus shook his head. "It is not your time and if you see more you will want to stay. There is much work to be done."

I glanced over my shoulder and through a gap between his 'wings' I saw the Man join the women. The last time I had seen him was in ancient Jerusalem. His wounds remained. His gaze turned to me and those eyes, eyes more beautiful than any green or blue or turquoise eyes would ever be. He nodded gently and I knew who He was.

He was my Savior. He was the God man who had become flesh and had endured all that I counted as painful and more. He was the Incarnation of God, love made flesh, Truth walking and talking, eternal, unending, and always loving. He was the Son who had shrugged off the power of his godhood to be born as a helpless baby, who lived a normal life, preached and healed and faced a betrayal far greater than I or any man could ever comprehend. And He had died. Death came to God, who was never to die.

God tasted mortality and said, "Enough!" He filled his Son with a new life, an everlasting life, a life eternal and unending, and He burst forth from the grave to destroy and conquer death forever. All of this I saw in one glimpse of the Son of God risen from the dead. This is what Theo saw when he chose to remain in Jerusalem. This was my Savior, my Lord.

We were moving away now and falling, tumbling still wrapped in white and snow returned and cold and pain. The wings unfolded and I slid back into my body. And with it the pain and the sudden lurching of my heart as it beat again. I rolled onto my back and tried to think, to know, to see, to feel who I was. The otherworldly experience was being swallowed by returning memories. It was like watching an old flickering movie with stuttering sound and scratches on the images. I saw bits and pieces of my life since the beach. But the images were sideways and backwards and reverse negative and I blinked and still I saw them.

"Help me!" I whispered. "God help me!"

Alphus appeared over me and looked to his left. "Yes, sir." He touched a finger to my forehead and pulled it back slowly. I screamed some more as the thing came out of my head. It was long and black like a torn spiderweb made of metal. The strands popped and screeched as they slid through the skin of my forehead until Alphus held the dangling strands of my implant above my head. He tossed it aside and knelt over me.

"I was given permission to remove your implant. But I have no idea what will happen now."

There was one memory that came early after my amnesia. The memory had been without context, a replaying of the moment I had given my life to the Son of God I had just seen. The story of my trial had no meaning to me, but now I began to feel it, see it. I was at that table in the courtroom. I was in the witness stand when the third demon took my mind, entering me like some slimy parasite, swallowing my soul and smothering me with its evil! I felt it all. I recalled it all, and I gasped in agony.

I had heard the words of my father in the video. But now, what happened after came thundering into my reality. I remembered it. I remembered it all.

———

The bailiff led me down the hallway to my holding cell. He locked me in and disappeared. My head ached with pain from the presence of the third demon. Before the demon had left me in a state of forgetfulness. The episodes in which he had used me to perform his evil deeds were lost to me. But this time, I recalled every moment of what just happened in the courtroom.

I had a brother? An evil creature who had killed our mother? My anger boiled and fury took me. I turned and pounded my hand against the cinderblock wall of the cell. I welcomed the pain. It helped me clear my mind. I would find my brother and I would kill him! If I was to face a murder trail it would be for a good reason.

"Son?"

I whirled. My father stood outside the cell door. The bailiff accompanied him and unlocked the door. He had a pile of clothing and a bag of my personal belongings.

"The judge has dismissed your case. Get out of those prison clothes. We're leaving."

I grabbed the jeans and the tank top from the bailiff and stripped down to my underwear. My father glared at the bailiff. "You were supposed to take him to his youth pastor."

"The Judge gave me other instructions when he left his office." The bailiff said.

"Never trust a demon." My father said.

"When were you going to tell me?" I growled.

"I did not know. Honestly, son."

I pulled my clothes on and took my possession bag and removed my watch, my socks, my sandals, my wallet and my car keys. They were all crusted with rust colored particles. It was only then I noticed the hard, dry clotted blood soaked into my clothes. I pulled my tank top away from my chest. "This is her blood, Dad! Hers! He killed her and yet you say you never knew he existed?"

My father motioned down the hall. "Not here. I've asked Kevin to meet us outside. I'll tell you more as we walk."

I followed my father down the hallway. But instead of taking me out the main entrance, he motioned to a service exit. "We're keeping a low profile. Your brother is very dangerous. Someone was supposed to have come and gotten you."

"Who?"

"Kevin."

"What is going on?" I stopped at the exit door. "Tell me now."

"We did not know your mother was having twins. Dr. Santiago hid that fact from us. You were born and there were no problems. Then your mother started having more pains and your brother was born. But he stopped breathing. Dr. Santiago took the body, and I never told your mother. As far as she knew, you were her only child. She almost died from bleeding, JJ. I never thought that your brother was alive."

"Who was Dr. Santiago?"

Something dark and foreboding crossed my father's turquoise eyes. "I never saw him again. I tried to track him down. He just disappeared. Now we know why. The demons orchestrated the entire incident."

"What?"

My father wiped his face and sighed. "We couldn't get pregnant. Your mother underwent embryo implantation. Two of them. Santiago always told us only one embryo survived. Now we know he lied."

The door opened suddenly, and a hand grabbed my arm and jerked me out into the shadows of an alleyway. The door slammed shut on my father.

"Listening to father's lies?" I looked into eyes that were turquoise and fiery. I looked at the ginger hair, the regal face. Dark circles rimmed my brother's eyes.

"You!" I hurtled at him, driving him back against the brick wall. He laughed as I pounded his head against the wall. He head butted me and I fell back onto the ground.

I was dizzy for a moment and Jeremiah leaned over me. He drew back his fist and pounded my face. Over and over until I felt the blood run down my throat. I had to fight back. This was the thing that had killed my mother!

I kicked his feet from under him and he fell on top of me, knocking the breath out of both of us. I crawled from underneath him, gasping for breath, and kicked him in the face for good measure. He grabbed my ankle and pulled me back toward him.

"I'm sick and tired." He gasped. "Of hiding because of you!"

I rolled over onto my back and tried to kick him in the face again. He dodged and caught my free foot and pulled himself on top of my legs. Blood dripped from his nose and his eyes were bloodshot. "Where do you think you're going to go?" He said.

"Wherever I want after I kill you!" I finally had enough breath to scream.

Jeremiah crawled up my body, pushing me underneath him until his face was above mine. "I knew you had it in you. It took a while to get up the courage. I had help from our demon. Yes, the one we shared." His eyes were bright with insanity. "She abandoned me and kept you! And after I take care of you, I will go after Father!"

"Go ahead." I spit in his face. "You'll have to wait in line for him." I shoved my knee into his groin, and he groaned and rolled away. Stumbling to my feet, I wiped blood from my face. Jeremiah rolled in pain on the pavement. One kick and I could cave his face in!

"JJ! Stop!"

I froze with my foot drawn back and glanced up at Kevin hurrying toward me.

"What are you doing here? Go away. I have to finish this."

Jeremiah gagged and then giggled and slid up against a wall. "Don't listen to him! Go ahead. Pound my head in! Slam my skull against the brick wall! Finish what you started."

"JJ, don't let his evil taint you any longer. That's not your brother talking. That is an evil spirit." Kevin said.

I looked at Jeremiah, my heart pounding. I wanted this. I wanted to end this creature who had taken my mother from me. "Kevin, go away!"

Kevin drew closer, and for a moment, I saw fear in Jeremiah's eyes. I blinked. What? Why was he afraid of Kevin?

"JJ, Yvonne called me. She asked me to come get you and take you

to my church. Your father wanted me to talk to you about your spiritual condition."

I froze and shook my head. "My father did that?"

"Don't listen to him, JJ." Jeremiah said.

"Shut up, you spawn of hell." Kevin said in a thundering voice. "Or I will send you back into a herd of pigs."

Jeremiah scooted away from Kevin. He licked his lips, and I saw him for what he was. A meat puppet. A pawn in the hands of an evil power that had destroyed my mother and ruined my life. I relaxed my clenched fists and lowered my foot. He slid away from Kevin, keeping his back against the wall.

I knelt in a pool of blood. Our blood. My head pounded and painful spasms racked my body. The pain cleared, and the fury and the violence slowly faded. Kevin squatted before me. He glanced once more at Jeremiah, slowly moving down the alleyway. The righteous anger gleaming in Kevin's eyes should have made the third demon tremble. Then he turned those eyes on me and they were filled with a brotherly, divine love as deep as the sea.

"Hey, man, I've come to get you. You need to come on home. Your friends and family love you. It's time to walk away from all of this. Would you like for me to help you?"

Down the alley Jeremiah stood up and glanced once over his shoulder and the look of utter defeat in his face almost made me want to cheer. But that look was a mirror of what I had been for the past few months. I was no better off than my brother. I had given in to the evil spirit within me. I did not want to be my brother any longer. I turned my gaze back to Kevin. He held hope in his hands. "I don't want to go on like this. Will you help me?"

"I promise." Kevin said.

MAX'S COMPOUND

Faye sighed in frustration. She was making little progress. Victoria knew the meaning of some words and some phrases. It was like she had the jigsaw puzzle pieces laid out on the table before her, but some were turned with the picture down and Victoria didn't know how to turn them over. She didn't know they had a side with information on it! Victoria's mind was a strange blend of lack of basic knowledge and too much knowledge that she did not know how to collate. What Faye needed was something that bound all of that together and pulled it into a cohesive hold.

To her credit, Victoria was not angry or frustrated, which was unusual. But she didn't know enough about her confused condition to have the context in which to be angry. Victoria sat alone at her small table, drawing again. If there was one thing she liked to do, it was to draw. But always abstract interwoven multicolored lines. Lucille had not changed. She would help Faye with certain cognitive tasks and tests, but never really seemed engaged with Victoria when Faye was with them.

Faye sat at Lucille's desk. Lucille had a large screen monitor showing a record of Victoria's results. "Lucille, thank you for helping. I know this is hard for you."

Lucille nodded, but remained silent as her gaze turned to the monitor. Faye cleared her throat.

"Maybe if I knew more about Victoria's past? For instance, I know she was an assassin, which is why you wanted to show her guns and knives."

Lucille crossed her arms. "Okay, if she had recognized them, they would have shown Victoria that she had violence in her past."

"And it wouldn't be a far step from that to infer she might be a killer." Faye said. "You haven't used her name, Raven."

"Her pseudonym. Her real name is Victoria Poe." Lucille said, uncrossing her arms. "We haven't said 'Raven' around her yet."

Faye nodded. "Quote the raven, 'nevermore'. Got it. But I get the impression there is something from deep in her past long before she became," Faye paused, "what she became. Something perhaps from her childhood that might trigger a response."

"Trust me. Her childhood was a horror show." Lucille said.

Faye sat back. A horrible childhood, life as an assassin, and her handler routinely erased her memory using brain implants from Dr. Monarch. Seemed like her entire life was a horror show. Maybe it was best Victoria never recovered those memories. But Max had been insistent they had to find out about those off the book jobs. If it weren't to help Jonathan Steel, she would walk away from Victoria and leave her to a new life. But her heart broke every time she looked at her. She saw her sister in Victoria's unfocused gaze and innocent smile. No, no matter what, Faye could never walk away from someone who need her help.

Lucille reached for her keyboard and opened a video feed on the screen. "There's a storm coming over the peaks, and I'd like to keep watch on the weather." She said. The video feed showed the driveway in front of the compound. Snow fell lightly in the gray light of afternoon.

Faye stood up and wandered over to a set of tables against the far wall. The basement of the chalet had only one set of windows along the western wall set high up. Through them she could see the far mountains if she stood in a certain spot. Otherwise, the walls were plain dull gray. In the northwestern corner a double set of doors led into the wine cellar. Right now, she longed for a drink or two of that wine. She was sure it was expensive and exquisite.

Faye paused before the rolling cart and pulled back the cover. She studied the various knives and pistols. Should she use them? Would they nudge some of Raven's memories up from the well assuming those memories remained? And if these were so useful and Max did not want to remind Victoria of her job as an assassin, why use them at all? Because Max was getting desperate.

For a moment she thought of Jason. Where was he? What had he found out about Drake? She touched where he had kissed her right before they parted. Something about the man was powerfully attractive to her. Not physically but in his very soul. Was she falling in love with him? She smiled. She could only hope so.

Faye paused before Victoria's sketchbooks. She had looked through all of them and the drawings were all the same: abstract interwoven lines that made no logical sense. She turned the sketches in all orientations and always there was nothing there. She even tried to imagine the lines forming some type of subtle, subliminal images. And no two sketches were alike. Multicolored lines intersecting. And at each intersection Victoria had carefully drawn a curve as if the lines were somehow interacting? That wasn't the word. She picked up the latest sketchbook and studied the image. This particular image Victoria had finished this morning and the lines were almost set at right angles to each other. In fact, the lines formed a grid. A grid. Maybe Victoria was trying to align the lines just as she was aligning her thoughts. Faye studied the intersecting lines. Why was there a little bump? A curve? It was almost like a, what, a knot? Faye felt that wonderful wave of cold realization that she had just maybe, just maybe seen a breakthrough.

Faye went back along the table and examined the tactile and hands-on items Lucille had used in her occupational therapy. Clay, beads, blocks in their respective holders. She glanced at Lucille.

"Lucille, do you have any occupational activity that involves strings?"

To her right she saw Victoria freeze. Victoria smiled. "I like strings."

Faye's heart raced. Yes! Her drawings were of strings! "Let's don't count our chickens before they hatch. What do you have?"

Lucille's surly attitude vanished and she retrieved a plastic handicraft holder. Inside where spools of multicolored strings. "We use these to make woven bracelets."

Faye motioned to Victoria. "Go ahead, Lucille. See what she can do with the strings."

Lucille looked at her and smiled. "Thank you."

Lucille sat before Victoria and placed five spools of the thick strings before her. Victoria smiled. "I like strings."

Victoria's hands moved deftly, unwinding a long strand from each spool. She cut the strands away with her teeth and laid each strand before her side by side. Faye sat slowly beside Lucille.

"What are you doing, Victoria?" Faye asked.

"Putting them together. The strings go together. They make a whole." Victoria paused and something foreign filled her eyes. She blinked a few times and frowned. "Father hated my strings. He hated them." She whispered.

Faye looked at Lucille who put her hand over her heart. "But, you like the strings, right?" Lucille asked.

Victoria nodded, her gaze never leaving the strings. "Yes. They are my life. They are my structure." She began working with the strings, interweaving them and tying knots as certain intersections. At first, the pattern made no sense. But with each knot, Victoria's eyes filled with new life. With each knot, her smile widened. When she was finished, she laid the final object before them. She had woven the strings together into a perfect grid with each square an inch wide.

Victoria sat back and studied the grid. She put a finger on one knot. "This was my lamb. It was in the cake."

Faye looked at Lucille and Lucille closed her eyes. "Oh, my! She is remembering."

"Remembering what?" Faye asked.

Lucille pulled Faye up and they walked to the far corner. "Her stepfather was a monster. Bought Victoria a baby lamb for her birthday and then baked it in her cake."

Faye put a hand to her mouth. "What?"

"We aren't sure, but we think Victoria watched her father strangle to death on a room filled with strings. The police report said the strings had been spread all over the kitchen."

Faye looked back at Victoria. She was touching an intersection point and mumbling to herself. "Then she is remembering. I hope that is a good thing."

"She needs to remember the off-the-book jobs, Miss Faye. That was his command."

Faye's face warmed with anger. "I don't care about those jobs right now. If her painful childhood memories are returning, there is no telling what that will do to her. She doesn't have the maturity to deal with that kind of pain. We need to take the grid away for now. Let her process what she is remembering. Slow this down."

"No!" Lucille said. "I'm getting the cart."

Faye grabbed Lucille's arm. "Wait a minute! You said 'he'!"

An alarm blared all around them. Faye froze. Lucille looked around, her eyes wild. Victoria screamed and put her hands over her ears.

JONATHAN STEEL

I recalled it all. Kevin taking me back to the church. Cleaning me up and explaining the Gospel go me. I prayed with Kevin and my heart changed, was cleansed, was renewed and the hatred and evil that had come into my life when I had found my grandfather's journal was replaced with the love, the forgiveness, and the Lordship of my savior, Jesus Christ. I was new. I was forgiven.

All of this hit me hard and sudden, for it was the most important memory that had returned. It was the transformational moment of my life. In time, I would explore the other memories that had prompted flashbacks of my father training me to defend myself. Memories of my father berating me for becoming a Christian. And yet, the video had revealed that my father had an ulterior motive in bringing me to Kevin. Only by becoming a Christian would I be immune to control by any demon! Only by showing me tough love would he force me to learn to defend myself, to trust no one, to become a loner. What a dichotomy he created in me! A man of God, a follower of Jesus Christ who would trust no one and who would live under a cloud of anger and fury. All to protect me from my brother! I glanced at the laptop. The screen filled with static. The hard drive was fried. The next video of my father's "story" was lost to me. I looked up at Alphus as these memories returned and realized I did not have the luxury to explore them any further.

"Sam and Yvonne triggered the EMP, and it affected me. They paralyzed the attackers, but I'm afraid they may not have gotten too far. I have to help them."

I tried to pull the surfacing thoughts together and suddenly, violently, without warning, a tsunami of more memories washed over me, driving the breath out of my lungs. I screamed again as the memories cascaded over me, threatening to drown my mind!

"Oh God, help me."

Alphus reached out carefully and took my hand in his. Warm and tingly. I squeezed it so hard if he had been human, he would have screamed in agony along with me. Images and people and deeds and pains and triumphs all mixed together like the debris from a flood.

I panted, drawing the cold air into my lungs until I tasted blood in the back of my throat. Slowly, oh so slowly, the flood waters subsided, and I slowed my breathing. The pain lessened, and I released the hand of an angel. Slowly, I stood up.

"I am Jonathan Steel, once known as JJ Stone. I am a man with a restored past. Guilt and shame taints my soul for the things I have done that I only now remember. I know who I am now and I know what I must do." I said. "There is nothing I can do right now to help Sam and Yvonne. They are more than capable of taking care of themselves. They taught me well after I ran away from my father when I was 18 and they reconnected with me." I said to Alphus.

"You recall everything?"

"I'm getting there. All those 'missions' I could not remember. I thought I was an assassin for my father. Now I know those deeds were at the direction from Sam and Yvonne to try and find my brother. I know that I masqueraded as an assassin to work with Raven. I know that on a mission to Africa I was imprisoned and my father had the implant placed so he could erase me memory and stop me from pursuing my brother."

Alphus nodded. "I have no knowledge of these facts."

"My brother thinks he is the chosen one for reasons I still do not understand. Instead, I am. But by giving me amnesia, my father misdirected my brother and other forces, looking for me. My father made my brother the special one to find. He has been on the run because of that. Now, all of that has changed. Since I was exposed in Switzerland, now they know I am the one they seek." I said all of this as much to summarize what I was remembering as it was to tell Alphus.

"Why do you tell me these things?" Alphus said.

"Because I need you take me to Dr. Monarch's lab in London."

"In your weakened condition, you will be damaged."

I stepped toward Alphus. "I heal quickly, Alphus. I am not an ordinary person. I can take the hit." I felt something crunch under my feet and looked down at the implant. I picked up the spindly metal fibers. The air shivered as another concussion shook the tunnel.

"Alphus, this is important. Can you take this implant somewhere else? It seems to have enough signal they can find me. I need you to take it somewhere else so they will look for it. And I need you to take that laptop with you and hide it in case they might recover the files. I assume you can teleport inorganic objects if you so desire."

Alphus nodded. "I have permission to help you." He took the implant and scooped up the laptop and disappeared. He reappeared empty handed. "I took the implant to Guam. I will not reveal where I took the laptop for now."

The sound of my laughter was foreign and strange, yet so welcome. I had not laughed in months. "I really like you,

Alphus. Now, before they break into this tunnel, can you please take me to London?"

Alphus paused and looked at the tunnel. "I am sorry, but you will not be helping Dr. Monarch. I will see that someone helps her. You are needed elsewhere."

I froze. "What?"

"Your brother did not go to the cœompound to enter the other tunnel and flank you. He went for another reason. Only you can help now." Alphus gestured and the rocks shifted down the tunnel. "I have unblocked the tunnel entrance. You must go now. The tunnel will emerge in a basement wine cellar and you must be there to help someone."

"The compound! I saw it under attack!"

"Yes."

"Who is there?"

"Raven." Alphus nodded and disappeared.

LONDON, England

Dr. Monarch screamed in agony as her shoe bounced off the chain and hit her in the face. She collapsed onto the floor of the Faraday cage and swore. She rubbed the bump on her forehead and swore some more. It had been only hours since the man had locked her in the cage.

The man was not Jonathan Steel. And yet he had Steel's eyes and looked almost identical to Jonathan. Who was he? Most importantly, how had he disappeared in plain sight? One moment he was there and the next he was gone.

Olivia once told her tall tales of demons and their ability to teleport humans through space. She had scoffed at such fantasy. But was it so farfetched? Given time, scientists would discover how to teleport people. Progress had already been made in that direction. She pounded on the door to the cage. But such an option was not available to her. If someone did not come and help her, she would die in this cage.

She stood up and craned her neck to look through the one small window near the ceiling visible from her angle. Evening was coming. She was in London alone. No one was waiting for her at the safe house. Olivia and Steven might try to call later but would probably leave a voicemail.

Monarch surveyed her empty lab. This had been home for months and now it was a cold, sterile reminder of the emptiness of her life. Since the death of her husband, Monarch's one objective had been to obliterate Olivia's epilepsy.

Nights had come when she would reach to the other side of the bed and imagine him lying beside her. Their love had been intense early on before he had become obsessed with the Proto-Virus. After seeing that name on the folder, it all had come back to her. What was the ProtoVirus? He had never told her. Secrets within secrets. Her entire life since their marriage had been layers of secrets.

"Help!" she shouted at the top of her lungs. She screamed and screamed until her throat was raw. No one could hear her. She chose this site because no one could hear whatever transpired in the basement.

Hopeless. Helpless. She mouthed the words. Just like Olivia and her epilepsy. Just like Steven's disappearance. And now Olivia had embraced God. She claimed to see demons. Monarch knew it had to be related to her abnormal brain activity. Demons did not exist! Right?

In the past few days, Olivia spoke often of her experience with God. True, her daughter showed confusion and anger because Steven's hands had been healed in Numinocity and her epilepsy had not. But how to account for Steven's healing? Was it a manifestation of the mental power augmented by Thakkar's virtual reality? Or could miracles be possible?

She gripped the wire of the cage door and peered out into her darkening lab. "God, are you there? Do you exist?"

For a moment, she did not feel silliness with her request. Jonathan Steel fought demons. Even she had seen things defying explanation. Was it possible? She needed a miracle. Problem was, she didn't believe in miracles.

Monarch sat down on the floor and crossed her arms. She wept and tears dripped from her cheeks. "God, if you are there let me thank you for healing my son. That is if you were the person who healed him. I mean, how could a computer program force your brain to heal your body? And Olivia. She still has seizures. But I see hope in her eyes. I hear joy in her voice. It has been a long time since I have heard and seen such things."

"Babe, you just need to open your eyes and ears." A voice whispered from the gathering shadows.

Monarch gasped and pulled herself up. The voice was that of her husband! How was this possible?

A figure moved out of the darkness and for a moment she feared he had returned. This man was taller and wore white and had long, blonde hair and eyes that glowed with power.

"No, I am a messenger from God." The man said. He gestured toward the lock and it fell away. Monarch pulled the chain from the door and pushed it open.

"Who are you?"

"Alphus. You would know me as an angel. I'm keeping a promise to Jonathan Steel. You are free." Then, he just disappeared from sight.

Monarch gasped and put her hand to her mouth. She then waved her hands in the space where the man once stood.

"Demons? Angels?" She smiled and laughed. Maybe it was time to start believing.

CHAPTER
FIFTY-SEVEN

COMPOUND

Right hand, second finger red. Left hand, third finger red. Why? Right thumb blue. Left thumb yellow. Green string around right wrist. White left wrist. Strings tightening. Pain! Lurching, jerking, standing. Dangling in the air. Pressure now. Strings tightening. Pulling. Lifting. Dangling. Moving.

No! Don't want to move that way! No! Let me be free. Not! A! Puppet!

Snapping, popping. Fingers flying away from hands. Dangling before her. Reaching for fingers and only palms! Arms snap away. Dangling arms. Legs dangling. Torso only? What is happening?

A knife.

A pistol.

Blood.

A lamb.

A lamb? Moving between the strings. Tiny lamb. Eyes filled with compassion. Wounds on the head. He is my lamb. My lamb. Slain from the foundation of the world? Yes.

Help me. God, help me. Please.

Fingers and hands and arms returning. Popping into place. The strings dangling still tight but hands working. Touching, moving. Strings tactile in hands. Tying a knot. Tying it down. Anchoring it so they can't pull it anymore! Yes!

Another knot tied. More freedom. The lamb is walking away but leaving behind a cloud of love. Compassion. Clarity? Another now and more freedom. Father? A monster? He's gone. Can't hurt you. Monarch. Monster. She can't hurt you. Faces. Eyes. Life fading. So wrong. So wrong. The lamb pauses and looks back. Forgiven. I am forgiven. Another knot in the strings. Dark eyes and long dark hair behind a surgical mask. Surgery. Implant. The Captain. Hate him. The Captain. Love him. Who is the Captain?

Turquoise eyes filled with hate. Ginger hair. Not the Captain! The knife slashes across the chest. He runs to live to see another day.

Vivian. Atchison. The cavern. Another set of turquoise eyes. Angry eyes, but different. No scar on the chest. You're not him! Who are you? The gun. The exploding bullet. I am forgiven? Pain. Lacerations and falling into frigid water.

Rebuilt. Another knot. The airplane to London. Josh. Josh! Another knot. I remember. Numinocity. I remember. The lamb disappears. Into my heart. Into my mind. Into my soul. Must help. Must help Jonathan Steel. Last knot. All connects. Grid complete.

"What is that?" Faye shouted above the alarm.

"Intruders!" Lucille said and smiled. "They are here."

"Who?"

"Jeremiah." Lucille threw back the cover on the cart. On the second level were boxes of ammunition. She picked up a pistol and checked the magazine. She pointed the gun at Faye.

Faye backed away and put her hands up. "Lucille? What are you doing?"

"He promised me he would love me, don't you understand?" Lucille walked toward Faye and her gun waved around in tiny circles. "No more, 'Lucille' do this. Do that. Take care of Faye. Change her diaper." Lucille's eyes widened. "Change an adult's diaper? Have you ever?"

Faye nodded. She remembered changing Josh's diapers while he was in a coma. "I have. You don't have to do this, Lucille."

Lucille closed the distance and pressed the gun against Faye's chest. "Oh, yes, I do. You don't know what he is like. He is repulsive and hateful, and I love him!"

"Are you going to kill me now?" Faye's voice shook.

"No, I'll let Jeremiah have that privilege. He'll take you out himself."

"No, he won't." Someone said. The voice was distinct, stronger, not at all that of a child. Faye whirled. Victoria jerked the pistol from Lucille's hand and pressed the pistol against her temple. "You never cleaned me up enough, sweetheart. Now, who is coming?"

"Jeremiah. For you." Lucille giggled and pushed her head against the pistol. "He doesn't need Faye. Just you."

Faye gasped. "Victoria?"

Victoria glared at her with eyes that were far different from the innocent child from before. "I'm back. Call me Raven." She grabbed Lucille by the arm and walked her toward the desk with monitors. She pushed Lucille down onto the chair and kept the pistol pressed against her head.

"Open the video surveillance footage."

Lucille shrugged. "Won't make any difference." She tapped the keyboard and a half a dozen video windows popped up. At least a dozen attackers in assault gear were making their way through the hallways. At the front door, one servant lay in a pool of blood.

"Where are the exits from this room?" Raven said.

"Up the stairs where they will be coming. Or, into the wine cellar."

Faye hurried after Raven. "Wait! You're back? Just like that?"

Raven paused and nodded at Faye. "You did it. The strings were the key. It's why I've been drawing them. But the feel of the strings in my hands made the difference. Thank you."

"What do we do?"

Raven's gaze swept around the room. "Windows lead where?"

"Outside." Lucille said. "Where they are gathered."

"They don't know about the windows, or that would have been the perfect entry point." Raven said. "You said those doors go to a wine cellar?"

Faye flinched at the sound of muffled gunfire. They were getting close. Lucille nodded. "It goes under the chalet into a chamber carved into the very rock. But there is a back stairway to the kitchen pantry. They'll be in the kitchen by now."

Raven nodded and slammed the pistol against Lucille's head. She slumped forward over the keyboard.

Faye gasped. "What are you doing?"

"Trying to save your life. Help me get her into the wine cellar." Faye took one arm and Raven the other, and they dragged her across the floor to the cellar doors. Raven opened the doors, and they placed Lucille inside. Tall wooden shelves filled with dusty wine bottles covered the walls. "Faye, you stay here. Hide behind one of those shelves."

"What are you going to do?" Faye said.

"What I'm trained to do. They want me. They get me. But, on my terms. Now go!"

Faye slid behind a shelf, and Raven hurried back into the room and closed the doors behind her.

———

Raven sat quietly behind the table with her hands out of sight. Just moments ago, she had been confused and lost in the aftermath of Monarch's deactivation of her implant. Now she was back. Unfortunately, her body was not as strong as she normally kept it. No exercise in quite some time. But they didn't know she was back.

The door to the basement blew open in a cloud of smoke and embers. Raven ducked behind the table. Four people in assault gear and helmets ran into the room with their guns pointed in her direction. They moved around the room and two more assault members moved up beside her. Six assailants, she noted.

"What is happening? My head hurts. You hurt my head. I want Lucille." She said in her most innocent voice.

"Shut up!" A man said.

"That hurt! You're a mean man."

The two attackers flanking her looked at each other as the other four secured the perimeter of the room. One paused in front of the double doors. "What's behind here?"

One of the four, a woman, held up a tablet. "Wine cellar. Clear it."

"Enough!" a man said as he walked into the basement. He wore a black jumpsuit and a black knit cap. A set of ski goggles covered his eyes. He studied a cell phone in his hand. He swore loudly and threw the phone across the room. It shattered against the far wall. "The other team just went dark. Something catastrophic happened."

"I tried to tell you to concentrate on them. Not her!" The woman with the tablet said.

The ski goggle man reached behind him and pulled a pistol from his waist. He pointed it at the woman and pulled the trigger. The woman's head snapped as the bullet blew out the back of her skull and she collapsed onto the floor. A warm drop hit Raven in the face and she tried not to flinch. The man looked at the others. "Sorry. I'm a tad angry. Any more suggestions?"

One of the other assailants picked up the tablet. "No." One

down, five to go, Raven thought. Plus the newcomer. He was in charge.

"Get through to them somehow. Now!" He screamed. The tablet person ran from the room. The man in the goggles drew a deep breath. "It's okay. I'm calm now." Another one down, four to go. And the unstable leader.

"Doris told me to clear the wine cellar." One of the remaining men said. "What do you want me to do, boss?"

The man shook his head. "Doris and her ideas are gone. You're in charge now. We have what we want. Forget the wine cellar."

Raven did her best to look vulnerable and helpless as the man in the goggles came to her table. The drop of blood tickled down her cheek. She resisted the urge to swipe it away in disgust. The man pulled up a chair and sat across from her. He took off his goggles, revealing bright turquoise eyes. Raven wanted to gasp in surprise, but she buried the shock.

"Who are you?" She managed, although with her returning memory, she knew exactly who he was.

"You don't recognize me?"

"No."

"Ginger hair. Turquoise eyes." The man sat back and crossed his arms. "I know, it's the grin. He never smiles. So grim and dour." He suddenly leaned forward. "And that temper, oh my! At least my temper is always under control and ready to be unleashed when appropriately provoked." He nodded toward the woman's body. Then, he reached forward with a gloved hand and wiped the blood drop from her cheek. "Now, that's better." He smiled and pointed to his face. "See. Smiling."

Insanely smiling, Raven thought. The man was psychotic!

"Okay, if I must, I will say his name. I'm not Jonathan Steel." The man said. "No, my name is Jeremiah Stone. Jonathan's better half. Literally. Max did a poor job of hiding you. She underestimated my resources."

The tablet person came down the stairs and paused beside

Stone. The helmet came off, revealing a woman with short hair. Her eyes were milky white. Raven hid her surprise. Now there were five again!

"What's wrong with your eyes? Does that hurt?" Raven said.

"No." She said. "The better to see you with. Boss, it seems they set off an EMP on the other side of the ridge. Fried all of our equipment. They got away." The woman cringed, waiting for the last sound she might hear, the snap of his pistol.

Jeremiah tensed. "Gudren, just who is 'they'?"

"The lawyer and the cop. Don't know if Steel was with them." Gudren said.

Jeremiah pursed his lips. "Oh, he was there. I tracked his implant."

"The EMP knocked out the drone. We can't sense his implant anymore." Gudren released her breath.

A muscle twitched beneath one of Jeremiah's eyes. "He was in the house."

"We have the house covered. No one is there. The computers are toast. There was a tool shed in back leading into a tunnel. The last signal from his implant was when they went into the tunnel. It was very weak, but it was definitely there." Gudrenn glanced at the tablet, and her eyes widened. "Wait! We've reacquired the signal." She blinked in confusion. "He's somewhere in the Pacific?"

Jeremiah jerked the tablet from her hands. "Let me do that. You incompetent idiot." He studied the screen and kept refreshing the feed. "Guam? He's in Guam?" Jeremiah's face twisted into a mask of rage and he hurled the tablet across the room. It shattered against the wall. "He must have teleported and the only way he could do that is if one of those messengers helped him." He roared in anger, and the remaining attackers backed away.

Jeremiah panted and closed his eyes as he slowed his breathing. He wiped sweat from his ginger hair and then drew one deep, calming breath. He pointed to the woman who had held the tablet. "He'll be incapacitated. Are you in touch with your demon?"

Gudren shook her head. "Not now. It comes and goes."

"Yes, I know. You Vitreomancers are very unreliable." Jeremiah squatted down and made eye contact with Raven. "But what can I say? I take help wherever I can get it. Gudren, go upstairs to the SUV and call the boss. Tell him to send a demon to Guam and see if my brother is there. Teleporting that far will weaken him."

Gudren nodded nervously. She pressed a hand to her ear and Raven saw the thin wire of a radio leading down into the woman's vest. "Sven just called and said they have the SUV's up and running. Should they go after the lawyer and the cop?"

Jeremiah rubbed his chin with a gloved hand. "No, let them go for now. Tell them to regroup at the farm in the valley. No need to waste time and money on the fugitives for now. Concentrate on my brother. Go find Dimitri and get the SUV ready."

The woman spoke rapidly with her hand on the radio receiver. She nodded and ran up the stairs. Jeremiah stood up and stumbled. He put a hand on the table to steady himself.

"Teleportation takes its toll. But I can handle it." He straightened and paced around the table. He paused beside the sketch pads and the other works of art. He picked up the string grid. "What have we here?"

"My strings." Raven said quietly. "I like strings. See the knots. Even and tight."

Jeremiah studied the grid and tossed it aside. "I heard you had lost you mind. Monarch really screwed you up, didn't she?"

"Who is Monarch?" Raven said slowly.

Jeremiah picked up a lump of blue clay and squeezed it in his gloved hand. Tentacles of clay shot from beneath his fingers and fell to the floor. He tossed the clay aside. "Looks like you were left with the mind of a child. What is your name?"

"Victoria." Raven said. "You made a mess. You need to clean that up."

Jeremiah turned and studied her from a distance. "Either you really have lost your mind or you're faking it. Either way, I must know if your memory of a certain off-the-book job remains." Raven tried to hide her surprise. An "off the book" job? Was that what this was all about? Then she recalled something Lucille had said earlier. Max was after the same thing. She smiled.

"I like books." She reached for a nearby book and one of Jeremiah's men slammed his hand down on the book.

Raven recoiled and her face screwed up into a frown. "That was mean."

A distant crashing noise came from the cellar. Stone nodded toward the door. "Check it out. Now!"

One of the assailants rushed through the cellar doors into darkness. With Gretchen gone, that left three men, plus Jeremiah. Raven tensed and Stone pointed to the two men beside Raven. "Take her to the SUV. We will finish this later. Important thing is Max didn't get what she wanted."

"Which was?" Raven said with a smile.

Jeremiah froze. "What did you say?"

Raven pulled both knives from their places taped beneath the table, stood up and plunged them both into the necks of the assault members on each side of her. She ducked as the one remaining attacker, positioned near the stairs, fired her way. Raven rolled under the table, taking the dying man's assault rifle from his hands as he collapsed beside her and sprayed bullets across the knees of the man by the stairs.

Jeremiah pulled a pistol from his waist and shot the man in the head. "Don't kill my prize!" He screamed. "Just can't get good help anymore." He turned back toward Raven.

Raven answered with a burst of fire toward the weapons' cart, but Jeremiah had already moved away. The last man in the wine cellar appeared at the doors and shouted at Jeremiah.

"This way! There's a rear stairway."

Raven let loose a volley of bullets at the wine cellar doors and the man fell back into the cellar. Jeremiah fired over her head and Raven hid behind the table as the bullets tore chunks of wood.

Jeremiah ran for the cellar doors while Raven was pinned down. Raven peered around the fallen table. The cellar doors were halfway closed. Had Faye made it up the rear stairs from the cellar?

Raven hurried across the floor to the cellar doors. She glanced around the door into the empty cellar. The remaining man groaned and blood bubbled from her lips. One of Raven's bullets had hit him. Jeremiah had left him behind.

"No! They're coming for me. I change my mind. Don't take me there!" The man hissed, and he stopped breathing. His goggles were gone and his white eyes faded away into cloudy, normal appearing eyes. They stared off into heaven. Or, in his case, hell.

Where were Lucille and Faye? Someone groaned across the cellar and Raven ran around boxes and supplies. Lucille lay in a pool of blood.

She tried to smile as blood bubbled from her lips. "He took her with him." She coughed blood. "He said he would meet me in hell." She smiled, and the life faded from her eyes. Jeremiah had shot her in the chest. But where was Faye?

Raven stood up and drew a deep, shuddering breath. She thought she had put this life behind her. She thought she had found freedom. But no! Behind her, a shelf filled with wine bottles tilted forward. She backed away quickly as the shelf crashed down on Lucille's body. A wooden door in the wall behind the shelf flew open and out of the darkness, a figure emerged. The man's breath filled the air with steam. Raven pointed her rifle at the emerging figure. The meager light in the cellar caught his eyes. Turquoise!

"Stop right there!" She screamed. "Where is Faye?"

The man halted and his eyes widened. "Raven? Is that you?"

Raven's trigger finger tightened, and it was only the familiar sound of the man's voice that saved his life. She blinked in confusion. The man before her had the same turquoise eyes as Jeremiah Stone, but he was dressed in blue jeans and a flannel shirt and wore a parka. And he wasn't smiling. He raised his hands at the sight of the gun.

"It's me. Jonathan. Don't shoot."

Raven hesitated and her hand began to shake. "You might be him."

"Who?" The man's eyes widened even more. "Wait! My brother! I thought he was with the people on the ridge. He was here?"

"Yes." Raven said. She lowered her gun. "Yes, Jeremiah was here. He took Faye."

"Faye Morgan?" Jonathan stepped over the broken wine bottles whose scent had filled the air with a heady cloud of alcohol. "Raven, what is going on?"

Raven ran back through the room and stepped over the dead man. She hurried up the stairs. As Jonathan followed, she heard his ragged breathing. There was a sound of a vehicle burning rubber in the parking area. The cold draft directed her across an enormous living room to an open foyer door. She ran out the door, her rifle ready as the SUV disappeared down the driveway, but she hesitated. She couldn't take a chance on hitting Faye.

Jonathan stopped beside her. "You can fill me in later. Car?" He pointed to another SUV in the driveway.

RAVEN RAN across the snow-covered ground toward the SUV. Its motor still pumped out steaming exhaust. She pointed to the driver's side.

"You drive. I shoot."

Steel slid behind the driver's seat and gunned the engine, sliding in a circle as he turned away from the compound toward the road leading down the mountainside. "Plan?"

"They're heading toward the valley." Raven looked in the back seat and tossed her assault rifle onto the floor. She grabbed another rifle from an open box and checked to see if it was loaded. "She said something about the farm in the valley. They will switch to a less than conspicuous form of travel. Train would be too risky. Probably a smaller car. Max planned this compound perfectly for isolation for just that reason. The town below has only one road in and one road out."

"I guess I should say welcome back?" Steel asked.

"My memory is back. I heard Lucille talking about it the past couple of weeks. Something about Switzerland has 22,000 dairy farms. The town is centered around a dairy farm. Quiet. Secluded." Raven paused and swallowed back emotion. "Lucille worked for Jeremiah. She was his plant." Raven glanced at him.

"Where did you come from?" Ahead of them, she glimpsed the van as it rocketed around a sharp curve.

"House on the other side of the peak. A safe house. I was teleported there by an angel. Same angel told me to come down a tunnel to the compound to help you." Steel said.

Raven grabbed the seat arm as Steel swerved around a tight curve. "Okay, I'll take your word for it. But I heard a toady with white eyes tell Jeremiah the fugitives had escaped, and you had teleported to Guam."

Steel sighed. "Good! Alphus, the angel, sent my implant to Guam. That is how they found me through my implant."

She gasped. "Your implant? It's gone?"

"It's a long story. But, Raven, I have my memories back."

Raven froze. "All your memories?"

"Well, they're there, just all jumbled up."

Raven nodded and drew a deep breath. "All of my memories are back, too. Which begs the question of why was your brother coming for me? He said something about an off-the-book assassination."

She felt Steel's gaze on her. "And that would be?"

Raven shook her head. "Not now. Like you said, my memories are all jumbled up. I couldn't tell you the ones on-the-book! I'm running on pure instinct and training. For now, we concentrate on getting Faye back."

"Why did he take her?"

"To get me to follow." Raven checked her rifle and pointed to the driver's side of the road. Below them, a small town filled the valley, and a lake sat at the entrance to the valley. Snow clouds filled the air around them and obscured the view as the storm came over the ridge.

Steel swerved to miss another car coming toward them and whirled on the icy road until they came to a halt on a scenic pull off. A couple taking pictures of the lake glared at them. Steel shot away from the pull-off as they spied the SUV going down a long, winding driveway to a snow-covered field on the near side of the lake at the base of the mountain. A dairy farm spread out along the valley floor beside the lake. Steel hit the road again, swerving and sliding as he tried to keep his SUV under control. Raven held on for dear life.

"What will be our approach?" Raven said.

Steel drove the SUV onto the main motorway into the small town. He slammed on the brakes as a red and white train shot across the track in front of them.

"We've done this before." Steel said.

Raven drew a deep breath as a memory surfaced. She glanced at Steel whose eyes were riveted on the passing train. "I remember. I looked different then."

"Before your plastic surgery." Steel said.

"I was different then." Raven said quietly. Her memories were slowly returning but in a new context. God was now a part of her life. That relationship was putting everything in a new perspective. "You're remembering the time I tried to kill you." She whispered.

"Yes." Steel said. "It was after you shot Monarch in London. I recall tracking you down in Versailles."

"At the café on the palace grounds." Raven said as the memories returned.

———

She was sitting at the table in the corner, just as he had suspected. Raven would make sure she could see anyone who entered the restaurant. Steel adjusted his tie and drew a deep breath. He had to make this work, or he would be dead within the hour.

She saw him and visibly tensed. She was nervous. Good! Raven rarely got nervous. Steel paused at the end of the table and motioned to the empty booth. "May I?"

Raven motioned to the empty seat. "Please."

He slid into the opposite seat and placed his hands on the table. "Where should we start?"

"How about I just kill you now?" Raven whispered.

"People are watching."

"You know I can kill you in a dozen different ways. I can kill you and get up and walk away from this booth, and the waiter would think you were still reading the menu ten minutes from now."

"Do you feel that?" Steel asked.

Raven blanched. She must have felt the metal tip against her stomach. "What is it?"

"A retractable blade. One thrust and you die."

"Not before I fire the pistol hidden in my purse. It has a silencer."

Steel withdrew the blade. "Then shall we call a truce for tonight?"

Raven studied him and nodded. "Very well. But if I see you tomorrow, I'll have to kill you."

"You didn't want to kill me six months ago." Raven flushed. "Don't remind me. I was foolish."

"We both were fools to think we could hide this from the Captain," Steel said. "We were doomed from the start."

"There is no place for love in our lives," Steel said.

"I realized that long before you did." Raven laughed and dabbed at her eyes with the napkin. "It's over, and all that is left for us is the day I finally kill you."

Steel felt his heart constrict with anger and disappointment. "If not my father, then who wants me dead?"

"Now, you know it isn't nice to kiss and tell." Raven picked up the menu. "What's good?"

The waiter came and took their order. Once he was gone, Steel placed his hands in front of him. "Do you ever grow tired of the killing?"

Raven reached for her purse and placed it on the table. She took out a mirror and lipstick and studied her face. Steel saw the glint of the pistol in the purse.

"My private life isn't up for discussion."

"Raven—"

"Don't call me that in public." She dropped the mirror back into the purse.

"Victoria," Steel continued. "I don't want to kill you. And I don't want to die. I only want one thing, to find the Captain. You work for him, and you can help me with that."

Raven laughed. "What makes you think I know where he is?"

"Because he hired you to find me." Steel leaned back as their meal arrived.

Raven toyed with her steak knife. It caught the candlelight and reflected it onto her face. "You have no idea who hired me to find you. Things have changed in the past few months."

She started cutting her prime rib, and its juices gushed onto the plate. Steel ignored his plate and reached out to put a restraining hand on hers. "Don't you think we should say grace?"

Raven jerked her hand away from his. "You want to pray?"

Steel watched her panic-filled eyes. "I know about your past, Victoria. I know about Lucas. I know about your stepfather."

Raven's knife clattered onto the plate, and she reached for her purse. Steel snatched it away before she could get the gun. She glared at him.

"What gives you the right to pry into my life?"

"You talk in your sleep." Steel reached into his pocket and pulled out the plastic bag. He placed it on the table in front of her. "You haven't been able to find me because I was in a prison camp in Africa. My father put me there. I escaped, and I know he's looking for me. Who better to find me than you?"

Tears trickled down her cheeks. Steel reached over and touched her face. She jerked away.

"Victoria, not long ago, all I wanted to do was to kill my jailer. But God brought me back to my senses. I know where you started, Victoria. I know you can stop this and get your life right."

Raven shook her head. "You're insane!"

"Maybe I am. But in my moment of deepest despair, when I was ready to give in to the chaos and the lies of Satan, I found this." He tapped the piece of paper in the bag. "I want you to have it. If I can stop you—if I can help you—you'll understand these people do not have to die."

Raven picked up the piece of paper. "Where did this come from?"

"It was a gift from God. Read it. Consider my words. Turn your back on the world you now live in. From this day forward, I want to help people, not kill them, Victoria. And finding the Captain is the first step in that process. If you won't help me, then let me help you. Turn around. Head back to the world you abandoned when your stepfather died. Find forgiveness before it is too late."

Raven stared at the piece of paper as Steel slid out of the booth. "I'll see you around." He walked out of the restaurant, afraid that at any minute he would feel the bullet pierce his skull. But he did not die that night.

———

"Things are different now." She said as the train finally passed by.

Steel turned his intense gaze on her. "Are they? We're both reliving our past, both recalling memories from when we both were very different people."

Raven nodded and put a hand on his right arm. Another flashback. His bare skin beneath her touch. His lips. His face. Was he recalling those moments, too? His muscles tensed, answering her question. She pulled her arm away and swallowed hard to slow her heart rate and concentrate on the battle ahead. "So many memories, Jonathan. Things I've done wrong. I have a lot of thinking to do. Because Jonathan, I am a new creature. I don't even need strings anymore."

"You returned the scripture from the bag to me in the amulet. It must have influenced you." Steel said.

"It did. It took some time. I take it you found the dossier?"

"Yes, it's safe in the hands of Max." Steel said quietly. The train had long gone by now. Steel relaxed and drove across the railway and turned toward the farmhouse. "I'm just hoping neither one of us relapses."

They both saw the farm off the side of the road at the same time. Raven readied the rifle as they pulled even with the SUV parked in the driveway. The doors were open, and the SUV was empty.

"There!" Raven shouted, pointed out the windshield. Over a nearby hill, she had spied another vehicle moving away on the one road leading out of the valley. She hoped and prayed Faye was in that vehicle. If they stopped to search the farm, they would lose Faye.

"No time to search the farm. We'll lose them. Let's go." Steel said as he drove after the receding car.

CHAPTER
FIFTY-NINE

FAYE GAGGED on the cloth in her mouth. She blinked and tried to focus on her surroundings. Her body swayed with motion and only a red ray of light illuminated the interior of wherever she was. She remembered someone pressing a gauze over her mouth and the horror of suffocation. She had passed out. Where was she?

More swaying as she took inventory. Faye was on her left side and her hands were tied behind her back. The cramped space around her left her in a fetal position. The sound of road noise filled the interior of a car trunk. She wanted to scream and kick but knew instinctively it was best to be quiet until she figured out more about what was happening.

Raven's memory had returned in the chalet and Faye marveled at the woman's speed and ability when she fought off the attackers. It had not been enough to spare Faye. But what had happened in the interim? The odor of manure and hay hung in the air of the trunk. Had she heard cows lowing? A dairy farm?

Okay, survival first. She worked her lips and tongue and managed to push the gag out of her mouth and down on her chin. She sucked in cold, sweet air. Her hands were bound with plastic ties. Thank you Lord I have taken stretching classes, she thought.

She slid her bound hands down and painfully worked them around her backside until she could feel the souls of her shoes. She pointed her toes down and flexed her back forward in the cramped space until her bound hands were sliding over the bottom of her feet. Faye bit back the scream of pain in her shoulders and back as her hands popped over her feet. She straightened and gasped for breath as the pain finally subsided.

Now, about the plastic ties. The meager red light from outside gave her enough light to see the interior of the trunk. Open metal edges were just rough enough to catch on the plastic ties. Faye pressed her hands against the edge of the rough metal and began to saw away.

She gasped in pain as the rough edge scraped her wrists. Keep going, she told herself. Finally, the ties popped loose. The car continued to sway with motion. It moved gradually, normally, not as if it were in a rush to get away. Whoever had abducted her knew enough to drive normally and not draw attention. Whoever that was!

Now, what to do? She had very little room to maneuver but feeling along the trunk sides near her feet she located the tire tool. The metal was icy cold and she realized she was shivering. Her breath steamed in the frigid air.

With the car moving, she had little options until it stopped and then what? Surprise her assailants? Behind Faye she felt a lever. She rolled over so that she was facing the back of the back seat of the car. Some light came between the seats! The back seat was designed to fold down for increased storage!

Faye quietly lifted the lever and grabbed the back of the seat as it started to fall inward toward the car. She pressed her face against the open crack between the seats.

Two people sat in the front seats. The passenger was a woman in a black knit cap. A man with long, blonde hair beneath a knit cap drove the car. The woman spoke loudly and pointed out the window.

"Where is the boss going? Divide and conquer, he said."

"We don't ask questions! We do as we are told or we die." The man said.

"Like Doris!" Gudren shouted and slapped the console. "She was going to transform me, Dimitri! I would have had the Vision!" She sobbed softly.

"You are too gullible, Gudren. Too ambitious. We do our job. We take the woman to the rendezvous point while the boss does whatever it is he does." The man said. "One day your eyes will be white."

"He spread us out too thin and now Doria is dead."

Silence fell between the two of them except for the woman's gentle sobbing. "I need a restroom." Gudren said.

Dimitri pounded the steering wheel and swore. "We don't have time for this, Gudren."

"Dimitri, we are out for a pleasant drive in the country. You are driving too fast and it will draw attention. I need to compose myself. I need the restroom. Now pull off at that store ahead."

The man swore again, and the car slowed. He pulled off the road and into the shade of a petrol station.

Faye clenched the tire tool in her right hand. If she moved quickly enough, she could hit the man in the head. Once the woman got out of the car, Faye could render the man unconscious and dump him on the ground and then what?

Faye shook her head in dismay. Her plan would never work. The woman left the car, and the man looked into the rearview mirror. Faye froze and held her breath. Would he see the seat pushed forward?

The man got out of the car and started toward the trunk. Now was her chance. She rolled over back onto her side. Maybe he was only checking on her. She pulled the gag back into her mouth and shoved her hands behind her still clutching the tool. She shut her eyes just as he opened the trunk.

The man smelled of cow manure from the dairy farm. Snow swirled into the trunk from a gathering storm and she tried not to flinch when his icy fingers tested the gag. He grunted and slammed the trunk.

Faye rolled over again and peered through the seat crack. She saw the man's head as he disappeared toward the store. Move, she told herself. She pushed the seat open and painfully crawled from the trunk. She peered over the edge of the front seat. The man and woman were still inside. She opened the back door and squatted down on the pavement. Now what? Run? Cry out for help? These two were dangerous. They had been a part of a crew who had killed everyone in the chateau. What would they do to the people in the store?

No, there was only one option. She opened the driver's seat and slid beneath the steering wheel. She glanced at the storefront. The man and woman were inside looking for snacks. She put the car in gear and let it back away slowly. She turned it so that it finally slid out of sight from the interior of the store. She put the car in drive and pulled out slowly onto the highway. Which way to go? Which way had they come from? She did not know, but to her left, the mountains and the road were being swallowed up by the snowstorm. She could lose herself in the storm. Once on the highway, she pressed down on the accelerator and took off down the road. She glanced once in the rearview mirror and saw the man and woman run out of the store.

CHAPTER
SIXTY

JONATHAN STEEL

The snowstorm swallowed the road ahead. I felt the tires slide in the new snow and reluctantly slowed down. "Belarus." He said.

"The ice storm. I remember." She said. "I was driving then."

"Off a cliff, if I remember correctly." I said.

"But we weren't hurt. Six feet of powdered snow provided a cushion." She laughed. "We stayed in that abandoned cabin in the mountains."

As the snow filled the air in front of us, I put the wipers on high. I recalled that night. She kept her gaze averted as I looked at her. We both remembered what happened. "Is that why you tried to kill me later on?"

Raven nodded. "I thought we connected. Then the next time I saw you, you tried to kill me."

"It wasn't me."

"I know that now. I knew it in the caverns of Transylvania. I suddenly realized what I had always suspected. You had an impersonator. I thought it was because of plastic surgery like I had. That clinic specialized in repurposing assets. He's not an impersonator. He's your brother?"

"Not a twin. Just looks enough like me to pass as me." The tires slid again on the slick road. From out of the cloud of swirling snow, a car appeared and crossed the midline. I swerved and felt the tires slide off the road onto the shoulder. The oncoming car spun around once and righted itself just as it sped by. For a second, the driver's face flashed through the frosted window and I saw Faye Morgan's features etched with fear.

"That was Faye!" I said as I slowed the forward movement of our car. A large, white moving van appeared from the snow and sped after Faye's car. Behind the wheel, I made out a woman with piercings and tattoos and an angry glare on her face. "That van? Driving too fast in this weather for a moving van."

"Probably stolen. That was Gudren driving. She was in the basement. They're after Faye." Raven said. "Turn around."

"But Faye is headed back toward town. The road's a dead end." I pulled the car onto the road and my wheels spun on the snowy surface.

"I don't know how she did it. Looks like she took the kidnappers' car from them." Raven checked her rifle. "I need a pistol." She stood up on her knees to look into the back seat. "Got it!" Raven checked the magazine for bullets.

"What are you planning?" I felt the car slide again.

"Catch up with the van and pass them? Maybe force them off the road." Raven wiped condensation from her side of the windshield. "And turn the heater up. I need a clear shot."

"Catch up? Force them off the road? We are heading into the worst of the snowstorm." I said. Wind buffeted us and the SUV lurched under the onslaught.

"Steel, use it for our advantage. They won't see us coming."

"And if we spin off the road and crash, we can't help Faye."

Before she could answer, red lights appeared in the swirling snow. I threw on the brakes and we slid sideways toward the van. It had stopped on the side of the road. I spun the steering wheel and barely missed the van with the rear of our SUV now pointing ahead and the front end pointing back the way we had come. The SUV slid sideways onto the shoulder and off onto the ground.

Raven wiped condensation from her window. "The van doors are open. Maybe no one is inside."

"Faye must have run off the road."

Raven threw open her door, and the full force of the snowstorm blew in. I grabbed the rifle from the floorboard and followed Raven out into the storm. We both made it to the side of the van. The bitter cold grabbed us both. Luckily, I still had on my coat, but Raven wore only a thin jumpsuit. For the first time, I noticed the infantile splashes of paint covering the jumpsuit.

"Therapy?" I pointed to the paint.

"Yes. Didn't work." She motioned to the driver's side window, and I nodded as she crouched out of the sight of the mirror. I waited as she duck walked to the door and stood up slowly to look inside.

"No one inside. Other door is open." She mouthed.

I motioned to the back of the van and then toward the front. We would split up. Like puzzle pieces falling into place, I was back in Belarus with Raven. We understood each other; each movement. We were a team again.

I eased around the back of the van as snow pummeled my face and made me squint. The van sat halfway off the road and fortunately the ground sloped gently away, unlike the sheer cliffs we had maneuvered along coming down from the mountains. The tracks of a car led off into a complete whiteout.

Raven and I made our way slowly along the ruts in the snow made by Faye's car. A wooden fence appeared out of the storm. Broken timbers covered the ground. Faye's car had barreled through the fence.

I stepped over the broken timbers and followed the ruts into the whiteout. Above the roaring wind, I heard voices and the crack of a gun. I could barely see Raven in the snow. Her hair was filled with snow and she wiped flakes from her eyelids as she motioned to her right and then to her left. We would flank the kidnappers.

The wind buffeted me as I made my way carefully down the snow-covered slope, moving away from the car's ruts. My feet tried to slip out from under me and I fought for balance. Raven disappeared in the storm to my left. Something dark loomed ahead of me and I pulled up the rifle. The lumbering form of a cow appeared in the snow. The cow paused and regarded me with large brown eyes. Snow covered her flanks, and she licked flakes from her snout. She sauntered past me toward the road. I relaxed and continued on my way until I felt something squish beneath my feet. I looked down at the fresh cow patty.

I tried to ignore the sudden warmth of my right foot. Through the swirling snow, I saw red lights flashing from the rear of Faye's car. I heard voices.

"You're not worth the trouble to me, sister!" A woman's voice came to me on the wind. "Cooperate, or I'll put a permanent hole in your head."

"Calm down!" A man's voice said. "The boss wants her alive."

As I drew closer, three figures appeared in the storm. Faye's hair was filled with snow and the two people with her wore gloves, coats, and ski masks. My feet flew out from under me and I fell onto my back and I slid right into the man. He fell on top of me and the woman swore. She pointed her pistol at me and I shoved the man up off me just as she fired. His eyes filled with surprise as the bullets buried themselves in his back.

I rolled away from the man's lifeless body and I grabbed Faye and took her with me, pulling her into the shelter of the car. The woman's boots were visible on the far side of the car. Faye's eyes filled with fear, and I put a hand over her mouth. I had lost the rifle, but if we stayed, the woman would find us.

Snow landed on the dead man's eyes and he did not blink. I

grabbed his pistol and pushed Faye toward the rear of the car as the woman approached the front. I pulled Faye to her knees and motioned into the snowstorm. We stood and ran into the maelstrom. White surrounded us and still we ran until Faye stumbled and fell. My feet slid out from under me and I slid down the snow-covered slope after Faye.

My head swam with dizziness, and I finally came to a halt in cold water. I sat up shakily and looked at a pond spreading away from me. Steam filled the air, mixed with the swirling snow. Where was Faye?

I stood up and searched the blowing snow around me. I could shout her name, but that would alert the woman. Somewhere up the slope, I had lost the pistol. Water splashed behind me and I whirled. The woman from the van had flanked me and was moving across the edge of the pond.

"Don't you move a muscle. I ought to take you out right now for killing Dimitri." She said through cold, stiff lips.

"I think you were the one who killed your partner." I said. Not the best thing to say.

She stood in ankle deep water. "Don't go there! Where's the woman?"

I shrugged. "Don't know. We fell, and I slid down here. She's up toward the road."

"Then I don't need you anymore." She pointed the pistol at me and the sound of the gunshot made me flinch. No pain. No impact. Blood gushed from the woman's forehead and she fell back into the pond water and floated away into the mixture of steam, snow, and water.

I whirled. Faye held the pistol, and her hands were shaking. I ran to her and gently took the pistol from her grasp. She looked at me and tears streamed down her face.

"My father took me to the gun range. Said I might need to know how to shoot someday." She looked at the pistol as if it were a poisonous snake. She began to shake, and I pulled her to me. I held her frozen form against me as she sobbed. "I've never killed anyone. Never! I'm a nurse practitioner. I save lives."

"Shh!" I said. "You saved my life, Faye."

I was still holding her when Raven appeared out of the snowstorm. She took one look at the woman's body floating in the pond and at the gun in the snow and put two and two together. "Let's get you somewhere warm." She said.

We made it up the slope to the van. My friendly cow stood in the lee of the van protected from the snow filled wind. She had left me another cow patty in appreciation. Raven opened the back end of the van. Blankets thrown haphazardly on the floor were normally used for covering furniture. She made a bed on the floor and helped Faye climb inside.

"Drive." Raven said to me as she climbed into the back. I shut the door and climbed into the driver's seat. I jacked up the heat and pulled the van back onto the road headed away from the small town. Behind me, Faye sobbed as Raven comforted her and wrapped her in blankets. Raven also shivered and pulled blankets around her shoulders.

"Just lay down and let the heat warm you up." Raven said.

"I took their car. They chased me. I'm not used to this." Faye said in gasping breaths. "And I killed that woman." She paused and studied Raven's face. "Is it all back? Your memory?"

"Yes. Thank God or you would be dead." Raven said.

Attached to the console was a cell phone. It was a commercial type with no password. I grabbed it and dialed Max's secure number.

"Who is this?" A man said.

"Jonathan Steel. I need to talk to Max."

The line clicked and whirred establishing a secure link.

"Jonathan?" It was Jason Birdsong.

"Just a minute." I said and handed the phone back to Raven.

Faye glanced at the phone in Raven's hand and grabbed it, and shoved it to her ear. "Jason! Oh my God! They kidnapped me. Raven and Jonathan saved me!" She said as she sobbed. I couldn't hear Jason's side of the conversation, but after a while, Faye calmed down. We passed a petrol station on the right side of the road and eventually left the snowstorm behind. Raven handed me the phone.

"Jason? She's safe. Raven is, too." I said.

"How did you get there? I mean, how did you save Raven and Faye?" Birdsong said.

"Long story. I'll catch you up once we get to a safe house."

"I'm sending you an address. Max said she will have a car waiting. You need to get off the road as soon as possible."

"No one knows we are in this van, Jason. But once this snowstorm passes, they will find the bodies, and the two abandoned cars."

"They? The police?"

"No. My brother and his henchmen."

"Henchmen, huh?" Birdsong said and chuckled nervously. "Sorry, haven't heard that one in a while. Got you on GPS and you're about twenty miles from the rendezvous point."

"This storm won't pass quickly. Should give us plenty of time to make the rendezvous."

"Wait a minute! Did you say brother?"

"Yes."

"Let me get this straight. This entire time we've been dealing with the cliché of an evil twin brother?"

"He's not my twin. But he is definitely evil." I said.

"Well, be careful. You know who your real brother is, right?"

"I'm talking to him." I said.

"Godspeed, Jonathan. And thank you for rescuing Faye." His voice cracked with emotion and he ended the call.

CHAPTER
SIXTY-ONE

JONATHAN STEEL

I stood on the balcony overlooking Place Du Trocadero. In the distance, the Eiffel Tower reached up into low-lying rain clouds. Christmas lights illuminated its structure. Were we that close to Christmas? The gentle breeze blew cold rain in my face and I tried to ignore them.

"You're going to freeze." Raven said. She closed the balcony doors behind her and handed me my jacket. I shrugged into it. "How are you?"

"Numb." I said, and Raven took me by the arm and gently pulled me back out of the rain. We sat on two wrought-iron chairs. I smelled coffee. Raven pushed a mug into my hands.

"I know you don't like coffee." She said.

"Makes me irritable." I sipped the black coffee. Bitterness filled my mouth. "But I need to be irritable."

"Max will be here within the hour." Raven sipped at her own coffee. "His eyes look just like yours. Talk about a rude awakening to come out of that mental fog and see him standing there with a gun."

Steel tensed. "I'm glad you didn't shoot me."

"Well, your voice is distinct, not as insane." She chuckled. "Much softer."

"Soft? I didn't know I could do soft."

"You were in the past. Look, we've both changed, Jonathan. That scripture you left me? I memorized it."

Raven drew a deep breath and then began to speak. "Who shall separate us from the love of Christ? Shall tribulation, or distress, or persecution, or famine, or nakedness, or peril, or sword? As it is written: 'For Your sake we are killed all day long; We are accounted as sheep for the slaughter.' Yet in all these things we are more than conquerors through Him who loved us. For I am persuaded that neither death nor life, nor angels nor principalities nor powers, nor things present nor things to come, nor height nor depth, nor any other created thing, shall be able to separate us from the love of God which is in Christ Jesus our Lord."

Raven smiled and even with the surgery, it was her original smile, one I missed. "That is the reason I went to Max for help. I put the verse in the medallion. I wanted to feel that kind of love in my life, Jonathan." She looked at me and put a warm hand on mine. "Thanks to you, I did."

I patted her hand. "I found that scrap of paper in the medallion. Truth came full circle." I said as Raven dabbed at her eyes.

She cleared her throat and drank some coffee. "Why is your brother after you?"

"I'm not sure." I said, and a shiver took me. "There are some gaps missing. Not from my memory, but from the information I could glean from my father's video confession."

Raven sat forward. "Confession?"

"From the trial."

"What trial?"

"When I was accused of killing my mother. Only it was my brother. My father claims everyone thought he died at birth." I said, and all of it was still surreal. "Turns out my mother and father underwent some kind of embryo implantation. Claims they implanted two but only one took. Turns out there were two of us. My father claims my brother died at childbirth. Obviously, he didn't. He's been in hiding. Now certain people know I am alive and that my father perpetrated a huge hoax on everyone."

"What do you mean?"

"Seems that someone is looking for me for some reason. So my father made it look like my brother was the special one and hid me away. At least once he realized my brother was alive. At the trial."

Raven raised an eyebrow. "And I thought my family was messed up."

"Now there are people who are looking for me because I made the news with that airplane crash in Switzerland."

"Your brother is looking for something also. He wants one of my memories." Raven said.

"What?"

"Of an assassination, off the books." Raven glanced at me. "I have to be careful, Jonathan. There were only three assassinations I did not put in my dossier."

"You remember them?"

"Not the names. Just the circumstances. That's why they aren't listed. I don't know who hired me or who I killed. Besides, those memories are still foggy." She looked at me and sighed. "Like a lot of memories. Memories of us."

I studied her face so different from the face I knew as Raven. Her eyes were the same and filled with such sadness and regret. "I remember some of those moments, Raven. But I'm not that person anymore."

Raven looked away quickly. "Neither am I. Thank God. And I mean that reverently. How did I lose all my memories?"

"Monarch used the nannomemes and tried to destroy the carbon matrix of your implant. Instead, she erased your mind." I looked away at the misty rain covering Paris. "At least we thought all of you was gone."

I felt her hand on my arm. "I'm back. Most of me. Jonathan, how do you deal with these memories? It's like I'm two people now. The killer from the before. The woman with regrets now."

"Do you remember what you told me before Monarch started the treatment?" I pulled my arm gently out of her grasp. She rested her hands in her lap.

"Yes. I told you to forgive your father. And, I told you I wouldn't. I was going to kill him." She sighed. "In spite of what I just told you, I'm still going to kill him. And, your brother."

"I don't know if I can forgive him. Even knowing what I know now." I looked away and rubbed my eyes. "Right now I have to focus on my brother and what he has planned next. He's the big bad now. Not my father."

"How does all of this fit in with the Council of Darkness?"

I shrugged. "I'm not sure. My father is supposed to be on the Council. He has the Ark of the Demon Rose which gives him some influence over the Council. What few members remain. But the Council will rebuild itself. There are only four more demons I have to deal with."

"Maybe you need to get help from your father?" Raven said.

"So you can kill him?"

Raven smiled. "I won't hurt the man until after we've dealt with your brother and the Council. I promise."

The doorbell rang. We went back into the hotel suite and I glanced through the peephole. Max and her assistant, Gamma stood outside. I opened the door. Max wore a long white faux fur coat and a headdress to match. She ushered Gamma in and shut the door behind her. Gamma pulled a cell phone size device from her pocket and began scanning the room.

Max pulled off her hat and her gray hair fell unhindered to her shoulders as if it had never been bunched up inside the hat. She took off her coat and Gamma nodded. "We are secure." Gamma left the room and stood outside the door.

Max wore a smart gray pair of slacks and matching blouse. A jeweled dragonfly brooch sat on her upper right chest. She turned to me and grabbed me in a tight hug. She finally pulled away and her eyes were wet with emotion. "I never knew about your brother. I would have told you." She whispered. I nodded.

"I believe you, Max."

Max turned to Raven and opened her arms. Raven fell into the woman's grasp and they hugged for what seemed like an eternity. Tears flowed. I found some tissues in the kitchen of our suite and put them on the dining table and sat at the end. And waited.

They whispered among themselves for a few moments. Raven touched the dragonfly brooch.

"Still on the side of angels." She said.

"Always." Max said as she wiped moisture from her eyes.

"I'm so sorry about those who died at the compound." Raven whispered.

Max nodded and wiped at her eyes. "We're still cleaning up the mess. Someone came and took the attackers' bodies. I'm sorry you have to recover your memory in such an abrupt fashion." She motioned to the table. "Now that is out of the way, sit. We have much to cover."

Raven sat to my right and Max slid into the chair at the opposite end of the table. "Gamma will ensure our safety. I have two security men downstairs in plain clothes. So, first things first. Jonathan, Faye and Jason are on their way back to the states."

"Faye was instrumental in my recovery." Raven said. "Max, Lucille was a plant."

Max's mouth opened slightly and her cheeks blushed. "That is impossible. Lucille has been in my employ for years. She was once a nurse in a clandestine clinic for the unsavory, shall we say. She came to me for help."

"I'm sorry. The way she acted toward, uh, Jeremiah he must have had some hold on her."

Max looked at me. "I understand from my security forces that you were in my chalet on the far side of the ridge?"

"Yes, taken there by Alphus, an angel. I met up with my two,

I guess you would call them, guardians." I said. "My lawyer and her investigator from when I was tried for killing my mother."

"Your lawyer?" Max raised an eyebrow.

"Yvonne Brown and her investigator, Sam O'Malley." I said.

Max blinked hard. "Yvonne Brown? That name rings a bell."

"You spoke to her and gave her the name of the third demon. Fifteen or sixteen years ago?" I said.

Max's eyes widened and she put a hand to her mouth. "I remember that, now. That was you?"

"Yes. I remember it all."

"You have recovered your memory?" She said.

"Yes. But the memories are like jigsaw puzzle pieces all piled on the table. It will take some time to put them together." I said.

A knock on the door interrupted us. I stood up quickly and Max raised a hand. "Gamma was supposed to text me if she needed me. No door knocking."

I moved quickly to the door and glanced quickly through the peephole. The person looking back at me was the last person I ever expected to see.

"Jonathan, it's your sweetheart. Truce, dear. I just want to talk. I have information you need."

I opened the door and the Crimson Snake stared back at me. Beneath a leather jacker, she wore a blinking Christmas sweater with a snowman and a snowwoman entwined in a kiss and a hug. Gamma sat unconscious on the floor by the door. "I'd put her on a bed if I were you. She'll wake up in a few. I'm here to see Max."

Before I could stop her, Snake pushed past me into the suite. I whirled and saw two things that startled me. Raven held a knife and Max held a pistol in her outstretched arm. Snake laughed. She pulled off a beret and her red hair fell down around her shoulders. She slowly removed her leather jacket. "I said truce, darlings. I'm here to help you out."

I checked on Gamma. She was breathing slowly, and I took

her and placed her on the bed in the bedroom. "What did you do to her?" I asked.

Snake held up her prosthetic hand. "Vulcan neck pinch. Now, can the two of you put your weapons away and let's have some tea and biscuits?"

Max lowered her pistol, and Raven took one step backwards, still holding the knife in her hand. Snake looked around the suite and moved into the kitchen area. "Ah, Earl Grey tea. I like it hot!" She bustled around the kitchen filling a kettle with water and dispensing tea bags into four cups. She opened cabinets and found a cache of snacks supplied by the hotel. "And, Biscotti's cookies. I love these."

I pointed to our seats, and we sat again as Snake made tea. Raven placed her knife on the table within reach. Max hid her pistol.

"I know this will come as a shock to you, but I'm out of the business as of yesterday." The kettle whistled and Snake poured steaming water into the cups. She took sugar and honey from the snack cabinet and placed them on the table, and served each of us a cup of tea. She retrieved a carton of cream from the refrigerator and looked at us. "What? You saw me make the tea. It's not poisoned." She put her good hand on her hip. "If I wanted you dead, we wouldn't be having this conversation right now." She sat at the table and took the tea bag from her cup and poured a generous amount of honey into the cup.

"How did you find us?" I asked.

"Oh, please!" She stirred her tea and added cream. "As if you have to ask." She sipped her tea and sighed. "Very good. Drink up. Then you can thank me."

"For what?" Max pushed her cup away.

"For Goudreaux." Snake tore open a pack of cookies and took a bite. "I turned her own organization against her. They arrested her, as you know, Max, and pinned the air disaster on her. As far as the Swiss know, she paid me to blow up the airplane. And they have lots of questions about her white eyes."

I gasped at the news and glanced at Raven. Raven shook her head and prepared her tea. I glared at her and she shrugged. "What? I like those cookies, too." She said.

"Well, don't everyone thank me at one time." Snake sipped more tea and crunched more cookies. "Now, about your brother, Jonathan. Or should I call you JJ?"

"How did you know that?"

"Your two friends told me." She said.

I bolted up from the table and my tea cup turned over spilling steaming brown fluid over the tabletop. "What?"

Snake waved me down. "Oh, don't worry. I was monitoring the compound from the ridge when I saw the mobilization of vehicles to approach a certain isolated chalet. When the EMP went off, my arm was useless. I saw the truck go over a ridge so I followed on my snowmobile. Analog. The truck broke down at the bottom of the ridge and I overheard your two friends talking about their hopes that you escaped. That's when I came to their aid and offered a ride down the mountain. You should have seen all three of us cuddled on a snowmobile. Perfect photo for a Christmas card. Oh, wait! I took a selfie."

Snake pulled her cellphone from her pocket and tapped the screen. She held the iPhone where I could see it. Yvonne sat behind Snake on a snowmobile, her face impassive. Sam sat behind Yvonne decidedly uncomfortable and his mouth was open, no doubt from just shouting out an obscenity.

Snake turned the screen toward Raven and Max. She smiled and sipped more tea as she pocketed her phone. She pried a piece of cookie from between her front teeth. "I took them to another small town and they caught a train for who knows where. Don't worry, I never told them I knew you." She got up and snatched a towel from the kitchen cabinet and tossed in on the table. "Now, clean up your mess and calm down."

I wiped up the tea. "Did they say where they were going?"

"They said nothing except for a thank you." Snake finished

the biscuit. "Although the big guy made a few sailors blush! What a potty mouth!"

I sat down and with difficulty said, "Thank you."

"Care to tell me who they are?" Snake asked.

"No."

She brushed her good hand against her artificial hand and crumbs fell on the table. "Now, down to business. I am here to help. I am done with the old life. I want a new life." She looked at Max. "Have you spoken to Vivian lately?"

"No." Max said.

"We made a deal. I would help Jonathan by getting rid of the charges against him and she would speak to you about helping me, uh, well, rehabilitate." Snake swallowed hard as if choking on the word. "Look, I'm tired of being hired, used, and then tossed to the wind. I'm tired of killing and spying. I'm tired of being me. I want a new me."

I glanced at Raven and then at Max. Max nodded. "Very well, then we will start now. Remove your prosthetic arm and hand it to Raven."

Snake tensed. "Why?"

"There will be no asking why from now on. I will only tell you to do so for our continued safety. I will decide when you will get it back."

Snake reached into her sweater and there was a snap. Her arm slid onto the table. Max pointed to it. "Raven, if you would be so kind."

"Gladly!" Raven took the arm and placed it her lap.

"There is important business to attend to first." Max straightened and looked at me. "Your father? What have you gleaned from your memories?"

I sat back and told them the long tale of my trial. "He had no idea my brother was still alive. I am wanted for some reason. My father took great pains to make it look as if my brother was the special one so forces would go after him. All of my memory loss was supposed to protect me with anonymity.

Until the air disaster and my face appeared on international news sites."

Max steepled her hands before her. "I gave your lawyer two names for the third and fourth demon. Those names were purely speculation! I wasn't completely sure they were genuine."

"They must have been. Yvonne used the third demon's name in court." I cleared my throat. "She also said you told her to stay away from Cephas Lawrence. You told her he was dangerous."

Max blinked and looked away. "I was wrong about Cephas, as we now know. I thought he had something to do with my daughter's disappearance." She sat up straight and nodded. "Now, let's move on. What does your brother want?"

"My memories." Raven looked at Max. "Just as you do."

"What?"

"I'm not stupid, Max. If Jeremiah wants those memories, then so do you. You're the light to his darkness. Besides, I overheard Lucille say as much to Faye. What is so important about these off-the-books jobs?"

Max's gaze moved slowly across Snake and rested on me. "Have you heard of the Penticle?"

"Yes." I said. "The unholy triad had me find out information about a member of the Penticle."

"I've heard rumors." Raven said.

"I've met a member of the Penticle, too. But he's dead." Snake said. "I killed him. Three years ago. Seems that the assassin hired to take him out failed." Snake looked at Raven. "You."

Max gasped, something I had never heard her do. "You know who the dead man is?"

"No." Snake said. "I'm sure Raven can corroborate this, but the job was an anonymous hit. The man's location at a certain time and place were given to me."

"And I was told to make it look like an accident." Raven finished. She looked at Max. "I knew it was a man but had no idea of his identity."

"You said there were two jobs." I said.

"Actually, three in all." Raven said. "It's coming back to me. I succeeded on two of them but the third man failed to appear at the proper time and place. Thus, the two completed off-the-books jobs. All three victims were anonymous."

"Why is this important to you?" I asked Max. "Or my brother?"

"You know the answer to that, Jonathan. Why did the three demons want to take out Faust?" Max asked.

"So they could put a demon possessed person on the Penticle. They claim the Penticle is demon free and they craved the influence."

"It's a good bet that one of the Penticle members hired me to kill that man three years ago." Raven said.

"And Max and your brother want that information to blackmail the Penticle member who hired me and Raven. Force him to retire and create a vacancy among the five seats." Snake said.

"Which is exactly what they originally planned to do with Faust. Use Raven's dossier to show he hired her to kill someone not on the Penticle and then blackmail him to resign and recommend a demon from the Council for his position." I said.

"Who killed Faust?" Raven asked.

"My brother." I said. I couldn't prove it but it made sense. "I'm not certain, but it makes sense. Then he can use this other information about the off-the-books job to secure someone a place on the Penticle. With Faust out, they would have a chance to fill Faust's spot and the spot of the person they want to blackmail into retiring."

"Fill the spots with who?" Snake asked.

"I don't know." I said. "This may turn out to be the Council versus the Vitreomancers. I'm pretty sure my brother was possessed by the third demon long ago. And the third demon claims to have. 'Legion' of humans he moves among leaving lesser demons as placeholders. My brother could still be one of the third demon's puppets."

"Which is why you wanted the information." Snake pointed at Max.

"The Vitreomancers are not as powerful as the Council of Darkness." Max said. "If the demons asked Jonathan to find out information on Faust so they could place a person possessed by a demon from the Council of Darkness on the Penticle, it stands to reason the person killed by Snake was possibly replaced with a Vitreomancer."

"Or, someone not possessed by a demon." I said.

"In any event," Max continued, "with the blackmail leverage, if the Vitreomancers are behind this, they could fill both spots."

"You're thinking my brother is working for the Vitreomancers?" I said.

"Possibly. Not likely. If two members of the Penticle are controlled by rival demonic councils, there would be hell to pay." Max said. "If would could identify the person who hired Raven and Snake to kill a member of the Penticle, we could discover if that person was in fact a Vitreomancer." Max looked at Snake and then as Raven. "Is there anything the two of you can remember about the job that might point to the person responsible?"

Snake looked at Raven. "We could compare notes. That is if Raven agrees not to knife me."

Raven raised up Snake's arm. "I don't need to knife you. I have the upper hand."

Snake smiled. "I am disarmed."

Max groaned and actually rolled her eyes. She motioned to the bedroom. "While you two talk, I'll check on Gamma. And find out how Snake got past my two men downstairs."

"Wait!" I said. "What will you do with this information?"

Max smiled. "Make sure the Council doesn't succeed in getting the empty seat."

"Who would fill it?" I asked Max. She blinked a couple of times and averted her gaze.

"I have a few candidates in mind." She stood up and disappeared into the bedroom.

What would happen if Max was a member of the Penticle? Could she shape events in the world to stop the work of the demons? Or, would the power go to her head? I shook my head. I trusted Max completely. I had no choice. She was the anchor I had in this demonic storm.

I paced restlessly around the living room suite while Raven and Snake talked. I had to get out. Leaving the suite, I made my way down to the ground floor. A dozen or so people moved around the lobby. I couldn't for the life of me pick out Max's guards. A group of hotel employees were putting up Christmas decorations. I walked through the doors and out onto the streets. The fine misting rain had turned into a gentle shower and I pulled my jacket hood up over my head. Just a short walk to clear my head.

I felt a tiny prick in my neck and I halted. I reached up and felt the small dart. Darkness took me.

CHAPTER
SIXTY-TWO

I AWOKE to nausea and retched. The odor of unwashed bodies and urine filled my nostrils from the bed I lay on. I sat up quickly, too quickly. My vision swam and I blinked to clear my eyes. Someone moved in the shadows and slid a curtain aside. Pale light filled the room through a grimy window, and I squinted to see who my captor might be.

"This is the room where Steven Monarch almost died." A familiar voice said. The Eiffel Tower was visible through the dirty windows. "Forgive my subterfuge. I didn't want to deal with Max just yet."

My vision focused and my father sat on a couch across the small room. "You are unbelievable." I growled.

"I understand you have recovered your memory." The Captain wore his ever present Panama hat and the fragrance of pipe smoke drifted from the pipe in his hand. "If that is so, then we need to put the past behind us and get on with a plan to stop your brother."

I tried to stand up and fell back onto the small bed. Dust surrounded me and I sneezed. "So that's it! We just forget what you've done to me?"

"It was for your own good, son. I had to protect you by

changing your identity. Surely you remember the years we ran from place to place?" He stoked his Meerschaum pipe and the red glow lit up his turquoise eyes.

"I remember them. Years of training and hiding."

"From your brother. You remember that now, don't you?"

"Yes." I felt the memories fall into place like dominoes tumbling. "And I escaped you when I was 18."

"Took me three years to track you down."

"And you put an implant in my brain." I said.

"Which I could have used to subdue you, but I needed your memory intact."

I tapped one of my temples. "I no longer have the implant. You can say that phrase again and it wouldn't touch me." I hoped, anyway. So I said it. "Beware the demon of the spiral eye." I said. I tensed, waiting for the inevitable nausea and headache. Nothing happened. I smiled. "See. I'm free of you."

The Captain looked away. "How?"

"An angel took it out of my head." I said. "Divine intervention."

"You weren't cooperating. I had to find some way to control you." The Captain said. "I have no regrets, son. I did it to protect you. Now you know why. We've put off the inevitable for fifteen years. Now, the time has come to pay the piper." The Captain stood up and moved to the window. "I brought you here to escape any surveillance. The demons are everywhere. And they may answer to your brother."

"Why would they watch you? You told Vivian you were on the Council." I said.

"A convenient lie, if you will. I was a consultant to the Council." He turned and his eyes burned with anger. "I had to do it, son! I had to sell my soul to Satan to protect you. Can't you see that?"

I stood up and wobbled. "There had to be other ways."

The Captain moved quickly to within arm's grasp. "And look at the man you are today. A Christian, a spiritual warrior fighting these powers of evil. If I had used any other 'plan' the Council would not be decimated. The powers of evil are being defeated. By you, JJ. By you. And the only reason you can stand here in indignation at my sins is because you are a righteous man. I made you that way." He looked away. "I and God."

"Yvonne and Sam were more of a parent to me than you've ever been." I said.

The Captain whirled and slapped me across the face. I felt the sting of the pain and recalled all the times he had slapped me before. I drew back my fist and fought for control. What good would it do to strike the man now? There were more pressing matters at hand.

I stepped back. "Violence is always your answer, isn't it? How many have you had killed in your quest to find my brother?"

The Captain's red cheeks glowed with anger and he stepped away and turned back to the window. "I had to enlist the help of the Vitreomancers." He said, avoiding the question. "They think I am on the Council. I've turned both groups against each other."

The Captain slowly turned around and tapped cold ashes from his pipe onto the floor. He slid the pipe into his pocket. "Your brother is working with the second demon. There is a master plan I am not privy to. I need your help, son. We must stop your brother from achieving his goal."

I released the tension in my fists and rubbed my stinging cheek. Jeremiah was not working with the Vitreomancers? That meant the replaced member of the Penticle would be a Vitreomancer. My thoughts were foggy from trying to keep it all straight. I glared at my father. "So you want me to put all of this between us behind me?"

The Captain took off his hat. He rubbed his eyes and for the first time I saw humility there. "I need you, son. We have to call a truce if we are to stop them."

"Fine! What should we do?"

"You will take number four and number three off the board."

He pulled an envelope out of his pocket. "Some Bible verses for you to read when you get to the courtroom."

"Courtroom?"

"When you arrive in Dallas, you will be arrested again for an arraignment before Judge Meridian to drop the charges. Drake will be at that same arraignment. Meridian wants to put on a show." He handed me the envelope. "When you two certain items from evidence, you will need to read the Bible verses."

I studied the envelope in my hand. Two items, I thought. He was being overly cautious. I looked around the room and wished Olivia was here. She would have seen if there were any demons to listen in on our conversation. Two items, one for each demon? My father had the Ark of the Demon Rose and within it were talismans for every demon on the Council of Darkness. Possessing a talisman could possibly give the holder an advantage. I nodded.

"I understand."

"Good, I will follow up on your brother and his plans. We divide and conquer. You make your court appearance and I will take care of some things on my end."

My father walked out of the room. It took me a while to maneuver down rickety stairs to the street. By then, the sun was setting and the misting rain had cleared leaving behind a sky filled with blood colored clouds.

I had no cell phone and I flagged down a taxi to take me to the hotel. I had to wrangle with the taxi driver while I called up to the suite. Gamma showed up and paid the taxi driver and escorted me back to our room. She looked now worse for wear.

Max ceased her pacing and Raven ran across the room when I showed up through the door. She grabbed me and hugged me then pushed me away and gazed into my eyes.

"What happened?"

"I went for a walk and was taken by my father." I stumbled over to the table and sat down. "Coffee?"

Max moved to a coffee pot and poured me a cup of coffee.

She sat beside me and put a hand on my arm. I sipped the noxious brew and hoped the caffeine would clear my head. "You shouldn't have gone out on the street, my boy." She said.

"I know that now." I whispered. "But my father and I had an interesting exchange." Raven sat beside Max. "What did you and Snake come up with."

"We compared notes and came up with two probable names based on the time and location of the assignments." Raven said. "Gamma is working on the search right now. Snake left." Raven motioned to the kitchen cabinet where Snake's arm lay. "But we kept her arm as collateral."

My head began to clear. "According to my father, I will be arrested the minute I arrive back in Dallas."

"Yes, you will." Max said. "We picked up the chatter just moments ago."

I put a hand on Raven's hand. "The two of you find out what you can about this assassination attempt. I'll go back and face Meridian. And, Drake."

HEATHROW AIRPORT

"You're hurting my hand." Faye Morgan said.

Jason Birdsong glanced down at her, hand clenched tightly in his lap. "I'm never letting you go."

"Relax, Jason. I'm fine." Faye said.

Birdsong blinked and studied the rain running down the window of the terminal at Heathrow. "The least Max could have done was fly us back to the United States on a private jet."

"We are flying first class, babe." Faye said. He felt her free hand rub his arm. He relaxed his grip. He had almost lost her. And he had just found her before all of this began.

"This isn't over, you know." Birdsong finally looked at her. Faye had pulled her hair up into a knit cap and wore a large sweater.

"Hey, I did what Max asked. I helped Raven recover her mind." She smiled. "And then, Raven and Jonathan saved me from his brother? Right?"

"Yeah, he hasn't explained it all to me. Yet." Birdsong studied her eyes. They hinted at something deeper. Something she had not told him. "Are you sure you're okay?"

Faye looked away. "I was kidnapped and almost killed, Jason. I need time to process it all."

He rubbed her back and looked back at the frosted windows. Christmas decorations hung around the terminal along with Hanukkah decor. But the festive atmosphere did little to allay his fear. Jeremiah Stone could be nearby.

He felt Faye's warm hand on his face and she turned him to face her. She planted a kiss on his lips. "The only reason Jeremiah took me was to get to Raven. That's over now. We're safe." Her voice broke with emotion and she nodded quickly. "We are safe, aren't we?"

Birdsong nodded numbly. "Yes." He said, but his heart wasn't in it.

"Mr. Birdsong?"

Birdsong jumped and stood up quickly. D.I. Holland walked across the carpet with a rolling suitcase. "Holland?"

"Heading home? God, I wish I could smoke." She glanced at Faye. "The missus?"

"Uh, my girlfriend, Faye Morgan." Birdsong said. "Where are you going?"

Holland actually smiled. "Your tip paid off. We found lots of trophies, including McGuire's medal at Drake's hotel room, along with enough DNA evidence to bury him." She motioned to a seat across from them. "Mind if I sit?"

"No." Birdsong eased back into his chair.

"I'm heading to Dallas, Texas. Yeehaw!" London wore a pair of jeans and a denim shirt. "I dressed for the occasion."

"What's in Dallas?" Faye said.

"Reginald Drake. He has been apprehended and your friend's son, Josh, is his name? He recorded essentially a confession from Drake that he killed Molly McGuire. I am personally escorting him back to London for his trial. I have all the extradition papers in my bag." He noticed a metal valise handcuffed to her other arm.

"And that?"

"Evidence I will present to the judge. Some of it may help implicate Drake in the murder of that poor doctor in Louisiana." She leaned toward him. "I made sure it was handcuffed to me. Chain of evidence must stay intact. Only problem is I'm in the rear of the airplane. Cheapest seat." She said.

"You told me the department was hurting for funds." Birdsong said. He wasn't about to tell her they were flying first class!

"Oh, the department refused to pay. They insisted a U.S. Marshal bring Drake back to us." She smiled. "So I paid for the ticket myself. It will be worth every pound just to see Drake's face when I show him what's in this little case."

"Good work, D. I. Holland." Birdsong said. "I respect you for that!"

Holland threw him a sideways glance. "You're not such a bad investigator yourself. If you ever decide to move to London and need a job, look me up. There are vacancies on the force."

Birdsong glanced at Faye, and she shook her head. "I think we've seen enough of Europe for a while. No offense."

Holland laughed. "None taken. I'll feel the same way when I get back on the airplane coming back to home."

"With Drake in tow." Birdsong said.

Holland nodded. "That will be one interesting trip. I have a Tazer I'll use on him if he doesn't shut up!"

JONATHAN STEEL

The courtroom was almost empty when Ruth Martinez and I walked down the aisle and to the first row of the spectator section. Bubba, the bailiff, stood stiffly at the edge of Martinez's desk. Behind me, the doors opened and Jason Birdsong entered, along with a woman I had never met. She was thin and carried a metal valise handcuffed to her wrist.

"Jonathan!" Birdsong grabbed me and hugged me. "Brother!"

My eyes misted, and I patted his shoulder. This man was my real brother! "I heard you had quite the adventure."

"In Drake's furnace, no less." He nodded to Ruth. "Ruth, Jonathan, this is Detective Inspector Holland from London." He motioned to the woman.

She shook my hand. "The infamous Jonathan Steel." She grimaced. "I was ready to throw you behind bars."

I lifted my ankle. "I'm not out of the woods yet." I pointed to the anklet. "They met me at the airport and put a new anklet on me." I introduced Ruth.

"Ms. Martinez." Holland shook her hand.

I stared at the valise. "What's in the case?"

Holland smiled. "Evidence that will put Drake away for life. Items we recovered from his hotel room. Souvenirs from his prior kills. I'm hoping something in here will link Drake to the murder of that doctor over in Louisiana."

"Dr. Moshander." I said conscious of the envelope from my father tucked in the pocket of my jacket. "When do we get to see what's inside?"

"During the arraignment. Is your justice system always this wonky? Having you appear at a hearing to decide your fate and then move right into Drake's arraignment?" Holland asked.

"Judge Meridian is rather ruthless." Ruth said. "He's a bit of a showman."

The side door to the courtroom opened and three guards came in, ushering Reginald Drake to the defendant's table. He was cuffed and manacled and wore a bright yellow prison jump-suit. Drake's two-toned eyes flashed with mischief as he glanced around the room. His gaze settled on Birdsong and his eyes widened. "How?"

"Yes, I am alive." Birdsong said.

Holland walked over to the table. "D. I. Holland. We'll be spending some time together when I escort you back to London with me. And you will bloody well pay for your crimes." She pointed at Birdsong. "Including attempted murder."

Drake shrugged. "Put it on my tab." He looked around Holland at me. "Mr. Steel! So good to see you are back among the living." The guards pushed him down into his chair. One guard attached his manacled hands and cuffs to a metal ring on the table.

Drake ignored them, his gaze never wavering from me. "You realize that once I am acquitted, I will track down your son and there will be payback for his betrayal."

I tensed. "He didn't betray you. He fooled you. Josh was clever and recorded your confession."

"Which will be quickly thrown out in court." He put a hand

up to the side of his mouth and the chains rattled. He winked at Holland. "I'm buddies with the judge."

"All rise." Bubba intoned. We were already standing and Drake remained seated. Holland huffed and crossed to the prosecution table.

"I can't rise, Bubba. I'm chained to the floor." Drake said and giggled.

The door to Meridian's office opened and Assistant District Attorney Bryan Nicholas appeared. His gaze was hooded and he glanced nervously at Ruth. Judge Meridian followed and snapped his fingers. The huge, black dog, Anubis bolted into the courtroom and ran immediately to Drake's table. He growled at Drake with his huge paws on the front edge of the table. Drake backed away.

"Good doggie. I promise you some liver later." He glanced once at me and threw me a kiss.

I resisted the urge to rip the man's head off. Meridian mounted his desk and towered over us.

"Anubis, heel." He said. Anubis ran back to the front of Meridian's desk and lay down, his huge pink tongue hanging from his mouth.

Holland leaned toward Birdsong. "What the dickens, mate? What's a bloody dog doing here?"

Meridian tapped his gavel. "I'm sorry, miss. Did you have a question?"

Holland marched up to the desk and ignored Anubis. "I'm D. I. Holland from Great Britain and I am carrying sealed evidence that will show that Mr. Drake not only killed Margaret McGuire but also murdered Dr. Moshander in Shreveport, Louisiana." She held up the valise. "And other evidence that will tie him to at least five murders in Europe and possibly more here in the states."

Meridian looked like he had swallowed a sour apple. "Miss Holland, we will get to you once the fate of Jonathan Steel is decided, and I will determine if I will allow this so-called evidence to be entered. D.A. Nicholas will prosecute Mr. Steel and Mr. Drake, and I am sure he is eager to see this evidence when I decide the time is appropriate. Now, will you take your place in the spectator's section until I call for you?"

Holland nodded. "Can I smoke?"

Meridian blinked behind his huge glasses. "I have no problem with that."

Anubis yelped as Holland stepped on his paw. The dog growled and Meridian snapped his fingers. "Down boy. Your turn will come."

Holland moved to the back of the courtroom and lit up a cigarette. Meridian settled into his chair. "Now some housekeeping. We are here today to decide the fate of Jonathan Steel regarding his recent fugitive status. And to officially dispense with other charges. I assume Ms. Martinez is once again representing you?"

"Yes, your honor." Ruth said.

"Then who is this other man?"

"My business partner, Jason Birdsong. He escorted D. I. Holland to protect the evidence." I said.

"Very well. First, let me say that Mr. Drake does not have a defense council. By the powers vested in me, I hereby appoint Ruth Martinez as his attorney for the duration of this hearing."

"What?" Ruth shouted. She glanced at Nicholas. He shrugged.

"I had no choice in the matter, Ruth. He called me into his office right before the hearing to inform me." Nicholas said.

"Your honor, I cannot represent Jonathan Steel and Reginald Drake. There is an obvious conflict of interest." Ruth said.

"Mr. Steel continues to have an outstanding warrant for his arrest in Great Britain as an accessory to the murder of Margaret McGuire. And accessory to Mr. Drake. Therefore, since you represent Mr. Steel, you will also represent his accused accomplice."

Ruth started to protest and Meridian rapped his gavel. "If

you do not accept this arrangement, I will have you removed from this courtroom and taken immediately to jail for contempt of court. Let me remind you that I am judge and jury for this case by your very request." His hand disappeared beneath the desk and reappeared holding a set of scales. The ancient bronze set of scales squeaked as he set it before him. I gasped. He had used the same set of scales in my trial.

"This ancient set of scales represents the law, Ms. Martinez. The concept of law goes back thousands of years. I represent the ultimate expression of that law and as solid and as reliable as these scales are, so will be my edict in this courtroom. Now, will you defend Mr. Drake or shall I have the three guards waiting in the anteroom take you immediately to a holding cell?"

I squeezed her hand back. I looked into her tear-filled eyes. "Ruth, you have no choice."

"But I've done this once and he was acquitted. Because of me, Jonathan. Those other people are dead because of me! I can't do this again."

I put my arm around her shoulder and pulled her close to me. "You have to trust me, Ruth. Drake will never leave this courtroom. Trust me."

Ruth pulled away and her eyes filled with confusion. "What? What do you have planned, Jonathan?"

I rubbed the tears from her cheek. "Trust me." I turned to Judge Meridian. "Your honor may I approach the bench?"

Meridian smiled. "I'd like nothing more, Mr. Steel. Don't step on Anubis."

I ignored the dog's growls and looked up at Meridian. "I know there are outstanding charges against me that you will now drop, if I am correct?"

"Yes, Mr. Steel. All federal charges have been dropped based on new evidence. There is still the charge of removing your anklet and leaving the country." Meridian held up some papers. "And, of course, D. I. Holland's charges regarding your actions in London."

I felt a tap on my shoulder. Jason Birdsong motioned toward the door. "Do you trust me, brother?"

I glanced at the door. What did he have up his sleeve? "Yes."

Birdsong moved between me and the judge. "Ms. Martinez would be free to defend Mr. Drake if you will allow another attorney to defend Mr. Steel."

Ruth hurried to my side. "Jonathan, what are the two of you doing?"

I looked into her eyes. "Ruth, trust Jason. He knows what he is doing." I hoped.

"Ms. Martinez, your decision?" Meridian said.

Ruth cast one anguished look at me and then at Jason. "I accept."

Birdsong took out his cell phone and tapped out a message. The back door of the courtroom opened and two people walked in, Yvonne Brown and Sam O'Malley.

"No! You can't do this!" I hurried toward them.

Yvonne put a hand on my chest. "Relax, JJ. Everything is out in the open. We were going to come in at the most opportune time, but Jason said you need me to defend you?"

I looked into her eyes and over her shoulder at Sam. "It would seem so. But I have a plan if things don't go our way."

Yvonne winked. "I do, too. I have total recall of certain names, if we need them."

Sam reached out his hand. "I'm glad you made it, son."

I took his hand and pulled him into a hug. "You didn't have to come."

"Of course we did." Sam said hoarsely. "Now let's take care of this demon duo."

The three of us walked up to Meridian's desk. Yvonne glanced down at Anubis. "Getting gray around the eyes, aren't you?" The dog growled at her. "The last time I saw you was when you were swallowed by the third demon."

"This dog is, in fact, Anubis number four. I'm hard on dogs." Meridian stood up slowly, and a sly smile lit up his face. "Well, what a family reunion. Mr. Drake, everyone has come home to roost. Except the Captain."

"Your honor, I am Mr. Stone. I mean Mr. Steel's attorney. I have been listening at the door and I understand that there is evidence in this courtroom that might clear my client of any charges of accessory to murder." She turned to Holland. "I will need to see the evidence from D. I. Holland before we proceed."

Holland stood up and shook her head. "It's a bloody circus over here, init?"

"A circus indeed?" Meridian sat back in his chair. My mind went back through the years to this very courtroom. I paused and looked around. I remembered it all, recalled every moment of the trial! I glanced at the defendant's table. I had been there, and not Drake. But the third demon had been here as well.

"Remembering all the details, are we?" Drake said, tapping his temple. "We remember everything, don't we?"

"You weren't there, Drake. Just your demon."

"Demon?" Holland said.

"Just present the evidence, D. I. Holland." Meridian said. "I am eager to see Mr. Drake's spoils." Meridian said. "Come forward D. I. Holland."

I moved back to the defendant's table and sat beside Drake. I smiled at him as he glared at me with his two-colored eyes.

"What is Ms. Brown up to?"

"We'll see." I said.

Bryan Nicholas shrugged and pulled out a chair for Ruth. "I seem to be superfluous here."

Holland placed her valise on the prosecutor's table. I motioned to Jason to sit behind me in the first row of benches. Yvonne stood stiffly by me.

"I hope you know what you're doing." I said.

Yvonne gripped my shoulder. "I hope you do, too. I'm buying us some time."

Holland took out a set of keys and unlocked her handcuff. I reached into the inside pocket of my jacket and took out the

Captain's envelope. Holland opened the valise with another key. Nicholas craned his neck to look into the valise. Holland glared at him. "You'll see everything, counselor. Patience." She glanced back at Drake.

"Your honor, the first item we found in Mr.Drake's hotel room was this jaunty hat." She held up a bright green Swiss Alpine hat with a huge white feather.

"Oh, that's my favorite hat." Drake said. "Can I wear it, please?"

Holland glared at him. "We have already identified your DNA and the DNA of Johann Sweitzer from Austria. He was found brutally murdered three years ago. His killer was never found but his DNA is on the brim of this hat along with Mr. Drake's."

"Let me try it on and I'll explain." Drake said.

"By all means." Meridian grinned. "Give the man his hat."

"Yes, let's see if it fits." Holland handed the hat to Birdsong.

"Because if the hat fits, he wore it." She said. Jason took the hat and came around behind Drake and put the hat on his head. It fit perfectly.

"See." Drake said. "I purchased this hat from a secondhand market. It was because it fit so perfectly." He leaned his head back and yodeled. "Oh de lady, oh de lady hooo!"

Meridian rapped his gavel. "Stop that nonsense."

Drake grinned. "Which nonsense would you like me to do?"

Holland looked at me and winked, a totally unexpected gesture. I tensed and glanced back at the hat. Was this one of the talismans? A hat? I opened the envelope and pulled out the letter. Holland proceeded as I read the contents of the letter. An icy wave passed over me as I read the first of the two sets of Bible verses.

"Your honor, I have four different watches. Two belong to two men and two belong to two women." She held up two plastic evidence envelopes. "We found these in Drake's hotel room. Each has been identified by the DNA of cold case victims from four different countries in Europe."

Holland placed the watches on the table. She took out the knife. I froze, and my heart skipped a beat. Drake leaned over and whispered in my ear. "Look familiar, honey?"

Holland held up the golden knife in its plastic envelope. "The knife used to kill Margaret McGuire. Originally, this knife had only the fingerprints and DNA of Mr. Steel. It was placed in our evidence room. Shortly thereafter, the knife disappeared for a time and mysteriously reappeared twenty-four hours before I flew here."

"So you are admitting your evidence is tainted?" Meridian said.

Holland ignored Anubis and approached the bench. She placed the golden, gleaming knife on the desk. "Go ahead and look at it, your honor. When it reappeared in our evidence box, we had it retested again. Mr. Steel's fingerprints were no longer there. Instead, two sets of prints appeared. One of an unknown assailant and the other," she turned and pointed at Drake, "Reginald Drake's."

She came back to the valise and removed a folder of papers. She passed them to Bubba. "Our evidence room attendant signed an affidavit stating he was paid to remove the knife and give it to an unknown man. A man with turquoise eyes." She turned and looked at me and I froze. My blood ran cold. "A man who resembles Mr. Steel but whose fingerprints and DNA from the knife are totally different."

Meridian picked up the knife and studied. "This is very confusing, D. I. Holland."

Yvonne spoke up. "I believe what D. I. Holland would conclude is someone who looked like Mr. Steel freed Mr. Drake from his anklet and then was his true accomplice in the murder of Margaret McGuire. And perhaps this unknown accomplice removed the knife from evidence so Mr. Drake could, uh, fondle it. You might recall a similar sequence of events occurred during

JJ Stone's trial with regard to his brother. They resembled each other. And Jeremiah Stone has never been captured since he confessed to killing his mother."

Meridian crossed his arms. "Nice speech, counselor. Are you suggesting that Jeremiah Stone is Mr. Drake's accomplice? How do you explain the original set of fingerprints on the knife from Mr. Steel?"

"He has already stated he picked up the knife from the artifact room of Hampton's museum to defend himself when he heard someone taunting him in the furnace room." Yvonne said.

"Taunting? It was more like inviting him to play." Drake giggled again.

Meridian leaned forward and tore the clear envelope from the knife and held the knife up to the light. Holland stepped back.

"What are you doing?" Holland shouted. "You've just contaminated the bloody evidence."

Meridian held the knife close to his face and golden light reflected onto his glasses. "I had to touch it. I had to feel all the evil and all the deaths this knife has accomplished." He closed his eyes and moaned in ecstasy. "Yes! Such evil!"

"Your honor, I protest!" Nicholas said.

Meridian opened his eyes and sighed. He put the knife back into its envelope. "Relax counselor. I will attest that I touched the knife and my fingerprints can be eliminated. I haven't removed the incriminating evidence. I concede Ms. Brown's points." He placed the knife next to his gavel. "Do you have anything else?"

"I have fourteen total items all linking Mr. Drake to the murder of as many victims in Europe." Holland returned to the valise. "I have five items that cannot be linked to murders in Europe but I believe they will be linked to murders here. I have already allowed Special FBI agent Franklin Ross to examine those items and he is currently correlating them with cold case murders." She held up a dark, rusted chain. "This chain, for instance, is very primitive, possibly from a museum and there is blood on it we cannot identify. We believe it was used to strangle a victim."

I tensed and read the second Bible verse again. Hope filled my heart. My heart! Yes, that was the key. Holland removed one last evidence envelope and held it up. "Finally, Margaret McGuire's St. Christopher medal. Her DNA and Mr. Drake's DNA are on it."

"It was a gift." Drake said loudly. "We had a thing."

"Oh shut it, you loony bin!" Holland said.

"Is that the extent of your evidence?" Meridian said.

"Yes. Along with the extradition papers to allow me to take Drake back to London." She sat down beside Nicholas.

Before Meridian could speak, I stood up. "Your honor, may I have a fifteen minute recess to gather my thoughts before proceeding?"

Meridian's gaze had returned to the knife. He tapped his gavel. "Fifteen minutes. But no one leaves this courtroom."

"I will need Mr. Birdsong to acquire an object of evidence if you will allow him to leave the courtroom?" I said.

Meridian looked up from the knife. "I will allow it."

I took Jason, Sam, and Yvonne to a far corner and told them my plan. Jason looked at me with horror. "You want to what?"

"Take Sam. He knows who I'm looking for, right Sam?"

Sam nodded slowly. "I think I can find him."

"Just do as I ask, Jason. Trust me."

Jason shook his head and he and Sam left the courtroom. I glanced at my left palm. It glowed a faint blue. I hoped this was going to work!

MERIDIAN CAME out of his office. It was only then I realized he had taken the knife with him. He sat behind his desk and placed the knife beside his gavel. "Let's get on with this, shall we?"

I put a hand on Yvonne's shoulder. "Pay attention." I whispered. I stood up and walked without hesitation toward his desk. Anubis growled at me and rose to his feet. I ignored him.

"Your honor, I appeal to the scales of justice. I would like for you to weigh my heart."

Drake chuckled. "This is better than anything I could have come up with."

Yvonne glanced at him. "Shut up, you fool."

Meridian stood up, and he raised an eyebrow. He snapped his fingers and Anubis jumped up and, before I could react, grabbed my shirt and ripped it from my chest. I stumbled back, putting a hand on my bare chest. I shrugged out of my coat and tore the shirt off me. Anubis growled softly with the remnants of my shirt in his mouth. I stood bare chested before the fourth demon.

"I bear my heart, Meridian. Call off your devil dog."

"Oh, Anubis will stay right where he is, Mr. Steel. You know what happens in the weighing of the heart." Meridian was no longer the judge. His eyes fairly glowed with evil and eager anticipation. I glanced back at the door to the courtroom and hoped and prayed Jason had accomplished his deed. I looked back at Meridian.

"Those gathered here may not be familiar with the weighing of the heart." I said. This was no longer a courtroom of law. It was a battlefield for spiritual warfare.

I turned and regarded the strange assembly of people. "In ancient days, the legend goes like this. When a person died, their heart was weighed on the scales of justice." I motioned to the scales. "Every deed, good and evil, was assessed and then the person's heart was placed on the scale. On one side, the person's life. On the other side, an ostrich feather. For if the person's good deeds outweighed the evil deeds, then the heart was light and would weigh less than a feather."

"That's bloody ridiculous." Holland said. She glanced at Nicholas. "You can stop this charade, can't you?"

"No, he can't." Meridian said. "Mr. Steel has agreed to the weighing of his heart. There is no turning back."

I heard the door open behind me. Meridian froze, and for a moment, his face twisted in fear. "His kind cannot come into this room!" He stood up. Anubis' attention wavered, and he looked beyond me. He dropped my shirt and cowered. He backed away until his tucked tail hit the desk.

Jason Birdsong, Sam O'Malley and the angel, Alphus, joined me before Meridian's desk. I glanced at Drake, and for the first time, he was speechless.

"You bring one of them to this proceeding?" Meridian growled.

"Your honor, I assure you that Alphus is here as a witness. You must allow me my defense." I said.

Yvonne joined us and smiled as she looked at Alphus. She pointed to Alphus. "Or are you afraid of one of your own kind?"

Holland cursed and shook her head. "What the devil is going on?"

"The devil, indeed." I said. "I'm sorry D. I. Holland. But what you and Mr. Nicholas are about to witness is something that is beyond the natural." I confronted Meridian. "Will you allow it?"

Meridian slowly sat back down. "No tricks."

Alphus wore a totally white three-piece suit with a red tie. His long, blonde hair draped over his shoulders. "My kind do not consent to tricks."

I held up my palm, and it glowed a faint blue. Yvonne smiled. Sam backed away along with Jason and they moved to the front row of the spectator section. "Not too long ago, I had an encounter with what is known as the shards of the Grimvox." I faced Yvonne and Holland.

"The Grimvox, from what I understand, is a repository of all the memories and deeds of demonic beings in our mortal realm."

"Bloody hell." Holland let out and pulled a cigarette from her purse. "Then you won't mind if I add a little fire?" She lit a cigarette with shaking hands.

Nicholas held out his hand. "I need one."

"I didn't know you smoked." Ruth said.

"I don't."

I opened my left palm and the glow grew stronger. "Somehow Vivian Darbonne transferred these shards of a fragment of the Grimvox from her palm to mine. Since that time I have seen things I personally have not experienced. But, as Mr. Drake said a moment ago, the two of us were at one time host and demon. There are memories recorded in these shards of my life." I turned back to Meridian.

"I have done many wrong things. I have committed atrocities against my fellow human being. With Alphus' help, I would like to show these to you, Judge Meridian."

Alphus joined me and Meridian smiled. "I'd love nothing more, Mr. Steel. We are going to weigh your heart, remember?"

I looked into Alphus' pale blue eyes. "Can you take the image of my sins and mold them into a heart?" I whispered.

Alphus looked to the side as if listening. "I have been given permission to help you."

I held out my palm toward Alphus. "Alphus is a messenger from God and he can extract the many sins from the memories stored in the Grimvox."

Alphus cupped my hand in his hands. The blue light intensified and I grit my teeth as the shards of the Grimvox ripped from the skin of my palms.

Each shard spun and images sprang forward as if from a slightly out-of-focus hologram. I saw the fights I had never experienced while in high school instigated by the third demon. I saw Mercedes, the young woman who had taken me away from the church that night, wrapped tightly around my body. More images of fights with my father, fights with people I now recalled were part of my response to his programming, more victims of my personal violence. I saw Josh, Claire, April, Robert, Raven all flickering in the air until it stunk of death and decay. The images all collapsed one at a time and formed something pale blue in Alphus' hand until the last image faded. Alphus held a pale blue fully formed human heart.

I was empty, void, weak and stumbled back. Blood dripped from my palm. Yvonne caught me and motioned to Birdsong. He hurried to her aid and held me up. Anubis ambled over to me, stood up on his hind legs, and put his front paws on my shoulders. He touched his hot snout to my cold chest. I felt his breath on my skin.

Alphus placed the beating blue heart on the front of Meridian's desk. Meridian picked it up and laughed. He opened his mouth and he roared. "Now, this is true justice."

"Just a minute." I whispered. "You need a feather."

Meridian paused and looked around. "A feather?"

"Yes, the feather for the other pan on the scales."

Meridian pulled the bronze scales to the front of his desk and placed the heart on one side. The pan bounced as it slammed down on his desk. Meridian motioned to the scales. "You actually think that one feather would weigh more than this heart?"

"I claim the right of the weighing of the heart." My voice was stronger. Anubis' hot breath had brought sweat to my chest. I looked at Yvonne and then at Holland. "We need a feather."

Holland nodded with a smile on her lips. She dropped her cigarette butt on the floor and stepped on it as she stood up. "Ms. Brown, if you will join me next to Mr. Drake."

Yvonne glanced at me and then at Drake and smiled. "Of course."

Drake glared back and forth as they stood behind him. "What?"

"Your jaunty hat." Holland said. "It has a white feather." She plucked the hat from his head. "Besides, this is MY evidence." She held it toward Yvonne. Yvonne pulled the white feather from the hat and glanced at me. I nodded.

Yvonne walked forward to the desk. "Your honor, as Mr. Steel's defense attorney I offer into evidence this feather."

Meridian glanced at the feather and then at her with a perplexed look on his face. For a second doubt clouded his features and then Drake spoke up. "Oh, get on with it, Four. It's just a feather!"

Meridian motioned to the scales. "Place the feather on the scales."

Yvonne stood on tiptoes so she could reach the empty pan of the scales. She released the feather and it drifted slowly down onto the pan. For a second nothing happened and she backed away.

Meridian smiled and giggled. "Looks like the scales of justice have spoken, Mr. Steel."

I watched as the pan with the heart on it began to rise. "I believe they have."

Meridian stood up, and horror and disbelief filled his magnified eyes. He pulled his glasses off and focused on the scales. The heart reached the highest height and the pan with the feather settled on his desk. "This is a trick!"

I reached out and grabbed Anubis by his snout and shoved him away. He backed away in confusion. I turned and grabbed the letter from my father off the table and began to read.

"When all the people were being baptized, Jesus was baptized too. And as he was praying, heaven was opened and the Holy Spirit descended on him in bodily form like a dove. And a voice came from heaven: 'You are my Son, whom I love; with you, I am well pleased.' Matthew 3:21 and 22."

I stepped forward. "That heart represents only a fraction of my sins, Meridian. I can do nothing to repay for any of my sins. It is impossible. The weight of the heart in your manner would always lead to the exile of the dead to the underworld, for no power produced by man can ever erase our sins."

I moved closer. "But the feather of a white dove represents the Holy Spirit, part of our triune God. God the father, the creator, the transcendent One. Jesus, the Son, the Godman, God fleshed out into our space-time dimensions. And the Holy Spirit, the spiritual presence of God in all those who have accepted the ultimate sacrifice of Jesus Christ on the cross and His subsequent resurrection. We spoke days ago of a game, of how you will one day rein in hell. I told you then, and I tell you again now, that you and your spawn are the walking dead. You were defeated on the cross. I was there. I saw my Savior for the briefest of moments and in His name, I now point your attention to your talisman, the talisman of the fourth demon. The white feather of the scales of justice held only by the most powerful Judge. Those scales represent the atoning love of God. And in His name, the name above all names, the name of Jesus Christ, I command you, known as the fourth demon, to come out of Judge Meridian and join Anubis in hell."

Meridian blinked, and suddenly, he shuddered. He cried out

in pain and his face elongated into the image of Anubis. Muscles bulged through his robes, and a powerful chest blossomed from Meridian. The form of the fourth demon rose upward and towered over Meridian in its ancient form.

Alphus grew in stature until he was taller than the judge. The fourth demon bared his fangs and growled. Alphus said something in a language that came before the stars were born. The demon cried out in pain.

"No! I am the Fourth Demon on the Council of Darkness. I am a member of Lucifer's inner circle. You cannot command me!" The creature shouted in deep, guttural tones.

Alphus spoke the same words, and they cut through the air with the force of a sword. The fourth demon's chest opened and his heart, a dirty black and gray lump of gnarled flesh, came forth and hovered in the air above Meridian's paralyzed form.

Alphus gestured over the spectator section. Shadows deepened and from the shadows, lurching, deformed figures emerged. Men and women shambled through the benches as specters of darkness. I saw Micah and Herod's priest. I saw Pharoah's sorcerers converge on Meridian's desk. Their chests were ripped open, empty of their hearts. They stumbled and staggered.

Holland and Nicholas froze and glanced at me with horror-filled eyes.

"They will not hurt you." I said.

Drake opened his mouth and laughed out loud. "Now, this is a true circus! Everyone pay attention to the center ring!"

The Fourth Demon moaned and then screamed in a throaty, deep shout that tore the surrounding air. The figures paused before the desk and then, as one, launched themselves at the fourth demon. His screams echoed around the room and I put my hands on my ears. The shadow demons fell upon the fourth demon, writhing, biting, clawing.

Alphus motioned to the wall behind the fourth demon and suddenly the wall opened in a gaping maw of darkness. A dozen dog like shapes appeared with glowing red eyes and hungry maws. Their teeth sunk into the substance of the demon, and screaming, dragged him off into darkness. The maw closed leaving the wall untouched.

Meridian shook his head in confusion. The man looked around the courtroom. He slowly stood up and put on his glasses. He blinked at us.

Holland and Nicholas muttered and moaned in horror. Meridian grabbed his gavel and pounded it on his desk. He pointed the gavel at me. "This changes nothing. I am still Judge Meridian and you will rot in jail for the rest of your days!"

A loud growl interrupted Meridian's speech. Anubis jumped up onto the desk. Meridian snapped his fingers. "Down, Anubis. Heel!"

Anubis growled louder and hurled himself onto Meridian. His jaws closing around Meridian's neck and both of them tumbled out of sight behind the desk. Bubba, the bailiff, had cowered in the corner the whole time and now jumped up and ran around to the back of Meridian's desk. He screamed in horror as the dog hopped up onto the desk. A beating heart hung from his mouth. The dog shook the heart, showering the room with blood, and then slowly faded from sight.

Silence fell. The heart disappeared from the scales. Holland plopped back into her seat, her hands shaking. Nicholas wiped the blood from his face. Yvonne smiled.

"Justice has been served." She said.

CHAPTER
SIXTY-SIX

A RATTLING from the table interrupted the uncomfortable silence. Drake was jerking at his manacles, his eyes wide in terror. "Get me out of here. Now! Four's gone, so free me!"

I shook my head. "Oh, no, number three. You and I have some business to attend to." I walked over to Holland's valise and picked up the chains. "Let me read you the other Bible verses in this letter." I slowly moved toward Drake, holding the chains in one hand.

> "They went across the lake to the region of the Gerasenes. When Jesus got out of the boat, a man with an impure spirit came from the tombs to meet him. This man lived in the tombs, and no one could bind him anymore, not even with a chain."

I looked up at Drake and held up the chain. "Look familiar?" I came closer to Drake and gently swung the chains back and forth like a pendulum.

> "For he had often been chained hand and foot, but he tore the chains apart and broke the irons on his feet. No one was strong enough to

subdue him. Night and day among the tombs and in the hills he would cry out and cut himself with stones."

I arrived at the table. "Are you afraid, Drake? Does your heart pound with fright? Every victim of yours; every person possessed by you and your Legion has felt this same fear. Yes, I am talking to the third demon. For not only is Drake feeling the fear, but so is Azzuzabel."

Drake's two toned eyes widened. He jerked against the manacles. "He's still here. Inside me. He's cowering in fear."

"I command the third demon to stay put." I said.

Drake shook his head and jerked at his manacles as I dangled the chain before his eyes. "He can't leave my body. Get out of me, number three! Go away!"

"He cannot leave because these chains are his talisman." I said. "He is bound to you until I allow him to leave. Let me continue."

I continued reading.

"When he saw Jesus from a distance, he ran and fell on his knees in front of him. He shouted at the top of his voice, 'What do you want with me, Jesus, Son of the Most High God? In God's name, don't torture me!' For Jesus had said to him, 'Come out of this man, you impure spirit!' Then Jesus asked him, 'What is your name?'"

I looked at Drake. "You said your name was Legion, right? Let me answer for you." I read some more.

"'My name is Legion,' he replied, 'for we are many.' And he begged Jesus again and again not to send them out of the area. A large herd of pigs was feeding on the nearby hillside. The demons begged Jesus, 'Send us among the pigs; allow us to go into them.' He gave them permission, and the impure spirits came out and went into the pigs. The herd, about two thousand in number, rushed down the steep bank into the lake and were

drowned. Those tending the pigs ran off and reported this in the town and countryside, and the people went out to see what had happened. When they came to Jesus, they saw the man who had been possessed by the legion of demons, sitting there, dressed and in his right mind; and they were afraid."

Drake was still tugging at the manacles. "Pigs! Pigs! They were unclean and our host was not to touch them and yet He sent us into pigs. But we survived and when the Master chose his twelve for his council, he chose us; he chose ME and made me number three for we had survived an encounter with the Son!" Drake's voice was no longer his own. Snorts and squeaks now punctuated his words.

I took one end of the chain and whirled it above my head. Releasing it, the chain wrapped around Drake's neck. He screamed in agony and squealed like a pig!

"There are no pigs in this room, Drake, but I will speak His name and you and your Legion will not find a home in this realm any longer. You will, instead, go on to your eternal punishment. In the name of Jesus Christ, I command Legion to leave this man!"

Drake froze and something hideous moved out of his very skin. A pig's head appeared with long, crusted tusks. Tiny eyes glared at me from pits of fat. The chain stayed around the creature's neck as it grew.

The hog like body grew out of Drake and hooves tugged at the chain. From the pinkish, hairy skin dozens of demonic heads sprang out of his deformed chest and abdomen. The same hideous heads now writhed and screamed in agony. Only this time, when the third demon appeared he was truly more like a pig than before. I handed the free end of the chain Alphus.

"These are the very chains you put on that man two thousand years ago. Now, they will bind you and take you to Tarturus." I said.

Alphus lifted from the floor on membranous wings and flew around the third demon. With each pass, the chains grew tighter and tighter. The third demon screamed in agony and looked down at me. "We were together. We could have done so much."

"We were never together, Three. I always wanted you to go."

It looked over at Yvonne. "Little Missy, at one time you loved me. Didn't you?"

Yvonne's eyes widened. "No! I killed your host and I would kill you if I could."

The chains tightened and number three dwindled in size, squealing and snorting until it collapsed into a dark hole. The writhing demon heads began to devour each other. He cast one last look at me from the Abyss. "I was in your brother when she died. He has the video." He smiled and disappeared from sight.

I gasped in shock at the revelation. I had forgotten about the video and I looked at Yvonne. Her face was stricken. I turned toward Drake. In the confusion the third demon had broken Drake free of his manacles. I whirled. Where was he?

Drake stood on the judge's desk with the golden knife in his hands. He shivered and wiped his face. "Well, I'm glad that's over. Three was a little overbearing."

Bubba reached for his pistol but his holster was empty. Yvonne stepped forward holding the pistol. I put a hand on her arm and she whirled and pointed the pistol at me.

"No, JJ. I'm going to finish him like I did with my kidnapper." She hissed.

"Yvonne, you can't do this!" I said. "You would be no better than Drake."

"I don't care. He is not leaving this courtroom." Yvonne said again and her lips trembled.

"That's right, little missy." Drake said. "He showed me everything he did to you." Drake tapped his temple with the golden knife. "It's all up here. That and centuries of atrocities. I can wallow in them all!" His insane glare shifted to me.

"And you, JJ Stone! I have a secret."

I wasn't going to play his games. But anything to keep him off balance would help. "What secret?"

He smiled. "Your brother didn't kill your mother."

I froze. "What?"

"He was supposed to. Initiation ritual. That's what the video was for. Proof. But he was too weak. They made him watch, though." Drake said. "Want to know who killed your mother? Then let me go and I'll tell you how to find the video."

Nausea gripped me. This couldn't be happening. "You're lying."

"Am I? You'll never know unless you see the video. It's all there. Now, tell your lawyer to back off and let me leave here quietly."

Sam had moved up silently behind Yvonne along with Holland. What was I to do?

"Your judgment is coming at a higher court, Drake." Yvonne pointed the pistol at Drake. Things happened suddenly. Both Sam and Holland went for the gun. All three of them lurched backwards and the pistol fired in Drake's direction. The man leaned to the side to avoid the shot and his feet caught in the golden scales. He stumbled, he lurched, he fell forward holding his hands before him to stop his fall. The man landed on the floor and screamed in agony. Blood poured from under his body.

I ran to him and turned him onto his back. The golden knife protruded from his chest.

"Where's the video?" I screamed into his dying face.

Blood bubbled from Drake's lips and suddenly his two toned eyes widened in fear. "No! No! Can't you see them? They're coming for me. No!" He cried out and then grew still. The color faded from his eyes back to dull brown. Reginald Drake had met his true master at last.

THE AFTERMATH WAS TOTAL CHAOS. Bubba rose to the occasion. He was glad to no longer be in the clutches of Judge Meridian. The judge must have held something over the man's head to keep him in line. But Bubba took over. He took the gun from Yvonne and fired it again at the ceiling.

"I need to make sure gunshot residue is on my hands." He said. Holland and Sam pulled Yvonne back toward the benches. She sobbed quietly as they sat beside her.

Bubba put his pistol in his holster. "Police will be here any minute after that ruckus. The lot of you follow my lead and we can all go home tonight."

When the police arrive, Bubba told them Judge Meridian had been viciously attacked by his own dog and the dog had run off somewhere in the building. He also said that Drake had managed to get a hold of the knife and was threatening to kill Yvonne Brown until Bubba had threatened to shoot the man. Drake had dodged the bullets, fallen on the knife and died.

It took five hours to get everyone's statements. I found that before his death, Meridian had signed off on all my charges so I was a free man. It was over. The fourth demon and the third demon were gone. I found out my father had talked to Holland and made sure the two talismans were in the valise. She was more than happy to receive two more solid pieces of evidence against Reginald Drake. I never told her that my father was not with Interpol as he had claimed.

Finally, Ruth, Jason, Yvonne and I left the courthouse. Yvonne and Sam disappeared to who knew where. The rest of us piled into Jason's truck. He took us to Ruth's house.

Ruth unlocked her door and I put a hand up to keep her from going in.

"Let me check first." I said. I made a quick survey of her house. Nothing unusual. When I came back into the living room, Jason was waiting at the door.

"Clear." I said.

"I'm taking Holland to the airport. She wants to catch a night flight so she can get the evidence back to London. This will go a long way to restoring her status in her department. I can swing back by in an hour and pick you up." He sighed. "And then we can talk about this supposed video."

Ruth had collapsed on her couch and I walked Jason out the front door. "I could go with you and save you an extra trip."

Jason shook his head. "Jonathan, Ruth has been through a lot tonight. She needs you right now."

I opened my mouth to speak but couldn't think of anything to say. He put his hand on my bare chest beneath the jacket. "Listen to your heart for once, Jonathan." He winked at me and walked off into the darkness to his truck.

I went back inside. Ruth had changed into a set of pajamas and sat on one end of her couch with her feet tucked beneath her. For a moment I was back in time right after Ruth had told me how Drake had manipulated her.

"This is déjà vu." I said as I sat beside her.

Ruth looked at me with puffy eyes. "Yes, that night you put your arm around my shoulders after I told you the truth about

Drake. Jonathan, that night I felt the warmth of your chest, heard the slow, steady thump of your heart. You let me cry and I nuzzled into your chest until you groaned."

I nodded. "That's right. I had broken ribs."

Ruth looked away. "I needed your arm around me, the solace of your beating heart, the warmth of your presence." She looked back at him. "I wanted nothing more than for you to sweep me off my feet and hold me and tell me it was going to be fine; that all of the bad men would never find me because you would protect me." Ruth shrugged. "I guess I'm a hopeless romantic."

"I felt the same way for a moment, Ruth. If you recall I told you I couldn't do this. I couldn't get involved. Now you know why."

"Demons and talismans? Yeah what was that talk about talismans? And why didn't you tell me about your plan?"

"Because I was making it up as we went along. My father had mentioned the talismans but he couldn't give me any details. Demons were listening. Holland came through and the Bible verses gave me the edge I needed. Each verse pointed to one of the talismans."

Ruth drew a shuddering breath and scooted closer to me. "Jonathan, can you forgive me?"

"For what?" I felt the warmth of her body.

"For doubting you. I know you have dealt with demons and I always believed it but what happened in that courtroom today could drive a sane person crazy." She said.

I drew a deep breath. "I'm sorry for that. This is the world I live in. At least for now. Two more demons and I hope I can have a normal life." I swallowed hard. "I have recovered my past and I'm trying to sort through it."

Ruth looked at me with moist eyes. "Jonathan, I have always believed in the law's power. The power of justice. Even when it goes the wrong direction, like it did with me and Drake. I'll never look at the scales of justice in the same way again. This entire ordeal with Meridian has discouraged me. I know we can abuse the legal profession. But who knows what wrongs Meridian did while he was under the influence of the fourth demon?"

I nodded, looking deep into the flames of the fireplace. "He didn't deserve to die like he did. But when you dance with the devil, the end can never be good. His side plays for keeps, and the only thing they have left to inflict harm on God is to take one of His children's souls."

Ruth shivered and leaned into me. The flames flickered in the fireplace and my face grew warm. Context. Now I had context. I looked back along my thirty years of life and saw more than just Claire and April and Raven. I saw girlfriends from middle school. I saw Mercedes, who took advantage of me. I saw my hatred of my father and my love for my mother. The emotions washed over me like a tidal wave and I gasped as the meaning of this touch from Ruth sunk in. I cherished it. I needed it. I wanted it.

"Now what?" She said.

I pulled her closer. "Let's not think anymore about it tonight." I said hoarsely.

Ruth put her head against my chest. "I can hear your heart beating." She sat forward and slid off the couch, turned to face me, and sat on the coffee table. She put her hands on either side of my face. She looked into my eyes. "Jonathan Steel, that heart of yours? God has blessed it. God has given you the incredible gift of forgiveness, and all those horrible things you did in the past belonged to JJ Stone. You are a new man. Guard your heart." She paused, and a tear trickled from one eye. "Because I want it!"

I opened my eyes, and for the first time truly saw her. The last time we sat here, I was a different person. I hardly recognized the angry, furious man bent on vengeance. My "heart" melted and with all my returned memories, I now had a proper perspective. I leaned into her.

"First, I'll give you my lips." I said.

She sat back and put a hand on my lips. "Really? That's your opening line?"

I shrugged. "I'm out of practice so it'll have to do."

CHAPTER
SIXTY-EIGHT

Christmas Eve

"Jonathan, thank you, thank you, thank you." Cassie said as I slowly walked her down the 'aisle'. The aisle was nothing more than a long, blue carpet laid out on the sand leading toward the beach.

"I can't think of a better venue than my beach house." I whispered in her ear. "Just wish your father was here."

"And, Renee." She sniffed.

Monty stood by Josh in a white shirt and black pants. The warm breeze tossed his hair. It was a perfect day. No too hot, not too cold. For once, perfect. Cassie wore a simple white dress and veil. She carried a bunch of red carnations. "Renee's favorite." She had said.

We reached the end of the aisle and she handed the flowers to Raven. Max was resplendent in her silver dress. She had the power to marry anyone. Was there anything she could not do?

———

A massive tent sat at the bottom of the stairs from my beach house. A portable dance floor took up the center of the tent. Cassie and Monty had invited one hundred guests, and they filled the tent with laughter and life. Cassie and Monty danced. Josh and Olivia danced. I declined and as the setting sun gave way to cool darkness, I left the tent and walked barefoot down to the water. The sky was clear, and the stars shone brightly. The crescent of a new moon reflected on the waters.

"Dad?"

I was almost used to that name. Josh ran up to me, his breath streaming.

"Josh, is there a problem?"

"No. I just missed you. Olivia wanted a dance with you." Josh wore a white tuxedo jacket and his white shirt was open to his chest.

"Josh, I don't dance."

"Are you sure?"

I tapped my head. "My memories are back. Trust me. I have two left feet."

Josh crossed his arms and shivered. "Yeah, how is that going?"

"It's a slow process. I can suddenly remember something, and it's not like a flashback. It's just there. But I have to examine it and relive it to make sense of it." I said.

"Olivia still wants me to fly out to Arizona and have a post-Christmas dinner with her mom and brother. And Jason. If that's still okay. He's found a safe house for them." Josh said.

I nodded. "You'll be safe with Jason. Has she seen any demons lately?"

Josh shook his head. "Not since you got back from Europe." He looked out over the ocean. "It's been quiet. Too quiet."

"Leave the paranoia to me." I said.

"What's coming next?" Josh looked at me.

"Two more demons and my brother." I swallowed and

rubbed my eyes. "But we will not dwell on that today. Today is about Cassie and Monty."

We were silent for a moment, just watching the rolling waves. Josh stepped closer and leaned his head against my shoulder. "Thanks for being my daddy. It started out pretty rough, but you grew into the role, bro."

It was totally out of character of the new me but somewhere in the past a feeling of warmth surfaced and I put my arm around Josh. "You turned into a pretty good son." I said.

Josh pulled away and faced me. "Just so you know, I love you."

I smiled. There was a time when hearing that would have made me uncomfortable. Not anymore. "Love you, too, son."

He walked back up the sand toward the beach house. That is when I smelled pipe smoke. My heart accelerated and I whirled. Not thirty feet away two figures in white stood at the water line. Red fire illuminated my father's face as he stoked his pipe and the reflection revealed Max's face.

I hurried down the beach toward them. "What is the meaning of this?" I said.

Max glanced at me. "We're almost done." She handed a USB flash drive to my father. "That is all I have on the first and second demon."

"And the Vitreomancers?" He said.

"Of course." She faced me. "We have decided to call a truce and work together. Your father and I are going to take down the rest of the Council."

"And the Vitreomancers." The Captain said. He drew one last lung full of smoke from the pipe and then emptied the ashes onto the sand.

"Are you going to shoot me again with a tranquilizer dart? Are do you expect me to believe you have made a 180 turn?" I said to him.

Max put a hand on my arm. I jerked it away. "The enemy of my enemy is my friend? Is that what you're going to tell me?"

Max crossed her arms and the cool ocean breeze stirred her gauzy wrap and her hair. The dragonfly brooch glittered in the starlight."Yes. We need to put the past behind us, JJ."

"I'm not JJ!" I said hotly. "I'm sticking with Jonathan."

"Of course." She said and for a moment I saw her resolve, her stoicism break. She looked out over the ocean. "I'm tired, Jonathan. I've been at this battle since I thought my daughter had died. Imagine learning your daughter did not die and spent her life under the influence of the eleventh demon. I should have looked harder. I should have been more like your father. It's been a long campaign. I'm ready to do whatever it takes to put the Council down."

"Selling your soul to the devil?" I said nodding toward my father.

"I did that already." The Captain said. "That spares you and Max from further tainting of your souls. Besides, you took the two talismans I sent and you made them work, didn't you?"

"A jaunty hat with a white feather?" I said loudly.

"The hat was already in the valise when I met D. I. Holland at DFW airport. She decided to put the feather on it. She was more than happy to take down Drake. You should thank me." The Captain said.

I looked away and calmed my racing heart. "Did you really think I would go with the 'weighing of the heart'?" I looked back at him.

"Now that was inspired." He said.

"By God." I said. "Not by my father."

Max put a hand on my arm. "That's enough for now. I have to go. I'm taking my private jet to an island for Christmas. Tonight."

"Spending Christmas alone?" I asked.

"No. There are three other guests waiting for me." Her eyes glittered in the star light. "Raven, Vivian, and Snake."

I drew a deep breath. "More dangerous liaisons?"

Max stepped close to me and put her hands on my shoulders.

"Look at me, Jonathan. This is a dangerous world we live in. There is only one source of light in this universe. We have to go to the Light, live in the Light, and trust the Light. We serve a God of second chances. All three of those women deserve second chances." She touched my face. "So do you. And, so does your father." She turned and walked away.

"Let's walk." The Captain said and started away from me. The waves washed up toward our feet. I couldn't believe I was walking along the beach with my father. "I reached out to Sam and Yvonne. How are your memories?"

"Painful." I growled. "Thanks to you. Are they okay?"

"Sam and Yvonne are safe for now. They told me to ask you about the other laptop?"

"There was an EMP pulse. It erased the laptop hard drive. Right before it messed with my implant which is why an angel had to remove it." I said.

"Yvonne told me you were supposed to watch my video." The Captain slowed down and turned to me. "Did you?"

"The part from Meridian's office. I understand what you were trying to accomplish."

"Tough love." He said.

"Love was never a part of it." I said harshly.

He paused and studied my face with his turquoise eyes. He pulled a small, black box from his pocket and opened the box. The inside was lined with red velvet. He placed the pipe in the box. "This is a Christmas gift for Josh."

"A pipe? Josh doesn't smoke."

"There's a card beneath the lining with the name of an auction house. I have arranged for them to auction off the pipe. It's worth an easy one hundred thousand dollars. But the decision to sell it is up to Josh." He tapped the Meerschaum pipe bowl. "I want Josh to have spending money for college. He doesn't have to know it's from me."

"He has a trust fund from Cephas Lawrence."

"I am aware of that. And the trust fund will be carefully

doled out. This will be for things like a car, computers, and his girlfriend."

He pushed the box toward me. "And, speaking of Olivia." The Captain pulled an envelope from his pants pocket. "This is for her. There is a neurosurgeon in Houston who has perfected an ablation technique. I arranged for him to review Olivia's records. He is certain he can ablate the seizure focus. She can be seizure free. He is waiting for the call after the first of the year."

I took the envelope. "Why are you doing this?"

"It's Christmas."

"You never allowed me to celebrate Christmas after the trial."

"We were on the run."

I looked at the pipe. "Yes. From my brother." I took the pipe from the box and held it up studying the face of an angel on one side and the face of a demon on the other. "These represent me and my brother, don't they?"

The Captain shook his head. "No."

"What do they represent?"

The Captain studied the pipe. "I had the pipe long before you were born. Your mother was fascinated with it. This pipe is how we connected. How we met."

"I never saw that video. The Story of Captain Stone."

"This pipe for me represents the love I had for your mother." He looked at me with moist eyes. "I am so sorry I blamed you for her death. Now we know it was your brother under the influence of the third demon. I still have questions of why he was motivated to kill her."

"Right before he died, Drake said my brother didn't kill our mother. Drake said there was a video." I said hoarsely.

The Captain stepped back and his mouth fell open. "I had forgotten about the video. Jeremiah didn't kill Christine?"

"Drake claimed it was an initiation rite gone wrong. Jeremiah couldn't do it. The video is supposed to show who really killed mother."

The Captain looked out over the ocean. He breathed rapidly

and put a hand to his chest. For a fleeting second I saw my father as the broken man he truly was. I saw his frailty, his weakness. He slumped and touched his eyes. This was my father, the man. My father who lost the love of his life and found out one of his sons was a demon possessed monster. Almost, I felt sorry for him. Almost, I reached for him but I held the pipe in one hand and the box in the other, a poor excuse for not showing my emotions.

After a few moments he calmed. "Drake was lying. He had to be. One last dagger to your heart, son." He turned back to look at me with moist eyes.

I swallowed back emotion. "If my brother didn't kill my mother, then who did? Who was his mentor? Santiago?"

The Captain looked away. "Santiago is dead. Long ago. They found his body not long after you were born. This is why we have to find your brother and stop him. We need to know who is pulling his strings."

The Captain pointed to the pipe. "The two faces on that pipe are not you and your brother. They are me and my father. The man was vile, evil, steeped in arcane practices. And, he is not dead. Watch the video and you'll find out. He faked his death."

"What?" I could hardly breathe. "Could he be Jeremiah's mentor?"

The Captain drew a deep breath. "Maybe. He was the one my father wanted, after all. Once I found out your brother was alive, I developed a plan to make my father think your brother was the special one. And your brother must have hidden away from my father. When your face surfaced on the news after the air disaster, your brother came forward out of the darkness."

"Jeremiah hid in the shadows and made himself a part of my life for months and months." I said. "People saw him and thought he was me. I am convinced he was in Numinocity with me. He taunted me and told me I had killed mother."

"Once he started working out in the open, he attracted attention. Now my father knows how to find you." The Captain said.

"What does he want from me?"

The Captain looked up the beach toward the beach house. "You have a life now. You have family and friends. Protect them. Take care of them. A day is coming soon when you will confront the last two demons and your brother. But you will not be facing them alone." He took one more item from his coat pocket and studied it. "This memory card has all the videos from the trial we recorded. If you didn't hear my story, then it's on this card." He held it out to me. "Watch it and you will understand everything, especially the pipe."

I took the card and slipped it into my pocket. "You just happen to have it on you?"

My father closed the box lid over the pipe and laid the envelope on top. I put them in my other pocket.

"The video on the laptop, the one you did not see, is me telling my story in Meridian's office." The Captain said. "I left some things out. Later, I decided I would tell the entire story to you." He looked away and cleared his throat. "In case something happened." He glanced at his watch. "I have a boat to catch."

Behind me, I heard an approaching boat motor. I whirled and out on the sea an enormous yacht had arrived with gleaming lights. A small pontoon boat slid up onto the beach. The Captain took one last look at me and nodded. "I'm off to find the Ark of the Apostles. With both Arks we can control the Council, son. Watch over your friends and family. Enjoy the holidays. You've done well, son. Keep it up."

Before I could say anything, he waded into the surf and into the boat. It pulled away and headed toward the yacht. My cell phone rang as my face burned with anger and indignation. I glanced at the caller ID and my heart slowed. My face cooled.

"Hey." I answered the call and started walking away from my father and away from the danger that waited. With my free hand, I touched the memory card in my pocket.

"Hey yourself." Ruth Martinez said. "I wanted to call sooner, but we were making fudge." In the background, I heard voices.

"Your whole family is there?"

"Yep. Christmas tradition. My brothers. Their significant others. My father and mother. And a few close friends. We're at the house on Lake Travis. How did the wedding go?"

I glanced up at the tent. Cassie was tossing her bouquet. Olivia caught it. "Beautiful. I wish you could have been here, but I understand. You don't know Cassie and Monty that well."

"Jonathan, they're your friends. I would have been there if I could. But you insisted."

"On doing something normal. Yes, I know. We needed normal, Ruth. Both of us. Me here with Josh and Monty and Cassie and you there with your family."

She was silent for a moment. "So Josh called this afternoon."

"He did?"

"To tell me he was going to Arizona with Olivia if you approved and he couldn't come to my house after Christmas. I told him I understood, but he assured me he had your permission. After all, he's not legal yet. But that was very thoughtful of him." She laughed, and the sound made my heart tremble. Out on the water, the yacht turned toward the open sea and made its way from the shore.

"So, are you showing me off to the family?"

"I know this is sudden, Jonathan. It just feels right."

"I agree." I said and emotion welled up in my chest. "It's been so long since I felt normal."

"Did you get Josh a present?"

"Yes. I took your advice and got him the newest MacBook Air." I said.

"Good. And?"

"And what?"

"Did you get a little something for me?" She said.

I glanced up at the wedding. Monty was shooting Cassie's garter into the men crowded around him. Josh caught it. I was fishing for a response. She laughed. "Got you."

"Ruth, the truth is, I barely had time to get Josh something with the wedding and all that." I said.

"Jonathan! I was kidding." She was silent. "Wait a minute! I can tell when you're lying. You got me something, didn't you? We said no gifts."

I smiled. "I need to work on my lying."

"Okay, so I got you something, too."

I looked out over the water. The lights of the yacht dwindled in the distance. "Being with you will be gift enough."

"Now that was the right thing to say. You're learning." She said quietly. A voice screamed in the background.

"It's spinning a thread, Ruth. We need you!" Her mother shouted.

"I have to go. We're making divinity and it's critical to get it right."

"Divinity?"

"Yeah, imagine a cloud filled with puffy sugar meringue and vanilla. Lucious. It's my mother's secret recipe."

"Ruth!" her mother called again.

"Got to go. I'll see you soon?"

"I'll be there."

"Love you." She said. I froze. A gasp over the phone. "Did I just say that?"

"Yes, you did." I smiled. "And it sounded just right." I whirled and glanced up at the wedding gathering. Josh and Olivia were dancing again, hand in hand. Cassie and Monty were getting ready to leave. "Guess what?"

"What?" she said nervously.

"I love you, too." I said. Ruth sniffed.

"Bye." The call ended. I looked at my other hand where the blue glow from my palm had not appeared in the days since the weighing of my heart. And right now, right here, my heart was as light as a feather!

CHAPTER
SIXTY-NINE

THE CRIMSON SNAKE rubbed the stub of her bare arm and stared up at the stars. The southern cross glittered above the horizon. She wore a two piece swim suit and felt the sun burn into her snake tattoo. Two snakes wound their way up her legs and onto her back with the two heads were intertwined and looking at each other.

"We're in the southern hemisphere." She said as waves washed up onto her bare feet. "How big is this island?"

"Big enough." Max said. "I need you to come back to the table."

"The Christmas dinner was pleasant." Snake said. She swallowed hard. "I haven't had a decent Christmas in years."

"Let's have Christmas tea." Max said.

Snake glanced over her shoulder at the woman. Max wore a one-piece swimsuit and a gauzy cover up that swayed around her feet in the sea breeze. A jeweled dragonfly held the cover together just under Max's chin.

"Isn't it too hot for tea?"

Max pointed to the lights of the nearby beach house. "Iced tea. Cold."

Snake followed Max up the sandy walkway to the deck of the

small beach house. Vivian Darbonne and Raven sat at the table. A servant had poured four glasses of tea and placed them on a wicker table. The remnants of their Christmas dinner were being cleared by another servant.

"We have a decision to make." Max pointed to a chair. She removed her cover with the dragonfly brooch and placed it in a pile on the table. "Sit."

Snake settled into her chair. Max stood behind the other chair and nodded to the servant. "Get the boat ready. We won't be long."

Snake picked up the glass of tea and sipped. It was cold and very sweet. "If you're leaving, why the swimsuit?"

"I don't get to travel to the tropics very often. When we return to my beach house on the mainland, I plan on a midnight swim." Max sat in her chair.

Snake sipped tea. "And, Vivian, dear, you're not dressed for the tropics." Vivian wore a long sleeve tee shirt and jeans.

"I'm heading to Colorado." She drank tea. "The next person on the list."

"And I am helping now." Raven said. She also wore a long sleeve sweat shirt and matching pants.

Snake drank more tea. The heat and humidity were relieved by a brisk breeze, but she was thirsty. "You didn't answer my question. How big is my island?"

Max pointed to the beach house. "One bedroom with a serviceable kitchen and a small den. You'll enjoy being out here more than inside. Solar panels on the roof for power. Fresh water from a well. If you choose to jog, it's about two miles around the entire island. I bought it from the owner ten years ago."

Snake turned her attention to the beach again. "I don't suppose you could swim to the mainland?"

"A heavy current between here and the mainland."

"Wherever that is. You kept me blindfolded the entire trip. When do I get my arm back?"

"When you have helped me pay back over 225 families." Vivian said.

Snake froze. "You're kidding."

"I don't kid." Max said. "Now look at this list." She pulled a piece of paper out of her leather satchel.

"I narrowed the lists down to the person who hired me to two people. One of these people is the same person who hired you." Raven said.

Max slid the paper across the table. Snake studied the sheet. "Aha! Yes! This one!" She pointed to one name.

Max smiled. "Just as I suspected. Now we know who is manipulating the Penticle. That means I have plans to make."

"Plans?"

"To stop this person." Max stood.

Snake looked at Vivian. "How did you do it?"

"What do you mean?" Vivian retrieved the paper and looked at it.

"Turn your back on your life? Found redemption?"

"It starts with genuine regret for what you have done. But I question whether or not you have a conscience. I had one. I had just locked it away so I could justify what I needed to do." Vivian passed the paper to Max.

"I had help with that. I had my memory erased. And then, my mind." Raven said.

"Trust me." Max folded the paper and tucked it inside her satchel. "By the time you've looked into the eyes of the survivors of that flight, you will find your conscience and it will either bring you to redemption or kill you."

Snake drank more tea and tilted her head toward the house. The dock they had arrived at was on the other side of the house at an inlet on the beach. "Will the servant be staying?"

"You'll have food delivered by drone every third day." Max said.

"How will I cook with one hand?"

"You'll manage." Vivian said.

Snake swatted at something buzzing behind her. "Bugs! Look, I am truly tired of this life. Selling myself to the employer with the biggest check. Killing people. Grows tiresome."

"And unfulfilling?" Raven said.

Snake nodded. "I want to find what the two of you did. You changed. I didn't believe it was possible."

"With God, anything is possible." Max said.

Snake looked back at Max. The breeze stirred the woman's gray hair. Her eyes gleamed intensely.

"You realize I have little use for God and after all I have done, he shouldn't have much use for me."

"This is true." Max said. "True redemption is undeserved. A gift. Grace. You can't earn it. You must learn how to ask for forgiveness. One prerequisite for redemption is regret. Do you truly wish you had never done what you did?"

The servant appeared at the door again. "The boat is ready."

"Bring me the present, Gamma."

The young man disappeared into the beach house and returned with a wrapped Christmas present. She placed it on the table. Max pushed it toward Snake.

"Vivian and Raven have already opened their presents back on the mainland. This is yours." Max said.

Snake blinked in surprise and pulled the box toward her. She tore the paper off and opened the box. Inside was a three-inch notebook binder and a slim laptop. Max placed a tablet on the table and tapped the screen.

"Do you remember David Boone?"

"You mean the movie star turned tech wizard? Died recently."

"He owned an island, as well. Much larger than this one." Max looked up from the tablet. "A powerful explosion equivalent to a nuclear blast destroyed the island. Sank the entire island. Along with David Boone and his prized technology."

Vivian cleared her throat. "In the interest of regret and conscience, I have to confess I was responsible for the explosion.

But Boone and his people were already dead. I barely escaped with my life."

"Yes, I know." Max looked up from the tablet. "Dr. Janice Manning was a very promising scientist who died some years ago. She developed the technology that Boone basically stole." Max tapped the tablet.

Snake gasped as the sensation took her. She felt the tingle course along her missing arm. She looked at the stump of her severed arm, but she felt, no; she knew her arm was back. She could feel the breeze across the skin of her arm. She felt goosebumps form on the invisible skin. She flexed absent fingers. "What is happening?"

"Dr. Manning created nannomemes for medical purposes. Boone used them for more sinister reasons." Max said.

The sensation disappeared, and Snake swore out loud. She felt a tear in her eye. For a brief few seconds, her missing arm was back. At least it felt like it was back! She glared at the tea glass. "What did you do to me?"

"In your tea was a healthy dose of these nannomemes. They can do quite a few things to your body. And your mind. If I want, I could give you leukemia. I can make your missing arm appear to feel like it is present. I can cause you excruciating pain or exquisite pleasure."

Max placed the tablet back in her satchel. "This is my insurance policy, Snake. I don't trust you. No one should. You have done nothing to earn such trust. If you are truly repentant, then you may find redemption. Open the notebook."

Snake glared at Max hotly and opened the notebook. A plastic sleeve held laminated cards. She pulled one from the sleeve. A photograph of a young girl filled one side of the card. She turned the card over. "Melissa Graff? Do I know her?" She read the name at the top of the card. Below it, more text detailed biographical information about Melissa.

"How could you? She is dead. Perished in the crash of your Swiss flight. There are 225 cards. The rest of the notebook has brief biographies of each victim. The laptop carries videos of those victims. These cards are basically flash cards. Vivian will return in two months. If you have memorized the biography of each of your victims and can give her those details based on the photograph alone, then you will have taken the first step on your journey to redemption."

————

Unnoticed by the women, the dragonfly brooch had twitched and come to life. It lifted quietly on buzzing wings and flew toward the nearest palm tree. The dragonfly settled onto the fronds of a palm tree. Its jeweled wings glittered in the sunlight. The eyes glowed and pulsed as its wing twitched, uploading the image it had just captured from the piece of paper. Far above, a satellite received the digital image and relayed it to its recipient. Upon receipt of the image, another pulse bounced back to the satellite and then down to the dragonfly. Its wings buzzed and it left the palm frond and flew through the humid air and settled on the wrap piled on the table.

————

Max stood up and pulled her wrap around her. "Two months, Snake. If you try to escape this island, I will activate the nannomemes." She picked up the satchel. "If you fail to memorize these victims, I will use the nannomemes. I will give you incentive to truly be regretful over their deaths."

Snake tossed the card onto the notebook and felt more tears sting her eyes. Why was she crying? Was it the face of this innocent child? Maybe she had hope after all. "I thought you said redemption was a gift."

Vivian stood up. "Honey child, you are not worthy of that gift. Yet."

Max nodded in agreement. "Snake, there is hope for you. But

until you acknowledge the true depth of what you did and realize how horrendous it was, you will never feel the level of regret you will need to receive the gift of forgiveness. I'll be in touch."

Snake watched Max, Raven, and Vivian walk into the beach house through tear-filled eyes. For the first time in her life, she felt sorrow spike in her heart as she studied the face of Melissa Graff.

EPILOGUE

"DO YOU REALIZE WHAT THIS MEANS?" Dr. Sno shouted at Nigel Hampton from behind her desk. Hampton was relieved to be out of the mansion but wished the circumstances were different.

"The fourth and third demon are no longer on the Council. That is good news for the Vitreomancers." He said.

Dr. Sno paused and leaned forward on her desk. "And now we know the Captain is not only *not* on the Council, he used us! He infiltrated the Vitreomancers, and he has the Ark of the Demon Rose. He used the talismans to help his son defeat the demons! We need that artifact and you had it right under your nose and you let it get away from you."

Hampton laughed and Sno froze. "What are you laughing at?"

Hampton took Pandora's box from his coat pocket and placed it on her desk. "You gave this to me. And, you, love, let Cephas Lawrence get his hands on the Ark."

"How dare you talk to me that way." Sno shouted but her efforts were weak. She looked away with her white eyes gleaming with anger. "Okay, you're right. I started this whole thing with the Pandora Stone and the Ark."

She sat back down. "I haven't told you everything."

Hampton put a hand on the box. "I think it is time you did. I'm tired of being your whipping boy, Dr. Sno."

"The Ark of the Demon Rose can't hurt the Vitreomancers!" Sno crossed her arms over her chest. "But there is more to this than you think."

"I know." Hampton smiled as he towered over Dr. Sno who looked suddenly small and powerless behind her desk. "There is another Ark, the Ark of the Apostles. If someone opened it in the presence of demonic forces, they will be subdued. It has more power over us than the Ark of the Demon Rose."

Sno glared at him. "I'm impressed."

"If you had listened to me instead of shoving me back into my little dungeon, you would see that I have something to contribute. I was searching for the Ark of the Apostles long before I met you." Hampton said. This was so gratifying to see Sno hug herself in discomfort.

"Well, we must have that Ark before the First demon gets his grubby little hands on it."

"The First demon!" Hampton raised an eyebrow. He wasn't expecting Sno to say anything about the first demon. "What must I do?"

"Keep the photo album and Pandora's box safe. Return to the mansion and lay claim to it. Use all of your sources to search for both Arks. I will see to it the police drop their search for you. I need you in public view and helping find the other Ark."

Hampton nodded and turned with relief to the wall behind him. He placed Pandora's stone against the wall and the Void appeared as the door to the cave under the mansion opened before him. He stepped through.

Dr. Sno drew a deep breath. She stood up and turned her gaze out over the open dessert beyond the windows of her office. She would have to kill the man eventually and assign his demon to someone else. The Vitreomancers worked much differently from the Council. Once a demon was assigned to a human, they stayed with that person until the person died. Sort of like mating for life!

Someone stepped through the open doorway, and it closed behind them. Sno whirled. The man standing before her held Pandora's stone in his hands. He slid the stone into the pockets of his jeans. He had red hair cut almost to the scalp. His turquoise eyes glittered with malice. "Hello, Sno."

Dr. Sno froze. "You!"

"Yes, me!" He giggled. "I regret what just happened to Dr. Hampton. I hope he recovers. Of course, that depends on how quickly I can get back to the chamber and call 911. I've done it before." He shrugged. "At least the third demon did. Now I am here to call a truce."

Sno sat slowly in the chair behind her desk. "Truce?"

"Between the Council and your Vitreowhatevers." He smiled. "What kind of truce?"

"We both know what is at stake here. We are looking for the same thing. I think it's time to put our differences aside and join forces." He said.

"Why?"

The man pulled a cell phone from his pocket and tapped on the screen. A monitor on her desk sprang to life and showed a bird's-eye view of a table with four women sitting and drinking beverages. He tapped the screen some more and zoomed in on a piece of paper on the table. Dr. Sno saw her name on the paper.

"What is this?"

The man closed the image. "My name is Jeremiah Stone. You might also know me as the Second Demon. Those three women now know who orchestrated the assassination of a member of the Penticle three years ago. And guess who took that person's place on the Penticle? The same person who paid for the assassination." He pointed at her. "That's right! It's you! The winner is Dr. Sno!" He laughed.

"Now, not long ago a Dr. Faust died in a terrible, regrettable tragic accident and there is a new vacancy on the Penticle." He stepped forward and perched on the edge of her desk. "I have something for you." He pulled an envelope from his pocket and placed on the desk.

"What is this?"

"A signed confession that I killed Dr. Faust. You see? I'm giving you leverage over me and I have leverage over you. Let's call it an exchange of trust."

Sno fingered the envelope. "What are you suggesting?'

"First, you sponsor someone of *our* choice for the Penticle. Second, we join forces to find the final artifact we are both looking for, the other Ark. Together, we can move past petty Councils and white-eyed demons."

Sno sat back and tapped her fingernails on the desk. "You're too young to be on the Penticle."

Jeremiah hopped up. "Well, physically, you're right. So there is another candidate." He slid over to the wall, pulled Pandora's stone from his pocket and pressed it against the wall. The door appeared and someone stepped through. As the man moved into the office, Jeremiah backed away. The man wore khaki safari clothing and a pith helmet. He took the helmet off, revealing white hair and his turquoise eyes glittered.

Jeremiah bowed and swirled his hand in a dramatic flourish. "Let me introduce you to my grandfather, Silas Stone, also known as the First Demon."

AFTERWORD

When I began the Chronicles of Jonathan Steel, my intention was in include "apologetic" information in each book. Apologetics is not the discipline of saying "I'm sorry". It comes from the Greek work "apologos" from 1 Peter 3:16 and refers to the discipline of defending the truthfulness of the Christian worldview through evidence from science, philosophy, and history.

I have gotten way from purely including such information but this book has two very important passages I want my readers to focus on. During Jonathan's essentially near death experience he had this to say:

He was my Savior. He was the God man who had become flesh and had endured all that I counted as painful and more. He was the Incarnation of God, love made flesh, Truth walking and talking, eternal, unending, and always loving. He was the Son who had shrugged off the power of his godhood to be born as a helpless baby, who lived a normal life, preached and healed and faced a betrayal far greater than I or any man could ever comprehend. And He had died. Death came to God, who was never to die.

God tasted mortality and said, "Enough!" He filled his Son

with a new life, an everlasting life, a life eternal and unending, and He burst forth from the grave to destroy and conquer death forever. All of this I saw in one glimpse of the Son of God risen from the dead. This is what Theo saw when he chose to remain in Jerusalem. This was my Savior, my Lord.

This passage, in essence, is the Gospel, the good news that God has not abandoned us to a world of chance and random events. Everything that has every occurred has done so as part of his plan to bring us redemption. Jonathan refers to this in another passage:

"That heart represents only a fraction of my sins, Meridian. I can do nothing to repay for any of my sins. It is impossible. The weight of the heart in your manner would always lead to the exile of the dead to the underworld, for no power known to man can ever erase our sins."

I moved closer. "But the feather of a white dove represents the Holy Spirit, part of our triune God. God the father, the creator, the transcendent One. Jesus, the Son, the Godman, God fleshed out into our space-time dimensions. And the Holy Spirit, the spiritual presence of God in all those who have accepted the ultimate sacrifice of Jesus Christ on the cross and His subsequent resurrection. We spoke days ago of a game, of how you will one day rein in hell. I told you then, and I tell you again now, that you and your spawn are the walking dead. You were defeated on the cross. I was there. I saw my Savior for the briefest of moments and in His name, I now point your attention to your talisman, the talisman of the fourth demon. The white feather of the scales of justice, only the most powerful Judge, holds in His hands. Those scales represent the atoning love of God."

Each of us must "weigh our hearts". Our every thought is either of evil, or contrary to God's will and work in this world. Or, our thoughts are good and aligned with God's will and work in this world. But no matter how dark our hearts may be, there is always an unending level of love and forgiveness for those dark deeds and thoughts and can be found in the saving Grace of our Lord Jesus Christ. He alone carries the scales of His justice and He has already paid the price to bring our hearts into balance with His love and forgiveness.

May you find such peace and hope in these dark days!
Bruce Hennigan
November, 2022

ABOUT THE AUTHOR

Bruce Hennigan grew up in Northwest Louisiana and became a physician practicing in the field of radiology. He was a church drama director for 15 years and wrote over 150 plays. He is a certified apologist, or one who defends the truthfulness of the Christian faith with Reasons to Believe and with the North American Mission Board in the role of a Certified Apologetic Instructor. He speaks on this topic on a regular basis. Bruce is also the author of nine books in the supernatural thriller series, "The Chronicles of Jonathan Steel" as well as "Death by Darwin", "The Homecoming Tree", "Our Darkness, His Light", and, with Mark Sutton, "Hope Again: A Lifetime Plan for Conquering Depression" and "Shadow Merchant: A Jack Merchant Medical Mystery".

Together with Mark Sutton, he participates in a seminar based on the book entitled, "Conquering Depression". For more information on the book and tool, "LifeFilters" go to www.conqueringdepression.com.

Bruce is married to the most incredible woman in the world, Sherry. They have two adult children and they live in Shreveport, Louisiana. Bruce and Sherry along with their daughter, Casey, are strong advocates of support for epilepsy patients and their caregivers.

For more information on books: hopeagainbooks.com